SLAVE SPY

The Youth and Times of Lazarus Perlman

An Historical Fiction

Byron Lee Wade

Cover Design by Kelli Ann Morgan
www.inspirecreativeservices.com

Interior book design by
Bob Houston eBook Formatting
http://about.me/BobHouston

ISBN: 978-0-9856376-0-6

Dedication

To my daughter Carrie Lee,
whose courageous and successful battle with cancer
at too young an age
helped me to alter my own little journey on this planet.

Acknowledgements

I am indebted to many, but mostly to my wife Carol, who sustained me throughout the process, yet remained discerning in appraisal. Rob Bignell at Inventing Reality performed yeoman editorial assistance. The remaining errors are my own.

Rev. Norman Hatter read an early manuscript and provided invaluable challenges on motivation and the African perspective. Suzanne Hines Levy performed some typing and provided feedback. She and husband Joe Levy advised on Jewish traditions and characterizations. I am also indebted to those who read parts or all of the manuscript and provided comments, criticisms and encouragement: Al Perry, Bob and Carol Allen, Frank and Jeanne Depiano, Ken and Maryke Guild, and Marsha Giomariso.

Authors and compilers of source materials are too numerous to list, but gratitude must be expressed to four: Ellen Gibson Wilson for her remarkable biography of Thomas Clarkson; James Walvin for his *Black Ivory: Slavery in the British Empire*; Hilary Beckles for *A History of Barbados: from Amerindian settlement to nation state*; and P.C. Coker III. My copy of his marvelous picture/history volume *Charleston's Maritime Heritage 1670-1865* has become a personal treasure and made a would-be salt of this land lubber.

To the reader:

This novel is set in the late 18th Century when people spoke more formally than they do at the time of its writing. Use of dialect in modern fiction is sometimes viewed as a sign of derision or insensitivity. Its use herein is not intended as disparagement, but to provide a sense of authenticity and in recognition of its own cultural and literary merit. It is hoped the reader will make allowances.

Reference to the Lord is spelled "G-d" when designating the Jewish deity. Despite the novel's British setting, I have used American spellings (e.g. "parlor," and "gray" rather than "parlour," and "grey")

None but the undersigned is responsible for the contents of this novel.

Byron Lee Wade
Houston, Texas, 2012

Table of Contents

PART FOUR: The Caribbean Correspondent

PART FIVE: Jamaica Bound

About the Author

Men from England bought and sold me,
Paid my price in paltry gold;
But. Though slave they have enroll'd me,
Minds are never to be sold…

Is there, as ye sometimes tell us,
Is there One who reigns on high?
Has He bid you buy and sell us,
Speaking from his throne, the sky?

from The Negro's Complaint by William Cowper, 1788
Sung as a ballad by the abolition campaigners

PART ONE: The Prodigy

London's East End 1775–1789

Chapter 1. Songbird of Brandenburg

Lazarus Perlman wanted a life.

He made that clear from months before his birth. He kicked, roiled and tumbled within his mother. At times she thought her one child might be two. His time seemed so very long in coming. Leah felt beyond discomfort, but she bore it well. In bed at night she often placed her husband's hand on her stomach. She had lost two other babies before their birth time and wanted his witness to the life motion within her. When the time to be delivered finally did arrive she thought her travail would never end. The crown of the baby's broad head appeared, but then retreated a little as if savoring birth.

Leah was a small woman and Lazarus a large baby. Their fevered stalemate continued throughout the night. At dawn, the probing midwife found the life cord looped around the baby's neck, freed it and completed the delivery. Lazarus was blue when finally extracted and his mother lay exhausted. Leah fought to live, but the birth took her blood and her life.

The midwife told Mordecai that the baby would likely join his mother within hours, but the child stubbornly refused to do so. He struggled silently for days but then gained strength, color and a voice.   At Mordecai's request, Rabbi Hirschell acted as the circumcision mohel – the wielder of the knife - to trim the baby's foreskin. When Lazarus did not bleed, the rabbi said the law required blood and he placed his mouth on the baby and drew a little blood, biting the baby's tender appendage in the process. Lazarus cried out as if coming fully to life. The rabbi then gave the baby the name of Moredecai's dead grandfather. Mordecai thought it an apt name.

Mordecai was not equipped to care for a baby, but he could not part with his Leah's child. With aid from the midwife, Mordecai found a wet nurse willing to help in the baby's care. The large-breasted Portuguese Jewess and her brood lived just round the alley from Houndsditch where Mordecai lived over his tailor shop. Mordecai instructed Mrs. Suares with difficulty.   The hard consonants of his Yiddish met her vowel-rich Ladino dialect on the common ground of broken English. Her ground, he thought, was more broken than his own.   Still, Lazarus thrived, so the arrangement continued well enough for seven years.

In the late winter of 1782 an epidemic spread in London and illness struck the Suares home. Mordecai had not heard of "agues and catarrh," but high fevers accompanied the disease. Learning this, he kept Leah's child at home where he hoped the boy would be safe. Mrs. Suares and her entire household died within three weeks. Mordecai's hands, devoted to his work, were now filled with an all-day child.

Mordecai acted dutifully towards Leah's child. He read to Lazarus from the Torah each Shabbat. He recited the Shema, confessing his faith. With his audience of one, he observed the holy days. He took pains to keep a proper diet for himself and for the boy as well.

Moored to tradition and lost in memories, Mordecai Perlman aligned each step he took with his own footprints. But he knew his obligation to teach the boy both the skills of his trade and the customs of his heritage. He used the same methods his own father had used and many of the same stories. It was the only way he knew.

Mordecai told stories about patriarchs and persecutions. Lazarus thought them unhappy accounts of unhappy people. Occasionally, Mordecai related a story or two about his own past. Lazarus fancied those stories better and sometimes requested his favorite.

"Tell me about the scar, Papa," Lazarus would ask. For the few minutes required to tell that particular story, the old man seemed younger – lifted from the passionless, instructive tone with which he usually spoke to Lazarus.

His son's prodding sometimes allowed Mordecai to add a new detail to the story. Lazarus would detect the new addition immediately. Neither Mordecai nor Lazarus knew whether these revelations were fresh recollections or just the result of Mordecai's advancing age, but Mordecai thought he remembered them. They usually enhanced the story, so a silent pact was formed and neither father nor son voiced any doubts.

The story of the scar pleased and pained Mordecai. He did not want to relive it often because it exhumed memories he held sacred. With some small boy pleading, however, he would eventually acquiesce - -

A decade and some years before the birth of Lazarus, a man and a pretty young girl lived happily in a tiny shtetl in the western part of the Brandenburg region of Germany a little east of the Elbe River. It was a perilous time as King Frederick II was trying to unite that region with Pomerania to its north and to his Duchy of Prussia to the northeast.

The man was named Mordecai the tailor. He had sewn for many years and set aside for a few spare comforts. They included a strong poster bed for which he crafted a lace-trimmed cover, a seven-candle menorah and a generous milk cow.

In the tailor's thirty-fourth year, the girl - the sixteen-year-old youngest daughter of the shtetl's cantor - became his "kallah" or bride. Her name was Leah and she was dark-haired and fair skinned. She seemed most willing to have the older man as her "chatan" or groom, or so her father had said. Leah sang at her work with a voice like no other, Mordecai insisted in his gruff, guttural Yiddish. Leah's voice was clear and soft. She sang as sweetly as a songbird. Not like the songbirds of England, but like a bird heard only in the pine forests of the Brandenburg.

At about this point in the story, Mordecai, if he were working, would set aside his shears, needle, thimble or awl and give himself only to the retelling - -

Leah and Mordecai fasted before the wedding. He recited from the Book of Psalms and asked forgiveness for the sins of his youth.

Festivities began seven days before the wedding. Their friends gave the kallah-to-be and her chatan wonderful but separate parties. They each received well wishers and the blessings of their families. The tailor gave his pledges to Leah's parents and broke a plate to seal his covenant. He promised to raise any children blessed to the union in a faithful Jewish home.

Leah was a small, graceful woman with a simple beauty often unnoticed by others. People loved the sound of her voice, but only Mordecai and her family truly perceived the tenderness of Leah's soul and the pleasure of her gentle gaze. When the wedding day finally arrived, Leah came sweet smelling as if bathed and scented. When Mordecai went forward to lower her veil, claiming her as his own, her clear eyes met his and her beauty stirred him. He counted himself of great fortune.

At this point Mordecai would often pause and sigh as though he were recalling some scene that he did not share with the boy. Then he would sigh again and say, "Where was I?"

"The chupah, Papa, tell about the chupah," Lazarus would prompt. The story would continue - -

Under a cloudless sky, the couple stood in the shade of the chupah, held up by a pole in the hands of a friend on each of its four corners. All the people of the shtetl attended, but the happy couple saw only each other. There Mordecai gave Leah a simple gold ring for the forefinger of her right hand as a symbol of her great value. He signed with his right hand and gave her a scrolled writing of his promises to her. He promised to work for Leah, to honor her and to provide for her.

Then the tailor and his bride received seven blessings. They each sipped wine and Mordecai smashed the wineglass with the boot of his right foot. Accompanied by two witnesses, the couple then retired inside and broke their fast together with a small meal, which they fed to one another. After a brief time, they reemerged and joined the entire wedding party in a feast. They danced and sang and again received the blessings and toasts of their friends. When all were exhausted, the couple departed to Mordecai's home and began a seven-day celebration of their union and their family to come.

Alone in the small house, they stared at each other at first and then talked in whispers. He began to call Leah "Songbird" with great affection. She played with his beard and received well his attentions.

Mordecai paused here again. He thought of his worry that the young girl would not find him to her liking, but he smiled silently behind his beard as he remembered how she had complimented him on his patience and his touch.

"Go on, Papa," Lazarus would urge. Heavy brows and a solemn frown quickly erased Mordecai's smile as the story proceeded - -

Suddenly, on the last day of their celebration, the shtetl came under attack from one faction or another of the combatants in King Frederick II's war with Russia and Austria. The people of the shtetl ran about crying that the Austrian army approached from the south, but some thought them to be French mercenaries. The village fell in a matter of minutes. An hour later, Frederick's Prussians valiantly counter-attacked from the north and repelled the invaders. But that was too late for the tiny shtetl. As they retreated, the mercenaries sacked the village and set it afire. Nothing remained but ashes and mud.

As the attack had begun, Mordecai had wrapped Leah in her shawl and sent her to hide in the nearby forest as he ran to save his milk cow. Leah watched the slaughter in the shtetl from some distance away. She was horrified, but there was nothing she could do. She crouched in a stand of saplings, startling at every snap of a twig, shivering in a light rain. After a while, she heard a shrieking chorus of men and metal. She rose cautiously, and looked on as the Prussians counter-attacked and routed their enemy from the clearing where the shtetl had stood.

As the pillagers fled, the Prussians pursued them and Leah ran back to the village. About half of the others of the shtetl had also managed to escape into the woods. One or two at a time, they reappeared and followed Leah back to the clearing. They found no one uninjured and few alive in the village. All of Leah's family and Mordecai's mother, his only family save his new wife, lie dead. At first, Leah could not find Mordecai and prayed that he had been taken as an impressed recruit - by either army. Perhaps then he was alive and would come back to her.

She ran about frantically searching for him. Within a few minutes she saw him lying face down at the far edge of the smoldering shtetl next to his dead cow. A long French sabre, still vibrating a little from side to side, rose with its hilt in the air and its point buried in Mordecai's back. Mordecai did not move and he was covered in blood.

Leah threw her hands to her mouth and gasped, but as she stepped forward to confirm her loss, she saw that the sabre was actually planted in the cow and not in Mordecai. Still, Mordecai did not move. Leah knelt and saw a long gash at the back of Mordecai's bloody head. She knew he was dead after all. She broke her silent shock and began to weep as she lifted Mordecai's head into her lap. Then she thought she felt him stir. She stopped her crying and turned his shoulders and head to see his face. As she did, she heard him faintly whisper something. He was near death though still alive. Leah leaned close, still cradling Mordecai's head in her lap. His mouth quivered again. She drew his face up a bit and turned her ear to his lips just as he softly whispered, "Songbird."

With tears streaking down her face, Leah wrung out her shawl and wrapped it around his head. Others seeing her came and helped. Mordecai didn't know much of what happened for the next few weeks. He did know that Leah dressed his wound, changed the bandages, nursed him and fed him. All the while she hummed softly and as pleasantly as a bird on a distant tree. Mordecai recovered to learn the details of that day from Leah – and that half the village had died that day or soon after of their wounds and burns.

Mordecai still bore the scar from the sabre. At this point Lazarus would part his father's gray hair to see it again.

"We must remember, both of us," Mordecai would slowly say with a tear in his eye, "that neither of us would be living at this moment, but for the courage of a dainty little songbird."

Lazarus was happy to end the story there. Mordecai, though, always insisted on continuing … the war later forced the newlyweds to flee down the Elbe River to Hamburg and eventually to sail for England. They had arrived in London destitute, he said, but had been aided by the people of the Great Synagogue at Duke's Place.

Following the story, Mordecai would instruct his son that every Jew must observe the commandments or "mitzvoth" and undertake sacrifices he called "mitzvah" to help others and thereby draw closer to G-d. He said the rabbis and people of London's synagogues perform great mitzvah when they help Jews seeking refuge from wars in Europe or from persecution.

Mordecai remembered their kindness. As other refugees arrived at the Great Synagogue from time to time, Mordecai would on occasion present one of them with a warm cloak fashioned from remnants of cloth. It was truly a mitzvah he told himself. He hoped his son would carry on the practice.

As Mordecai instructed though, Lazarus would be in a daydream - trying to imagine a sound he had never heard - the melody of the songbird in the pine forest of Brandenburg.

Chapter 2. The Jews' Free School

Lazarus worked in his father's small shop every day except Shabbat, which began at sundown each Friday, and other holy days. Mordecai was particular and would fall into an earnest lecture to the boy at any time. Lazarus seemed ill suited to tailoring. With his clumsy boy hands, he would draw the stitch too long and run his needle out of thread. He would sometimes stain his workpiece with blood from a punctured thumb. Lazarus was not allowed to make cuts - not because the long, sharp scissors might be a danger to him, but because Mordecai feared he would waste cloth.

To Mordecai, Lazarus was a perplexity. He grew constantly. He questioned frequently. He tired of routine easily. He took little comfort in the familiar. He preferred the new, the unusual and the strange. When something captured his attention, Lazarus dwelled on it with single-minded, trance-like concentration that made him all but oblivious to his surroundings.

As he worked, Mordecai sometimes heard the boy mumbling to himself. One day Mordecai had gone to the back of the shop to sharpen his shears. As he quietly returned to the work area where the boy sat near the tailor's jacket mannequin, he overheard the boy's whispers. Lazarus seemed to be speaking to the headless mannequin. "Hear, Israel, the Lord is our G-d, the Lord is One. And you shall love the Lord your G-d with all your heart and with all your soul and with all your might and you shall teach your chil …" He stopped there when he noticed that his father had returned. Mordecai smiled at Lazarus. The lad, who was two left hands with his training, could recite his father's prayers.

Lazarus had something of Leah's gentleness and a soft voice. He made an awkward apprentice, though, always in the way and underfoot. After just a few months of Lazarus in the shop all day, Mordecai determined that he must find another Mrs. Suares to care for the boy. Lazarus could continue to learn his father's trade in the evenings.

Mordecai knew that the Great Synagogue sponsored a small school. Perhaps, he thought, the school might be a place for Lazarus. While at the synagogue one Shabbat in August, he approached the leader of the community. Rabbi Hirschell first advised that the school had been established with orphans and the unfortunate in mind. Then, recalling that the boy was motherless, the rabbi gave his consent. He cautioned that the schoolmaster must consent as well.

Mordecai pled his case with Rabbi Solomon, the schoolmaster of what was soon thereafter named "Chevra Kadisha Talmud Torah," but commonly called "The Jews' Free School." The schoolmaster was reticent. He alone instructed the boys and his home parlor classroom was full. He regretted that the school could not accommodate Mordecai's son.

A few weeks later, after further discussion and with Mordecai's pledge of a fine frock coat for the schoolmaster - wool dyed black, full length with ample lapels, pocket flaps and three large buttons down the front - Lazarus was admitted for the first year of instruction. Some of the boys at the school were as young as six. Lazarus entered the Jews' Free School just before his eighth birthday.

Lazarus still helped his father in the evenings and assisted in the making of the schoolmaster's coat. He had difficulty with the heavy wool. Lazarus doubted that his hands would ever become as skilled as his father's or that they could be content in the completion of tight little stitches on some gentleman's or rabbi's coat.

As Lazarus prepared for his first day of school, he caught sight of himself in the mirror where Mordecai's patrons checked the fit of their new clothes. There he saw brown hair curled defiantly atop his broad head. He had pale, clear skin and meaty hands. His big dark eyes were soft and steady. Between them sat what Lazarus viewed as the flaw of his appearance, a ridge of a nose. It protruded away from his eyes almost at the bridge and then ran down his face, splitting in two the landscape of his otherwise pleasant boy's face. Mordecai walked him to school, nose and all. Rabbi Solomon's home was near the synagogue. Lazarus soon learned to walk there on his own.

Rabbi Solomon's first lesson was discipline. After that he taught Hebrew, lessons from the prophets and readings from the Pentateuch, the first five books of the Torah. He drilled the students in the reading and memorization of scriptural passages, the same passages for every boy. He required standing recitation. He seldom allowed questions and often interrupted a recitation or questioning student mid-sentence. Then without looking at the student he would demand, "Go on boy." He spewed the word "boy" through his tight lips as if it were an accusation.

Lazarus learned his lessons, but could recite them only in measured spurts. When called upon, he rose reluctantly. As he recited, he spoke lowly with his eyes on the floor and his mouth drawn. The schoolmaster prodded his students with a slender stick. He called it his "pointing baton" but he wielded it as if driving headstrong cattle.

"Perhaps this will loosen your tongue," Rabbi Solomon would say as his pointing baton struck across the back of Lazarus' legs. "Do not mumble boy and straighten up," he instructed as the baton whistled against Lazarus' back.

Lazarus tried to respond to the schoolmaster, but still stammered at each juncture in his speech. The more the teacher demanded of Lazarus, the less he seemed able to deliver. It was not really a stutter; for once he managed to begin he could recite a memorized passage while his breath lasted. Once his air had been spent though, he stopped as if concluded, even if in the middle of a sentence. Starting and restarting became more and more difficult.

School mornings became struggles as well. "I do not want to go to that school," Lazarus protested to his father, without ever telling the reason. Mordecai prided himself on obtaining a place there for the boy. He would not listen to protests.

Some months following Lazarus' admission, the school was suddenly reorganized. A controversial new Board of Governors now ran the Jews' Free School independent of the Great Synagogue. From separate sources, both Mordecai and Lazarus heard rumors that Rabbi Solomon had been reprimanded for harsh treatment of his students. The new governors hired a second teacher. In a strange compromise, though, they also designated Rabbi Solomon as the head teacher. Immediately, he began to insist that the students call him "Headmaster Solomon." He cautioned the boys that the new teacher was not a rabbi and that he reports to "The Headmaster."

The new teacher was to instruct the boys in secular studies – with a focus on English and mathematics. The purpose was to "Anglicise" the boys enough to cope with their life in England without risking their assimilation into non-Jewish culture. The headmaster, though, remained singularly committed to "setting directionless youth on the traditional path of an obedient Jewish life."

The boys suffered through Rabbi Solomon each morning from nine o'clock until noon. After their midday meal, which each student brought for himself, the boys marched in line behind Rabbi Solomon around the corner to the synagogue to stand for prayers.

After prayers, custody changed as the boys filed out and followed the new teacher from the synagogue to his house two streets away. Master Symmons did not require marching in line and he looked straight at his students as he talked with them. He seldom interrupted a recitation except to provide a hint and he smiled easily – especially when a student responded well.

Master Symmons appeared to be perhaps twenty years junior to the headmaster. Like Lazarus he had a high, broad forehead. There the similarities stopped. The new teacher was a tall, thin man with a boney frame. He wore dark-rimmed turn-pin spectacles that made his eyes appear large. He often folded and dropped them into his breast pocket. He trimmed his brown beard much shorter than Mordecai or the rabbis. His slender wife looked younger still, perhaps just twenty. She also wore spectacles – with delicate umber frames and thin lenses - that did not distort her already big warm brown eyes. Lazarus had never seen spectacles on a woman or one with such rich auburn hair.

Even after its reorganization, the school's primary goal remained preparation for the Bar Mitzvah and no student could stay at the school more than six months following his thirteenth birthday - the age of responsibility. The headmaster fussed about that preparation. The new "English teacher," as Rabbi Solomon referred to him, seldom mentioned it.

Instead, he instructed the boys each afternoon in proper English, some rudimentary science, and occasionally mentioned events from both Jewish and secular history. He said he might introduce the older boys to some classics of literature. He left mathematics to his wife. He said that Jewish history and English history had sometimes intersected. He told the boys that Jews had been expelled from England in the English year 1290 A.D. and not readmitted until the time of Oliver Cromwell, just a little more than one hundred years ago. "One hundred years seems a very long time to a boy of ten," he said, "but in the history of our people it is only a moment."

In his early days at school, Lazarus decided that he was no better a student than he was a tailor's apprentice. Whenever he stood before the class, he trembled and his throat tightened as if someone were choking him. Asked to rise and recite anything from memory, he spoke haltingly. In the mornings he could hardly recite at all. In the afternoon he was hesitant and required help to get started with nearly every sentence. Once given the first word, though, he could blurt out the rest of the line using all the air in his lungs. Then he would stop, drop his chin to his chest as if to hide his nose, draw a deep breath, and require another prompt before he could begin again.

In the afternoon, Master Symmons, at the suggestion of his wife, took to allowing Lazarus to recite from his seat. This proved more successful. Master Symmons hoped it would eventually provide a cure for Lazarus' frailty.   Yet on occasional return to his feet, Lazarus would immediately regress to his former paralysis.

At least twice each year the headmaster would summons Mordecai for a review of Lazarus' progress. This always resulted in deliberations about whether Lazarus should continue at The Jews' Free School.

Reports of his son's poor recitation surprised Mordecai, since the boy had shown no hesitation at home. "Oy, oy, oy, vas a boy," he said to Lazarus when recounting the headmaster's report. "So much to say at home, un so slow to speak at schul." The headmaster reminded Mordecai that Lazarus was occupying one of a limited number of seats in the free school and that each year the school was more in demand. The headmaster would have to consider whether another candidate might merit Lazarus' place.

The headmaster said that the school had many needs and, as he noticed some spot on his trousers, he would suggest that Mordecai consider how he might provide some assistance that could weigh in the decision. Incidentally, he was in need of some new trousers. He could come to Mordecai's shop one afternoon the following week to be measured. Mordecai said he would be honored.

At the measurement a few days later, the fate of the boy was again the topic when the headmaster inquired about the cost of the trousers. He should have replaced his trousers earlier, he said, but it is a pity that we do not better pay those entrusted with the minds of our sons. "Now, what will be the cost of the trousers?"

There was no cost, Mordecai assured him. Making the trousers expressed Mordecai's gratitude for the headmaster's patience with Lazarus. Each year the headmaster acquired more new clothes. For the father of Lazarus Perlman, the "free school" had its cost. His son paid a price as well.

Chapter 3. Marmalade and Chess

From two o'clock until five each afternoon, the boys of the Jews' Free School studied in the home of Master Symmons. As the weeks passed, he broadened his approach to teaching English. Rather than commit his students only to rote exercises in grammar, spelling, vocabulary, syntax and composition, he began to regale them with literature, historical accounts and even assigned recitations from contemporary political writers. "There is no better way to learn how to organize one's thoughts into words," he said, "than to examine how thoughtful people have done so."

There was no pointing baton in Master Symmons' home. He seemed to put his entire self into his teaching. He was not alone.

From the beginning, Mrs. Symmons assisted in instruction of the students, though she said she understood it was not her place. When the time for mathematics lessons arrived, her husband readily deferred to her. Master Symmons would say, "Gentlemen, it is time we pay a visit to Euclid, Archimedes, Pythagoras and perhaps that upstart Isaac Newton," then he would step aside and his wife would conduct a lesson in simple arithmetic. Lazarus thought it peculiar to be instructed by a woman, but he liked it.

Mrs. Symmons soon determined that mathematicians are not made in large groups. She began inviting the younger boys into her kitchen in ones and twos as the others studied with Master Symmons in the parlor. She reviewed their ciphers by asking them to count little treats on a plate. After they summed them up, then her pupils gobbled them up, a few at a time, recounting as they went in a lesson in subtraction.

In her kitchen Lazarus learned to add loganberries, multiply black currants and to divide by sectioning Spanish citrus when Mrs. Symmons could obtain it. Well, it was not as often sectioning as much as cutting, for Mrs. Symmons preferred sour oranges from Seville that she transformed into a delicious marmalade. And the lesson was not so much division as an introduction to fractions.

One afternoon she asked Lazarus for "the pleasure of your company at the kitchen table." There she placed before him a bowl of oranges with two lemons on the top. "I boiled these for hours this morning," she said, "they should be ready. Will you please help me?"

Lazarus picked up one of the oranges, stuck in his thumbnail and grabbed at the thin peeling. The orange was soft and had swollen in the boiling. Watery juice flowed over his thumb.

"No peeling," Mrs. Symmons said, "for this recipe we keep the skin." She stepped from her counter, placed a wooden cutting board on the table and a knife on the board. "First cut it in two as evenly as you can … fine, now where you had one there are two. And each piece is called what?"

"One half," Lazarus said.

"Yes, now cut each half in two. Very nice, now what are these?" she said, pointing at the result.

"Quarters," said Lazarus. The quarters then became eighths and the eighths were cut across to become sixteenths. She scooped the small sixteenths into her cupped hands and across the kitchen to the boiling pot still over her kitchen fire.

"You are fine with this," Mrs. Symmons said. "Slice the rest, but be careful not to cut yourself. Remove the seeds and put the fruit in this," she instructed, setting an empty bowl next to the oranges. "Same with the lemons," she said.

As Lazarus sliced, Mrs. Symmons talked through her preparations. "Now I am adding the sugar to the boiling water," she said as she heaped large spoonfuls into the pot. As Lazarus finished the last lemon he watched Mrs. Simmons facing her fire. He sliced his left first finger. In the surprise he let out an "ouchhh," drew back the injured finger and wrapped it up in his right palm. Now he felt the lemon juice and he winced.

Mrs. Symmons insisted on examining the bloodied finger. The cut was not deep, a shallow scrape of skin really, but it bled. She made a little fuss. She wrapped it up in the corner of her apron and clamped her hands around his. Connected by the apron, the two of them waddled across the kitchen like geese. There Mrs. Symmons washed the injured digit in her basin, dried it and wrapped it in a cloth that she split and tied above the knuckle. The scraped finger now bore the bandage of a severe laceration.

Mrs. Symmons said she was sorry and did not scold him except to say with a smile, "You were to cut the lemon, not sever the finger." He returned the smile and they turned to the table to inspect the diced lemon. It was spoiled with spatters of blood and a bit of

Lazarus' skin. Mrs. Symmons looked at the lemon, then at Lazarus and said, "Master Perlman, are you as able at keeping secrets as you are at fractions?"

He looked at her but did not know what to say.

"I think I can trust you," she said. "This is an eighty-year-old recipe from Scotland - it requires two boiled lemons." With that, she scooped up the bloody lemon, dropped it into the bowl with the other sliced citrus, stepped across the kitchen and emptied the entire bowl into the pot. "When that comes to a boil, we shall have our Dundee Delight ... about two hours with cooling time. The secret," she said, "is the skin."

"My skin?" Lazarus asked.

"Well perhaps with this batch," she said with a wide, toothy smile. "No, I mean on the marmalade. When it is cooked enough, a spoonful on a cold plate will form a skin and will wrinkle as it cools. If there is no wrinkled skin, keep boiling." The next day, everyone in the house sampled the marmalade. It tasted tart and sweet at the same time.

"This is the best Dundee, yet," Master Symmons said to his wife, "how did you do it?"

"Mr. Perlman gave me a hand," she said. She winked at Lazarus and they both suppressed small giggles. They kept their secret.

Lazarus was not the only student to share a secret with Mrs. Symmons. From each boy she extracted a promise not to tell the headmaster or anyone outside the house of her complicity in the education of the young males of Israel. She need not have had concern. Lazarus did not know any boy who confided in the headmaster ... or any boy who would betray Mrs. Symmons.

Over time, Mrs. Symmons became more and more involved in her husband's work. She seemed at times strangely distant from the traditions that were the centerpiece of the morning lessons. Lazarus thought that she sometimes gave him extra attention. It was subtle, hardly noticeable, really. She would look in his eyes to see if he understood a lesson or spend an extra moment over his shoulder as he wrote a few sentences in English.

In little ways, Mrs. Symmons did not seem to defer to her husband. Yet she would sometimes rise to his aid when a student was unruly, inattentive or provoking another boy. She would invite the offending student into her kitchen while Master Symmons continued his lesson. She would hand the student a cup of hot tea with a saucer and she would take up one herself. She would share some of her marmalade. While the student and the schoolmaster's wife juggled their cups and sipped the hot liquid, she would engage her kitchen guest in some little conversation that had nothing to do with his offense.

She would inquire whether the student was feeling well and she would set her tea on the table and place her warm palm on his forehead as if to examine him for fever. Then she might ask whether the boy had found disagreeable anything he had recently eaten. She would hold a few fingers in the air before the boy and ask him to focus on them while she moved them left and right, all the while examining his face with her gentle brown eyes.

Within a few minutes, she would reassure the boy that he seemed just fine to her. By the time the tea in the cup had cooled, the temper in the boy had usually done the same - his sour face sweetened with orange marmalade. Having confirmed the boy's physical health, she would then bolster his confidence. "You are a fine lad," she would say.

Then she offered some simple challenge that called for agreement from the student. Among her standbys were: "You can be an example to the young ones. Will you help us a bit in that way?" or "Master Symmons tells me that you have a keen mind when you stay awake. Do you think you can manage it?" When she spoke, no matter how simple the charge, it never sounded condescending. She seemed to know just how long to wait to ask the question. She always got the same answer.

Lazarus cherished the afternoons. Somehow they were much shorter than his mornings. He also grew fond of his afternoon teachers - both of them.

* * * * * * *

One afternoon, Lazarus stayed late in Mrs. Symmons' kitchen. When he emerged all the boys were gone from the parlor. Master Symmons sat at a small table and across from him sat a man Lazarus had not before seen. The man talked seriously about Africa. Before him on the table were more than a dozen small black statues. There were little white statues before Master Symmons. As the two men talked they moved the statues about on a black and white board which sat between them on the table. Lazarus stood silently and watched. After a few moments, the man with the black statues noticed Lazarus and nodded, drawing the attention of Master Symmons who turned and said, "Mr. Perlman, I did not know you were still here."

Lazarus apologized and started to leave.

"Perhaps you should take my seat young man," said the man with the black statues. "I seldom manage to stay long in a match with this cunning Cambridge champion."

"I never thought of that," said Master Symmons. "Hold there Mr. Perlman, this might be just the cure for you. If you can stay a while tomorrow, we shall see."

Then Master Symmons turned back to the man and said, "Fine suggestion, Thomas my friend, really. Fine suggestion but poor move." As he said it he slid a white statue across the table toward his friend, lifted a black statue and rested his white one in its place. "Check," he said.

"As I was saying ..." said the man with the black statues, shaking his head.

Lazarus quietly left out the door.

The next afternoon Master Symmons introduced Lazarus to a game that soon became their regular after-school pastime. The complexity of the game, and the seemingly infinite variety of situations produced by the play of its 32 pieces on 64 squares captivated Lazarus. He wished his own life were as limitless.

Master Symmons would often catch Lazarus' pieces aligned, abreast or on file, and place his rook or queen on line with them. Lazarus was thereby forced to either move the nearer piece, placing the far piece in jeopardy, or stand and sacrifice the leader. Lazarus learned to mind his alignments and to value each piece, lowly pawns included. Master Symmons excelled at waiting for Lazarus to make an error. Then he would pounce without delay. Lazarus learned from his mistakes and seldom repeated one.

As Lazarus rapidly improved, Master Symmons was required to employ more elaborate strategies. He thrived on pin and fork attacks, simultaneously threatening two or more of Lazarus' pieces with a single well positioned knight or bishop of his own. Sometimes he stationed two or more pieces so as to limit Lazarus' movement while skewering him from an entirely different angle.

Lazarus began devising his own attacks and even disguising them with decoys he seemed to come by instinctively. He secretly named some of his schemes after constellations of the stars. His favorite he called "The Scorpion," so named because it employed what he thought of as "pinchers" attacking each side followed by a deadly "stinger" striking from the back.

Within five months from the day he had seen Master Symmons and his friend playing chess, Lazarus was as often victorious as his mentor, though the two ended many matches in a draw. Master Symmons never boasted of his own mastery. Neither did he permit Lazarus any vanity at his growing prowess. "It is a game, to be enjoyed but never perfected," he told Lazarus. "Once you think you have it in hand, it will quickly humble you, no matter how clever you think you are ... not unlike one's little journey in this universe."

Unlike her husband, Mrs. Symmons gushed. "You are among perhaps a handful of men in England who play at the level of my husband," she told Lazarus. "I doubt any of them has come to it as quickly." Her compliment charmed Lazarus – not that she noted his chess skills, but that she had called him a man.

Chapter 4. Blood Libel

Perhaps because of Lazarus' difficulty with recitation, his prowess at the chess board puzzled Master Symmons. "Young Mr. Perlman is a contradiction," he told his wife. "He sometimes struggles to recall a lesson, but he learns games extremely well."

"He learns math quickly and he loves to read," she said. "I'm not so sure the problem is his memory."

Each student was encouraged to read on his own from a large collection of books in the Symmons' home. Lazarus read rapidly and widely. Noting their preference for gentile writers and their struggles with the language of their fathers, Master Symmons took to calling the boys his "Hebrew Heathens." He maintained the title was no contradiction as it applied to them. Since he used the term fondly, his students viewed it as an affirmation. These two attentive teachers often issued challenges, but Lazarus observed, they also bathed their students in approval.

Mrs. Symmons was absent for a few days each month and sometimes stayed in her kitchen. She was there one day when Master Symmons undertook a somber lesson. He taught that Jews had been the objects of intolerance throughout the world for generations. In ancient times they had been exiled from their homelands. In more recent times, he said, they had been enslaved, burned, robbed, raped and persecuted in nearly every one of the many countries to which they had migrated.

Even in England, Master Symmons said, Jews had at times been forced to wear some badge or means of immediate identification. They were often forced to pay special taxes not paid by gentiles. After their earlier expulsion from England, Master Symmons taught, they had been expelled from France, Hungary, Germany, Austria, Lithuania, Spain and Portugal. Some Jews were forced to appear to have converted to Christianity or be killed. This was especially true of the Sephardic Jews of Spain and Portugal.

Then an older boy asked Master Symmons, "But why were Jews expelled from England?"

As if waiting for the prompt, Master Symmons turned and gazed earnestly into the eyes of his pupils. He said that Christians believed that the Messiah had come and that Jews had betrayed him and enticed the Romans to kill him. Master Symmons illustrated English hatred and suspicion of Jews with a story he called "blood libel." He said that frightened Christians apparently believed liars who said that Jews were not only killers of Christ, but killers of Christian babies as well. It was incredible! Men of Norwich had accused some Jews of kidnapping a baby and draining its blood. They used the child's blood, it was charged, for marking their door posts.

"But why would anyone tell such lies?"

Master Symmons said he could not answer for certain, but said that there was great jealousy and hatred. He said some people had envied Jewish merchants and their prowess. In those times, he explained, the church had prohibited Christians from making loans at interest. Since no one would lend money with the risk of loss but no opportunity for gain, there were few Christian lenders. Jews, on the other hand, were prohibited from owning land and from certain ventures. They were not prohibited, however, from providing risk money at agreed rates to other businessmen. Many Christians, Master Symmons said, had therefore borrowed from Jews and did not want to repay. Others resented competition from Jewish merchants; some in the clergy wanted to convert Jews or destroy them.

"In these circumstances," he said, "perhaps that particular slander originated from a misunderstanding about the source of blood on door posts." Then he asked, "What is it that we celebrate at Pesach?"

"The Passover," answered a student.

"Yes, when the children of Israel were in bondage in Egypt, the Lord sent Moses to the Pharaoh who was the king of the land. Do you remember that reading?"

Several heads nodded.

"And what did Moses say to Pharaoh?"

He extended his hand to a very small boy who answered, "The Lord said, 'let the people go.'"

"Yes! Of course, Pharaoh immediately obeyed and set the people free, didn't he?"

Perturbed looks descended on young faces. Heads slowly shook and a few hands rose in the air. "What is it?" Master Symmons said, feigning impatience and again recognizing the same small boy.

"Sir," the boy said in a pure little voice, "um ... Pharaoh did not let the people go. I mean ... he did, but not at first he didn't."

Now the schoolmaster's head shook and his face twisted into a mask of confusion. "Well, what happened then? Those people or their descendants are not still there in Egyptian bondage to this day are they?"

Heads shook and a murmur arose, but no hands were in the air.

"You remember, of course," said Master Symmons, "that Pharaoh refused to let the people go though the Lord sent plague after plague into the land." Then Master Symmons retold the story. The boys heard again about the bondage and the plagues G-d visited upon the keepers of the slaves.

The schoolmaster described each plague in detail, amplifying the Scriptures. The boys imagined a river of blood, a sea of frogs, a plague of lice on men and beasts and the sky darkened with swarms of flies. Master Symmons described huge boils that eat a man's flesh. With each new pestilence the boys liked the story better and better. Hail stones of fire rained on hard-hearted Pharaoh. Swarms of locusts covered the land of Egypt and invaded the houses of the Egyptian slavers. In Master Symmons' telling they climbed in nostrils when people tried to sleep. They devoured bowls of porridge before Egyptian boys could take even a spoonful. They crawled in clothing, covered the skin and bit at people's private parts. They completely darkened the land, Master Symmons explained as he drew the parlor draperies, darkening the classroom.

Plague after plague, through eight plagues so far, the eyes of the boys had gotten bigger and bigger and their attention more and more intense. As he continued with the plagues, Master Symmons stepped around the room and blew out the lamps one by one. Just as he reached the last one ... the Lord in Egypt turned out the light. The land of Egypt laid in total darkness. The Symmons' parlor classroom stood in darkened, breathless silence.

After much suffering by the slave keepers, all carefully recounted to the spellbound young students, it all came, whispered Master Symmons in the dark, to the events recorded in Exodus the Twelfth Chapter. "Let us read that chapter once more," he said, and he asked the same small boy to stand before the Torah. The room remained still.

"But Master, it's too dark," pled the sweet voice of the boy.

"Precisely," said the schoolmaster, "and there is more than one way to be left in the dark. At this moment we are without benefit of the sun, are we not? We are also without benefit of the Scriptures," he said. "He who provides the one has also provided the other."

"Well, let us see," Master Symmons continued, "when we left them the people of Israel remained in bondage, so I suppose we should finish the story. Let there be light!"

At that cue the door from the kitchen opened and Mrs. Symmons entered the room carrying a large, bright oil lamp as Master Symmons parted the draperies. The story reached its crescendo - the Lord passing through the night to smite all the firstborn in the land of Egypt - save those with the blood of the lamb on the door posts of their houses. There were deaths in nearly every house, except those that had been marked with lamb's blood and passed over. The boys could almost smell the rotting flesh. Finally, with this tenth plague, the children of Israel were delivered out of the land of Egypt. Terrible Pharaoh reversed himself and managed to get his army swallowed up by the Red Sea, but Moses and the children of Israel finally escaped their awful slave masters.

It was a gruesome recounting of the history, especially for boys of six to twelve years. It was hardly a new story, but this retelling commanded attention like no story before it. Lazarus had heard this same story from Mordecai. Somehow, now it seemed more than just a story.

Master Symmons discussed observance of the Passover and traditions arising from it. He said the tradition of lamb's blood on door posts could have been misunderstood by some. "And do not let the point be lost," he said, "men who persecute and enslave others steal their lives. They are the criminals, not those who honor their history by marking their door posts each year."

The bloody wrath of the Lord on those who kept the children of Israel in bondage made Lazarus shudder. The plagues were horrible - but they also seemed justified. So it should be for those who make slaves of others, he determined.

"What became of the descendants of those slaves?" Master Symmons asked. All of the boys knew the answer to this question. For perhaps the first time, Lazarus also felt it ... he was a descendant of slaves.

Chapter 5. Master Shuckles

As his thirteenth birthday approached, Lazarus worried that he would never be able to complete his Bar Mitzvah. He knew the Hebrew words, but he knew he could not perform the reading.

Despite his difficulty with oration, Lazarus had continued to learn quickly. His frustration with speaking on his feet only increased his determination. Mrs. Symmons seemed always sympathetic to Lazarus, if she took note of his deficiency at all. Master Symmons also tolerated Lazarus' weakness and tried to avoid unnecessary humiliation. The teacher knew that his chess partner possessed an exceptional mind, even if he blanched and froze at recitation.

During his fourth year at the school, Mrs. Symmons began to take a special interest in Lazarus' recitals. What she had ignored before, she now turned to her specific attention. She began to call Lazarus alone into her kitchen for a few minutes nearly every day. She would have him sit at one end of her table and read silently, then aloud. After a while, she began to ask him to recite from memory, as best he could, something of what he had just read while remaining seated at the table. She was astonished that he could proceed at great length without perceptible error.

"You have an amazing mind, Mr. Perlman," she once told him. "When you recite, perhaps it would help if you looked up at me and not down at the table. You have such a proud, manly nose. The rest of you should be as proud as your fine nose, so try to look up at those for whom you are reciting."

"A proud nose … a fine and manly nose," Lazarus repeated to himself that day and for several days thereafter. He had never been proud of his nose and certainly had not thought of it as "manly."

A week later, Lazarus again sat reciting for Mrs. Symmons while she busied herself in her kitchen. She had asked him to look at her, so he held his head higher now and his eyes followed her movements. He liked to look at her but until now felt self-conscious, afraid she might catch him staring. He now sounded a little stronger. Casually, Mrs. Symmons interrupted his recitation and asked him to, "Go on, but fetch me the teapot from the top shelf, please," as she pointed to the far end of the room. Lazarus did not hesitate but stood and walked the several steps to the shelf and back returning the tea pot to her, continuing his recitation as he did so. Then she asked for a large baking iron and after that a ladle, then a fourth item and still a fifth until Lazarus had completed his recitation while continually traversing the room and returning to her.

As he finished, he stood extending a soup bowl to her with his right hand. She did not take it. Instead she folded his left hand into both of hers and held them to her heart. "I knew you could do it," she sighed. Only then Lazarus realized what had just happened. He had completed the recitation while on his feet, and he had done so with ease.

"I've noticed that you keep very still, with stiff knees when you stand before the class to recite." She paused for a moment and then asked, "When you say mid-day prayers with the men in the synagogue, you stand do you not?"

"Why, yes, we all stand," he said, not sure why she asked.

"And do you manage your prayers?" she asked.

"Yes, I suppose I do," Lazarus answered, now intrigued.

"Do you stand perfectly still when you pray?" she asked. They both knew the answer.

"No, no I do not. I move some to and fro'."

"Show me."

"What? … um …" Lazarus hesitated.

"Do you move like this?" she asked as she began to twist and shifted her weight from side to side.

"Not quite," Lazarus said, and he began to bow and straighten at the waist in a rocking motion, "a little more like this," he said as he demonstrated with the soup bowl still in his hands.

"Yes," she said, altering her movements to mimic his, "your feet may stay in their place, but you do not stand still. You move about, rocking from your waist and perhaps you turn a little to the left and right, but mostly back and forth, do you not?"

"Why … um … yes, I suppose I do, but all the men and the other boys…"

"You say your prayers while shuckling … like the flame of a candle," she said as they both continued to sway in the same rhythm. "The next time the master calls on you to recite a lesson, try to move about a little when you stand. Even close your eyes and pretend you are praying and no one is listening to you except G-d. Just speak a little louder so you may be heard."

Lazarus stopped his shuckling and watched Mrs. Symmons as she continued to sway back and forth, now with her eyes closed. It was a revelation.

The very next day Master Symmons said, "Our reading has brought us to consider three forms of government – monarchy, aristocracy and democracy. The ancient statesman Cicero warned that combining these forms of governments would end in failure. Mr. Perlman, will you kindly stand and recite from William Blackstone's reply?"

Lazarus knew the assignment. He stood slowly and with a little more confidence, but the same old tension grabbed him by his throat.

Then he spotted the feet of Mrs. Symmons standing in the kitchen doorway. He looked up at her. She stood erect with her chin held high. Then she nodded at him and rocked her body back and forth, demonstrating their shared shuckle of the previous afternoon.

Lazarus shifted his weight and bowed a little. Then he increased his movements and closed his eyes. Without a prompt, without further urging, he spoke.

"Happily for us of this island ... " he said - his recitation came in little spurs at first, *"... the British constitution has long remained ..."* he breathed deeply, *"... and I trust will long continue, a standing exception... "* He again paused, standing motionless, but opened his eyes and again followed the lead of the lady in the doorway, rocking from his waist and knees. Then the words came again and again and yet once more. Within a few moments he had repeated Blackstone's argument that the British Crown, the House of Lords and the House of Commons combine the three forms of government.

He paused briefly one more time, glanced again at Mrs. Symmons, and then deliberately pronounced, *" ... there can no inconvenience be attempted by either of the three branches, but will be withstood by one of the other two; each branch being armed with a negative power, sufficient to repel any innovation which it shall think inexpedient or dangerous. "*

Lazarus then came to a full stop. He strained a moment, but he did not know any more – then he realized he had completed the entire recitation – while standing.

Classmates buzzed and murmured. Master Symmons smiled broadly but otherwise acted as if nothing unusual had transpired. "Thank you, Mr. Perlman, you may be seated," he said.

Lazarus looked toward the kitchen doorway as he took his seat. Mrs. Symmons was staring straight at him. She now stood still, except that her hands were pressed together in prayer posture. She dipped her forearms pointing the fingers of her hands toward Lazarus and then back skyward, touching her forefingers to her lips. Then she repeated the motion as if she were drawing and redrawing a line between G-d and Lazarus.

That line seemed to strengthen as long as Lazarus remained at school. He rocked and flickered his way through the following year with much success. The other boys mocked his recitation style, aped his mannerisms and took to calling him "Master Shuckles," but they could not match his memory. Lazarus felt as though the weight of the Tower of London had been lifted from his shoulders. He seldom stammered or stuttered again.

Just as Lazarus had come to feel truly comfortable at the school, even before the headmaster, he heard disturbing rumors about Master Symmons. An older boy at school said that the master had pursued learning at Cambridge, that there had been some charge of fraud and that he had resigned or been expelled. Lazarus dismissed the rumors and grew angry at boys who repeated them. Current-day libel, he thought.

Lazarus' days at school came to an end too soon for his liking. Upon reaching his birthday that year he recited and read in Hebrew at his Bar Mitzvah in a manner found competent by all in attendance. He stood erect and looked past his manly nose, directly at his audience. Though just thirteen years of age, he spoke like a man.

Mrs. Symmons beamed. She faced him with a hand on each of his shoulders and said, "My dear Mr. Perlman, now you have found your voice."

Chapter 6. Fish Oil

After he left school, Lazarus found his daily schedule reversed. He now continued his apprenticeship with his father in the daytime and read books in the evening. Clothes making didn't require much concentration – at least, he didn't give it much. While sewing, he mulled other matters that paraded across his always active mind.

Mordecai accused him of being overly curious and sometimes distracted. To please the old man, he applied himself as best he could to tailoring and his skills improved. He cut from bolts of cloth now, tracing Mordecai's patterns that had been used over and over. He could make a satisfactory stitch and his knots held, but buttonholes remained a challenge. He managed to complete a few garments on his own from start to finish.

Though Lazarus and Mordecai worked side by side, Lazarus did not think of himself as a tailor. He held a vague conviction that his father's trade was not, somehow, at the heart of his future.

While Lazarus made some small headway with his father in those months, he made strides in his studies. He was aided by a personal friendship with Mr. and Mrs. Symmons. Beginning in the springtime after he had left school, Mrs. Symmons often invited him to spend an evening in their home. Master Symmons directed that Lazarus not call him "Master" any longer. "You are not a pupil in this house Mr. Perlman, but a guest," he insisted. Before many months had passed the three of them attracted a small group of young men from the community who entertained themselves with shared readings and discussion.

Lazarus admired the mind of Mrs. Symmons. She seemed in all intellectual respects the equal of her astute husband. Why that surprised him, Lazarus could not say. Perhaps Mrs. Symmons was different because she was not from the congregation of the Great Synagogue. Lazarus did not think he knew any of her family or even their name. It had never been mentioned. Outside her home, she was reserved as the other women. In her house, she seemed to be as much her husband's colleague as his wife.

Somehow then, it did not surprise Lazarus when he learned that it was Mrs. Symmons who obtained the stacks of books that were kept about their home. She did not provide any particulars, but said that her father possessed a large private library. A number of the books she produced from time to time interested Lazarus. As a friend of the Symmons' household, he was allowed to borrow one or two at a time. He read them diligently between his now weekly evening visits to the Symmons' home.

Lazarus wondered about the library of Mrs. Symmons' father. He imagined its grand stacks of books and polished wood cases and sadly compared it in his mind's eye to his own father's small shop and few stacked bolts of cloth. He longed to see such a collection.

Since Mrs. Symmons had always seemed to favor Lazarus, he managed the courage to ask her. She said it would not be possible for Lazarus to visit her father's house. "I am very sorry my sweet boy," she said. She was unhappy to disappoint him. It showed in her eyes.

At their next encounter Mrs. Symmons was very attentive. During the evening's discussions at her home, she repeatedly solicited Lazarus' views. She put a little honey in his tea. When she served it, she cupped her hand beside her mouth and near his ear. Then she whispered, "I should like to have a lad like you." Lazarus thought it an odd comment. He was not sure what she meant by it.

Then, on Thursday evening of the following week, Lazarus and a few other former students again gathered at the Symmons home. At the end of the evening Mrs. Symmons brought Lazarus his coat. As she did so, she placed her lips almost on his ear and whispered. The whisper tickled and sent a chill through Lazarus. He was not even sure what she had said, but he thought it was, "Can you keep a secret?"

He looked into her face. "Yes, certainly," he said, "you know that I can."

She spoke softly, "I have arranged a treat for you, but do not tell the others." Mrs. Symmons then helped him don his coat and brushed her hand across his shoulders as if to straighten its wrinkles - and perhaps, he thought, to admire the breadth to which his shoulders had now grown. As Mr. Symmons fetched the wraps of the other guests, she then turned Lazarus by those shoulders until he came about to face her.

She smiled fetchingly as she took his left hand, turned his palm upward and placed a folded paper in it. As she pressed it into his palm she curled his fingers about it and said, in a faint voice, "Do you know Leadenhall Street?"

"Yes, I do," he whispered back.

"Good, then follow the directions in this note," she breathed. "It is a healthy walk to the west. Wear your overcoat and remain as inconspicuous as possible. Be there at half past ten tomorrow morning if you are able, but tell no one. This is just for you."

Now his hands trembled and he perspired a little. What intrigue was this, he wondered. Then came her quiet parting words. "I trust your discretion, and I will meet you there." Was this a riddle? What did she mean by it?

Lazarus could not sleep when he went to bed that night. He was to meet Mrs. Symmons at some secret location the next day. He read her note and placed it under the corner of his thin mattress for safekeeping. Then he retrieved and reread it. While she had called it a "note" and it provided directions, it was the length of a letter. Mrs. Symmons had taken some pains to construct it. There could be no doubt that she had given serious thought to their meeting.

What a prospect! He respected Mr. Symmons, but he also admitted to himself that he had feelings for the schoolmaster's young wife. Perhaps she felt the same and had requested the meeting to discuss their dilemma. Perhaps there would be fond embraces and even tender kisses. Perhaps he would have some experience as men and women share. He knew little of such things, but he knew that a mysterious union was a part of love. He understood, either innately or from some snickering he had heard at the free school, that the private parts of women and men were engaged in the union. That fascinated him.

When Lazarus finally did sleep, he partly woke sometime later, hazily suspended in the night somewhere between sleep and consciousness. He lay still in his narrow bed with his eyes closed, but rather than darkness his eyelids were arrayed with soft auburn hair and full brown eyes. His breath was deep and strong. He could feel his heart beat throughout his body. Each heartbeat seemed to levitate him slightly from the bed. Then he realized that he was turgid and throbbing against his bed clothing and heavy covers. His head seemed to whirl about lightly as if he were approaching some high precipice. He did not recognize this condition, but he did not want it to end.

He thought more of Mrs. Symmons and her soft pale skin. He

felt just a bit pinched and he moved a little for comfort. The movement did not free him so he reached with his right hand to check his condition. Just as his fingers made contact, he spontaneously gasped and his back almost arched. He tingled and stretched and bloated. It felt strange and yet wonderful. He touched himself a little more. It provided great pleasure and somehow seemed apt accompaniment to his visions of Mrs. Symmons.

He had felt himself before, but for some reason he took much greater interest in it this night. Instinctively he patted and stroked. He quickened the pace as he slightly increased the pressure. Suddenly, without premeditation, he gasped and almost cried out as he lurched involuntarily and spurted in three, no four strong spasms. The sensation was incredible and compelling. He settled back into his bed and panted deeply. He lay without moving for some time. Then his hands and nose told him he had emitted some warm and sticky fish oil that soaked the area about his groin.

What an unusual and pleasing feeling it was. It was at once new yet not unfamiliar. He did not recall that it had ever happened before. Yet, thinking on it, he felt vaguely as if he had experienced a similar dream several weeks earlier. Had that dream produced the same result? He was not sure. He felt a little uneasy in his stomach and he itched a little. He knew he was not ill. He thought about his meeting with Mrs. Symmons in the morning. He sensed that somehow his night sweat and his appointment were not unrelated. He breathed easily and edged back away from alertness as if he had ingested some sweet sedative.

Then he slept.

Soon after sunrise Lazarus awoke. He thought for a moment that his nighttime experience had been a mysterious dream. He felt below and discovered it had been quite real … the sticky fish oil had hardened some and matted his few short dark hairs. His night clothes adhered to him and his movements pulled at the mat of hair.

He slowly crept out of bed and freed himself enough to deposit a strong and steamy stream into his chamber pot. Then he cleaned himself in the washbowl. Though he was alone in his room, he felt a little embarrassed and secretive about his nighttime experience and soiled bedclothes. He had soaked a smaller area than it had seemed the night before, but it was no dream. He held the evidence of its reality in his hands.

Chapter 7. The Rendezvous

The next morning Lazarus left the shop to "return a borrowed book to a friend - I forgot to return it last evening." His father protested, but the son pretended to not hear him and trotted into the street with a book in his right hand.

With his off hand, Lazarus shielded the unfolded note from the light mist falling on the city. He took long strides, three streets south toward the river until he came to a broad street. Then he checked the note. "Walk west on Leadenhall Street past Grace Church and continue on Cornhill" the note directed. "At Princes Street, bear to your right and proceed to Gresham." Lazarus did so. "Follow Gresham Street to the left until you reach Aldermanbury and turn right."

So many streets, so many turns - by this time Lazarus knew he was on his way to some hidden retreat to be shared with the auburn haired woman with the soft brown eyes. He breathed more heavily than dictated by his pace. "Proceed a short distance until you see on your right a tall building with large steps. Do not stop there but walk around it to the smaller north-side building. Please wait at the side door entrance."

Lazarus located the place. He waited near the side entrance for several minutes. Then the door creaked opened. From within a barrel-chested little man wearing a red vest appeared. He looked up and down at Lazarus, puckered his lips to a point and said, "Pardon sir, are you to meet Miss Baring?"

"Why, no sir. I am waiting for Mrs. Symmons."

"Yes, of course, I do beg your pardon. Please follow me," chirped the little man. Once inside he said, "Please come this way. The lady awaits you in an upper room that is little used these days."

The little man walked a few steps down a hallway, turned to his left and nearly hopped up a flight of stairs on his short legs. Lazarus followed him until they turned into a small rounded room. At the room's center and behind a rectangular table sat a woman. Her hair was styled neatly beneath a fashionable molded hat. Its brim was folded up at one side and a large feather along the other side protruded toward the rear. For a moment, Lazarus did not recognize the lady. Then she smiled at the two men - the toothy smile of Mrs.

Symmons. Only then Lazarus noticed her thin spectacles.

There were three chairs on either side of the table. A sumptuous fur coat the color of her eyes was draped neatly around the chair opposite her. On the table before her sat a large leather handbag with its two strap handles looped in the air. No one else was in the room.

The little man said, "Is this the gentleman, Miss Baring?"

"Yes, thank you for your courtesy Mr. Robin," she replied.

"Very well Miss," the little man said. He looked sternly at Lazarus and hopped about. As he left, he started to close the door behind him, then apparently thought better and left it ajar.

From the doorway, the hat, the draped coat and large leather bag had hidden all of Mrs. Symmons but her face - and provided some little privacy. It was a clever precaution, Lazarus thought; and she was using a false name - no doubt another precaution.

Mrs. Symmons stood slowly now and extended her arm. Lazarus walked to the left end of the table, dropped his book there and quickly rubbed his hands together.   Then he took her small hand between both of his. He held it like a trophy and slowly applied a fond press with his thumbs.

This woman looked unlike the Mrs. Symmons that Lazarus knew. Today she wore a gown of delicate dark green fabric. It featured puffed sleeves and was fluted from just above her waist to the floor where it was hemmed with a golden ribbon. A matching ribbon encircled the sleeves and marked the neckline that fell lower than usual and exposed the white skin covering her collarbone.

Today, there was a fragrance about Mrs. Symmons. Possibly lilacs Lazarus thought. Perhaps it was her new attire, but she also seemed to glow. Her pale skin was always somewhat luminous, but today her skin and something about her whole bearing was different. She looked to Lazarus almost like a painting in which she stood in a soft descending light and all about her remained dull, blurred background. Today, her brown eyes sparkled and her cheeks were flush.

She gently pulled back her hand. Lazarus had said nothing. Now he spoke. He wanted to respect her precautions and not use her true name, so he called her "Madam."

"It is a pleasure to see you, Madam," he said, copying the affectatious style of Mr. Robin.

"I see that you found your way," she said.

"Yes, thank you," Lazarus answered.   He was anxious to
confirm the nature of their meeting, but he was also curious. The
luminous woman before him was not the simple wife of a
schoolmaster. She looked to be an English lady, though Lazarus
knew he was no judge of ladies.   Could she have attired and
perfumed herself for their encounter? Before he calculated another
way to ask it he said, "What is all this?"

"It is, I think, a good place to begin an adventure," she said with
the gentlest turn of a smile at her pink lips. Did he detect that they
bore a little rouge?

Lazarus had meant her new name, her fine clothes, her styled
hair - and that hat. It was surprising, but quite pleasing and she had
already confirmed that they were to have an adventure. His breath
came a little shallow now. She looked down at the bag. Lazarus
wondered what was in such a large handbag. Perhaps it was ample
so as to accommodate some female things as might be required for
an adventure.

Lazarus was but near fourteen years, yet he was man enough to
have noticed Mrs. Symmons' thin, comely body. Her new attire
revealed a new woman. Now she looked softer, with a fuller bosom.
He decided that she was not too thin at all. She seemed to have
rounded out a bit. Now, he thought, she was just about perfect.

Lazarus did not know whether this room was private, but it
seemed to him near secret enough for almost any adventure. His
stomach tumbled. His mouth was dry. He wanted to embrace her -
to hold her and press her body tightly against his own. Here they
were alone. Perhaps this place would do. Still, the door remained
unlatched and he could not be assured that someone might not enter
at any moment. Somehow that made the moment all the more
delicious.

"Come, sit here next to me," Mrs. Symmons said, resting her left
hand on the back of the wooden chair next to her. Lazarus walked
around behind her and pulled the chair away from the table. He
stepped next to her, between their chairs to sit, and their bodies
brushed each other. Lazarus tingled at the touch and she turned
toward him. There was a moment of pause, of expectation. He was
now close enough to smell her sweet breath. Neither of them spoke.
He thought to whisper to her or perhaps to lean in and kiss her

blushing cheek. Then she broke the tension.

She leaned back a little and motioned for him to take his seat. He sat slowly as she did the same. Their chairs both now faced the opening to the room across the table in front of them. They, however, turned to face one another. He stared at her. She was beautiful he now thought - radiant and beautiful.

They just looked into one another's eyes for a moment. Then she leaned a little toward him and spoke with her soft voice, "I have sensed that you have a thirst that is difficult to quench."

How knowing she was, he thought.

"I understand," she said, "I have an appetite myself."

It was what he had hoped to hear.

"That presents us with something of a predicament, does it not?" she asked.

"Why, yes, I suppose it does," he acknowledged. Clearly she wanted to talk before they proceeded. He sighed deeply. He understood. Even improprieties must be carried out properly.

"You do recall that I am trusting you, counting on your discretion?" she asked.

"You shall never be disappointed on that score," he assured her, "I shall never betray you."

"Very well then," she said, "I have a grand surprise for you."

Indeed you do, he thought, but his throat tightened and he could not even speak. This was much as he had expected. What happened next, however, was not.

She stood again and walked around the table. She faced him from behind her draped coat. She whisked up her coat from the chair as if unveiling a statue and announced with a wide smile, "These are for you."

Lazarus was confused. She saw his astonishment. "Wha - what?" he said.

"Why these books here on the chair," she said. She laid her coat aside, one chair over, and grabbed up a few books that had been hidden on the seat of the chair beneath her coat. She placed them on the table and then reached and stacked on several more, perhaps six or seven in all. She bent and slid the stack halfway across the table, next to the leather bag. Then she returned to her original seat, reached out to the stack and drew it toward her.

"There are a few others from my father's collection in the carry bag." She smiled broadly.

"What?" Lazarus said. He was stunned. "Wh - wha - what do you mean? Books? I thought, I mean ... why?" He was bewildered and reduced to stuttering like he had as an eight-year-old.

His heart almost stopped and he knew it missed a measure or two. He didn't hear what she said for the next few moments. He did not really know if she said anything at all. His head seemed to spin about. He felt crushed and completely humiliated. It was fortunate that he was seated, he thought. Otherwise he might have fainted to the floor.

He struggled to catch his breath. He grasped the edge of the table and put his head down on the backs of his hands.

"This is better than I had hoped," Mrs. Symmons said gleefully, "you are overcome."

"Steady," he told himself, "steady." Then, after a moment, he realized that he had not really said anything that disclosed his expectations - or had he? He thought quickly about it. No, he didn't think he had said anything to give himself away. She had done most of the talking. He retraced her words, or as many as he could recall in an instant. Didn't they indicate that she shared his expectations of this encounter? He thought a little more on it. Perhaps ... perhaps they did ... not ... not necessarily ... not really. He would have to think more about it later. His posture at the moment might itself become an embarrassment if he could not recover - and do so hastily. He drew a deep breath and slowly raised his now pale head. He could not look at her. He looked instead at the table and the stack of books and the large leather bag.

He sighed deeply. Then he was back with her.

"I know you love to read," she said. "You looked disappointed when I told you that you could not visit my father's private collection. I thought this place might be a fine substitute."

"Yes, well, I ..." he did not know what else to say.

"I am so glad you are surprised," she said.

He looked about the room. Shelves and cases lined the walls. Entranced as he had been, he had not even noticed. It was not like him to not notice books, but the spell was broken now. Now he saw that the shelves about the room held rows of books and binders of papers.

"What is this place?" he finally managed to ask.

"It is a magical place," she said. "It's Guildhall Library. The offices of the City of London are next door at the Guildhall. This place is usually restricted to use by scholars, researchers, men of government and teachers requiring resources for their studies. Before my father and his brother became established and when I was a girl, my father brought me here regularly."

Lazarus glanced at her now. Her eyes were shining. "We would sneak in the side door, just as you came, and he would deposit me in this very room while he attended to his business next door. Just as now, there were no schools for girls, so my father arranged for one of the aides to watch over me. I think he paid them. Mr. Robin whom you met served as one of my informal tutors. When I was a girl and he was younger, he would fly up the stairs and feed me one volume after another, then soar back below with those I had finished. This," she said looking about, "was my cozy little nest." She caught herself and paused.

"Well," she started again, "it is a place I love. My father cares for it as well. It is one of the few things we still have in common." She bowed her head a little and cleared her throat. Then she continued. "My father now sits on the Board of Governors here. Even though he is engaged always in his business, the people here know him well. He is their employer in a way."

"I see," Lazarus managed to say. But he did not really understand much at all.

"The three volumes in the bag belong to my father," Mrs. Symmons said. "I have borrowed them from his private collection. Please return them to me after you have looked at them. I thought you might like to know what such a man reads."

"Why, yes," he said. He began to know what this was all about, though he did not have any thought on Mrs. Symmons' father. His always active curiosity began to replace his disappointment and embarrassment. Actually, he felt some relief, Lazarus told himself. He sighed. "What have we here?" he asked, motioning toward the stack on the table before them.

"I sent a list to Mr. Robin yesterday," she said. "It contained some things I thought you might like or which might be to your benefit. Let us see how he is coming along on it, shall we?" Before Lazarus answered, she stood and the wooden chair squeaked against the wooden floor as her legs slid it a little rearward. She reached and one by one she took the books from the stack before her, introduced them to Lazarus, then recreated the stack in front of him. There was a long titled book by Thomas Hobbes, *A Fragment on Government* by Jeremy Bentham, *An Inquiry Concerning Human Understanding* by David Hume. Lazarus couldn't suppress a smile at Hume's title. He had so misread the intentions of his hostess that he thought he could well use some insight into human understanding.

Mrs. Symmons lifted the next volume, held it to her breast and sighed. Lazarus was again amused, just earlier he had actually thought he might occupy the position of that book. "How I loved my first encounter with Jonathan Swift," she said. "This one is called *Gulliver's Travels*. I found it most fanciful. My father said that perhaps I did not understand Swift's satire. Perhaps he was right, but I enjoyed *Gulliver* none the less. Sometimes we can enjoy what we do not understand, do you think?"

Lazarus thought this incredible and too ironic. If she but knew. He was relieved that she did not. He answered simply. "I am quite sure of it."

Mrs. Symmons next held up two thin volumes, one in each hand. "Perhaps you should read these two together," she said. "The first was written by Dr. Samuel Johnson and the second by his traveling companion, Mr. James Boswell. They are separate accounts of a tour of the Scottish isles that the two men shared." Then she said, "It's a real lesson, I think, that the two people viewed the singular, shared experience so divergently and relate it so differently."

Was she teasing him now or was this some fantastic coincidence? He dared not ask. When she finally finished with the stacked books, he breathed a sigh of relief.

Then she reached for the large leather bag. "These," she said, "are among my father's favorites. They are quite serious so they may appeal to your nature." She fetched out three volumes from the bag. With these she repeated the introductory process she had followed with the stack. The first of her father's books was by an author Lazarus had heard of, John Locke. The second was by one to whom Master Symmons had made mention, Jean Jacques Rousseau. The third was *An Inquiry into the Nature and Causes of the Wealth of Nations*. Its author was one Adam Smith.

"This last one is quite contemporary," said Mrs. Symmons. "My father truly treasures it. Please be careful with it and return these three to me as soon as you complete any examination you wish to make of them." Mrs. Symmons paused.

Was it over now? He wondered. He had anticipated this rendezvous more than any encounter in his life. His longing – his mistake - his own stupidity had made it a most uncomfortable meeting. Still, Mrs. Symmons stood over him as if awaiting a reply.

Lazarus sat up a little straighter. Then he decided to stand so he would not have to look up at her. On his feet, he didn't feel at all himself. He couldn't find the right words, so he said too many. "I shall take care with these wonderful treasures. I am most grateful. I am not worthy of your thoughtfulness. Thank you. I am quite pleased, really."

"Your response has made it all worthwhile," she said. She cleared her throat, and then added, "I have made arrangements with Mr. Robin. You may come here to study as you like. He may want you to use the side door, just as I have always done."

"I see, th-thank you again … dear lady," Lazarus sputtered.

"I'm afraid I have an appointment," Mrs. Symmons said. "I shall leave you to your explorations and I do hope you enjoy yourself." With that she was gone.

Lazarus just sat there. He had, he thought, narrowly escaped making a complete fool of himself. He vowed he would not forget this lesson, once he figured out exactly what it was. For the moment he was just relieved. As he later walked home toting Mrs. Symmons' leather satchel, he remained a little confused and more than a little troubled. He decided that this was a day he should just like to forget.

Chapter 8. The Shikseh

He could not forget. In the few weeks following his rendezvous with Mrs. Symmons, Lazarus thought of little else. He relived the experience over and over in his mind. It left a bad taste in his mouth - worse than regurgitation. He dwelled on questions left unanswered that day. What was it, if anything at all, that Mrs. Symmons had meant when she had said before their meeting, "I should like to have a lad like you?" It was a strange comment, was it not? Why had she dressed as an English gentlewoman and a prosperous one at that? Why had Mr. Robin called her "Miss Baring?" And who, pray tell, was her father?

Lazarus preferred musing on these questions to further recounting his near disastrous presumption that he had been an object of the woman's affection. He was relieved that he had not betrayed himself to her that day - or he hoped he had not. Since then he had not visited at the Symmons home.

Now he just stared at the leather bag in his small bedroom. He peeked into the bag each morning, just to confirm that the books were still there. Then, he remembered that he would have to return them - and likely have to face her. He would, he decided, look her straight in the eye with a steady gaze and thank her for the loan of the books - as though nothing had happened except the borrowing of books. Well, unless she could read his thoughts, nothing else had happened. Still, from her comments of that day he wondered whether perhaps she did, indeed, know his mind.

Wait though, he could not return the books unread. He realized she would ask his opinions and he would sound as ridiculous as he now felt. He would have to look at them a little.

Lazarus read the Rousseau. The translation seemed strange at first. It was not like anything he had read. He did not know what he had expected, but it was not that either. This Frenchman argued for the nobility of what he called the "natural man" by which he meant mankind before the advent of political states and institutions - or at least in the absence of them. Rousseau laid blame for man's inequality and oppression on governments and the phenomenon of private property.

He next absorbed John Locke. Locke maintained that man's

knowledge comes only through the evidence of his physical senses. As he thought on it, Lazarus developed a suspicion that those who rely on faith as a basis of knowledge might strongly disagree with Locke.

If there was a theme emerging from the favorite books of Mrs. Symmons' father, Lazarus did not yet see it. There was, however, some consistency in that neither of these works was the least bit respectful of the prevailing social order.

Finally, he turned to Adam Smith and read about the efficiency of self-interest. Lazarus had left the Smith volume until last because he knew the name was identified with some theory of economics. He did not expect economics to be so interesting, but Smith advanced a remarkable theory of wealth. He wrote of all the goods that an entire nation produces and consumes assuming the self-determination of each man to select the most efficient application of his talents. There were no natural rights to royal and upper class riches in Smith's world. Neither were those of oppressed minorities born to poor refugees from places like Brandenburg destined to have their future determined by the circumstances of their birth. Lazarus had growing doubts whether he was suited for the life which seemed selected by his own birth - or whether that life was a fit for him. Smith helped him realize something he already knew. There was some lack of efficiency and misapplication of resources in his life as a tailor.

Lazarus by now had almost forgotten why he had started to read the three volumes. They were eye openers - mind stretchers to be sure. Perhaps they were worth even the embarrassment he had suffered in procuring them ... perhaps.

He took particular interest in the ideas of Smith. It was not just the logic of the man's theories. It was also the absence of distinctions of class. Lazarus understood that for Englishmen and continentals alike, the realities were a distinctly structured social order. Nobility, wealth and privilege didn't come from one's industry or virtue. While merchants might find some measure of wealth, the vast hordes of the people were set in narrowly fixed positions established by the circumstances of their birth.

There truly were messages for him in these books. Some passages reverberated in him like a tuning fork. He selected and copied to note papers a few of the best parts. His favorite from among these favorites was an excerpt from Adam Smith:

> *Every Individual is continually exerting himself to*
> *find out the most advantageous employment ... It is his*
> *own advantage, indeed, and not that of society, which he*
> *has in view. But the study of his own advantage*
> *naturally, or rather necessarily, leads him to prefer that*
> *employment which is most advantageous to the society ...*
> *he is in this ... led by an invisible hand....*

Lazarus had often felt as though he were guided by an invisible hand. He felt less guilty now about his lack of devotion to his father's trade - and to his father's old ways.

He finished the Smith volume on a Monday evening. On Thursday evening he called at the Symmons' home. Mr. Symmons admitted him as usual, but as he entered he could see that Mrs. Symmons was ill at ease. She still had the glow he had seen at Guildhall Library, but she looked a little bloated and uncomfortable, as thought her supper had not agreed with her. With his mind still troubled by the meeting at Guildhall, Lazarus prepared himself for the worst. It never came.

"Where have you kept yourself?" Mr. Symmons asked.

"We have missed you," said his wife.

He told them that he had been providing some additional help to his father in the evenings and reading the books belonging to the father of Mrs. Symmons. He handed her the leather bag.

"Did any of these writers interest you?" asked Mrs. Symmons.

"Why, yes, all three of them."

"And which interested you the most?"

"I think Mr. Adam Smith."

"Well then," said Mrs. Symmons, "your tastes run to those of my father, for he much favors Mr. Smith."

Here was his opening. "Please tell me about your father. Where does -"

At that, Mr. Symmons' ears pricked up and he immediately interrupted. "How did you manage John Locke?" he asked.

"Well sir, he was difficult for me, more so than even the translation of the Frenchman."

"Indeed," said Mr. Symmons, "were you able to complete the volume then?"

"Why yes," Lazarus answered, "and his 'empirical' evidence of knowledge was provoking, but I do not know that it is as bold as the other two. Their ideas surely must be viewed as revolutionary."

"Revolutionary? Truly, but did you see no challenge to established order in Mr. Locke?"

"Well, Mr. Symmons, I do expect that advocates of faith may find him some annoyance."

"Some annoyance? Some annoyance?" Mr. Symmons began to laugh. "Well said Mr. Perlman, he is surely an annoyance! My goodness, an annoyance."

As they talked, Lazarus became comfortable again in their presence. He had thought perhaps his visit would be awkward, strained or that he would not be welcomed. He sensed none of that. It was as though nothing at all happened at Guildhall except the borrowing of a few books. Then he forced himself to remember - indeed, despite his excited state at the time, that was all that had actually transpired.

There was really no other opportunity that evening to ask Mrs. Symmons the questions that remained from the encounter. Things went so unexpectedly well that he now doubted that he wanted to risk asking her any personal question at all.

Still, in the following days, those questions remained and would not leave him at peace. Then it occurred to him how to investigate the questions without posing them to Mrs. Symmons. At the first opportunity he returned to Guildhall Library. Now that he knew the way, it was just a twenty-minute walk. Last time he had made the journey it had seemed much longer - in both directions. No prior arrangement for this visit had been made, so no one met him at the side door. He was not sure why he was not to use the main entrance anyway, except that he looked more a boy than a scholar and, perhaps, for the same reason he had been asked to be "inconspicuous." That term he understood. It meant not readily identifiable as a Jew. Fortunately, he found the side door unlocked.

Inside, standing at a tall desk facing the main entrance, he found Mr. Robin. Lazarus walked to the side of the desk. "Good day Mr. Robin," he said, "you may not rememb -"

"Mr. Perlman," Mr. Robin replied, "Good day sir, how may I assist you?"

As Lazarus though just how to word his question, Mr. Robin

said, "I must beg your pardon sir. When we did not see you these past few weeks, I reshelved the books Miss Baring selected for you. I have kept her list however, and will be pleased to produce any of them you may require."

Lazarus hadn't thought of that. He had ignored Mrs. Symmons' invitation to study at the library. Mr. Robin now seemed to confirm the invitation. At the end of his first visit Lazarus had never wanted to see the place again. Now he found the idea intriguing, but that was not why he had come. Besides, Mr. Robin had again referred to her as "Miss Baring." It was his chance.

Lazarus asked it as he had quickly planned. "When I was here earlier ... um ... with Miss - Miss Baring, she also loaned me a few books belonging to her father. I found them fascinating and would like to understand a man who collects such works. How can I learn about Mr. Baring?"

Mr. Robin showed the hint of a condescending smile - despite his position of service. "Why Mr. Perlman, surely you know of Mr. Francis Baring?"

"I am afraid not, Mr. Robin," he said. "Can you enlighten me?" It was the right approach Lazarus thought.

"Why, of course," Mr. Robin said as he tugged at the hem of his red vest. "Mr. Baring is a rather famous Londoner. He and his brother established a trading house some years back. The house of Baring now serves as established banker to England's most successful merchants. It is one of but a few banks to enjoy direct account with the Bank of England. Mr. Francis Baring, Miss Baring's father that is, also acts as an advisor to the Prime Minister. It is rumored about that he may one day be elevated to the peerage. If you go about in London, surely you will hear of his prominence."

Then Mr. Robin puffed out his chest, "We are most pleased that Mr. Baring was, just two years past, appointed the Chief of the Board of Governors of this 300-year-old institution." Mr. Robin unfurled his arms, "About these premises you may hear him referred to as 'Governor Baring.' He takes particular interest in our work. Both our collections and our patronage have grown under his direction."

"Mr. Robin, you are a most knowledgeable gentleman" Lazarus said. "I am in your debt. Now can you tell me why you do not refer to his daughter as Mrs. Symmons as I know her to be?"

With that Mr. Robin abruptly exhaled and his chest fell. He scowled and his mouth resumed its narrow point. He hesitated, then he said in a lower voice, "Follow me if you please, sir." He walked passed Lazarus and into an aisle between two high rows of shelved books. He kept his back toward the tall desk, and he motioned for Lazarus to stand abreast of him. Then, without facing Lazarus, he whispered, "You understand that Mr. Baring is my ultimate superior here at the library, do you not?"

"Why, yes, I understand," said Lazarus. Perhaps he had made a misstep, he thought to himself.

"Then surely you must appreciate, young Mr. Perlman, that I am bound to please him at the risk of my position."

Lazarus assured him, "Mr. Robin, I have no intention to expose you to any risk whatever."

Mr. Robin pulled at his vest and looked down as if addressing the floor, "I shall be pleased to assist your studies here, Mr. Perlman, just as Miss Baring requested." Then there was a long pause. Lazarus did not know what to say. Just as he was about to excuse himself, Mr. Robin cleared his throat a little and started again, speaking lowly, "Miss Baring has been one of our most devoted patrons and we remain most fond of her, of that you can be certain. Her father has instructed that she is to retain all her privileges here. But he has also instructed that we do not comment on the private life of Miss Baring since she left his house. That shall remain our practice unless Governor Baring cares to instruct us otherwise."

"Very well," said Lazarus. He knew he had been too direct. "I can see that you are a man of discretion." He hoped it was the proper retreat. Then he thought again and added, "If I may, I shall accept your kind invitation and soon commence some studies here with your assistance."

"As you wish Mr. Perlman, now please excuse me," Mr. Robin said as he walked away.

Lazarus had not come up empty. He had learned that Mrs. Symmons was the daughter of a leading banker - an English gentleman. Why had it not occurred to him before? If Mr. Baring had been appointed a Governor of Guildhall Library, he was a public official, and surely a member of the Church of England. Mrs. Symmons was not Jewish at all. She had married far beneath her social station and farther yet from her religion. She had been raised a Protestant - a gentile girl. Lazarus searched for the word ... Mr. Symmons had married a "Shikseh!"

As he walked home from Guildhall his mind raced. He should have known or at least suspected. Mrs. Symmons' secular knowledge, her lack of servility to her husband and all her unorthodox ways were clues he should have detected. Wait though, he had noticed them. He was a devotee of her uncommon manner. Indeed, these were traits he admired about the woman, but he had failed to catch their significance - or at least the heart of it.

Gentiles do not masquerade as Jews. He had never heard of it. He could be forgiven his oversight. She had pale skin and auburn hair. Still, he knew many fair skinned Jews. He was one himself. The entire Rosenberg family of the community had blondish red hair and they were not the only ones. The signs had been there, he admitted to himself. None of them was telling in itself, but taken together they now seemed obvious.

Mrs. Symmons was passing as a Jewess! He did not know how he felt about it. It was strange. He had heard many times of Jews trying to pass as Christians. He understood why some felt that necessary at times. They did it to avoid persecution, sometimes even deportation and banishment or just to advance themselves. Mr. Symmons himself, it was rumored, had posed as a Christian in order to attend an English university.

But it was not he who was trying to pass now. It was his wife. But why? Why would a Christian woman, particularly one of position and advantage, pose as a Jewess? Perhaps it had to do with her husband's position. Would a Jew married to a gentile be selected as a schoolmaster at the Jews' Free School? She must truly love him. How mistaken Lazarus knew he had been. Perhaps her adoption of Judaism and her observances of the holy days were also a matter of conviction. He would like to think that they were.

Lazarus had some answers that he had not had the day before, but they raised still more questions. Oh my, he thought, what does she do about the Mikvah, the ritual communal bathing of Jewish women following their time in the moon's cycle? Does she participate? Does she hide her identity from the other women? That was one mystery about which he knew he would never inquire.

Lazarus' wanted to share his discovery with someone. But wait!

Lazarus remembered that when Mrs. Symmons had met him at Guildhall Library she had pledged him to honor her trust in him - to act with discretion, did she not? His mind had been elsewhere at the time, but he thought he remembered that - and that he had probably given his assurance. Wait again! He recalled it now. He had thought she was swearing him to secrecy before beginning a romance with him. He had sworn he would never betray her, but they had been speaking of two different matters. This is what she meant by it, he thought. She must have meant that she required his discretion as to her true identity. Once she appeared as "Miss Baring," attired as she had been, and told him something about her father, she knew he would realize that her parentage was not what people assumed it to be. Those at the Great Synagogue and at the Jews' Free School thought her to be Jewish, just as he had. The point of the oath he had given had been lost on him - due to his misjudgment about the reason for their rendezvous – and, he thought, because he was an ignorant boy who had never heard of the famous Francis Baring.

A narrow miss - a near disaster.

Lazarus had not known his mother; if she were alive, would she have warned him to greater caution where women are concerned? Are they all such dangers? He wondered. What other learning was imparted from mothers to sons? Whatever it might be, he was ignorant of it. As a child he had never missed the presence of a mother. How can one miss something one has never known? Now, as a young man, he felt deficient for not having known her.

Chapter 9. Rumors of Cambridge

As time passed Lazarus tried, successfully he thought, to put fondness for Mrs. Symmons out of his mind. He arranged with his father to again perform his work in the evenings as he had while at school. He added early morning work to overcome his father's objections. He visited at the Symmons home just one evening per week, on Thursdays, when others were there for the discussion group.

He spent most days at Guildhall Library where Mr. Robin retrieved the books on the list for him. They included some that had not yet made their way to the table stack on his first memorable visit. One by one he consumed them. A person without guidance from a mother, he thought, must find his bearings elsewhere. He felt himself growing just a bit with each book he ingested.

Mrs. Symmons seemed to be growing a little each week as well. One Thursday evening her proud husband announced that she was "with child." Lazarus sincerely congratulated them both. Mrs. Symmons then turned to Lazarus and whispered, "I should be happy to have a lad like you." Lazarus knew those words. Weeks earlier, he had completely misunderstood the same whisper. This time her meaning was unmistakable. He felt relieved. All his lasting questions about her could remain a mystery. He was again at rest with his two good friends - his mentors. Their history was their own. He was privileged to share some of their present and he knew it.

Now that Lazarus was content to leave the Symmons' past undisturbed, Mrs. Symmons shared their story without so much as an inquisitive glance from him. Late that evening, she motioned him to her kitchen. He followed her there as he had when a lad in school. This is more classroom than cook room, he thought. Once alone there, she turned to him and said, "You seemed a little troubled when we met at Guildhall some weeks ago. I later thought how confusing that all must have been to you since I had to hurry off on my way."

"Not at all," - he lied. "It was ... um ... stimulating, new to me," - he told the truth.

"I'm sorry that I couldn't stay that day to better explain.

Actually, our meeting came just in advance of my examination by my father's physician. I could not postpone that engagement."

"Certainly not," Lazarus acknowledged, as he looked at her stomach.

"Yes, well, you must now know the identity of my father and perhaps suspect me a bit," she said, searching his face.

"Mrs. Symmons, you can be confident that I would never --"

"Oh, I have no doubt of it, Lazarus, honestly I don't."

"Nor need you," he said, pleased that she called him by his given name.

"I just - I would like you to know something more - particularly of Mr. Symmons."

"That is not at all necessary," Lazarus said.

"Yes, I understand it's not necessary," she said, "but I need to tell some – to tell you." She seemed unsteady, not at all the confident gentlewoman he had encountered at Guildhall Library. "Shall we sit?" she said, and they took their customary places at the table.

"My husband's boyhood was spent near here," she began. "Following his Bar Mitzvah and completion of school, his days were spent helping his father, a candle maker. While delivering candles at St. Paul's Academy, my husband made the unlikely acquaintance of a student there. Both of them were just about your age at that time. I say 'unlikely' because the student was from a devout Anglican family. After grammar school, he had come to London from his home in the north of Cambridgeshire to attend St. Paul's. Since it is on the grounds of the Cathedral, fires were not allowed, but the students and masters burned candles constantly."

Mrs. Symmons studied Lazarus, then continued. "Usually my husband came and went without any notice. On one occasion, though, he came upon a young man perusing a chessboard. The student engaged him in conversation and then in a game of chess. This led to more matches and more conversation. The young man never acted as though he viewed my husband in any way inferior. Over time they became friends."

"Who was the young man?" Lazarus asked.

Mrs. Symmons ignored the question and continued. "This young man of St. Paul's had lost his father, an ordained Anglican and a schoolmaster, early in his life. When my husband first encountered him," Mrs. Symmons said, "he was a guest in the house of a wealthy family by the name of Gibbs. I cannot tell all, but it was through this friendship that, some years later, certain arrangements were made, at no expense to my husband, for the admission of both young men to St. John's College at Cambridge University. I suppose you have heard gossip to this effect."

"Yes," Lazarus conceded, "there have been rumors of Cambridge, but I did not know it was St. John's."

"Well, each young man distinguished himself there. One won the prestigious annual Latin essay contest. Actually, he won it twice and became the first student ever to do so. The other won St. John's annual chess tournament," Mrs. Symmons proclaimed a little proudly.

Lazarus did not need to ask which won the chess tournament.

"As it happened," Mrs. Symmons continued, "it was through this same friend that I came to know Mr. Symmons, though he then spelled and pronounced his last name differently. The two young men were a lovely pair. Our friend was serious and tireless. He enjoyed the humor and sarcasm of my husband, just as you seem to do. In fact, you remind me of him at times."

"Indeed," Lazarus said, "but how did you meet Mr. Symmons?"

"A group of young men gathered around these two. It was not unlike the debating societies one now sees on occasion in London. Our friend undertook to include persons of all perspectives so long as they were willing to do the shared readings and attempted to contribute to the discussions. I was something of a student myself, having been encouraged by my father, though not of their caliber."

Lazarus suspected she was too modest, but he didn't want to interrupt the story.

"I was spending the summer with my aunt and encountered our friend at a party given at her country estate on St. Ives Road near Cambridge. Our friend discussed philosophy with me; quite unlike men are usually willing to do. When he found me to show interest and have some small exposure, he invited me to join the group one afternoon. Our friend, you see, actually believes that females are capable of rational thought." She paused, perhaps conscious of her exuberance.

Lazarus, though, liked her fervor.

She slowed her breathing and continued, "At his invitation, I came to join in some of the discussions of the group. Only two females were included and my aunt objected to my attendance without a chaperone. I confess that I took to misrepresenting my whereabouts to her while attending the group discussions. Somehow, that practice repeated itself regularly over some weeks."

Lazarus' eyes were fixed on her lips, awaiting every syllable.

"Though I never played chess, my husband and I did share debates before we became drawn to one an --" she stopped short. "Well," she said, "I do not know that is literally true, for I liked young Mr. 'Simmons' right away." She now pronounced the first syllable of her husband's name to rhyme with "crime" rather than its usual pronunciation rhyming with "him." Mrs. Symmons heaved a sigh and started in again, "Candidly, only a few weeks had passed when I realized that I had fallen in love with him." She paused and took a deep breath. Lazarus did the same.

"Mr. 'Simmons' discerned my feelings," she said. "He took me aside and disclosed that he was not 'Mr. Lawrence Simmons', an Anglican, as I had been given to understand, but instead 'Levi Symmons, a poor London Jew.'" She mocked her husband's voice as she said it, then resumed her own. "As you know, both of England's great universities admit only Anglicans. Then as now, Jews especially are not allowed."

She looked down at the table, "I had not learned much of prejudice from my father, except that it was prevalent. Still, I was shocked to learn this secret. In truth I felt hurt," she said, again looking up at Lazarus. "Mr. Symmons apologized and said that while I was not the target of his deception; neither should I become its victim." Mrs. Symmons sighed again. Lazarus did as well.

"After a short time, I realized that while Mr. Symmons may have deceived me, he had not intended to do so. He had not even encouraged my affections toward him, not really, except as imagined in my own mind."

Lazarus nodded. He understood only too well how one could mistakenly imagine the affections of another.

"Actually," Mrs. Symmons said, "in telling me the truth he also had entrusted me with his very life at Cambridge. A life he so well loved." She spoke unguardedly, as though Lazarus were her dearest friend. "Well, as you might imagine, that made me admire him all the more, and I kept his confidence. Indeed, sometime later, I confessed to him that my affections were no less."

"And what was his reaction?" Lazarus was bold now.

Mrs. Symmons spoke slowly. "At first he said that I could not love him. Then he relented. He said he felt powerfully drawn to me; that either I should leave Cambridgeshire and not return while he remained at college, or that he must leave the university, because he feared he could not be trusted in my vicinity. He said he felt helpless, as he could not convince himself that he did not love me … with that I was sure that I could not give him up."

Lazarus detected a little water in Mrs. Symmons' big eyes. He patted his empty pockets for a kerchief as she went on. "My father took a holiday and joined us at my Aunt's home. The day after he arrived, I told him that I had feelings for a young man at St. John's." Here she winced and said, "That, I'm afraid, instigated a disaster."

"Did you tell your father that 'Mr. Lawrence Simmons' was actually 'Mr. Levi Symmons,' a Jew?" Lazarus panted. He was breathless.

"No, I most certainly did not!" she exclaimed. "I was not ashamed; I just wanted to keep the confidence of Mr. Symmons. I suppose I also wanted to avoid any risk. Unfortunately, my father, as a matter of course and intending to ferret out any fortune seeker, commissioned an investigation of 'Mr. Lawrence Simmons.' He quickly discovered the truth for himself. At first, he took an understanding tone. He informed me of his findings and seemed prepared to console me." She paused here for several deep breaths. She gulped and blotted her eyes with her sleeve.

Recounting these events had seemed to be such pleasure for her a few moments before. Now she seemed to feel an equal measure of pain. "Forgive me," she said, "I've thought about those days a thousand times, but I seldom speak of them."

"Thank you for telling me," said Lazarus, "you need not continue." He longed to hear it all, but not if it grieved her. He started to rise.

"Please," she said, "keep your seat. I will be fine. I want you to understand. My husband knows that I planned to tell you. Let me finish."

It was as if she had waited to tell this story until sure of her audience. Lazarus felt honored. He resettled in his chair and looked softly at her. She was irresistible, but he now felt sympathy and, he told himself, not one bit of lust.

"Let's see … my father was consoling, even apologetic, but he said that of course I would not want to place myself in the position of giving my heart to a Jew. I told him that I knew Mr. Symmons was a Jew - that he had told me so himself - but that it was now too late. I told my father that my heart was no longer my own and that I would place myself in any position for my love." Mrs. Symmons ran short of breath and paused.

After placing a hand at her breastbone, she continued, "My father was stunned. He said he admired the young man for his earlier disclosure to me. He was convinced, however, that I underestimated the rigors and limits of the life I might have as the wife of a Jew. Whether we two were in love had little to do with it. He said Mr. Symmons could not forever maintain his deception, and I knew little of the struggles of the Jews. He was certain that we would both become outcasts … he insisted he could not allow his daughter to undertake such a life."

Lazarus thought to comment, but wanted to hear every detail.

"When I persisted and said it could not be helped, my father summoned Mr. Symmons to my aunt's home. In my presence, he repeated his arguments to Mr. Symmons. When he concluded, Mr. Symmons actually thanked my father for the audience and for his concern. He told my father that, while he had not formally proposed marriage, he intended to do so upon his graduation; and he looked at me, rather than my father, when he said it. He said he knew he was not worthy of me, but that it had little to do with being Jewish. He said that I should, indeed, consider my father's arguments since I would soon have a decision to make.

My father then became angry. He said that both I and Mr. Symmons should know that if I accepted any proposal without his consent, I would not have so much as a penny from him.

Mr. Symmons didn't even raise his voice. He told my father that, while he would prefer to have my father's blessing, neither the absence of money nor of consent would prevent his proposal.

My father fumed. Then he set down an ultimatum: He held out some papers and said that his investigation included evidence that Mr. Symmons had perpetuated a fraud in his application for Cambridge. He flung the papers on the floor before Mr. Symmons. He said that Mr. Symmons could not have me. He said that if Mr.

Symmons persisted, he would disclose Mr. Symmons' true identity as a Jew, provide the evidence of his lies to St. Johns, and ruin his scheme.

This young man loved learning. You, above all our friends, can I think understand his love for it." Mrs. Symmons looked pleadingly at Lazarus. He nodded. Finding affirmation, she continued, "He had subjugated his own heritage, which he cherished, in its pursuit. He had done exceptionally well in his studies and was but weeks from receiving his certificate."

She stopped a moment. "Then ... then Mr. Symmons stooped and gathered the investigation papers from the floor and slowly straightened them. He stood erect and stepped in front of my father, looking him directly in his face. He handed the papers back to my father and said, 'May G-d help me sir, but I treasure your daughter as well as my own breath. Do as you must, I will not renounce my love.'" Tears now ran freely down Mrs. Symmons' pale face. Pregnant and teared she shone with more beauty than ever. Lazarus moved his sleeve to his own eyes. Neither spoke. He could not break such a reverent silence. In a moment more, she did so.

"My father had put his own honor at stake. He did just as he had threatened. Mr. Symmons was disgraced and dismissed from the university."

"Thank you for telling me," Lazarus said. He had never been more earnest.

"There is a little more," she said. "My father is not a demon. When I left him he told me that his heart and his home would always be open to me, but that he would not provide any allowance to benefit Mr. Symmons." She placed both her hands on her belly and patted it with her fingers as she said, "I think I am ready to see my father's reaction to this little development."

Lazarus smiled with her.

"Still," she sighed, "Mr. Symmons and I have learned that my father was right about many things. We found it impossible to live in separate worlds; and my husband was not welcome outside his own. I studied my husband's traditions - it helped me to know him better. In them I found many of the same values I already knew. They may have different names and shades of meaning, but even some of the stories used to teach them are familiar. I've found compassion, humanity, respect for past sacrifices, rules for behavior, a present but unseen G-d, and … and love in both traditions. Clearly there are differences, but we have managed to share our lives. For me, it has been a discovery, but much of it has been rediscovery."

Lazarus nodded.

"I admit," Mrs. Symmons said, "I like my husband's manner of celebrating Shabbat. I enjoy its observance more than I appreciated the Sabbath in my father's house. That may be my own doing, but it is true.

The Jews, as we both know, have often found persecution at the hands of so-called Christians," Mrs. Symmons said, as if she belonged to neither group rather than to both, "but I have never thought it defensible. The Christian Messiah advocated love, not just for one's own kind, but even of one's enemies. I have found no enemy to His teachings in the traditions of my husband and no dishonor to my faith in my husband's rituals. Somehow, I have never felt that I have betrayed my Christian faith." Mrs. Symmons' voice had now gone from near sobs to approaching defiance. "Perhaps I twist my mind seeking justification," she said, "but my heart is at ease."

Her face was dry now and her voice resolute. "Words," she said, "fail to … in my heart I remain a Christian. At the same time, I love my husband and his ways, as a man … and as a Jew. I know it is strange, but do you think that perhaps you can understand just a little?"

"Yes," Lazarus said, "I believe I truly can … and I treasure your trust." It was all he could say.

It seemed all she needed. "Well, Mr. Perlman - my dear Lazarus - you are most welcome," she beamed at him. "You have been – you are a pleasure to both my husband and myself … as a student and I dare say as a true friend."

It was the best compliment ever, due in great part to its source. He did not think he deserved it. Now he felt guilty for his earlier longing for her.

Mrs. Symmons seemed to sense his discomfort, but she continued, "True friends are rare. Fortunately, from the day we left Cambridgeshire, we have had the support of our Anglican friend. It was through his assistance that we were lawfully wed. These days though, he keeps himself too busy to do much more than correspond with my husband. Oh, one more thing," she said, and she waited for

Lazarus to look at her, "I want you to know that my husband has never spoken ill of my father. He says that he had already gotten his learning at St. John's and that a degree was of little meaning to him. He now, with his lovely wit, tells me that he has had 'much the better of the bargain in trading a common paper certificate for a most uncommon wife.'" She blushed.

Lazarus silently chastised himself. How could he have missed her great devotion to her husband? He marveled at how his young man's urges had temporarily blinded him to everything else. He marveled, too, at this woman, and at his failure to perceive the character of her husband. He knew he loved them both, but in a way much different from what he had thought.

Even before it ended, Lazarus realized that the evening was a landmark ... one of those moments one lives for during the long stretches of unremarkable days and nights ... and this precious woman said that she hoped to have a son just like him.

Chapter 10. The King Solomon Club

More graduates of the free school began to join the Thursday evening gatherings at the Symmons' home. Review of news journals and discussion of contemporary writers remained the core activity. Sometimes, Mr. Symmons separated his guests into two groups, each assigned to argue one side of a question. He also began to invite guest speakers to address the group.

The first lecture came from Mr. J. G. A. Reinhold. He told of the journeys around the world of Captain James Cook and his ship *Endeavour*. He related both adventure and deprivations experienced by the crew. Lazarus and some other regulars - there were now nearly twenty - took particular delight in Mr. Reinhold's description of a strange animal. In the land of Australasia or southern Asia, which the immigrants to the newly established colonial settlement there had shortened to "Australia," there lived a most peculiar beast. Its short fur took on earthen hues and it stood sometimes as tall as a man; but it bounded about on huge hind feet and carried its young in some sort of sack at its ventral side. Mr. Reinhold said that even its name meant "I do not know what it is" to the aboriginals of the land. He pronounced it "kang-a-roo."

Mr. Reinhold demonstrated the strange animal. Placing his heels close together and his feet out-turned, he hopped about the room a little while holding his clasped hands low before his belly to simulate the kangaroo's young. As if they were still in school, some of the boys joined his game, as did Mr. Symmons. He held his hands out, inviting his wife to join him. She declined and kept her seat. She laughed at her husband and put her hands on her big low belly as if her baby tried to join the game on its own.

Later that evening, after Mr. Reinhold had left, one of the fellows suggested that the group name itself "The Kangaroo Debating Society." "Since," he said, "we are as unique as that animal."

"Actually, we are not," said Lazarus. "I've read that a number of 'Reform Clubs' and 'Revolutionary Societies' here in London meet to consider matters such as the situation in France, but I don't know of another Jewish group …" he said, extending an open hand toward Mr. Symmons.

"Unhappily," said Mr. Symmons, "if Rabbi Solomon has his way, our group will soon disband."

"How can that be?" asked Mrs. Symmons and she rolled her eyes. "This group is not sponsored by the free school. He has no say."

"You are right, of course," Mr. Symmons assured her. "However, Rabbi Hirschell tells me that old Solomon has complained to the Governing Board and to the rabbis at the synagogue. He claims that we lead these young men here away from the traditions that - "

"Excuse me," Mrs. Symmons interrupted, "but no one outside this room need have any concern about this gathering of friends. These young men are no longer students of the free school. They are graduates, men - here of their own free will."

The boys readily agreed. Rabbi Solomon's attack on the group didn't surprise Lazarus. "Are we not a self-formed society," he asked, "like a club?"

"If we are a club, then we should have a name?" said the boy who had earlier suggested one.

"Quite so, how about 'The Club of Dog-eared Pages?'" another suggested.

"Or 'The After Dark Discussion Society'," said a third.

The one discussion in the room disintegrated into several, all humming at the same time. Lazarus glanced at Mrs. Symmons who looked perplexed. She shook her head and hunched her shoulders as if to signal for his help. Lazarus knew the discussion had strayed from her concern - Rabbi Solomon.

He pulled at his chin. "How do we deflect Rabbi Solomon's intervention?" he asked himself. For some reason he thought momentarily of the great king of the Torah who was famous for his clever solutions.

Lazarus slid to the edge of his seat and blurted out, "Let us call our gatherings 'The King Solomon Club.'"

There was momentary silence.

"What better name for seekers of wisdom?" he asked.

"Yes, indeed," said Mr. Symmons.

"And - and," Lazarus continued, "if anyone wonders whether we respect our traditions, he can take comfort in that the very name of our group honors a great king of our forefathers." Some favorable comment arose, but Lazarus was not finished. "Moreover ..." he said, regaining attention, "moreover, Mr. Symmons could say to Headmaster Solomon that his former students insisted that we name our little society to indicate our respect for our former headmaster of the same name - Solomon - and his, um ... his contributions to our discipline and education."

The room buzzed.

"Any authority might certainly conclude that such a group should be perpetuated. Am I correct?" Lazarus said and leaned back in his chair.

The words were hardly out of Lazarus' mouth when Mrs. Symmons said, at some volume, "I like it! Well done Lazarus, well done my sweet boy." Then she caught herself as though she did not want to cause Lazarus embarrassment by her show of enthusiasm. Lazarus had known embarrassment. It was nothing like he felt now.

Soon the rest of the group joined in congratulating Lazarus. From that moment, the members of the group began to call themselves "The King Solomon Club."

* * * * * * *

It may have been her upset at the threats of Rabbi Solomon. It could have been her baby joining the game of the bounding kangaroo. Whatever the cause, just a few moments later that very evening Mrs. Symmons cried out, "Levi, it is time." She turned to Lazarus and smiled, but her smile quickly turned to a look of surprise and then of pain. He and Mr. Symmons took her, each by an arm, and helped her to her bed. Then Lazarus ran for the midwife as Mr. Symmons held her hand. When the midwife arrived, the others left, but Lazarus lagged.

"May I stay?" he asked Mr. Symmons.

"If you like," he replied.

Pacing in the parlor with Mr. Symmons, Lazarus suddenly feared for Mrs. Symmons. He remembered what childbirth had meant for his own mother. At around midnight, Mr. Symmons sent Lazarus home. The following morning, he learned that the Symmons' were parents of a healthy girl. The mother was doing well. Lazarus felt relief.

The meetings of the King Solomon Club were suspended for several weeks. When they recommenced, the first week centered on the new arrival. Given current events and world turmoil, Lazarus wondered what kind of a life she might live.

Lazarus heard no more about the threat from Rabbi Solomon. Perhaps it had ended. The King Solomon Club, though, was far from ended. Now it really began.

The next inquiry was a predictable one given the interest in it throughout England. Earlier in the year, the peasants of Paris had stormed the Bastille and much of France stirred in a continuing chaos. It was now October and word had just come that the women of Paris had marched to the Palace at Versailles to demand bread. Once there, they took the royal family hostage. They declared that they acted out of hunger and in order to prevent retribution or a counter revolt. Along with General Lafayette and 20,000 French guardsmen, they "persuaded" King Louis to return to Paris where it was believed he would face the charges of the revolutionary patriots. In France some 20 million peasants and commoners were seeking out the nearly half-million nobles and elitists who had worked, taxed and starved them to maintain their extravagances. The entire region, indeed all of Europe, was on edge.

Most of those in attendance at the King Solomon Club wanted to argue for the French peasants. Mr. Symmons divided the group into halves. This time, however, in recognition of the name of the club, he dubbed the sides the "Rehoboams" and the "Jeroboams." Still the teacher, Mr. Symmons interjected a short review of how Israel became divided after the reign of Solomon between his son Rehoboam who repressed the people of Israel and Jeroboam be Navat who led the contest against Rehoboam to relieve the burdens placed upon the people. What a talent Mr. Symmons has for casting the ancients into present-day controversies, Lazarus thought.

He was assigned to the Rehoboams and required to argue for King Louis XVI. Clearly he could not directly argue for repression of the peasants. He decided to take a different approach. He argued for reform in lieu of revolt. The revolt, he asserted, was tyranny of the masses. It was mob rule. He argued that the "natural man" is not "noble," as asserted by the writings of Rousseau, but rather a "savage." Had not the mob of "natural" Frenchmen without rule marched around Paris carrying the bloody heads of Foullon, the Minister of Finance, and deLaunay, the Governor of the Bastille, high on staves? The crowds had reportedly cheered at the sight.

This was not liberty; it was anarchy. Support of the lawless, bloodthirsty mobs of France could lead to the exportation of disorder. It must be stopped.

Lazarus made the arguments. He did not believe them, but he enjoyed the debate. No winner was declared. The Rehoboams were left to consider the arguments of the Jeroboams and vice versa.

In the days that followed, Lazarus became troubled. It was not that he had been assigned to argue against the peasants. It was, he decided on reflection, that the whole idea of sitting in debate, however heated, seemed somehow detached. Just across the channel people were fighting and even dying for the hope of a better future. It was not just debate to the people of France or even to their privileged class. It was life and death. How trivial my little life would seem, he thought, to either the people crying for *"liberte, egalite et fraternite"* or for those seeking to retain the order of sovereign rule.

Lazarus did not have long to enjoy his little misery. Soon another matter was identified for debate. Discussion followed discussion, punctuated by the occasional guest lecturer. It was at once exhilarating and, Lazarus thought, a little pathetic.

Mrs. Symmons was now occupied with her child. The baby, sometimes in her arms and sometimes asleep in the next room, reminded Lazarus that her gender was excluded from the free school and from the community's councils. Except for Mrs. Symmons, they were absent from discussions of the King Solomon Club as well. It was as if men assumed that women had no worthy thoughts to share. Lazarus knew the child's mother. He knew that any such assumption was quite erroneous.

Lazarus felt somehow uneasy. Perhaps, he thought guiltily, he was a little envious of the attentions taken from the group - from him - and devoted to the child. One must never be jealous of a mother's devotions to her child, Lazarus knew, though he had never enjoyed a mother's devotion.

Whenever Lazarus gazed at the flawless infant, a strange emotion came over him. He thought about her life to come and the lives of all the other girl babies in all the lands - and of their mothers - each one in her time at risk for her life in the perpetuation of her lineage. As Mrs. Symmons' baby slept in her mother's arms, he thought, there are causes worthy of more than debate – worthy of action, even of risk. Here he sat in Mr. Symmons' parlor, though, as safe and comfortable as a sleeping baby.

PART TWO: Other Knights' Dragons
London 1789–1792

Chapter 11. Coffin Space

Lazarus Perlman wanted a larger life.

His seemed comparatively trivial, but he saw nothing to alter the path before him to become a tailor. He passed the winter taking pleasure in the readings and discussions of the King Solomon Club. They involved significant, sometimes momentous matters. At the same time, mere discussion felt antiseptic and removed.

Lazarus smelled change in the air, a reordering of things. Feudalism, long the economic and social order of Europe, was being transformed. France was exploding in revolution and the peasants of the world seemed ready to ignite. Even in South America, the journals reported, natives were revolting against the heavy hand of Spanish rule. Lazarus sensed that a fantastic game was underway on the global chessboard. He wanted to suggest a move, perhaps a gambit, and to have a hand in its execution. Yet he felt restricted, destined to retread his father's worn steps.

With the spring, however, came new hope. One Thursday evening in late April, a visitor appeared at the gathering of the King Solomon Club.

"Young gentlemen," said Mr. Symmons, "our guest this evening has recently returned from France where he was received by the Marquis de Lafayette, Minister Necker, Monsieur Mirabeau and other notables in the pursuit of his cause. He is an ordained Anglican clergyman yet he is well received by men of many faiths and traditions ... even ... um ... 'heathens' such as yourselves." Mr. Symmons paused. The boys ignored his attempted humor; the visitor did not smile. "I have known this man since we were both your age," Mr. Symmons said. "Mrs. Symmons and I know him as a unique and generous friend."

Those last few words struck a chord in Lazarus. He was normally attentive, but now he concentrated on the man. Lazarus guessed him to be no more than about thirty years of age. He looked familiar; no ... yes, at least his face looked familiar. He was dressed all in black save a high-necked white blouse that frilled some over his double-breasted jacket with a high collar. He wore black stockings and his black breeches were buttoned tight against them just below the knees. He was seated, yet obviously tall and he sat somewhat rigidly as if uncomfortable. His eyes were quite blue and his features were strong but not striking. His reddish-brown hair was stylishly short at the sides and collar, yet ample enough to curl about some on the top of his head.

Curiously, on the floor to the man's right, between his chair and that of Mr. Symmons, sat a leather bound trunk with two unbuckled straps. It was nearly as high as the seat of his chair.

Mr. Symmons continued, "These past four years, this gentleman has engaged himself in the compilation of evidence to be placed before Parliament concerning the cruelties of the African slave trade and in agitating for its abolition. I am pleased to present Mr. Thomas Clarkson."

Lazarus knew of this man. *So this is the activist Clarkson.* Lazarus had read of his exploits in the slave trading ports of Bristol and Liverpool and of his association with William Wilberforce, the spokesman for the abolitionists in the House of Commons. *Could this abolitionist intellectual be the mysterious friend who had introduced Mrs. Symmons to her husband and been an accomplice in their unconventional marriage?*

Mr. Clarkson remained seated. He thanked Mr. Symmons in a soft but strong voice not unlike Lazarus' own. He feigned embarrassment and protested that Mr. Symmons had been excessive in his introduction. He nodded at Mrs. Symmons and smiled at her baby; and then his face grew somber as he looked slowly about the room.

"You gentlemen are fortunate to have had Mr. Symmons as a teacher," he said. "I know him well, both mind and heart. Were you at Eton or even at Oxford you could have found no better."

Now it was Mr. Symmons' turn to protest, shaking his head in modesty.

"Let me tell you of some recent history related to me by a teacher of my own past," Mr. Clarkson continued. "My teacher's name was Peter Peckard."

At this, two young men in the far corner of the room snickered and one whispered too loudly to the other, "Did he say 'Peter Pecker?'"

Hearing this, Mr. Clarkson looked plain faced at the offenders and said, at greater volume, "No, I said 'Peter Peckard' ... Dr. Peter Peckard, actually. The name is spelled P-e-c-k-a-r-d." Then he continued in softer tones. "Eight or nine years ago, probably before most of you could read very well, Dr. Peckard read in the London news journals a report of the ship *Zong*." He looked back at the two offenders and said, "That's Z-o-n-g." Chastised, the two lads soberly nodded, and Mr. Clarkson continued.

"The *Zong* was owned by British subjects and had sailed from the west coast of Africa with a cargo of some 417 souls. These people were not refugees or emigrants. They had been taken by force from their homes and were in chains. The *Zong* had set out for Jamaica where the ship's captain intended to sell the African captives as slaves. Do you know where Jamaica is located?" His question seemed to be directed to the far corner of the room.

There came a rather sheepish reply, "Um … a … why, yes sir. It is an island in the West Indies … um … I should think."

"Indeed you should!" Mr. Clarkson dryly replied and those not in the far corner smiled. "And if you so thought, you would be quite correct," he said.

"As you may know, the winds of the middle Atlantic circle around like a great clock, driving the currents with them. England is located at about one o'clock on this great Atlantic timepiece. Halfway round, located at about seven o'clock, sits a string of small islands known as the Lesser Antilles. The first island usually encountered by English ships reaching the West Indies is Barbados. The crown has maintained an outpost there since colonists settled the island in the year 1625. These islands run along the circumference of our imaginary clock until just past eight o'clock. As they do, they become much larger and gather at something of a loose cluster in what are called the Greater Antilles. Principal among these are Puerto Rico, Saint Dominique, Cuba and, beneath it, Jamaica. All together, the region is known as the West Indies.

On its journey from Africa to Jamaica, but before the *Zong* reached sight of land, disease broke out onboard. That may not be too surprising given the conditions aboard slave ships." At this juncture, Mr. Clarkson leaned to his right, lifted the lid to the trunk beside him and produced a drawing on a large sheet of heavy paper. He then rose, approached the two lads in the far corner and held the paper before them. "This is the plan of the ship *Brookes*, of Liverpool," he said. "It is a slave ship like the *Zong* but just a bit larger. On this diagram, you can see the cargo packed aboard.

Please examine it and tell us what you see."

The same boy who knew the location of Jamaica spoke, this time with no hesitancy, "Why there are black bodies laid about every part of the ship. They look to be packed closely together like fishes at the market."

"Quite right, this plan depicts 482 Africans on the planking and the poop deck, but the *Brookes* has actually carried as many as 609 Africans on an Atlantic crossing," said Mr. Clarkson, "please show the diagram about the room if you will." Then he retook his seat as the young man complied.

Before each onlooker there were exclamations - "Horrible!" "Terrible!" "Disgusting!"

"The *Zong* had been under sail for twelve weeks from Africa with no sign of land," said Mr. Clarkson. "Do you suppose you might enjoy a twelve week voyage so accommodated?"

Heads shook but none spoke.

"The officers had their cabins and the crew their quarters safely below decks. Food, marine supplies and any cargo then got shelter. The slaves were caged in any remaining space in the hold, on levels of planking below decks and then aligned as closely as possible on portions of the open deck, exposed to all the Atlantic hurled at them. These Africans would have more space if they were each in a coffin. Can you imagine the sanitary conditions on board such a vessel?" he asked but did not await an answer. "Each slave performed his bodily functions in a tub, or in one of a few pots passed about for that purpose, often in full view of the others and the crew. With the often-rough seas of the Atlantic, the occasional upending of a pot or two was inevitable." Then nodding to Mrs. Symmons he said, "My apologies to the lady."

He continued, "Among these captives were many whose innards rebelled at the waves and found themselves in need of evacuating their stomachs overboard." The picture was now vivid in Lazarus' mind, but Mr. Clarkson pushed the point. "As you can suppose, that proved most difficult to accomplish, since these captives were shackled in place or together, and many on lower planking had no access to a deck rail. So now we have the contents of stomachs mixing on board with the contents of necessary pots. The result could well be serious discomfort as well as disease, do you think?" Again it was a rhetorical question and again Mr. Clarkson begged pardon from Mrs. Symmons who readily bestowed it.

"Aboard the *Zong*, the captain concluded that some of the slaves were too ill to fetch any value in a sale and that some would die as a result of the disease. Death for such captives and even among the seamen of such ships occurs with far greater frequency than most suppose," Mr. Clarkson said. "Now as it happens, merchants of the sea often insure their cargo against loss. The owners of the *Zong* had procured such insurance."

Lazarus began to get a queasy feeling as if he were aboard the *Zong*.

"This policy of insurance was typical of such arrangements," Mr. Clarkson said. "It would not pay for sick slaves or even for the death of slaves on board. It would pay only for the loss of cargo. Knowing this, the captain gave orders to cull out the weakest slaves. Some 54 of them were chained together on the deck. At his order, the crew threw them into the sea, as if they were rotten cabbage." A collective gasp arose from the room.

"This practice continued until some 132 living souls had been discarded into the sea," Mr. Clarkson continued. "Each soul that was so mercilessly drowned, each and every such soul...." he paused here and seemed to choke a little. He cleared his throat and slowly continued, "Each soul was a father, a mother, a son or a daughter. Each was no doubt loved as each of you is loved by a parent or a sibling."

Lazarus felt his throat tightening.

Mr. Clarkson turned on the edge of his chair, and his blue eyes again surveyed his little audience as he resumed. "When the *Zong* completed her voyage and was back in England, her owners made claim against the insurers for the loss of cargo. Well, a legal trial on the matter ensued. The court found for the ship's owners. It relied upon precedent that animals could be discarded at sea for the safety of a ship. The insurers were not satisfied and took their appeal. The appellate court ruled that the cargo was human rather than mere chattel property and denied the owners' claim."

Mr. Clarkson paused then added, "Whatever sort of animal an African may be, I rather calculate, he was so made by the same creator as made each of the animals in this room." Mr. Clarkson leaned back in his seat. The room remained uncommonly quiet.

Then Mr. Clarkson looked about as if to assess his impact in each face. He now spoke softly, almost pleading. "Wonderful young men," he said, "the people of Africa have been subjected to just such treatment as I have related, most of it no doubt never having come to light in polite society, since the Atlantic slave trade began about 150 years ago. This decision, though, marked the first time in the history of England that an African slave, other than those relatively few brought to England herself, had been determined to be human rather than just someone's animal property.

In any event," he continued in solemn tone, "the facts, young gentlemen, are these: The slavers of this nation and of other European countries have long been and continue to be engaged in the mass forced exile of the native inhabitants of Africa. They have caused the souls so enslaved to be scattered across the ocean … except those sent to its bottom."

This mass exile and scattering of a people sounded familiar to Lazarus.

"We might well say," pronounced Mr. Clarkson, now seemingly proud of his point, "that we are engaged in the 'Diaspora' of the Africans - no less than that committed by the Romans and others in the land of your forefathers more than a millennium ago."

Lazarus knew well of the scattering of the tribes of Israel. It was the only use of the word "Diaspora" he had ever heard. It was a part of him and, he knew, a part of every member of the King Solomon Club. He was not sure how he felt about Mr. Clarkson's use of the term.

The room was alive with chatter. Mr. Clarkson raised his voice, "I dare say history will not look kindly upon England - upon us. Moreover, men of conscience, of all faiths and traditions, cannot ignore these continuing crimes."

Mr. Clarkson's speech was provocative, disturbing Lazarus thought. The King Solomon Club sat in stunned silence. Sensing this, Mr. Symmons said, "Let's take a little recess, then Mr. Clarkson has agreed to answer questions."

Chapter 12. The Scrotum Cinch

After a short interval, Mr. Symmons settled the boys of the King Solomon Club. "Gentlemen, Mrs. Symmons is concerned that we do not tire our guest, so perhaps just a few questions …"

Several hands flew into the air. Thomas Clarkson had captivated the King Solomon Club like no previous guest. To the first question he answered, "No, not every slave ship shares the fate of the *Zong*. Some do, though, and all such ventures have as their purpose the life long enslavement of once free men, free women and free children."

To another query he replied, "Yes, other countries have been and are yet involved in the trade. Spain, Portugal and France are among them. Britain, however, is most efficient at it. Our island nation has long been the home of daring, heroic seamen. In this trade of slaves, however, we sully their honor."

A question now came from Mrs. Symmons. Her question startled Lazarus, but neither her husband nor Mr. Clarkson seemed surprised. Mr. Clarkson replied, "Yes, there are some Jews among those involved in the slave trade. Jewish lenders have a hand in financing much of the commerce of this nation."

If Mr. Clarkson had the attention of these young men before, he was now hypnotic. "Many people invest funds to build and maintain our merchant fleet and its slave ships," he explained. "They include the houses of landed noble families and lesser men of means, bankers and merchants both Jewish and Christian, tradesmen, judges, clergymen, members of Parliament and even the estates of widows. No class or quarter but the impoverished appears free of blame if investment be the criterion. To most people, the slave trade is simply a part of our marine commerce - usually a highly profitable part. Still, those most committed to it also happen to be Anglican like myself. They are the owners of the West Indies plantations. It is these, some of them from noble families, who most oppose my work."

Then Lazarus posed his questions. "Since slavery is so cruel, why does G-d allow it to continue?" Thinking of the plagues upon Pharaoh, he added, "Why doesn't he punish the slavers?"

Mr. Clarkson gazed a moment at Lazarus. "Such questions," he said, "keep me awake at night. Perhaps you should direct them to

Mr. Symmons." He grinned at Mr. Symmons and said, "He and I have argued them for years." Mr. Clarkson slowly shook his head and said, "So far, it appears, God has not intervened ... at least not lately."

"Perhaps he has spoken," Mr. Symmons said.

Mr. Clarkson's face seemed to twist up a bit.

"Ah, the debate continues," Mrs. Symmons interjected. "Well then, how about a different question: What drives men to such cruelty?"

Mr. Clarkson smiled a little at her and looked relieved. "Greed for the profits obtained is primary, no doubt," he answered. "Also, two factors seem to dull our sensitivities. The first is distance. The taking or purchase of slaves happens after weeks of sailing and their resale occurs still many weeks more away from our shore and far out of our sight. Part of my mission is to help provide that sight."

"Are there other questions?" Mr. Symmons asked.

"Yes," said Lazarus, "our guest said that two factors dull our senses, the first being distance. Please sir, what is the second?"

"Quite right," Mr. Clarkson said. "I often omit the second one, but thought to mention it here because I doubt any of you will take offense. The other factor is the class structure in our country." Then he pointed his nose in the air, assuming a posture of mock superiority, and said, "Here in England we well know that some men are of lower station than others, so selected by their birth and thus given to the service of their betters." He looked straight down at Lazarus and said, "It is not difficult for us to suppose that there are others born of still lower station and destined for bondage to their superiors. Some in my own Church of England have argued that God placed a curse upon black Africans. I shall provide you with a pamphlet on my departure that addresses this rationalization and some other errors."

One of the boys in the far corner then said, "But these blacks are fierce savages."

"I believe," said Mr. Clarkson, "the greatest savagery is the brutal treatment of native Africans at the hands of the slave traders. I do not deny that the chiefs of some African tribes are known to sell competing tribesmen to slavers. There have even been sad reports of tribes in difficulty being persuaded by desperation and strong drink to sell members of their own tribes.

Often, we 'civilized' English introduce guns to tribal chiefs,"
Mr. Clarkson lowered his head and shook it slowly. "In effect," he
said, "Africans are given the choice of one end of the gun or the
other. 'Either take our fire arms and capture slaves for us - or
become slaves yourselves.' They are given no way out. And the
methods are truly barbaric. Journals kept by former slavers tell of
nighttime village raids and of scalding unruly captives with boiling
water. I shall not catalogue all of these tortures, but they are
remarkable in their ingenuity and in their cruelty."

"Mr. Clarkson," the corner boy persisted, "how would you
propose to tame these fierce captives?"

"My dear sir," Mr. Clarkson immediately retorted, "I would
propose that they not become captives at all. It is the very purpose
of my mission to end this practice. We cripple not only the
Africans, but ourselves and our souls in its perpetuation." While his
fervor was unmistakable, Mr. Clarkson appeared calm. The room
remained quiet.

Mr. Clarkson began again and spoke very softly now. "There
are some tools of this trade you must see for yourselves." He
motioned to the questioner in the far corner and asked, "Will you
please assist me?" Mr. Clarkson reached into his chest on the floor
and retrieved some noisy contraption. He held up for inspection
some chains that he said had been liberated from a Bristol slave
ship. He handed the chains and asked his recruited assistant to show
them around the room. The couplets at their terminus were so small
that the group concluded that they must have been intended to
secure a child or a small woman.

One after another, Mr. Clarkson produced a startling assortment
of the devices of the slave trade. One by one the club members
examined the items as Mr. Clarkson's new assistant passed them
about the room.

Most shocking were a metal muzzle with leather straps all about
as if it were intended for a mad dog, a hideous thing Mr. Clarkson
identified as a "thumb screw," and a section of a metal cone. The
cone resembled the funnel Mrs. Symmons used to bottle her
marmalade. Mr. Clarkson said slavers used it to force striking
Africans to eat, sometimes resulting in the slave ingesting some of
his own teeth along with the forced porridge.

Mr. Clarkson pulled from his trunk a choke harness, a wooden hobble and a cudgel not unlike the clubs carried by police constables. He handed each item to his assistant who supervised their examination.

While Mr. Clarkson answered a question about stains on the cudgel, his now anxious assistant reached into the trunk and said, "What is this thing?" The assistant straightened and held up a short, slender metal bar with a hole in one end and ribbon of small chain with a metal pin at its end affixed to the other.

"That is not for this evening ... I mean, I wasn't expecting to display it to this group," Mr. Clarkson said to his assistant. "Please put it back."

"But what is it?" the boy persisted, and he held it up near his eyes for closer inspection.

Mr. Clarkson cleared his throat, "Well," he said, "actually ..." Then he shifted, turning toward Mrs. Symmons and said, "My apologies, truly Madam."

"Accepted, sir," she replied. She smiled broadly and seemed to suppress a laugh. "Please proceed" she coaxed.

Mr. Clarkson sat silently for a minute. Then Mrs. Symmons stood. "I'll make it easier for you," she said and left the room for her kitchen.

Mr. Clarkson half stood as he watched her leave. Then he reseated himself, shook his head at Mr. Symmons and said, "Very well. This ... well ... it is a device used to persuade ... that is to ... you see ..." He retrieved the device from his assistant and dangled it out away from himself with thumb and forefinger, "It is placed about a male's private ... about a male slave's genitalia and tightened by inserting and twisting this little toggle." As he said it he laid a link on the pin with his opposite hand, inserted it in the hole in the bar and turned it like a toggle. The small chain wrapped about the toggle, shortening the chain. He then secured it by inserting one end of the pin in a link of the shortened chain. "It is called a 'scrotum cinch.'"

Boys chattered as Mr. Symmons cleared his throat for quiet.

Unexpectedly, Mrs. Symmons returned from the kitchen. She walked the few steps to Mr. Clarkson, and said, "Why don't you demonstrate for these young men?" as she handed him an orange which she may have boiled and intended for her marmalade.

"Well, um, that is probably ... I should think that not necessary, thank you."

Mr. Clarkson had not completed the sentence when several boys sang out at once. "Please sir," they begged.

Mr. Clarkson looked trapped as if he himself felt the contraption. "Um ..." he looked at Mrs. Symmons. Her mouth kept the smile with which she had earlier left the room, but she firmly reseated herself.

Mr. Clarkson looked pleadingly at Mr. Symmons, but he, too, offered no relief. Mr. Clarkson again slowly shook his head in what Lazarus now saw to be a characteristic manner. "Very well," he conceded in a low voice. He dislodged the pin in the device and laid the chain across the top of the orange.

"Thomas, please stand so all our guests can see," said Mrs. Symmons.

He looked sharply at her, then grinned a little at her wide smile and stood. He held the orange before himself and wrapped the little chain around it. Then he fixed the loose end without any slack in the chain. Then as he held the chained orange between the fingers and thumb of one hand he began to turn the little toggle with the other.

After a twist or two the orange became deformed.

The boys became quiet.

With another turn the orange began to resemble the shape of an hourglass.

The boys stared intently.

With just one more twist, the skin of the orange broke and a squirt of juice shot into Mr. Clarkson's eye.

The boys gasped.

As he retrieved his kerchief and dried his face, Mr. Clarkson began an explanation. Then he stopped short. He needed nothing more. He carefully retook his seat and crossed his legs.

At the end of the parade of terribles, Mr. Clarkson allowed his assistant to return to his own seat in the corner. "If men completely strange to you and perhaps of a different color came ashore near London tower, caught you by stealth and bound you and your fellows here on board a sea vessel, what would you do?" he asked the boy.

The boy looked at him and raised two fists, "They would have their hands full, make no mistake of that."

"I surely shall not," said Mr. Clarkson, "but you - you might behave in a most fierce and warrior-like manner, would you not?"

"I dare say!" replied the boy.

"Yet you are not a savage," Mr. Clarkson said. "I do believe you, though. If you were taken as these men of Africa are, you might well seek to defend yourself and to escape your capture by the most violent means, even if it meant inflicting bodily damage upon your captors. Can we then expect any less of these Africans? Remember, too, their women and children are also taken captive."

The room was again silent. Then the sound of chains rattled as they were passed about; and again Mr. Clarkson's mellow voice spoke. "Most of these devices were presented to me in the port of Liverpool, from which has sailed for some decades now the largest fleet of slave ships ever assembled in the history of the world. Ships line up on some six miles of dock front at Liverpool. Imagine it, six miles – about the distance from the Tower of London to Westminster Hall and all the way back again. It is a great port of trade to be sure. The most profitable vessels, among those which sail from there, are the slave ships which number more than a hundred. It is difficult to count them because, in addition to vessels designed as slavers, many merchant cargo vessels and decommissioned naval ships have also been put to use in the slave trade. Not all of them carry slaves on the open deck, but some do as you have seen. While Liverpool is the largest home port for slave ships, there are a few others as well. Bristol is also prominent in this business." Mr. Clarkson then leaned back and re-crossed his legs.

After a brief lull in the room, Mr. Symmons suggested, "Thomas, tell them about the essay."

"Very well," said Mr. Clarkson. "Now as to Dr. Peter Peckard – he was sickened by the reports concerning the *Zong*. As it happened, he was on faculty at a certain university. He determined to draw attention to the slave trade. He therefore set forth a question for the annual Latin essay contest among the senior bachelors at his college. The question was, *'Anne liceat invitos in servitutem dare?'* which means, *'Is it lawful to make slaves of others?'* This tract has been excerpted from my essay on that question." Mr. Clarkson reached again into the trunk and brought forth a few copies of a pamphlet. He handed them around the room.

So this booklet is the heart of the famous work that won

Clarkson one of his two essay prizes at Cambridge, Lazarus thought, and he laid his hands on one of the pamphlets and immediately skimmed it. According to the tract, the cost of providing a single slave laborer in the West Indies could be many other lives lost in the perils of capture, removal, ocean crossing, exposure to tropical diseases, training and supervision of the enslaved worker.

As Lazarus read, Mr. Clarkson continued. "Mr. Symmons introduced me this evening as his friend, as indeed I am. In the circles of our younger days Mr. Symmons here was respected as a scholar, a master of chess, and also as an advocate of tolerance."

Yes, this man did know Mr. Symmons, Lazarus thought.

"Indulgence of others, regardless of their faith and its harmless observance, must be at the core of any civilized society," he said. "As Jews living in this Christian nation, I'm sure you appreciate the need for such tolerance."

Mr. Clarkson had conferred with Lafayette and addressed leaders of Parliament, Lazarus realized, yet he had planned just how to address this small audience - who were no more to Mr. Clarkson than a few powerless Jewish boys.

Now Lazarus remembered having seen this man before. It had been in this very room some four or five years earlier, the first time Lazarus had seen a game of chess.

"With due respect to my friend," Mr. Clarkson said, again nodding to Mr. Symmons, "I submit for your consideration that slavery is the epitome of intolerance; and bondage is the embodiment of inhumanity. If we, who witness it, though we do not advance it, also do nothing to stop its spread then are we not, as my legal friend Mr. Granville Sharp might call us, 'accomplices before the fact?'" With that, Mr. Clarkson ended his remarks.

As usual, Lazarus was the last of the King Solomons to depart that evening. He was also last in the customary line formed to express thanks to the guest lecturer. As he did so, the tall Anglican took Lazarus' extended right hand and encased it in the two of his own. "So you are Mr. Perlman," he said. "You, then, are the prodigy of whom my dear friends have so highly spoken. I am greatly pleased to make your acquaintance young sir."

"A prodigy?" Lazarus thought. He was nearly speechless. He didn't tell Mr. Clarkson that they had once briefly met. Instead he said, "I, uh, I am honored to meet you as well Mr. Clarkson."

Having finally spit out a single sentence, Lazarus departed straight away.

On the short walk home in the chilly night air of spring, Lazarus marveled at what he had heard - all of it. He had been stirred and a little depressed by Mr. Clarkson's solemn message; but he understood why the Symmons were so enamored of their friend. Lazarus also knew, as he had suspected, that the Symmons thought highly of his mind. He knew that at his father's craft, he had been but a clumsy boy who was just now developing some limited ability. At his studies, though – the endeavors he loved - those who knew him best and whose opinions he most regarded thought him a prodigy ... the same boy who had failed at recitation a few years earlier.

Chapter 13. 18 Old Jewry

Lazarus expected that the uneasiness inflicted on his mind by Thomas Clarkson would soon wane. It was a familiar pattern. Whenever he read a novel idea or a clever concept, it captured his attention while he mulled, digested and catalogued it in his head. As he moved on, he would remember the matter, but his mind would give chase to some new inspiration.

Lately, he seemed to follow a similar pattern when he happened upon an attractive woman. She captured his imagination for a while. Then he would encounter another beauty and his attention would shift. He measured beauty by comparison to Mrs. Symmons. With the juices of youth coursing through him, he judged it generously.

But the images provided by Mr. Clarkson stayed with him. Sewing in Mordecai's shop, reading at Guildhall or resting in his bed, he found himself imagining rows of chained Africans being thrown into the sea. The vision seemed indelible. Before Mr. Clarkson's lecture Lazarus had maintained some sympathy for the unfortunates of France. The treatment of captive Africans now rudely pushed lesser miseries aside. He turned the matter this way and that in his mind. Concentrating even all his intellect on it did not reduce the massive slave trade to some capsule he could swallow. The more he wrestled with it, the more it troubled him. He tried to file it away in his memory under the category of "atrocities," for he knew of many in history. That did not provide any tranquility. The slave trade was not just historic – it continued every day and night. He feared the inaction against which Mr. Clarkson had warned – he did not want to be a silent "accessory" to the horrific slave traffic, but what could a fifteen-year-old lad in a tailor's shop in east London do about it?

Clarkson's case was overwhelming. When he had opened his chest of torture tools, he had uncorked a bottle that Lazarus could not reseal. Lazarus now recreated scenes of torture in his head – and he could not stop.

Lazarus finally appealed to his father for help. G-d had punished the Egyptian slavers of the Jews. Would any deity aid the Africans? Were there such rescues ... or were they just stories?

Mordecai impatiently instructed his son to devote himself to his own work. African slaves were no part of his world. He simply could not deal with such questions, except to say all was in the hands of G-d. To Lazarus, waiting for G-d while people were drowning seemed just an excuse. He had never before felt called to action in such a compelling way. He wanted to help, but he wielded no power.

Lazarus had developed a pattern for dealing with difficulties. As he retired at night, he would muster the relevant considerations and array them across his mind, like pieces on a chessboard. Usually, in the soft light of early dawn, just as he regained a little consciousness, he could see the pale outline of a solution that had evaded him. He tried his method to ease his anxiety concerning the slave trade. The images he revisited in doing so led not to peace, but rather to still more turmoil.

Lazarus' bed had always been home to his greatest security. There, as a small boy, he had envisioned his mother. In his bed at night he could recite like a poet when his tongue had betrayed him at school. In his warm bed, Lazarus could read from the Torah like a rabbi long before he had managed it at his Bar Mitzvah. In the secret safety of his bed, Lazarus had hazily entertained fantasies of beautiful women and fleshy confections conjured up by the erotic imperatives of his age and gender.

Night sweats of a wholly different sort now preempted those tender visions. It was repeatedly the same nightmare . . . he had just plunged into a dark sea. He strived to swim to the surface but a shackle around his ankle pulled him deeper and deeper and he could see the light at the surface fading as he fell father from it. He held his breath. He fought, struggling with every bit of his strength, but it was no use. He was doomed and sinking fast. After no more than a few minutes, he knew he was a dead man ... and at that moment he would awaken with a jolt and find himself sitting fully upright in his bed, soaked and gasping for breath.

He felt haunted. His ghosts were black souls of bondage brought to his attention by Thomas Clarkson.

Desperate, he decided that rather than try to forget, he would delve more deeply into Mr. Clarkson's claims. Perhaps the man had exaggerated the horrors of the slave trade. Perhaps it was not so widespread as the partisan Mr. Clarkson would have him believe. Perhaps he would discover some as yet wholly unknown circumstance that moderated the situation to a point from which he could deal with it.

Besides, if he needed a cause to possess him, Lazarus already knew of one - having been born to it. Were not his own people persecuted and reviled? Had not his own progenitors suffered bondage, inhuman torment and ostracism? Did not the very term "Diaspora" define their history? Were there not yet Jews in the current world who suffered for Lazarus' own traditions or simply because they had been born Jewish? It was true enough and its history was much longer than a mere 150 years.

Still, Lazarus somehow felt a little guilt for dwelling on it. Jews in England may not be permitted to own land and they have no say in the government, he recounted. They are barred from English universities and they have to sneak into the side doors of libraries. Jewish merchants may have to live inconspicuously. Jews may be denied many of the privileges of Englishmen. Lazarus recognized, though, that many Jews - himself included - were little molested and could observe their customs and holy days. They could pray at a synagogue and learn at a school. They could live full, long lives. Some, he realized, were even prosperous. No Jew he knew had to fear being sold into slavery; or being shackled, chained and thrown into the middle of the sea.

With the thought of ending his drowning dreams, Lazarus set about to examine Mr. Clarkson and the African cause more closely. Mordecai would never understand, so Lazarus related his intentions to Mr. Symmons.

"Well," said his mentor, "I believe you have Mr. Clarkson's booklet. You may also wish to speak to the man himself," he suggested as he scribbled on a paper. "Give this to Mr. Clarkson," he said as he folded the note, placed it in an envelope that he did not seal and upon which he printed an address. As he handed it to Lazarus he said, "This place is not far from Guildhall Library; it lies just before King Street. Mr. Clarkson has associated himself with the friends there." The address on the envelope said "18 Old Jewry Street."

The following midday Lazarus found himself standing before 18 Old Jewry - a small stone building, grayed with soot and standing close by the street. He mounted three steps and knocked at the large door. He knocked again ... no answer. He raised his hand to rap louder, but as he drew it back he was startled by a voice from behind him.

"May I help thee friend?"

Lazarus wheeled about and found a small old man with a thin face and gray whiskers. The fellow dressed in black and gray and wore a broad brimmed black hat with a half sphere at its center.

"I was told I might find Mr. Thomas Clarkson at this address."

"Hmmm," said the little man, "and who told thee?"

"A friend," said Lazarus.

The little man raised a suspicious brow.

"Mr. Levi Symmons of the Jews' Free School. Mr. Clarkson knows him well."

"Oh yes, that sort of friend. Did thy friend schedule thee a conference with Friend Clarkson or provide thee with an introduction?" the man asked.

"No ... I mean yes," Lazarus said, clutching the envelope Mr. Symmons had given him.

The little gray man motioned Lazarus aside, twisted his skeleton key in the door lock and invited Lazarus inside. The interior consisted of a single large room, more than twice in depth as in width. One large table centered near the room's front was the only place within sight clear of paper. Several smaller tables arranged at irregular angles with an assortment of mismatched chairs divided the rear half of the room.

"Now young man," said the old one, "May I see thy introduction?" as he eyed Lazarus from head to toe.

Lazarus held up the envelope. "It is for Mr. Clarkson," he said.

"Yes, well, I must examine it first," said the man as he snatched the envelope and extracted the note.

Lazarus thought to object, but before he could say a word, the little gray man started to read the note aloud:

> *T.C. - With your gracious appearance at our little gathering you renewed our admiration and gratitude. It appears you may have also piqued the interest of the worthy young man bearing this missive. I trust his attentions will not distract from your quest. If he tarries, perhaps you may find him of some use or another - assisting your compilations - aiding your correspondence*

H.B.S. conveys her love – as do I.

L. Sym

"Hmm, very well," said the gray man. He refolded the note and returned it to Lazarus. Then he stroked his chin as he slowly examined Lazarus again, head to heel. "We must be careful. Friend Clarkson has enemies," he said. "It is my duty to inspect packages and correspondence."

"Enemies?" asked Lazarus.

"Yes, I'm afraid so," the gray man said, "but it appears they do not include thee."

"Certainly not," Lazarus protested.

"Well then, may I have thy name and business friend?"

"Of course, I am Lazarus Perlman. I recently attended a lecture by Mr. Clarkson and wished to make further inquiry. Mr. Symmons suggested that Mr. Clarkson may be willing to assist my - ."

The man interrupted. "Mr. Clarkson is not here today, friend. I fear thou hast only myself to thy service. However, if thee wish to make inquiry concerning the trade in Africans, thou hast come to the place."

"I do beg pardon, sir," Lazarus said, "but what place might this be, exactly?"

"This is the office of the Society for Effecting the Abolition of the Slave Trade. I am Friend John Garling, secretary to the Society."

"Where may I find Mr. Clarkson? I was told - ."

"Thou wast told correctly," the man said. "When Friend Clarkson is in London thee may often find him here, with Friend Phillips at Lincoln's Inn or else near there in Chancery Lane where he often rooms. He is traveling at present but he may soon return. In the meantime, I bid thee welcome. Let me just deposit my hat and coat." The man briefly waved his hand toward the open room and stepped off toward its tables.

Lazarus slowly followed him, peering about. Tall open bookcases of dusty wood lined the walls, interrupted by a fireplace at the middle of the right wall and windows on that wall and at the rear. Two tea pots with stacked cups and saucers stood on a round table near the fireplace. Wrapping materials protruded from the edges of two or three waist high shelves. Shuffles of papers sat askew on the other shelves. Disheveled piles of books rose from the floor around the edges of the room. All about, scattered pamphlets, tracts, leaflets and handbills looked like the splattered droppings of some huge ancient bird.

Askew of a far rear corner, near a rear doorway, sat a larger edition of the trunk Mr. Clarkson had brought when he visited the King Solomon Club. Near it sat open crates and heavy shipping boxes. Mr. Clarkson had been so organized, Lazarus thought. This place is all clutter.

"Friend," the colorless little man said as he stepped to a nearby shelf and retrieved a small booklet, "this may be thy best introduction."

"I have read that one, thank you," Lazarus replied, recognizing the offered item, "though that is the only publication Mr. Clarkson left with my group. I had hoped to initiate a more comprehensive study."

"Well then," the little man said, "let me consider … ah yes." He walked toward the rear of the room and looked about as if scouting for a lost pet. "They were just back here I thought," Lazarus heard him say to himself. He returned to the front with shrugged shoulders. "Forgive me Friend, but I cannot just now locate the - wait." He dropped a shoulder and veered to his right. He slowly got onto creaky knees and retrieved three booklets from under a littered side table. Returning to face Lazarus he extended them to his visitor. "These were written by Friend Anthony Benezet of Philadelphia. I am told that Friend Clarkson began his study with this one," he said, touching a finger on the topmost book. "Thou are welcome to these so long as they are put to use. If thee would prefer, thee may study here. I am here from noon until nine in the evening on all days except the Sabbath."

With that awkward beginning, Lazarus said farewell to Guildhall Library and began to frequent the Abolition Society. The single meeting room at 18 Old Jewry Street replaced the tombs of Guildhall Library as the scene of his studies. He stationed himself at a rear table from which he had free run to sort among the papers, books and pamphlets strewn all about the room. This humble office compared poorly to Guildhall Library, but in it he found the most comfortable chair. Its woven back gave way to one's shape and its padded seat rested on a similar weave.

"It's mahogany with a 'cane back' made in the French style by Thomas Chippendale of St. Martin's Lane," Friend Garling told him. "It is one of three – from a broken set donated by Friend Sharp."

On Wednesday evenings Lazarus read at his rear table while a group of about a dozen men, the governing committee of the Abolition Society, gathered about the large table in the front. They hardly noticed him, or so he thought. He became a fixture.

Chapter 14. The Abolition Society

At the Abolition Society, Lazarus discovered that the majority of the governing committee were followers of George Fox, the religious dissenter. When Mr. Symmons had said "Mr. Clarkson has associated himself with the friends," he had meant "The Society of Friends," commonly called "Quakers." Until he visited 18 Old Jewry, Lazarus had never known a Quaker. He did know of them though. They dressed simply and spoke strangely. They would not comply with even simple social conventions such as calling nobles and gentlemen "my Lord," "Sir," or even "Mister." They openly advocated the equality of all men. They were industrious and some were prosperous merchants.

With the help of Friend Garling, for that is what he preferred to be called, Lazarus studied the Abolition Society's literature and investigated its origins. He learned that a group of Quakers had banned together four years before Mr. Clarkson had committed himself to the cause. Their efforts had been substantial, but largely ineffectual.

Mr. Clarkson and a few associates had broadened and expanded both the committee and its activities. Since his arrival, the Abolition Society had become independent of the Society of Friends. It was non-sectarian now and Mr. Clarkson alone had some 400 correspondents, most of whom favored abolition. He had established most of them in his frequent travels around England. They included some notables – Reverend James Ramsay in Kent, evangelical Christian leader Henry Thornton, and playwright Hannah More who penned poetry against the slave traffic. Mr. Clarkson's essay though, in its various iterations, stood as the centerpiece of the Abolition Society's arsenal of literature.

Lazarus examined an English translation of Clarkson's prize winning piece. It filled 256 pages and bore the title *Essay on the Slavery and Commerce of the Human Species, Particularly the African*. In addition to the points raised by the summary tract, it assailed notions that Africans are racially inferior. It argued that despite biblical references to slaves, Christianity does not condone slavery. One can not own another human, the essay maintained, for men are accountable to God. In order to be so accountable, a man must be free.

Lazarus continued to attend the weekly meetings of the King Solomon Club and kept the Symmons abreast of his activities at the Abolition Society. They did not discourage him.

Mordecai tried. "This Clarkson fellow is a radical," he had been told. Reading at a gentile library was one thing, but consorting with abolitionists – it was wasteful, improper and dangerous. "Keep to your work and to our own people," he pled.

Lazarus made an effort, but ignoring Mr. Clarkson was like trying to unring a bell. His travels filled the news journals. The King Solomon's tracked his exploits. Within a few days Lazarus found himself back at 18 Old Jewry. Friend Garling began to view him as a confederate and answered his questions. Mr. Clarkson, he revealed, had been charged by the governing committee with locating and preparing witnesses and exhibits for Mr. William Wilberforce, the Member of Parliament who spoke for the Abolition Society in the Commons. Mr. Wilberforce was not officially a member of the Society. He worked around the river's bend at his Westminster office near the House of Commons chamber. Many of the efforts undertaken at 18 Old Jewry, though, were in direct support of his activity in Parliament.

Mr. Wilberforce was a frail little man, said frail little Friend Garling, but not so his political stature. In the government, he and his allies were not to be dismissed. Mr. Wilberforce had earned the respect and the close association of the Prime Minister, William Pitt the younger. While Mr. Pitt supported the cause, his agenda was crowded and his attention dispersed. Lazarus had seen a portrait of the Prime Minister at Guildhall Library. He looked to be a tall young man with a thin face and a mouth puckered up as if he had just taken a bite of an especially bitter lime.

Mr. Wilberforce advanced other causes as well, but he could without much discomfort lead the abolitionist cause in Parliament, said Friend Garling, because he represented the large district of York. The district's port city was Hull on the Humber River near its mouth at the North Sea. "Hull," Friend Garling advised, "is the only major English seaport not engaged in the slave trade."

Mr. Clarkson traveled much of the time and, when in London, still moved about the town. He visited 18 Old Jewry Street sporadically. When he had first seen Lazarus there, he placed the lad immediately and offered a gracious welcome, but was immediately called away. Each time he reappeared, he seemed harried and too busy to give Lazarus more than a brief greeting.

From his vantage point, at the rear of their office in a comfortable cane back chair, Lazarus learned as much about the abolitionists as about their cause. He watched, he read, he overheard, he made notes. One Wednesday afternoon, Lazarus looked up from a journal to find Thomas Clarkson standing over him.

"Are you still here, these many weeks, then?" Mr. Clarkson said. Without waiting for an answer, he began to question Lazarus on his own sentiments in the matter. Then he suggested that, if Lazarus wished, he could be of service in the cause. Lazarus had never had an opening to give Mr. Symmons' note to Mr. Clarkson. Even so, Mr. Clarkson outlined the same duties as the note had suggested.

"I am afraid I must assist my father for at least a time every day," Lazarus informed Mr. Clarkson. "He indulges me as it is, for I am his apprentice."

Mr. Clarkson was undeterred. "If one has limits, one does what one can." He spoke frankly to Lazarus about the personal risks of allying with the abolition cause. The only compensation, he said, would be recompense for small expenses incurred and a clear conscience. "Take your time to decide," he said. "I myself considered the matter for a year before undertaking such a daunting task. But I couldn't escape, I felt compelled. I cannot envision any higher calling, any bigger life." Something about this man reverberated in Lazarus.

For all their dedication, Lazarus noted, these abolitionists have had great difficulty advancing an end to the slave trade. Mr. Clarkson laid blame at the feet of plantation owners, slave ship owners and those trading with them. Their "West Indies lobby" mustered powerful forces against abolition in Parliament, throughout Britain and expended considerable sums in their battle. By contrast, the Abolition Society was modestly funded by prosperous Quaker merchants and a few others.

Lazarus considered Mr. Clarkson's invitation. After an early start each day in Mordecai's shop, he was already spending most late afternoons and evenings at 18 Old Jewry. He had met most of the members of the Society's governing committee – nine Quakers and three Anglicans, including the famous Granville Sharp, the nominal chairman of the committee. Mr. Sharp had been the first British author to denounce African slavery. He had obtained a court ruling that freed the nearly 15,000 slaves who had been brought to England by their masters. It was based on the premise that men within England could not be held as private property.

Lazarus admired Mr. Sharp and found the Quakers charmingly peculiar. They readily engaged an unfamiliar Jewish boy.

Lazarus fixed on these twelve men, their cause and on whether he could be of any aid to them as he retired one night. By morning he knew his answer. He did not want to be viewed as impetuous, so he waited two weeks to give his positive reply.

His study had further compelled him. As informed as he was for a young man, Lazarus was shocked to discover the numbers of Africans captured in the slave trade or killed in the attempt. Some commentators estimated that when the British trade was added that of other nations dating from well over a century earlier, the total likely exceeded 10 million. Lazarus had read that the population of the London area was estimated at 780,000 and that the entire population of England and Wales was about 8 million. He could hardly imagine the total misery of the slave trade, inflicted on one poor victim at a time.

Yes, Lazarus wanted to assist the abolition cause. Perhaps his nightmares would end. He told Mrs. Symmons of his new endeavor, but nothing of his dreams. His dreams were the one thing Lazarus could never share with her.

Lazarus now threw himself each evening into his new duties assisting Friend Garling and Mr. Clarkson. The product of the Jews' Free School, the prodigy of the King Solomon Club and the recluse of Guildhall Library became the budding scholar of the Abolition Society.

At his very first Wednesday night meeting, the governing committee resurfaced an old debate. Over the strenuous objection of Mr. Sharp, the committee decided to limit its objective to the cessation of the slave trade rather than to the abolition of slavery itself. They reasoned that expanding the agenda of the Society would forfeit any progress at all. Lazarus preferred Mr. Sharp's position. Slavery's evils could not be overlooked in any degree.

Still, he understood that the first step toward justice must be to end the flow from Africa.

Lazarus brought efficiency to 18 Old Jewry. Its once dusty shelves shined and became the tidy home to the materials that had been scattered about the floor and on the tables. The reams of correspondence, stacks of books, boxes of evidence and piles of pamphlets found new order. Lazarus knew them all and could immediately retrieve any document requested by a committee member. Thomas Clarkson's tireless work made him the untitled leader of the committee. Lazarus Perlman's facility with documents made him the ideal aide.

Friend James Phillips, a member of the governing committee, ran a printing house from George Yard at nearby Lombard Street. It spat out one or another reprint of the more popular among the dozens of essays, pamphlets and books utilized by the Abolition Society in its campaign. Lazarus made the time to suggest the ingredients for new pamphlets consisting of excerpts from anti-slave trade books. The members of the Abolition Society and others in the cause continued to complete written appeals and the collection at 18 Old Jewry grew rapidly. Lazarus consumed and quietly critiqued each proposed publication as it was offered up. Within months, the committee came to rely on him to select and edit its new publications.

The Phillips' Printing House and the Abolition Society stocked themselves for the Parliamentary battle - with a fifteen-year-old Jewish scholar as their chief supply officer.

Chapter 15. Wrestling with Parliament

The Seventeenth Parliament of Great Britain began its first session in November, 1790. As tension built the following spring, Mr. Clarkson took rooms at No. 9 New Palace Yard in order to be near the lawmakers.

He supported Mr. Wilberforce by providing information on each point the abolitionists planned to address and evidence to refute the West Indies lobby. Lazarus stayed at 18 Old Jewry Street. Friend Garling, with the aide of a similarly clad young recruit, shuffled back and forth with notes of request from Mr. Clarkson and reams of response from Lazarus.

Now fully adopted into the Abolition Society, Lazarus helped Friend Garling with the correspondence. Though the governing committee included a dozen men, Mr. Clarkson received most of the letters. He asked Lazarus to read them and to draw prompt attention to any information useful in the campaign. The third letter Lazarus opened read:

> *You sniveling bloody negroe lovers – Stop your
> Whining! Tom Clarkson, you self righteous fool, be
> warned - - Wisbech fires in the middle of the night await
> those who press at the Commons - -douse THAT from
> Westminster Hall - -hard to escape for them what's
> crippled.*
>
> *Truely,   Firebug*

When Mr. Clarkson briefly returned, Lazarus showed him the letter. Without a moment of pause he called Friend Garling over and handed him the letter, "Please show our young friend here where we file away the threats."

"With pleasure," said Friend Garling. He crumpled the letter, stepped across the room to the fireplace, bent down and flicked the crushed paper onto the small fire under the teapot.

Mr. Clarkson smiled, and asked, "How many does that make Friend Garling?"

"I am sorry," said Friend Garling, "but I'm afraid I lost count sometime back at around sixty-three."

"But what did the letter mean?" asked Lazarus. "What's this about 'Wisbech fires' and 'them what's crippled?'"

Mr. Clarkson shook his head. "Nothing," he said, "just ignore these stupid threats."

A while later, after Mr. Clarkson left 18 Old Jewry, Lazarus asked his questions again of Friend Garling.

"Oh," he said, "Friend Clarkson's mother lives in Wisbech, she is badly twisted up with the rheumatism."

"My Lord," Lazarus said.

"Indeed," Friend Garling replied.

There were many threats, but most of the letters were responses to Mr. Clarkson's epistles to chairmen in the towns where he had established local abolition committees. Well represented for their size were Watford, Northampton, Coventry, Birmingham, Stoke-On-Trent and Stafford - all towns along the road Mr. Clarkson often traveled from London to the world's largest slave ship port, Liverpool. Much the same was true of Reading, Swindon and Bath, along the road to Bristol.

Occasionally, a letter would arrive from a West Indies island where a traveler or resident had witnessed some brutal act against a slave. Lazarus set aside particularly gruesome ones. The West Indies lobby denied the activities alleged in these reports ... "fabrications" they claimed. When the events were undeniable, they called them "aberrations" or minimized their severity.

Lazarus determined that the name "West Indies lobby" sounded too grand, as if their cause were legitimate. With his lead, the abolitionists came to call their opposition simply "the slave lobby."

Lazarus was astonished that members of Parliament remained so ill informed – and that many seemed to prefer it that way. Most of them did not understand the magnitude of the slave traffic.

"Acknowledgement requires accountability," Mr. Clarkson told him. "So long as they remain incredulous, they can justify their inaction. We must inundate them with evidence of the truth."

Those willing to listen were aghast to learn that the number of slaves on the few British West Indies islands, as last estimated by the military in 1775, exceeded the slave population of mainland North America. The truth was diluted by 4,000 miles of ocean water and dulled by communications that reported events only months after they had occurred. It was then further obfuscated by denials of the perpetrators and their allies.

Despite many proofs of torture like those in Mr. Clarkson's sample trunk, the pool of witnesses for the abolition cause began to dry up. Lazarus soon opened anonymous letters which revealed the cause - the slave lobby had deployed henchmen to intimidate, bribe, or waylay informants and they bought "evidence" of their own.

"Procuring false witnesses," Lazarus muttered as he read, "these scoundrels are no better than Pharaoh and his Egyptians."

One witnesses already surprised Mr. Wilberforce. The man had given a favorable interview, but once called to testify, he supported the slave lobby. Mr. Wilberforce abruptly ended the man's appearance and challenged his veracity. "My opponents have resorted to meddling with my witnesses," he complained. On his instruction, Lazarus began to take down an affidavit from each potential witness, summarizing his evidence. The abolitionists could now demonstrate perjury if a witness later lied during examination.

The Abolition Society had by now held hundreds of meetings at 18 Old Jewry and all around England. In a single year it had distributed 51,432 pamphlets, books and supporting documents. Churchmen of several stripes repeated its themes. It attracted opponents to slavery in nearly forty British counties.

Prime Minister Pitt had taken to referring to Mr. Clarkson and his closest supporters as "white negroes." Mr. Clarkson bore the Prime Minister's jest as a badge of pride. Lazarus counted himself an undistinguished but authentic part of that group.

Despite all the activities of the Abolition Society and its sympathizers, its objective had not been reached. The problem did not seem to be the quantity of support so much as with the quality of the Society's information.

Providing recent and specific evidence that would be unassailable before the scrutiny of Parliament and the attacks of the slave lobby, however, continued to present difficulty. It became the greatest challenge of the cause. "Broad accusations will not do," Mr. Clarkson lamented. "A clear account of a single, recent and gruesome cruelty seems to catch more attention."

At last, on April 19, Mr. Wilberforce's motion for a law to abolish the slave trade came to a vote. The House of Commons defeated it by a count of 163 to 88. Mr. Clarkson urged the members of the governing committee and Lazarus to take heart. They had succeeded in placing before the Commons a bill for vote. That feat alone, Mr. Clarkson consoled, had seemed nearly impossible when they had first undertaken their work.

The matter now fell squarely on the national conscience, Mr. Clarkson said, and he believed that with the Society's best efforts, Parliament would likely pass an abolition bill later - if not in the current session, then surely the following year. "Much legislation is presented repeatedly," he told Lazarus, "before it is enacted. We will not take 'no' for an answer. We shall press on, but we need first-hand accounts of recent slave mistreatment." He called such information "exact intelligence."

The Seventeenth Parliament then ended its first session on June 10, 1791 – without reconsidering the slave trade – its majority claimed evidence of cruelty remained unclear.

Lazarus knew one way the Abolition Society could obtain better evidence, and it involved him directly, but it was impractical. He kept the idea to himself.

During the ensuing summer, and at Mr. Clarkson's request, Lazarus consulted with the committee as it selected standard bearers to appear before Parliament the following year and speakers for both public and private debates in the meantime. Lazarus found irony in this given his personal history at oration. Still, he gave it his earnest attention.

Mr. Sharp had served well in this regard in the past. Former slave ship Captain John Newton and Alexander Falconbridge, an articulate one time slave ship surgeon, had also spoken out.

Newton had captained a slave vessel twenty-five years earlier. Since leaving the sea, he had found God or rather, he insisted, he had changed his life such that God had found him. He eventually joined the clergy and took up songwriting and poetry. Late in life, he penned lyrics for a twenty-eight line hymn. The first four lines were these:

> *Amazing Grace, How sweet the sound*
> *That saved a wretch like me!*
> *I once was lost, but now am found;*
> *Was blind, but now I see.*

Parliament and the public had long heard the stories of Newton and Falconbridge, and the West Indies lobby asserted that their charges were stale and no longer accurate. The practices of the slave trade, they claimed, had improved since the times related by these old witnesses. The abolitionists determined that they needed new voices with new evidence.

Lazarus admired the writings of Anthony Benezet. The bold American Quaker opposed even the widely held belief that black Africans are an inferior race. Few abolitionists made that argument.

"What a witness Anthony Benezet would be at Parliament," Lazarus said to Friend Garling.

Mr. Clarkson overheard. "Actually, Benezet would not do at all," he said, "nor would any American. You are too young to remember, but it has been less than a decade since King George withdrew English troops from those colonies. The general view at Parliament remains that Americans are disloyal, crude and hardly qualify as models of behavior for Englishmen - especially in the matter of Africans."

Mr. Clarkson explained the "American problem" to Lazarus with a reference to Dr. Samuel Johnson, widely accepted as one of the best minds of the era. In his essay, *Taxation No Tyranny*, Johnson had asked: *"How is it that we hear the loudest yelps for liberty among the drivers of the negroes?"*

Lazarus understood. Collectively, the Americans were guilty of hypocrisy. They revolted to establish their own nation. Its cornerstone, they said, was the equality and liberty of all men. Yet they denied liberty to large numbers of Africans whose lives they'd stolen by enslavement and acquired more slaves each passing year.

"Beside that," said Mr. Clarkson with a grin, "Friend Benezet died a number of years back."

Lazarus blushed, he should have known. He tried diversion. "Since you mentioned the king," he said, "where is the crown in this matter? Could it be a friend to the slaves?"

"King George has been battling an illness," Mr. Clarkson said. "I am told some strange disease has turned his piss to a royal purple."

"Purple piss?" Lazarus asked.

"Yes, but worse, he has gone a little mad as well, as you may have heard it rumored."

"Aha," said Lazarus, "perhaps G-d has sent at least one little plague."

"What?" Mr. Clarkson said. "No, it would not help, for the power lies with the Parliament. The House of Commons must be our focus."

Lazarus knew that the best friend of the slaves was Mr. Clarkson himself. He was a mainstream Anglican, but also a man of action - a risk taker. Lazarus sensed that if he were to be of real use in this cause himself, he would need to take action as well. Even he might become exposed to some risk. Being born a Jew, he had learned very early, imposed certain dangers. Now he had managed to align himself with the advocates for an unpopular cause against powerful and ruthless forces. Here at 18 Old Jewry, he was the lone Jew. He could not have been more out of place. Still, he felt on the verge of a larger life.

* * * * * * *

As 1791 ended and a new year began, the Abolition Society encountered a new challenge – keeping members of Parliament and the public from diverting their attention away from the slave traffic. Almost disabling distractions paraded before the nation. The ongoing revolution in France had already commanded attention throughout Britain, but people now began to take sides as the crisis deepened. Two spokesmen, in particular, gained Lazarus' attention.

Edmund Burke, a man of considerable renown, had published his *Reflections on the Revolution in France* in late 1790. More than a year later, it became a focal point for the debate.

England had progressed to a state that some called "Constitutional Monarchy" - entailing the notion that the people consented to be governed by the crown so long as they were not unduly oppressed by it. Burke chided those beliefs and argued that the consent of the people had nothing to do with the hereditary right of the royal family to rule them.

One reply to Burke came from a man of considerably less stature – the self-educated son of a Quaker corset-maker. He had gone to America and fomented trouble there and had since returned to England. He published a brief tract simply entitled *The Rights of Man*. His name was Thomas Paine.

His booklet put London and all of Britain on its ear. It rapidly became by far the best selling piece of writing in the history of the nation. Peasants pooled their pennies to share a copy. As contrasted with Burke's laborious piece, Paine's reply read easily and quickly. In a few paragraphs here and there, Paine showed Burke's arguments to be absurd. Paine captivated the whole country with one little booklet. The abolitionists had been unable to do so with entire libraries. That alone earned Lazarus' admiration.

The king, Thomas Paine reminded readers, was a descendent of William and Mary who became rulers when Parliament had passed a resolution bestowing the crown upon them and their heirs. They ruled by assent of the people's representatives who could as well revoke the consent – not by divine right. On that score the government denounced Paine's little book.

Mr. Paine found great favor, not only with Lazarus, but with Mr. Clarkson and nearly all the abolitionists. Mr. Clarkson made the mistake of saying so in public. He drew strong cautions from allies in the government that by espousing support for such a radical, he damaged the cause of abolition.

Lazarus wondered what Thomas Paine thought of the slave trade. Researching, he discovered an article by the man that had appeared in the *Pennsylvania Journal and Weekly Advisor*. The author passionately assailed slavery. He noted that apologists for slavery argued that God condoned slavery because the Jews of the Old Testament were permitted to practice it. For two weeks the King Solomon Club debated little else. Paine argued that the Jewish experience served as an example of retribution rather than of slavery. Ancient Jews had merely turned the tables on those who had first persecuted them. Scripture provided no permission for Europeans to enslave Africans who had never injured them. To a man, the King Solomon's concurred with Paine, but his pamphlet stole the public audience from the abolitionists.

Amid the unrest, there came news of a bloody revolt by slaves in the French colony of Saint Dominique – the prize colony of France in the West Indies. The revolters had burned plantations and murdered some of their owners in what appeared to have been a completely indiscriminate manner. This news troubled the usually unshakable Mr. Clarkson.

The London "white negroes" and abolitionists throughout the country were put on the defensive. The public widely and quickly condemned the bloodshed – when the blood was that of white men. Lazarus took quite another view. Slaves turning on their masters seemed just retribution to him. To himself he called the phenomenon "the Pharaoh corollary."

In a painful irony, the members of the Society who had fought to gain the ear of the public suddenly had more attention than they could handle. The slave lobby charged that abolitionists encouraged slave revolt and placed white people in the islands in danger. After having gained such promising momentum, then taking a back seat to the commotion in France, the Abolition Society found itself reeling. Lazarus took a hard lesson from these events: Despite all one can do, one's fortunes can turn in an instant.

At 18 Old Jewry Street, meetings were called and elaborate responses were debated. In the end, the governing committee listened to its hardest working functionary, Thomas Clarkson. He reasoned that the Abolition Society must stay the course and not allow events it could not control to distract it.

As the slave trade continued, parliamentary committees debated the honor of just one man - Warren Hastings. He had been the Governor of Bengal before being elevated to Governor General of India which he ruled for 12 years. He now stood accused of corruption – rumor held that he looted India's treasures. The scandal titillated the public, but Lazarus fumed that the government lavished attention on the reputation of just one man rather than on the enslavement of thousands of humans every passing month.

As if all these distractions were not enough, Lazarus faced others that troubled him alone. He found himself preoccupied – almost obsessed with secret thoughts about sex. His companions were almost all men, but he thought daily, hourly it seemed, about women. He furtively ogled girls he happened to encounter walking to and from 18 Old Jewry Street. He became aroused at the rustle of a skirt or nape of a slender neck and he still, involuntarily, dreamed of Mrs. Symmons.

His compulsions demanded attention and shamed him some – surely not every man of sixteen years is so captured by lust, he thought. He worried that he might be depraved. It is difficult, he thought, when your heart seems to have relocated to your groin. Still, he guiltily confessed to himself that his personal distraction was a sweet diversion. He wrestled with it and carried on as best he could.

Chapter 16. Rancid Rum

The fame of Mr. Clarkson's sample trunk had spread so that he became the beneficiary of donors, both known and anonymous, who sent him skin-piercing manacles, choke collars and branding irons. Few of the donors brought their gifts in person. Fewer still agreed to testify to their origin or use. While public audiences gasped at the inhumane tools of slavery, without authentication the pieces in the collection remained of little value before Parliament.

Roger Benbow of Kingston, Jamaica donated frequently. Mr. Benbow exported Jamaica's goods to Europe, mostly to Britain. He traded with the cane sugar planters, the cocoa growers and the rum distillers. Slave labor produced all the commodities he traded.

He did so successfully, but apparently also guiltily for, Lazarus learned, Mr. Benbow was also Mr. Clarkson's most reliable correspondent in the West Indies. While he wrote nearly every month, often sent gifts and provided information helpful to the cause, he would not swear an affidavit or travel to London to testify. Mr. Clarkson was nonetheless appreciative. "Jamaica is a dangerous place," he told Lazarus, "Mr. Benbow already puts himself at risk with his regular correspondence sent to this address."

According to Friend Garling, the Jamaican slavers knew Mr. Benbow to be sympathetic to their forced laborers. They called him a "traitor," an "informant," a "spy." Like some others before him, he had received repeated threats from planters who managed to monitor the destination of his correspondence – 18 Old Jewry Street, London, an address known to partisans on both sides of the contest.

Known abolitionists were at risk from the wealthy planters anywhere in the West Indies. Planters threatened abolitionists and even beat some and sent others home to England against their will.

Lazarus studied on Jamaica. The island had experienced more than its share of slave related violence. Runaway slaves hid in its interior mountains and sometimes struck back at the slavers who ruled their brothers on the island's large plantations. Lazarus did not condone violence, so he faulted himself for the satisfaction he felt that the Jamaican slavers simmered in a stew of their own making.   One who enslaves another can never sleep well, he thought. The situation seemed predictable, and just another example of the Pharaoh corollary.

No matter how many times Lazarus had seen shackles and muzzles, the arrival of a box or bundle containing a new restraint or blood stained lash disturbed him. Then, with reflection upon the dreary lives of those who had actually felt the sting of the whip or turn of the screw, he would become angry with himself for his own little discomfort.

Lazarus learned to value Friend Garling for his seeming dispassion. The little gray man's habits were untidy, but he did not shrink from sorting Mr. Clarkson's growing collection of torture tools. To be sure, Friend Garling also enjoyed sharing in the gifts that were delivered to the Society with some regularity. He helped himself to the figs, nuts, cocoa, molasses and citrus as it arrived from the West Indies. Mr. Benbow apparently sent most of it. The citrus was often spoiled, being usually two months off the tree by the time of its arrival, but Friend Garling did not chance that any of it still edible had further opportunity to rot.

Lazarus' mornings in his father's shop passed without demarcation or distinction. His afternoons at the Abolition Society buzzed with activity. Lazarus knew he would always remember this campaign and his part in it. He held that very thought one Tuesday when a large barrel arrived at the Society. It just appeared with a loud knock at the door, but no drayman could be found to explain its arrival.

Lazarus and Friend Garling were alone at the time and the two men rolled the barrel to the back left corner of the room and set it on end. As they did so, the contents of the barrel sloshed with a sound and feel indicating it contained some liquid. A tap had been screwed into the end and a small wooden spigot was strapped next to the tap. The end of the barrel bore some purple markings. Friend Garling tilted and turned it and read, *"R. Benbow – Jamaica."*

"No doubt Friend Benbow has sent some of Jamaica's fine rum as a gift," he said.

"Perhaps," said Lazarus, "but it seems rather large for a keg of rum. We'll discover soon enough. The committee meets tomorrow evening and Mr. Clarkson can investigate."

"We should save Friend Clarkson the trouble," said Friend Garling. "Let us tap in, then we may report the contents."

Lazarus did not care for this proposal, but he also knew Friend

Garling's habit of sampling the edibles. Friend Garling had misplaced the mallet and pry bar kept on hand to open crates, so he tapped in the spigot with a broken piece of bookshelf that splintered further in the effort. Lazarus reluctantly helped him set the heavy barrel across a crate and block it from rolling. Lazarus then returned to his table and his work. Friend Garling walked to the side of the room and returned with two cups. He stood at the barrel and extended one of the cups toward Lazarus. "Please join me, friend," he said.

Lazarus knew that Friend Garling wanted an accomplice in case Mr. Clarkson disapproved of the sampling. He was curious to see if Friend Garling was making a joke, for he knew the man to be a pious Quaker. "Quaker's do not drink spirits, do they?" Lazarus asked as he stood and joined his friend at the barrel.

"We are told to drink strong spirits only in moderation, and many Friends choose not to drink at all, but there is no prohibition on taking a taste. Friend Benbow, no doubt, thought a little taste might lighten our heavy duties, doest thou not think?"

"Perhaps," Lazarus allowed.

Friend Garling turned the spigot and filled both cups. The drink smelled strong and looked dark. Lazarus, and he suspected Friend Garling, had no experience at the drink. He did know to offer a toast. "To abolition!" said Lazarus.

"Hear! Hear!" said Friend Garling. Then both men raised their cups and drank down several gulps as if it were water. Both simultaneously choked and gagged a little but managed to swallow without spewing it out. It had a disagreeable odor and tasted even worse. Neither man wanted a second taste. Both left their cups half full and later discarded the rest hoping that the other would not notice. Neither commented to the other on his displeasure with the experience, though Lazarus wondered how men come to tolerate, even crave such drink.

The following evening, Friend Garling alerted Mr. Clarkson to the barrel, still astride the crate. "Shall I fetch thee a cupful?" he asked. Mr. Clarkson and the committee took their meetings quite seriously and so deferred until their conclusion. Then four or five approached the barrel and cups were filled and passed among them.

Mr. Clarkson and Mr. Sharp looked at each other as each detected the odor. "It smells rancid, perhaps," said Mr. Sharp.

This forestalled any tasting and just then, Mr. Clarkson saw the faded purple markings on the barrel end. Mr. Clarkson set his cup down and held up one hand like a military commander signaling his troops to halt. "Indigo content marker," he said to Mr. Sharp. A pale look came upon both men. Then they upended the barrel, spigot skyward. Lazarus had located Friend Garling's mallet and pry bar just hours earlier; he stepped forward and handed them to Mr. Clarkson, then deferentially stepped back so that committee members could gather around. As all stood about, two with lamps, Mr. Clarkson loosened the top iron rim from the stave ends and lifted the end off the barrel. He peered into the barrel and looked away.

Each man leaned forward to do the same and Mr. Sharp said, "My God." Then he sent Friend Garling to fetch a constable. Lazarus knew something was terribly wrong. He walked to the barrel, looked in it and saw the folded body of a naked man suspended in the rank liquid. The top of his head and shoulders were at one side and his knees pressed against the other in the position of a fetus. Lazarus immediately turned pale. He ran outside into the street where he vomited and shuddered until Friend Garling returned in the company of two police constables.

Lazarus trembled for days. Mr. Clarkson told him that planters and other Britons who die in the West Indies and desire to be buried in England sometimes provide for their bodies to be shipped home in a large barrel filled with rum in order to preserve their corpse from worms and decay. Mr. Clarkson could not identify the corpse in the barrel, but he had not received his regular correspondence from Mr. Benbow and he feared for his West Indies correspondent.

After some time, the suspicion grew and was finally confirmed to Mr. Clarkson's satisfaction by a ship's captain who described the export agent Benbow he had met in Kingston. The captain made no positive identification, as poor Mr. Benbow had by then been interred at the expense of the Abolition Society. Letters to Kingston later confirmed that Mr. Benbow had been missing since nearly three months before the arrival of the barrel. Mr. Clarkson and Mr. Sharp accused the West Indies lobby of complicity in the treachery. They denied any knowledge.

If the Society's opponents thought the death of Mr. Benbow and the delivery of his body to the Society's office would intimidate the abolitionists, Lazarus observed that they were wrong. At least on the surface it produced the opposite effect. To a man the abolitionists serving on the governing committee were angered and claimed to be more resolved to press on in what each believed to be the right.

The murder of Mr. Benbow shocked Lazarus. Despite his knowledge of drowned slaves, he had never seen a corpse. Roger Benbow, who informed but would not testify in life, provided a testament with his death. And perhaps, Lazarus thought, he may have done even more. He may have shown Lazarus a path for himself – or confirmed one.

As Lazarus watched the leaders of the Society in the coming days, though, he began to grow concerned. Their rhetoric was now strident, but Lazarus feared that below the surface, in their bellies, they had been weakened. He believed he could detect a little despair in their eyes.

The death of Roger Benbow, especially since it came at the hands of the slavers, troubled all the abolition leaders, but it particularly pained Mr. Clarkson. He had lost more than a friend. He had lost his best source. Evidence from the West Indies, he lamented, would now be difficult to come by. Reliable informants, resident in the West Indies, are precious and near irreplaceable, he explained, as nearly everyone there relies on the sugar trade in one way or another.

Lazarus tried to cheer Mr. Clarkson. "We just received a report of a recent event," he said, "a report that a slave ship captain flogged two slave girls to death."

"Who are the witnesses?" he asked. "Will they swear an affidavit?"

"Well, the witnesses are sailors," said Lazarus, "and when they came forward they were sent back to sea."

Mr. Clarkson nodded but lowered his eyes. "These sugar criminals not only enslave thousands upon thousands of people," he said. "But they put us in the position cherishing evidence of their butchery."

"Yes," said Lazarus. "Something must be done."

Chapter 17. Exact Intelligence

Mr. Clarkson rejected his plan. "It is a resourceful and a courageous proposal, Mr. Perlman," he said. "Visitors to the West Indies and, on occasion, a few residents have provided information in the past, but we have never sent anyone there for the purpose of observing and reporting." Then he paused. "Perhaps - no we could not spare you here at the Abolition Society. You are young and it is a danger."

Lazarus protested that he could likely provide some of the "exact intelligence" so desperately needed, but he would have to witness it himself or locate those who had.   He thought to say that the West Indies slavers were an evil Goliath and perhaps he could be a youthful David slinging stones at their head.   That sounded presumptuous, so he said, "I am told your own brother entered the naval service at the age of thirteen."

"You are correct," said Mr. Clarkson, "and I do not doubt you might be of service in the islands. Still, my first objection is that you are too valuable here. The Parliament will convene for its 1792 session before February, and we must move through its committees and build our attack for action in the spring – this is our best opportunity. Your assistance, your uncommon aptitude is needed." Then Mr. Clarkson placed a hand on Lazarus' shoulder as he had not done before, "We have a new challenge for you. Perhaps public protest will supplement our evidence."

Lazarus' new assignment proved to be formidable.   With Lazarus as records keeper, the Society amassed a mountain of petitions. He counted and organized 310 petitions from English cities and towns, 187 from Scotland and 20 from Wales. One from Manchester bore nearly 20,000 signatures.

Examining the piles of petitions, Mr. Clarkson said, "Well done! The British public has never so widely expressed its opinion,"

"Unfortunately," said Mr. Sharp, "the slave lobby has gotten wind of our petitions and appears to be marshaling opposition. Our petitions are freely offered - I expect they'll pay a tower of pounds sterling for theirs."

On a Sunday evening which happened to fall on All Fools Day – April First, Mr. Clarkson called together the Abolition Society's central committee, its most ardent supporters and its office volunteers in a special service. So as not to favor one denomination or another, the group convened at 18 Old Jewry Street. He asked all to put aside their differences and unite their faith in prayer for Mr. Wilberforce who planned to make a push for abolition the following day.

Mr. Sharp came forward. He motioned Friend Garling toward him and placed his left hand on the old Quaker's head as he said that the battle against slavery is not merely a protestant cause. Then he called Lazarus forward. Lazarus had come prepared and wore the prayer kippah Mordecai had made for him years earlier. Mr. Sharp reached toward Lazarus' head and just as Lazarus thought his kippah would be removed, Mr. Sharp instead placed his right hand on top of the Jewish kippah covering Lazarus' skull. "Ending the slave trade," he said, "is not just a Christian cause, but rather a matter of conscience and justice concerning all humanity." Then with his hands on the two heads, he bowed his own head and offered a stirring prayer. He not only asked that Mr. Wilberforce be given strength and eloquence, but he prayed for understanding from the opponents of abolition in the House of Commons and throughout the nation. His prayer seemed to touch all present. It penetrated one youthful Jew under his right hand.

Following the service, Mr. Clarkson reported that Mr. Wilberforce felt fully prepared and ready, thanks to the volunteers at 18 Old Jewry Street, and he invited Lazarus and Friend Garling to accompany him to the gallery of the House of Commons the following morning as a reward for their valuable assistance. If God were willing, Mr. Clarkson said, the old gray man and the bright young one would see history in the making – and would know that they had played a vital part in the moment. "But you must remain quiet no matter what happens," he said. "The Commons have long had a standing order to exclude strangers from their chamber. It is seldom invoked for routine matters, but this may get heated."

Lazarus could barely sleep that night. He left early without any explanation to Mordecai. He rode from 18 Old Jewry Street to Westminster Hall in one of the coaches hired by Mr. Sharp.

On a hard narrow bench in the crowded strangers' gallery, Lazarus sat next to Mr. Clarkson as a carriage stood ready outside in the event Mr. Clarkson felt the need to dispatch his right-hand aide back to the Society's office for any unforeseen reason. Friend Garling sat at Mr. Clarkson's left. The chamber below was divided with rows of chairs at each side, a raised speaker's seat near the far end and two red lines, about eight feet apart down its length. As the members of Parliament convened all seemed cordial. But the moment the topic turned to the slave trade they fell into disarray, even with no motion before them. While each side stayed behind its red line, several members jumped from their seats at one time. They spoke over one another and waived fists and papers in the air. If one managed to gain the floor, others facing him across the way shouted disparagement and laughed out loud to show disapproval. A few toed the red line and pointed across, railing at their brothers.

If the House of Commons has rules of behavior, they are insufficient, Lazarus thought. No wonder the committee had begun this battle with prayer.

Throughout the morning, Mr. Wilberforce could not stand without creating a storm, so he resumed his seat. "Waiting for the right moment," Mr. Clarkson said.

"What are the lines?" Lazarus asked.

Mr. Clarkson whispered, "They are said to be two sword lengths plus one foot apart . . . to make dueling impossible, though I don't think it has ever come to that."

"Spirited," Lazarus said.

"Much at stake," said Mr. Clarkson.

When the afternoon settled some, Mr. Wilberforce stood again and tried to make a formal motion, but those across the floor immediately became reanimated and began to shout at him to be seated.

"Hear him! Hear him! Hear him!" his allies shouted back at their opposition. Finally, at near six o'clock in the evening, Prime Minister Pitt intervened and recognized Mr. Wilberforce. Over constant attempts at interruption from across the floor, he moved for the abolition of the slave trade.

"It makes cruel brutes of gentlemen," he said.

"Not this stale old charge," an opponent yelled at him.

At that, Mr. Wilberforce raised his hand high and glanced up at Lazarus. "I have in my hand new information. A report of a recent atrocity," he said.

"A report, a report – reports are but rumors put to paper," a man across the way yelled at him.

"Sailors of Bristol provide a direct account," said Mr. Wilberforce. "A slave ship captain flogged not one, but two fifteen-year-old African girls to death because they resisted his advances – and," Wilberforce pointed across the way, "the captain is none other than John Kimber, well know constituent to a certain Member from Bristol."

Suddenly, a red-faced opponent jumped to his feet. "Slander, it is not true," he cried.

Wilberforce pressed on, "Is this the England the slave trade has brought us, where members of Parliament come to the defense of murderers?"

Lazarus thought Mr. Wilberforce spoke as well as anyone could under the chaotic circumstances. The abolition side held the floor with a parade of speeches throughout the night. Lazarus and his fellows left only for a small bite of food and to visit the necessary chamber. For Lazarus, the long night so filled with expectation that he didn't know when the sun rose. As it did, Prime Minister Pitt punctuated the pleas of the abolitionists with his own support. Lazarus smelled victory.

Then a previously quiet member of the Commons rose. Mr. Clarkson whispered that his name was Henry Dundas and that he was respected, having served as a secretary of state. He shrewdly agreed with Mr. Wilberforce and the abolitionists but urged moderation. Then he moved to amend the Wilberforce motion by insertion of the word "gradual" and a definition of that term to mean "over a period of six years."

Suddenly, fiery words such as "bamboozle," "trickery," "chicanery" and "deceit" flew about the chamber.

When it appeared the motion to amend might carry, Friend Garling leapt to his feet and pointed down at the opposition side. "Bollocks," he screamed. "Bollocks, bollocks, bollocks!"

Immediately, the speaker called for silence and pointed up at the gallery. "The Sergeant at Arms will clear all strangers," he ordered. Within a minute, a big brute grabbed little Friend Garling at his arm and everyone remaining in the gallery at that hour filed out, down and away under watchful eyes. Once outside, Mr. Clarkson procured the release of Friend Garling and asked Lazarus to take him back in a carriage.

As they departed, Friend Garling returned to his familiar Quaker demeanor and apologized. "I don't know what came over me," he said.

"I do," said Lazarus. "You were quite right. I'm not sure those puffed-up politicians will ever get it right. I was screaming at them as well, from the inside. I did not have your courage."

Friend Garling looked surprised at Lazarus. He sat silently, but seemed at ease.

Within two hours, Mr. Clarkson and the rest of the group returned to 18 Old Jewry and reported the news. By a final count of 230 to 85 the House of Commons had voted to abolish the slave trade ... gradually. A dour faced Mr. Clarkson called for thanksgiving and said the victory had not been complete, but it remained a victory all the same. He did manage a smile at Friend Garling, though, and asked, "Who knew our meek little lamb could be such a lion?"

Lazarus did not feel jubilant. He did not know whether to celebrate the victory or mourn the delay in its implementation. Six years seemed a very long time if measured by the past six – and the matter would not be settled until also passed by the House of Lords.

The Lords took up the matter in the following weeks. Mr. Clarkson reported the progress almost daily to his aides. The House of Lords, he said, had never before directly debated the slave trade. It did so now only with great difficulty. Many of the Lords appeared unwilling to acknowledge the very same evidence that members of the House of Commons had difficulty ignoring. They dismissed the report against Captain John Kimber. "Not credible," they said "It is for the Admiralty to investigate, but they will likely acquit him if they bring a charge." Adopting a theme of the slave lobby, some of them characterized the remaining accounts of abolition witnesses as not timely. They charged that the accounts that might be true related to incidents that had occurred some years and even decades earlier. Surely, these Lords argued, treatment of slaves had become more civilized.

Lazarus thought this rationale ridiculous. How can taking an unwilling man captive, forcefully removing him thousands of miles from his home and selling him into a life of slavery be said to be in any way civilized? There was no answer. Mr. Clarkson said that the Lords have a talent for not hearing questions they do not wish to address. Some of the Lords found even taking up the subject of the slave trade inappropriate. A vocal majority found the evidence old and stale. Abolitionist clamor, they said, had already resulted in better treatment for Africans, so they saw no need for intervention by Parliament.

It was not true, charged Mr. Wilberforce's allies in the House of Lords. Abuse of slaves continues, they charged. As the debate dragged on, the Lords added the terms "further testimony," "careful study," and "dutiful deliberation" to the lexicon of injustice. In each case the phrases actually meant indefinite delay. The Lords then repeatedly refused to decide the matter, even as amended. On June 5, 1792, and over abolitionist objections, the House of Lords put the matter aside without a vote. Then they administered the coup de grace for the year with one more dreadful word - "prorogation" – the Parliament's unique term for adjournment.

Until then, Lazarus had innocently believed that some real measure of victory had been at hand. The already somber Thomas Clarkson was angry. "The gradualists are enemies to our cause, make no mistake," he advised. He appeared to Lazarus to be gaunt and drawn from his efforts.

"The charge of 'stale evidence' is an excuse," said Mr. Sharp, "but still one we must eliminate."

The Abolition Society and its central committee again congratulated itself. It had managed to proceed as far as the House of Lords and vowed to fight on to its goal. To Lazarus, it seemed clear that the failure had disheartened the movement's leaders, despite their brave face.

As the committeemen broke for respite, Lazarus evaluated where this set back left the cause of abolition and his own place in the suddenly struggling movement. He realized he should not take the defeat as personally as had Mr. Clarkson, but he couldn't help it.

Mordecai welcomed the failure. "An end to your foolishness has come at last," he said.

The Symmons consoled him. "Understudy to Thomas Clarkson is good preparation for teaching," Mr. Symmons said. "That was my intent in sending you to him. Perhaps it is time you move on to that."

"I am so sorry, Lazarus," said his wife. "My father always said politics is a messy business."

"These members of Parliament, these mighty Lords," he told her, "none of them is the equal of Thomas Clarkson."

"Yes," she said, nodding her head, "I know."

After reflection, Lazarus rallied. He had seen Mr. Clarkson do it time and again. Mordecai would see. This was not the end. Lazarus and the abolitionists would still prevail.

Lazarus determined to lift Mr. Clarkson and the governing committee with his resolve. He had never before been in a position to do so. Mr. Clarkson had never before seemed so much in need. He bided a little more time to allow his leader to recover – and to dilute his father's resistance. He then resurfaced his proposal. He told Mr. Clarkson that he would travel to the West Indies and endeavor to gather "exact intelligence" that the Society must obtain. He could help fill the void that had been so evident during the Parliamentary sessions. The shoes of the late Roger Benbow were sizable, Lazarus admitted, but he offered to try to fill them.

Mr. Clarkson was still weak and, for once, ready to rely on another. He reluctantly assented, but with reservations. Financial support would be limited, but Lazarus thought the stipend suggested would meet his modest needs until the next session of Parliament.

Mr. Clarkson insisted that Lazarus agree to certain conditions:

"First," Mr. Clarkson said, "you must guard your affiliation with the Society and your sentiments or the plantation owners will destroy you. You will need some cover, a pretext for your presence. It must be convincing – not an obvious pretense."

"I can pass as a tailor," he assured Mr. Clarkson. "I know there are Jews in the West Indies. I am practiced at making their garments."

"That will do nicely, I think, and even slavers need clothes. You will need some means for yourself anyway," Mr. Clarkson advised. "Secondly, you must secure your own passage."

"Perhaps I can sign as a crew hand on a cargo vessel, I think it is often done," Lazarus said.

"Yes, and by lads your age," said Mr. Clarkson, "but do not think to crew on any slave vessel as they present far too great a risk. Even on a merchant vessel, the work and the passage are rigorous. You must understand that."

"Of course," Lazarus said, though he really had not much considered it.

"Thirdly, you must remain in the Lesser Antilles. Barbados, I think and not travel to Jamaica. It is far too dangerous."

Lazarus had, indeed, thought of Jamaica, the home of the late, sacrificed Mr. Benbow. "Why Barbados?" he asked Mr. Clarkson.

"It is the vanguard of British presence in those isles – and of the slave trade." Mr. Clarkson explained. "Earlier, we had correspondence from a few residents. Of late, I fear they have lost interest or may have been compromised. There is one unlikely sympathizer, but he is not really an informant."

"Am I to call on him, to assist or – "

"No, certainly not," Mr. Clarkson cautioned. "You should suppose no allies exist. Earlier correspondents may have been found out or even turned against us. I will not tell you any of their names so no one could possibly accuse you of revealing them. Neither shall they know of you. I'm afraid we do not know the situation there – we have had no intelligence of it for many months and the last proved unreliable. Trust no one! You will be wholly on your own with no safe quarter. It is a well settled place, though, not known for recent rebellion as in Jamaica. Its planters feel unthreatened. I calculate they may, then, be unguarded as well. Do your famous research and think on it."

"Actually, I have done some reading on the history and trade at each of the British possessions in the West Indies," Lazarus said. "Barbados was my first inquiry."

"Aha, I am not surprised," Mr. Clarkson smiled and shook his head.

Lazarus already knew - Barbados was small, the eastern most of the West Indies, but the seat of British rule over its possessions in the region. Its chief port, Bridgetown, was often the first place ships for the West Indies stopped, even if bound elsewhere. Besides, it had been the first site of English plantations in the West Indies, the first place British settlers had brought slaves. It might do very well. "Well, you mentioned Barbados when you spoke at the home of Mr. Symmons," he reminded Mr. Clarkson. Then he agreed. Barbados it would be.

Mr. Clarkson had still more conditions:

Lazarus would route his correspondence through a third party, so that it would not be apparent to anyone monitoring the post that he informed for the Abolition Society. "Do not underestimate the slave owners," he warned. "If they suspect you are engaged in espionage, you will likely disappear. Other informants have, but you know that."

Yes, Lazarus could answer truthfully that he had considered that risk. He had not thought of secretly informing on the slavers as "espionage," though. His prospects appeared more exciting by the minute.

"Oh, and one more thing," Mr. Clarkson said with an urgent voice. "Your father must consent."

It was hopeless then. Mr. Clarkson had no reason to know that Mordecai objected to Lazarus' very presence at the Abolition Society. His father would never consent to this adventure. But Lazarus had learned from the slave lobby – he delayed a little, then he lied. "Well, we shall see," he replied. "My father knows I am not truly a tailor."

Mordecai knew no such thing. Lazarus retired to his chair in the back corner of the Society's office to meditate his dishonesty: My father constantly presses me to spend my days – my life – just as he has spent his, he recounted, to ignore my conscience and live only, as he says, "with your own traditions and in your own occupation." For him, yes it is enough. But, perhaps I have not told such a big lie. He knows my discontent as a tailor. He knows I have other dreams. Besides, my father has opposed my work at the Society from my first day at 18 Old Jewry Street. He has not stopped me before, nor will he now.

Still, his chair felt less comfortable than usual. I shall have to devise a strategy, Lazarus thought.

When days later the solution still escaped him, Lazarus deployed more of his chess skills - he reassessed his position and refocused. The failure at Parliament would not be allowed to stand – but the defeat provided him the chance to play an important role. There was no easy solution, but the answer was clear: Mordecai must be persuaded – or overcome. Lazarus' days as a rearward supply officer were finished. No longer a pawn – he would be a rook or perhaps a devious knight – and he now had his opening to attack. He would not surrender - would Moses? Well, he knew he was no Moses, not even a Thomas Clarkson – still, he would find a way. He was, after all, a prodigy.

Chapter 18. The Concession

Lazarus sat with Mrs. Symmons at her kitchen table. He told her that he had news. He explained the defeat in Parliament and the charge that the Society's evidence was stale. He said he had conceived a plan how he might help remedy this deficiency. It involved a journey.

She anticipated him and said, "I think it is quite courageous of you, but I fear for your safety and that I would miss you too dearly – much too dearly."

"But I would be quite safe if the source of the information were kept secret. That is why Mr. Clarks – it is why I am asking you to relay my correspondence. I shall return once the Parliament abolishes the slave trade. It might be but a year or two."

Mrs. Symmons looked into Lazarus' face and saw turmoil. Consternation was not new to Lazarus, nor was her detection of it. Mrs. Symmons just looked in her soft way at him for several moments. "What troubles you?" she asked.

"I have not determined how to tell my father … or Mr. Symmons."

"My, that is a problem, isn't it?" She just stared blankly for a moment. Then she looked directly at Lazarus. "I suppose," she said, "that a young man heedful of the prophets and the great rabbis might do well to find a suitable mitzvah - a good work upon which to direct his life – a selfless one that promotes a worthy cause. It is the law, am I right?"

"Why. yes, of course," Lazarus said, discerning her drift but not all of her meaning.

"Among the hundreds of commandments Jews are to obey, one might well find one consistent with striving to put an end to bondage," she said with a hint of a smile.

Now he understood. She was giving him the means to advise his father and Mr. Symmons of his plans. Amazing, he thought – and she does not even play chess. He smiled with her. "One might indeed," he said. "You do not know what you mean to me, Mrs. Symmons." His voice cracked between boy and man as he said it.

"Nor you to me Mr. Perlman," she said with a twinkle of a happy tear in her eye. She moved a trembling finger to dab her eye.

Her caring face now brought a glisten to Lazarus' eyes as well. Both breathed deeply. It was thrilling to be near Mrs. Symmons, he thought. It was also torturous.

"It would be my pleasure to relay your correspondence," said Mrs. Symmons, just as her husband walked into the room.

"What correspondence?" Mr. Symmons asked. He was not a creature of the kitchen, yet here he was this evening suddenly standing over the table.

"His reports to Mr. Clarkson," Mrs. Symmons looked up at her husband as she said it and then back at Lazarus, "he intends to undertake a mission to the West Indies."

Mr. Symmons seemed to bristle at the use of the word "mission." "Is that what you have come to?" he asked.

"Yes, perhaps I can sign for Barbados aboard a ship this month," said Lazarus.

"It is all arranged then?" Mr. Symmons asked.

"Not entirely," said Lazarus, "but I am told Mr. Clarkson has his eye on a fine ship. She is set to sail for Barbados on fifteen September, if the load be tight and the tide be right."

"My, you sound like a seaman already," said Mrs. Symmons with a smile.

Her husband frowned. "Two days after Rosh Hashanah, the week before Yom Kippur," he said, looking some place over Lazarus' head and then down at him. "And what does your father say?" he asked.

"He understands little outside his shop," Lazarus said.

Mr. Symmons scowled, "He may understand more than you know," he grumbled. "Come," he said, "I am for a match if you are able."

Lazarus was always ready for chess. He excused himself to Mrs. Symmons and followed Mr. Symmons into the parlor where the chessmen already stood black facing white on rows. Without choosing pawns, Mr. Symmons sat at the whites and stared across at Lazarus as somberly as did his white king. He advanced his king's pawn one space with the comment, "Now, what is this West Indies business?"

Lazarus matched his move and replied, "We failed at Parliament, as you know. Mr. Clarkson and Mr. Wilberforce did all that could be done, but we need better evidence, more recent."

"But why must you be the one? You are a young man of promise. You would be an able teacher. Should you not acknowledge G-d's gifts by employing your talents in the service of his people?" As he said it, Mr. Symmons boldly brought out his queen and sat it on a diagonal to Lazarus' protected rook.

There was Lazarus' opening. "Is it not a good service, a mitzvah, to oppose bondage of the innocent, though they not be among the chosen people?" he meekly asked. He stayed back - he would not mirror reckless moves.

"I think it's indeed a fine service, and a mitzvah if you will, to oppose bondage, but the Lord has likely prepared a different work for you, though it may not be clear to you at present. I fear Clarkson has snared you in his fervor." Mr. Symmons sounded stern, not like the schoolmaster Lazarus knew. As the game proceeded, Lazarus realized that this was neither Mr. Symmons' usual tone nor his usual game.

During the next few moves, he asked Lazarus the details of his plan. There were few details, more of a general purpose. "The islands are dangerous," he said. "You know what happened on Saint Dominique!"

Lazarus had studied it. "Yes, but my destination is Barbados. There, the last rebellion of Africans occurred in 1692, exactly one hundred years ago," he said, "and that one was aborted before any serious violence."

Still the questions came. Lazarus admitted that he had procured no position in the islands, he had no sponsor in Barbados, and he was not even certain that he could earn his passage as a seaman. Mr. Symmons found deficiencies in all of this, but Lazarus sensed that was not at the core of his objection.

"It is said the Africans sometimes sell their fellows to the slave hunters in Africa," said Mr. Symmons. "How can one take pity on such a people as turn on their own?" He placed a pawn out for easy capture.

The pawn was offered too readily, Lazarus thought, likely clearing a route or laying a decoy. He did not take it. "Yes, they are sometimes given a choice of their own freedom or their brother's."

Mr. Symmons looked up from the chessboard as if he had scored a capture. Then Lazarus continued, "Joseph of old was sold into slavery by his own brothers. Is that not how our people found themselves in bondage in Egypt? You taught me yourself that the Lord cursed Egyptian slavers. Does he deny slaves to pharaohs but allow them to sugar planters?" He matched his mentor's boldness.

"Do you feel compassion only for Mr. Clarkson's Africans?" Mr. Symmons said as he slid his queen and captured a knight's pawn.

Lazarus jumped his knight over the queen and offered it in lieu of the trapped rook. "At the present, I know of no greater wrong than the slave trade," he said.

"The Africans face a monster in the sugar planters, a dragon difficult to slay," Mr. Symmons said, he captured the black rook leaving his queen in the corner in its place.

"Well then, the more swords, the better," said Lazarus as he moved his queen to guard his rook's pawn and blocked the retreat of the white queen.

"Monsters and dragons in need of slaying abound," said Mr. Symmons. "I understand what draws you to battle those afflicting the Africans, but they are not your dragons."

"A dragon may devour any man," said Lazarus. "Are they not enemies of all men?"

Mr. Symmons sat silently looking at the board, contemplating his next move - and his next argument.

Lazarus did not let him rest. "Besides," he pursued, "Jews are in some measure responsible for the Africans of Barbados."

"How is that?!" Mr. Symmons almost shouted.

"Fully half of all Africans transported to the British West Indies went to Barbados during the first 75 years of its settlement. A majority of those were sold to the British settlers there by Dutch merchants, most of them Jewish."

"You know that Jews were limited in their choice of trades. We cannot now be held - "

"True enough," Lazarus interrupted. He did not recall having ever interrupted Mr. Symmons. "If slaves had not been transported by the Dutch Jews, they would have been supplied by other slavers. Still, the fact remains. I do not suggest my own guilt in this, or yours, but I see some small redemption - no that is too strong a word, some small recognition of the fact in my work with the abolitionists, my observance of this … this mitzvah."

"Perhaps I should not have introduced you to Mr. Clarkson," Mr.

Symmons said. "Certainly I should have not recommended you to him."

"I never gave him your letter, your recommendation," Lazarus said. "I will return it to you if you wish to disavow any -"

"It is not necessary," Mr. Symmons said. Then he rubbed his chin as he looked at the chess pieces and said, "Mr. Clarkson says he is called of his God to aid the Africans, are you not called by your own G-d to serve your own kind?"

Lazarus thought to remind Mr. Symmons that his wife had not stayed among her own kind and that Mr. Symmons himself had gone so far as to pass as an Anglican while at Cambridge. Before he determined the best tact to take, Mr. Symmons spoke again. "It is said the Africans are as children, that they do not cover their nakedness and that they worship pagan gods. Perhaps they are a people not worthy of your sacrifices."

Lazarus suppressed a smile. Then he answered, "The children of Israel worshiped a golden calf, dancing naked before it, even after the Lord had freed them from bondage in Egypt."

Mr. Symmons' eyes left his queen and focused across the board away from her.

Lazarus moved a black bishop on line with the corner, but left his knight between the bishop and the cornered white queen. He asked, "Are they not our brothers who worship other gods?"

"Thou shalt have no other gods," Mr. Symmons said, and he took another black pawn to his left.

Lazarus moved his blocking knight, leaving the path clear from his bishop to the white queen. This gave Mr. Symmons the choice. He could stand and surrender her to Lazarus' bishop or he could take the bishop and still lose his queen to the black queen guarding her bishop.

As Mr. Symmons considered his predicament, Lazarus looked up at his beloved but now troubled teacher and said, softly but in great earnestness, "At school, a wise teacher taught me the *'Oath of Maimonides'*. I recall it all, especially the parts about watching over the life and health of the Lord's creatures, remembering the lofty aim of doing good and standing ready for one's calling."

Mr. Symmons blushed a little and sat back, surveying the chess board.

Lazarus pressed on, "One does not forsake one's own tradition by extending his hand, however feeble, to those in need of it, whether they worship his same G-d, gods unknown to him or no god at all. No prophet or rabbi said it that I know of, but I believe it."

Mr. Symmons looked up at him. His eyes were wide now. Almost without looking down he put his finger on the top of his white king - and tipped it down on its face.

Mr. Symmons had no sooner conceded when his wife came into the room carrying the strapped grip sack that she had first loaned to Lazarus, along with a few of her father's books, nearly three years earlier. It had passed between them carrying other volumes many times since then. She extended it to Lazarus. "This is for you," she said, "a gift, along with its contents."

He rose, took the bag, thanked her, nodded respectfully toward Mr. Symmons and turned to leave. As they said their goodbyes, Mrs. Symmons again protested that she would "despise" his absence. Lazarus had never heard that word used so well.

Mr. Symmons asked, "How will you make a match out among the islands?" Tonight he was uncommonly blunt.

"I expect to return once the Parliament has acted," he said, "then, perhaps I may meet a banker's daughter." He looked at Mrs. Symmons to see if he had erred. She smiled and turned to her husband.

"Yes, I had forgotten that you knew about that," Mr. Symmons said.

Lazarus did not say some other things he knew. Chess was not the only passion he shared with Mr. Symmons.

* * * * * * *

Lazarus lied again to Mr. Clarkson and told him he had made progress with Mordecai. In truth, he had postponed telling his father of his intentions, but he could delay no longer. He was determined and would not be deterred regardless of his father's reaction. Mordecai was usually at his best in the mornings. Lazarus came to him late the next Monday and too abruptly said, "Father, I have decided to strike out on ... I mean - I must leave England for a while."

"Vas is das?" Mordecai demanded.

Lazarus heard his father's accent return as it did at times of great stress. "I shall return in a year or two," he added. This was not how he planned to say it, but he shied from a more truthful approach. Besides, the old man did not understand Lazarus' work for the Abolition Society. He surely would not appreciate a further involvement.

"Where vould you go, what vould you do?" Mordecai asked in an almost dismissive tone.

"I believe I shall go to Barbados, in the West Indies, for a time and learn to rely on myself."

Mordecai scowled.

Hoping to relieve the tension Lazarus added, "I shall also continue in the tailor's trade as you have taught me, even in my absence."

Mordecai waved an upturned palm to his side and behind himself as if motioning to display the shop to someone who had never before seen it - though Lazarus had been in it every day of his life. "Someday," the father said as he returned his eyes to his son, "someday dis shop vill be yours."

"Papa," said Lazarus, "I must tell you … I must tell you that the shop is truly not what I want."

Lazarus knew his words hurt Mordecai. Both men knew that the words were truthful. Lazarus wished he had begun the conversation differently. He had meant to tell his father that his departure was part of a good work, a mitzvah, and that he saw it as in keeping with following the prophets and the law of his people. Now he wanted to simply tell his father the truth, but in a way that Mordecai might find at least some merit to his son's purpose.

"Papa," he said, "my purpose in traveling to the West Indies would be to provide much needed information on the treatment of Africans by the slave merchants and the plantation owners. I would earn my keep as a tailor, but at the same time I would observe what I could for the cause of abolition."

"You should go un see Rabbi Hirschell." Mordecai was in earnest. "He can tell you vat you should do."

"I cannot explain it," said Lazarus, "but I believe this is a mitzvah which I must do. Besides, I shall return when the slave trade is banned. Many believe that may come soon."

The old man crooked his head to one side and pounded his temple with the palm of his hand as if clearing water from one ear. Then he squared his jaw around and simply shook his head. "And how vould you pay for your pazzage?"

"I am told passage may be provided in exchange for services on a merchant ship."

"Oy, oy, you know nussing of ships," proclaimed Mordecai as if that put an end to it. "You vould not be able to attend de synagogue. It vould not do."

Lazarus had prepared himself for these objections. "I have read on sailing," he said. "I shall watch the lead of the others. I will do well enough." Then he looked at the floor. "Papa, there is a synagogue in Bridgetown, the chief city of Barbados." He did not add that the synagogue was a Sephardic community affiliated with nearby Bevis Marks, London's Spanish synagogue.

More of the sounds of his native tongue in Mordecai's words signaled to Lazarus that he had wounded his father. Lazarus regretted the harm. With a single word, Mordecai returned the blows, "Impozzible!" he said.

Before he thought on it Lazarus said, "I would unburden you for a time with such a journey." It was the wrong thing to say.

"Ven have I said dat the child of my Leah is un burden?" There was silence, but Mordecai's usually steady hands trembled.

As the middle of September approached, Lazarus contented himself that he had finally procured Mr. Clarkson's approval of his planned journey. The Abolition Society had even provided a modest allowance. It was unfortunate that he had resorted to a little deception in the effort – a note from Mordecai, actually penned by the left hand of his son - but it could not be helped.

Mrs. Symmons seemed to admire his devotion to the abolition cause. Even Mr. Symmons begrudgingly conceded the worth of his undertaking. He knew to expect no such concession from Mordecai. When he left, Lazarus realized, it would be without his father's blessing.

Lazarus remained unsure whether his father's stubborn ways were born in faith or merely ritual, but he dutifully celebrated the coming of the Jewish New Year with the old man. Neither man spoke of sailing ships or of Africans. Three days later, Lazarus appeared downstairs in Mordecai's shop with a packed duffel and a shorter leather satchel, a gift from a friend. He deposited them near the door and turned to his father. Mordecai averted his eyes.

"Papa," Lazarus said in a pleading tone. He took a step toward the table where Mordecai sat. Lazarus thought it proper to embrace the old man. Mordecai did not rise. With his eyes still on his work he said, "Vill you leave me then?"

Lazarus had not thought of it as leaving Mordecai, nor did he view it that way now. "You will be fine, Papa," he said, "I shall return and find you still at your work."

Mordecai did not look up or answer. He did not even stop his work. Lazarus shook his head slowly, lifted his baggage and simply left.

PART THREE: The Passage

Shipboard - September–November 1792

Chapter 19. The *Maidenstone*

Lazarus Perlman thought he would die.

Fortunately, he had purged every morsel and drop in his innards, because he had no strength left to pull himself up to the starboard rail that had been his station since the previous day. He had streaked and smeared the bulkwark below the rail, but the bow-down spray had washed it shiny clean. He gagged at nothing but the wind and the rise and fall of the ship in the turbulent sea just five days out of London. He had been well enough at the second sunset as the ship passed Plymouth, and at first, he had thought himself a likely good seaman. That was before the majestic, three-masted *Maidenstone* had cleared the channel.

Now, he found himself on his back like an overturned turtle, soiled in his own vomit, with his head aft and his feet forward. His body shifted from his left shoulder to his right and back with the incessant roll of the deck. His stomach spasmed and wretched, but he emitted nothing except mucus and some blood, which oozed from his bowels into his breeches and out of the right corner of his mouth onto his not-yet-a-beard. His clothes, his hair and his skin were saturated with body fluids and sea spray. Between the storm of the waves and the storm of the stomach, he was helpless.

This was not at all how the voyage had begun. Just a day clear of Lands End a fair north breeze, well abaft the beam, had promised to deliver the *Maidenstone* and her 200 ton burden to the Cape Verde Islands, a key marker in her planned journey, ahead of schedule. Seaman Novice Perlman was assigned to the first watch crew. When four hours had passed, the second watch came on deck, but Lazarus was much too absorbed to go below. He had done little as the ship had put out. The work had been slow. The tide and the Thames had performed most of it.

He had but four hours to sleep until his watch came again, as it would three times from each sunrise to the next. Still, Lazarus stayed topside at watch change but out of the way. He found a comfortable place leaning against the starboard bulwark just aft the mainmast. From here he could see not only the crew, but most of the helm and even up on the raised forecastle deck at the front, which he had already learned to call the fo'c'sle.

The channel could be rough, but it had been smooth for this novice as the *Maidenstone* slowly rounded Ramsgate. After she cleared Dover, she had crawled along the coast of Kent, around Dungeness and off Sussex toward the open sea. Day one and all had been well with the *Maidenstone* and with Seaman Novice Perlman.

That night Lazarus' duty crew had been in high spirits. Off Portsmouth, Able Seaman Percival Nugent on the main bellowed toward the fo'c'sle, "Recon she's still there with open arms, Georgie?"

From the fo'c'sle Seaman Apprentice George Parker looked sheepish under a bright moon, turned toward the distant town and dropped his head.

His fo'c'sle mate, Hugh Duncan, shot back toward the main, "It weren't her 'arms' what held Georgie tight, now were it boy?"

Then others laughed and Nugent shouted, "Ye lifted her skirts then, did ye George?"

As the laughter quieted, Captain Rodney Graves walked a few steps forward and barked, "Belay the talk o' floozies lads; in the morning there'll be other skirts for yer lifting." Then he pointed up and drew eyes to the mainmast's supporting shroud lines where a few brightly colored strings had been tied at one end. The strings were almost colorless in the moonlight, but they could be seen dancing toward the bow. "The telltales speak," yelled Captain Graves, "the winds is aiding."

The wind had aided yet at sunup. The captain climbed slowly to his station, relieved his mate near the pedestal and looked down at the gimball and the compass suspended from it to check her heading. It was habit. That morning there was little need to gain bearings as he recognized the shoreline of Weymouth Bay and Bill of Portland over his right shoulder. He faced forward again and bellowed to his fresh crew, "Let us give the lady her tops, lads, and if her bosom fills we'll give her gallant hats and spirits as well."

Almost together the crew yelled an enthusiastic, "Aye, cap'n, aye."

Over the next hour the crew scuffled about, repeating to confirm deck orders. Hands unwrapped cleats and tugged on halyards and sheets. Blocks squeaked and yardarms rose aloft. Young legs climbed, and square sails came unfurled and gently filled.

Then a little later there were more orders. Booms swung away, and two fo'c'slemen manned the foot of the bowsprit. Guy lines guided spinnaker and other spars while triangles appeared fore and a spanker sail was outhauled aft.

The crew shook itself out a little as it shook out and secured the sails. Fully outfitted, nearly two dozen sails in all moved the *Maidenstone* through the water.

Lazarus and his first watch mates had come back on duty. He helped on the fo'c'sle and pulled on lines as he was told. Here and there a new man, or one hung down from tavern nights, would trip and stumble on a deckplate, a stay or a mate. No hand was extended to men who fell. This crew worked together, but each man stood on his own.

By the time a few more watches passed, the *Maidenstone* had passed Start Point. A few more and she bore down on what Lazarus took to be Land's End. He pointed at it and asked confirmation from an older crewmate. "Nawr," the sailor said, "that be Lizard Point; Land's End be but a small bay beyond as ye'll see soon enough."

"Aye, that be Lizard," said another. "And do ye know why they calls her that?"

"No sir," Lazarus said.

The sailor grimaced a bit while his eyes shined. "Lads," he said to the hearing of several about, "this new dog says 'e are not familiar wi' the lizard land."

"Perhaps, 'e should."

"Give 'im the lesson."

"Likely 'e will," and other such came replies.

The sailor looked down at Lazarus and pronounced, "Lizard be the last point to put ashore in a boat fer new dogs, mummies boys and them what's lost their grit. Them what passes Lizard becomes men or dies in the doin'. Them what puts ashore slithers home on they bellies ... that be why she's called the point o' the lizard."

"All to the boat who's for shore and safety," one nearby cried. Then all about laughed and two stepped forward and firmly slapped Lazarus on the back, as one man does another.

Lazarus was not clear whether he was singled out for slander or for acceptance. He thought quickly and decided to act as if it were the latter. "Hum," he said loudly, "Some go ashore on their bellies, do they? Well, I'm for the sea and Barbados, I'm avowed." His people had seen worse than the sea, he thought. Surely he could manage this little crossing.

"Aye, so be it," said the sailor, and he sang, *"Out to the sea and the devil with ye – come 'round again on yer bended knee. "*

Lazarus did not know what the sailor meant by the rhyme. He let it pass. As she later cleared Land's End, the *Maidenstone* was neither for the devil nor on her belly. She stood tall before the full breeze that had now rotated a few degrees counterclockwise to come from the north. As the hours passed, the wind continued to swing some and grew stronger. It freshened yet again and swung some westerly so that the vessel could not run fully down but had to pinch the wind.

Through the next watch, the wind continued to rotate and strengthen. As it did, the helmsman began to tack, but the darkening horizon and shifting wind had alerted the captain and he ordered the crew to strike the jibs, spirits and stay sails. He surveyed the horizon again and barked orders that sent hands to the halyards to lower the high royals, then the topgallants and the topsails. Finally, as the wind had become angry and near nor'westerly, the crew tugged on lines and pulley blocks gathered sheets against their yard arms. A few lads scrambled above and secured them in place. With the fore course and the mizzen course furled, only the mainsail remained. The helmsman brought her bow up, close-hauling the ship at a tight angle against the developing west-nor'westerly gale.

The captain had remained on the quarterdeck as the rains then came and the mainsail, with her arm lined fine on the wind, had begun to luff. During the storm the sun had gone from behind the westward clouds and it was dark under a low sky. The ship had started to yaw hard and had heeled to larboard.

The captain had looked up into the rain, shook his head and cupped his hands near the ear of his mate. "Batten 'er down," he ordered. Then to the helmsman he said, "When the lads are down - bring 'er up straight." Crewmen grabbed at rope cleats and a few of them began to climb quickly aloft in the dark storm to help furl the mainsail. Suddenly, the wheelman turned to west, nor-west, directly into the wind. In the whistling wind, he had not heard the first part of the captain's orders. The turn was too soon and the storm gusted just as she came full into it and backwinded the mainsail. The mainsail snapped sharply back against the mast and split from top stayline to near bottom at the center. The ship jerked and the mast seemed to straighten back up from its slightly forward rake. Three men were thrown down to the deck. Not all could see what had happened, but all could feel the ship groan and shudder. All could hear the flapping rent sail. Each man of the watch felt his way to some hope of safety.

Two who had been thrown down were able to roll about. One clung to a raised chain plate, the other to a docking chock. Each man hugged one or another of the ship's masts, fastlines or rails. A few men ended up with arms and legs woven into the ratlines of the lower shrouds and webbing. All hands were secure - all save one. He had been aloft. The snap of the backwinded mainsail had thrown him away, backside down, and he landed with one foot chest high off the deck, caught by a turnbuckle, and his head diagonally below fixed on the bolt of a shackle which impaled him by his skull. His wet face looked to heaven and his eyes shined wide open.

After a few moments of clinging with no more disaster, the captain pulled himself upright, slid down on the main deck and pumped up his lungs. He bellowed fore, larboard and starboard, and the young fo'c'sle crewmen came slowly down to help on the main. After much exertion the wet, whipping sail was secured in its two halves, one bunched on either side of the mainmast yardarm. Four crewmen, under the captain's directions, then freed the body of their impaled fellow and wrapped it in canvass that whipped in the wind and made the gruesome task difficult. Then the soaked and somber fellows strung it about and secured the shroud to the same chain shackle that had rendered it a ghost. The wind howled. The crew was done, as was their captain. All secure on deck, he sent but a few below and remained himself with the skeleton watch to make sure she kept her nose to the wind.

Within the hour the rain had become sideways and had seemed to blow upward as it swirled around the fo'c'sle onto the main deck. The storm played the rigging like a discordant flute and percussion symphony. Staylines whistled, crosstrees and booms creaked, deadeyes squealed, furled sheets strained against their wraps and a few blocks banged against masts and caps.

Lazarus, though, had seen none of the teamwork of the crew as it had hauled down the sails from top to bottom, fore and aft. He didn't know the mainsail had split. He was ignorant of the impaled crewman, dead and wrapped on the side of the deck opposite him. He alone had been fast against the weather side bulwark. First, he spewed into the wind with his arms spread like twin booms along the rail. Then he rolled up in a fetal ball against the bottom of the bulkhead, trembling as his intestines jerked and contracted. His stomach heaved with the waves that crashed against the front belly of the ship.

Busied as they were, no officer or crewman noticed him there in the night. They would have thought him below deck, had they thought on him at all.

The night had passed slowly for Lazarus Perlman. Even though the storm abated by morning, his ailments lingered. Sunrise found him still within a few feet from the site of his most violent misery. The ship was not underway. Like its new crewman, it rocked in place - due now to a spent crew and ruined rigging rather than to weather. The shadow of the mizzenmast and its still furled topsails passed back and forth across Lazarus' eyes as the ship rocked. He stirred a little from his sick stupor. "This is a pretty mess," he thought to himself.

He lay in what seemed like a giant, smelly whirlpool. From the back of his knees to his waist his backside was coated in his own excrement. He hadn't even managed to pull himself to a waste tub when he had been vertical a few hours earlier.

The dizzying light - dark - light of the mast shadow added to what still seemed to Lazarus to be the alternating bow high, stern high pitch of the ship as it, or maybe just this one new crewman, was tossed about. Though the waves had gentled as the sun had risen, the storm within Lazarus did not subside. Even now, each wave of the constantly moving sea felt to Lazarus like a breathless fall swooped back up by a gasping rise. The passing shadows, the rolling, the chill wind pillowing the legs of his breeches and fatigue all made him a little delirious and disoriented.

Then there was a new shadow. "Well 'ebrew Laddie, are ye fit fer a sailor then?" said the shadow from somewhere above his head. "Ye'll learn to find the leeward rail to empty yer belly I'll wager."

"Stand aside," said another shadow with a Scottish brogue. Lazarus recognized the voice of the first mate. "Welcome aboard the great sea," the mate said, from somewhere above Lazarus' head. "Looks to be some blood 'n' mutton on this face," he said, pointing to the slime on Lazarus' chin. "Wash 'im down, help 'im below and fetch 'im some curd and bael. He may have brought the grippe aboard afore the ill winds. Tell the surgeon to look in an' report."

The shadows walked away. Two sailors reluctantly lifted Lazarus by his shoulders as two more threw pails of seawater on his fore and aft. The result was a new putrid pool on the deck at Lazarus' feet. Then the pail hands emptied a few buckets on the deck and rinsed her down and through the scuppers with as much regard for the deck as for the new hand. The two at Lazarus' shoulders then took him below with his feet dragging. It had been a long night for Lazarus Perlman. The coming month, more likely two, would be a long voyage for him as well … a very long voyage.

Chapter 20. The Waste Pot

The First Mate was partially correct. The ship's surgeon determined that Lazarus might have been infected before the *Maidenstone* had put to sea. But it was not the grippe with its influenza like symptoms. The diagnosis was possible dysentery and, of course, seasickness. Lazarus was quarantined to a hammock stretched across a small forward storeroom and given some vile smelling grog. He was not too ill to ask what it was. "Oil of pressed codfish and root of ipecacuanha," the surgeon answered. "It will clean out any infection. Then ye'll get some curd and bael to set ye straight. The bael should clog things up again. Eat it all or yer guts'll shrivel and ye'll wither. Sick as ye are, ye be a fortunate lad," said the surgeon. "Thar be one o' youre years already asleep with the fishes."

The surgeon held greater concern than he told Lazarus. Dysentery was not typhus fever or cholera as had ghosted whole towns on shore, but it was the scourge of the sea which sailors called "the bloody flux." It could kill over a few weeks if its victim could not hold his food. It was said that British vessels, naval and merchant, had been lost to it before. Aboard slave ships, Africans died more often of the bloody flux than from any other cause. It was a threat that every ship's captain and surgeon understood. If the mucus and blood issuing from Lazarus' bowels did not abate, it would mean that the bloody flux had already come aboard.

The *Maidenstone* would not chance an outbreak for the sake of a mere novice. Captain Graves was a veteran of His Majesty's Navy. He knew to quarantine one rather than risk the crew.

Lazarus managed to slowly consume the soft curd, in other circumstances a treat that lasted only the first half of a passing, and the dark green bael mash, which was no treat. At least it was not cod oil.

Lazarus thought he might never tolerate the incessant rocking of the ship. Still, he told himself he had no complaint. Had he been an African aboard a slave vessel when the storm and the illness struck, he knew there would have been no hammock, no bael mash, and certainly no soft curd. Rather, he might have been dropped into the dark rolling sea. He took some comfort, too, that Mordecai could not see him in this state – nor could Mrs. Symmons.

As Lazarus lay below for the next week, he learned to gulp down bael mash quickly without smelling it. He slowly began to recover some strength, but he could not leave his hole. The surgeon watched the consistency and color of the stool in his pot. His station did not aide his recovery, for as the voyage continued, his forward room, hammock and its occupant pitched up and down with the striking of the bow into the waves. Now he knew why captains' quarters were always far aft above the transom.

Early in the confinement, the captain ruefully reflected on why he had taken on this novice. When this Hebrew lad appeared, he had been ready, and he claimed able, to stay aboard that instant to sail as the captain ordered. The boy's face was unweathered, but his hands were callused at the fingertips and he appeared sound. Best though - he had no mother. There would be no woman to wail and squall if the lad met some misfortune and returned absent a limb or failed to return at all.

Captain Rodney Graves had not spent more than a score of years safely under the admiralty and at the merchant trades without following the regulations and a few guides of his own conviction. One of the captain's own rules was to avoid signing a deckman for a long voyage unless he had some weeks aship and his sea legs about him. Lesser vessels were not as particular. Older ships and vessels with fewer masts or those with nearer ports-o-call could serve as schoolers. Slavers were of a lower class still, plying their crews aboard with kegs.

No, he had first thought, this lad was not for his deck crew. Still, he had lost at least a few hands on each crossing when they were unable or unwilling to return, and a few more that could simply not be found.

"The sea be a strange home for a Jew," he had challenged the boy. He knew this sort to stay among their own.

"In what land is a Jew at home?" the boy had replied in a respectful tone.

An extra hand, particularly an anxious fellow, might be a prudent reserve, the captain had thought to himself. This Hebrew lad, upon examination, was some learned of nautical matters.

The captain and the ship had been ready to get underway. Other vessels awaited the *Maidenstone*'s mooring and her allowed time there was past. She were ballasted and crewed and her cargo was up, stowed and tight. The morning would bring a ready spring tide and the next able tide would be of a Friday. Captain Graves never embarked on a Friday. He knew it was not ill fortune, but he respected the traditions of his crew. He had decided then, that the *Maidenstone* would depart as scheduled on the morning tide. Of lesser interest, he had also relented. As he held and stroked his tiger-striped cat, Captain Graves had nodded at the Hebrew lad and said, "novice on the fo'c'sle then, if you will, and cordage boy."

The boy had beamed and gave his "Aye, sir" and his mark. He began to extend his hand to the captain, but the captain just stroked the cat so the lad withdrew his hand. The serious-browed captain, though, had grinned inside. The lad did not know shipboard courtesy. Still, this captain knew that the forty-and-some days at best, perhaps twice that number, and nearly 4000 nauticals to Barbados would either disenchant the lad or ready him for real use on the return. The captain, too, had liked the looks of the boy, in particular the cut of his prominent jib that split his earnest face.

The cord boy had soon learned just what his extra title earned him. In addition to novice seaman on the deck, his were the young legs required to go below and fetch whenever any of the first watch crew called for line or other supply from the ship's stores. Still, the captain thought, the lad had seemed ready for the task. That same ready boy was of no use now. While he lay quarantined, others could mend the mainsail, fix some battens across her and repair rigging.

If the repaired sail did not hold, the ship's twenty other sails could carry the *Maidenstone* if balanced fore and mizzen. She would not stand so proud, but she would make her way. The rigging were fouled, clogged and at loose ends. A novice would learn his lessons in untangling her shrouds, stays, sheets and guys if he were able. Now though, the boy would miss this chance to demonstrate his talent – if indeed he had any. Worse though, he threatened the ship unless his stools firmed and he kept his stomach. "We should know within a week," the surgeon had reported. In the meantime, the surgeon and the captain fretted some over the waste pot of a Jewish lad who, the captain knew, he should have left ashore.

Chapter 21. Over The Barrel

Lazarus lost track of days and nights in his dark storeroom isolation. Ten days passed by as a month to him. Slowly his watery discharge firmed and he excreted dark green ordure. His reward was the addition to his victuals of a small bowl of rice once a day. The tempest in his stomach began to calm. His innards felt wrung and too weary for further upheaval. A week later he held a crew's meal of dried salt beef, a few soaked beans and a half measure of scurvy water flavored with lime.

By the time the *Maidenstone* dropped anchor off the Portuguese Isle of Madeira, three weeks following the disabling storm, Lazarus had resumed his bunk in the fore of the two crew bays with the other younger sailors. He managed the strength to serve a deck watch while a small detail went ashore under Robert McAllister, the first mate. Lazarus felt weak and unsteady, but either the cure had worked or the surgeon had misdiagnosed one of the worst cases of seasickness the *Maidenstone* had ever seen.

The stop at Madeira did not appear on the ship's itinerary with which the *Maidenstone*'s owners had charged the captain. The captain, all understood, could put to sea or to shore as he judged prudent.

As in his prior passages as captain, Rodney Graves judged it prudent to take on fresh water – and a few dozen 30-gallon casks of brandied Madeira wine, treasured both in the Caribbean and by the captain himself. The "Madeira commerce," as he called it, was for his own account. If his two mates minded their watch and served well, they would share in the wine and in its profits. His log and his eventual report in London would omit any count of Madeira wine.

From the deck of the anchored ship, Lazarus breathed wholesome air. He extended his arms, limbered his legs and counted himself within a half measure of sound. The stop was a brief one and once all crew were aboard and the boat secure, the *Maidenstone* got underway again before the sun set. Kegs of island wine now replaced Lazarus in forward store room quarantine, save one keg which stood in a corner of the captain's quarters.

A few days later the crew peered over the larboard bow at two of the Canary Islands. The ship did not slow or swerve but kept her head at near due south. Captain Graves knew that the longest, most difficult part of the crossing lay ahead.

Once the *Maidenstone* caught the trade winds off the West African coast, the current and the winds would turn almost due westerly and cross the middle Atlantic a little north of the Equator. There would be no land to be seen for weeks. If God were willing, the winds would hold and storms abate and would bear the *Maidenstone*, eventually, to the lower stretches of the Antilles. As planned, Captain Graves would tie up at Cape Verde, let the crew catch its breath, again refill water barrels and inspect the ship before diving into the middle Atlantic abyss.

Three days south of the Canaries, the *Maidenstone* crossed into the tropics where the summer sun rises to straight overhead. The crew undertook to initiate three of their number that had not before sailed south of the Tropic of Cancer. With Mate McAllister on the quarterdeck and the captain below, Percy Nugent determined to be master of the ceremony.

Nugent was a storm cloud of a man. He had little forehead and the brow at the base of it looked permanently swollen. One continuous thick black eyebrow sprouted across it from side to side. Beneath it were two cavernous shadowy sockets which hid his eyes. Nugent's dark hair surrounded his face except for a wide swath of leathered skin that extended from beneath his nose to his huge Adam's apple. He twisted the hair on the left side of his head into a greasy braid that hung down and brushed back and forth across his shoulder as he worked. He pulled at the lines with thick hairy hands which looked as rough as the ropes.

Nugent's thunderous voice now clapped out from his station on the main deck, fore and aft, "It be the time fer new dogs to taste the kiss o' Neptune's daughter. Say ye so lads?"

The still recovering Seaman Novice Perlman looked confused as he and another fellow from the fo'c'sle were for some reason congratulated with slaps on the back, then grabbed on each side and escorted down to the main deck. Within a few moments a boy from the second watch was produced on deck from below. His hair was pushed into a pile and he was still rubbing sleep from his eyes and protesting. Others of his watch followed on deck but none came to his aid.

His protests earned him the first seat on a wooden chair that

Nugent's charges lashed to a long loading plank. Then the boy was tied to the chair and wrapped all about. One of Nugent's hairy hands held fast Lazarus' arm as other hands at his order unlatched the draw bolts from either end of the starboard rail gate and hauled the gate off its step and inward, depositing it near the middle of the main deck. With the gangway open, just the deck step, lower than a man's knee, stood between the crowd of men and the sea below. Lazarus knew this game would be a dangerous one. Crewmen lifted the chair end of the loading plank, swung it outboard and slid it away so that the chair end was extended several feet over the starboard side.

The boy tied to the chair now protested in a higher key as crewmen manning the plank slid it further outward still so that its middle rested on the edge of the low deck step. Each time the ship rocked to the right, the boy's feet dangled just above the water. The plank crew laughed at their prey perched on the chair and joked that their hands grew tired and that the new dog should cease his whining or be thrown, plank, chair and all, into the deep. After but a minute of this amusement, Seaman Able Nugent cried out something unintelligible to Lazarus' ear and the men on the plank walked a step or two closer still toward the sea as if they were to slide the entire length of the plank overboard.

As the first of them neared the deck step, they all sang out together, *"Into the sea and the devil with ye."* As they did so, they stopped their march and lifted their end of the plank above their heads causing the boy on the chair to be suddenly and completely submerged. Lazarus shuddered. Since he first learned the fate of captives on the slave ship *Zong*, drowning had been his greatest fear.

Nugent tightened his grip on Lazarus' trembling arm and the crew held their arms high for several moments. Lazarus squirmed to free himself and Nugent grabbed the back of his neck and held him now with both hairy hands. Just then the crew manning the loading plank reversed its motion and pulled back down in a vertical rowing-like motion. As they did, the sea reluctantly gave back the far end of the plank with chair and a not so sleepy novice seaman still intact at its end. The boy gasped for air and looked daggers toward the ship, but before he could speak he descended again. This time he emerged with a humbled, pleading look and he started to beg - but not for long. The chair dropped and the boy with it a third time. As he emerged, he offered neither a look nor a sound other than coughs of water and gulps for air. Water cascaded from his once disheveled hair that sat atop a silenced, sodden, slouching figure that might not have seemed alive except that it struggled to breathe.

The plankmen then hauled in the initiate and welcomed him to "the tropical brotherhood" as they untied him and lifted him to his feet. Seamen's hands next grabbed Lazarus to bring him to the chair, but Percy Nugent tightened his hairy grip, pulled Lazarus back and bellowed, "No, this one last, bring the other forward."

From just behind Lazarus, his fellow fo'c'sleman began to plead as his bearers brought him around Lazarus and plunked him down on the plank chair. "I never learned to swim," he cried as wrappings flew about him.

Nugent hollered at Lazarus loud enough for all to hear, "And ye?"

"What?" asked Lazarus.

"Do ye swim Jew lad?"

"No, I cannot," Lazarus confessed.

Nugent raised his heavy brow, feigning a look of concern. Then he proclaimed to all gathered in a mocking tone, "Hold now laddies. Take pity on these two - for, alas, they do not swim." That brought a roar of laughter from the party. Then Nugent continued his direction of the festivities, ordering the seated lad to be bound up on the dunking chair.

Staring down at his captive, Nugent yelled, as much to the crew as to Lazarus, "It be a pity that ye do not swim." Then he laughed and howled, "Do not trouble yerself about it, Jew lad. If Neptune's daughter likes yer looks she'll loose yer bonds herself. It will not matter one whit if ye swims er no. If she embraces ye, ye'll be in her bosom fer good, even if ye wiggles like a fish." This brought a louder roar.

The boy on the chair then turned his face to the hands wrapping the cords about him. He changed his pleas. "Tie me in good and no grannies with the knots, hear me please, make the knots good and tight and put another rope about me, my brothers."

"Ye be no kin to us - not yet," sang out Nugent, "not until the daughter o' the deep throws ye back thrice."

"Better not smile Reggie," said another, "er mebbe she'll fancy yer looks."

Lazarus looked at the face of the terrified boy in the chair. There was no danger that he might smile.

Three long dunks later and he was hauled back on board. He seemed to try to be proud of his trial, but was too wet and exhausted to keep up the pretense for more than the first moment out of the chair.

Hands grabbed at Lazarus again and this time Nugent relinquished his prey to the crew. Lazarus prepared himself for his turn on the dunking chair. As he was brought forward near the chair, though, Percy Nugent held both hands high in the air and quieted the crew. "This new dog deserves a special introduction," he announced. "Remember well lads, this no-help cord boy laid below and was served up his victuals in a private cabin whilst you 'n' me cleared and restrung the lady's corset," he loudly preached as he pointed back up at the rigging of the ship.

"Aye," cried one and then another.

"What treat will ye, Percy?" sang out Hugh Duncan, whose voice Lazarus recognized from his own fo'c'sle first watch crew.

Lazarus stood silent. No plea was asked of him and he had none to offer. He understood that his words could probably not help him, but perhaps cause him greater harm.

Nugent put one foot on the lowered loading plank and stood up on it so all could see him. He looked about and a grimace fell upon his face. He peered up over the heads of the crewmen and thundered, "Across the keel. It be time for this new dog to inspect the hull. What say ye lads?" Nugent looked about at the assembled crew and his braid flipped back and forth as he did.

There was a pause, and Hugh Duncan pulled at Nugent's arm as if to get to his ear. Nugent resisted stepping down from the plank, but did look down for a moment at Duncan. "He'll not make it Percy, let's find another test," Duncan said. Nugent stopped and turned to Duncan for a second or two as if awaiting the suggestion of another initiation. Both men knew that keel hauling was reserved for severe punishment and usually meted out only by a vessel's captain. None other could impose the very real risk of life it presented.

Duncan stared wildly as if his mind were racing, but he did not speak. Nugent turned back to the crowded crew and repeated his challenge. "This boy is but a Jew devil. 'E can use 'is gills if 'e gets caught up, I say 'e's for the keel and a double line wedding with the sea. Sons o' fear stand aside and fret, what men be with me?"

Without waiting for an answer Nugent began to bark orders. "Fetch the lines, to the bow with 'em." Used to complying when ordered about, a timid few began to follow and do as they were told, and then a few more. Lazarus had been resigned to the dunking and had not spoken until now. He sensed that real danger now threatened him. He thought he should speak up and explain his mission for the Abolition Society. He could admit that, though he was a Jew, he served a group led by Christian men and that he was on a journey of Christian mercy. That, though, would reveal his secret and compromise him before his mission even started. Besides, his commitment to the cause was centered more on what he viewed as Hebrew justice than Christian mercy. Lazarus doubted any plea would make a difference. He would keep his silence … if he could.

Like a growing squall, Nugent's orders now came rapidly and without a break of more than a few seconds. Seaman Nugent gave orders as if he had long practiced and awaited the chance.

Two men lifted and set aside the larboard rail gate opposite from the still open gangway used for the dunking. Four other men took two stout long lines forward and tied them together beneath the bow spar. They gave slack on both lines and lowered the knot joining the lines into the water. Then the four divided and on each side of the ship, two men walked a line back along the rail to an open gate, giving slack from the coil as they walked. Those on the lines now stood at mid-main deck, just before the broadest point of the ship at her beam. On Nugent's signal, a man held the end of each line and one line was given out under the ship while the other was hauled in from the water until the knot joining them emerged from the starboard side just a few feet inside the rail gate. Lazarus looked for the duty mate up on the quarterdeck for help, but he could see no mate and no help.

Nugent directed the lines to be held up with some slack while the knot that joined them was loosened. He pointed and shouted and at his command Lazarus' handlers raised his arms and looped the end of each line around his chest with sturdy knots.

"Prepare to haul away," Nugent shouted across the deck to those manning the shorter ended line near the larboard rail. "Prepare to lower away," he instructed those near Lazarus and the gaping starboard gate.

Just then Lazarus spotted the blondish head of Robert McAllister as his body slid down the ladder rail from the quarterdeck. It disappeared as he landed on the main deck, but a loud Scottish brogue cried out, "What be ye aboot lads? Step aside, what tricks 'ave we 'ere then?"

"All ready, loose the starboard line," Nugent called out, ignoring the mate.

"Seaman Nugent, what be ye aboot?" McAllister called out as he finally cleared the crowd on the starboard side and came upon those at the rail. He looked at Lazarus and the two lines about him. "Who ordered this?" he demanded.

Without pause of a second Nugent spat a reply at him, "A God fearing crew. This crew demands it, as does the Almighty. This be a proper crossing of the line of Cancer for a Jew. We'll not sail to the west with this Christ killer unless 'e passes a test o' God's mercy, will we lads?"

"Stand down and untie 'im," McAllister ordered.

"This dog an 'is like showed God the cross. We'll spare the crucifix 'e deserves if 'e crosses the keel and keeps 'is breath," Nugent cried, almost hysterical now.

"Fetch the captain," McAllister ordered, but no one moved. All looked to see what was about to happen. McAllister looked about and then back at Nugent. The mate stepped forward, looked at Lazarus and repositioned himself, pushing Lazarus back away from the gate with an open palm against a heaving chest. Then he turned his body to face Nugent, squared his shoulders and looked up at the brawny seaman. "This offender be but a lad. Look at 'is face ... 'e ne'er killed a soul I'll wager."

"'e be a Jew dog, borne of them what did. Blood suckers all they be says me." Nugent looked about the gathered crew for support; a few nodded their heads and mumbled.

"A blood sucker, ye say?" McAllister, too, turned his head to the crew and motioned behind himself at Lazarus. "Look at 'im, 'e's but a few years from sucklin' 'is mother's teats." Then he refaced Nugent and replanted his feet as if bracing to make a blow or to take one.

"'E's a bad seed," Nugent pronounced, "'e'll bring ill fortune to the vessel as carries 'im. With 'im aboard, we be cursed and bound fer the deep. I say we haul 'im across 'er belly. If 'e survives we'll have our sign."

"A crew has the right to initiate new dogs to the tropic winds, I'll grant ye that, but only the captain can order men to be hauled across the keel. Ye be not our captain now, do ye Mr. Nugent?" McAllister challenged.

"Aye, that be the point on it," came a stern, familiar voice from behind Nugent. All eyes followed the voice and found Captain Graves standing with his hands on his hips atop the starboard side ladder to the quarterdeck. In the face-off between Nugent and the mate, no one had noticed the arrival of the captain. Lazarus wondered how long he had stood there and what he had heard. "Mr. Nugent, ye and the mate stand as ye are, the rest o' ye lads back to yer stations. Now!"

The crew slowly but immediately disbursed, leaving McAllister, Nugent and Lazarus alone standing near the railing. The captain then stepped slowly down the ladder stairs and motioned his mate to approach him. They conferred at the bottom of the ladder for a moment. Then McAllister said, "Aye sir," and turned away. He walked to Lazarus, and untied the lines. He directed Lazarus and three others to haul in the lines and to coil them. Then McAllister slowly pushed Nugent back from his little perch on the loading plank, enlisted a few others and his work detail unlashed the dunking chair and replaced the rail gates. "Slide them bolts in full laddies," he directed. "We wouldn't 'ave 'er fall away when one o' ye leans on 'er."

As the gates were secured under the mate's eye, the captain stepped to Nugent and the two men spoke. Lazarus listened but could not hear except to discern that the captain did most of the talking. The captain called out, "Mr. McAllister," and the mate joined the conference. It broke up momentarily.

The captain climbed back up to the quarter deck and disappeared toward his helm. Nugent stood silenced but still defiant as the mate called, "All hands to the main," reassembling the crew. McAllister busied himself and a few others as the crew gathered and looked on. Two of McAllister's charges rolled out a large, fat barrel and stood it on end at the middle of the main deck just in front of the quarter where the captain now reappeared. He stood tall and held something behind him. He stared down about the main deck to settle the crewmen and get their attention.

"Be at yer ease," McAllister yelled at the crew.

With all eyes again on him the captain spoke with the same stern voice. "There be but one captain aboard this ship lads. He stands afore ye. Does any man among you say nay?" He looked down on the main from side to side. No one stirred. Then he looked directly down at Able Seaman Percival Nugent. Nugent did not speak but lowered his heavy eyes. "Ye have been warned afore Mr. Nugent. If ye heed not my rank nor my words, perchance ye'll learn a lesson riding the hog."

Nugent now looked up at him. "Put him o'er the hogshead," the captain ordered as he moved his eyes to his first mate. McAllister strained, and with two hands aiding him, tipped the large barrel over on its side. Then he directed the two aiding crewmen, who each took an arm and walked Nugent to the barrel with his back to the captain. The crew stirred and moved about, shifting their attention from the captain up on the quarterdeck to the barrel on the main. Lazarus looked on too, unsure what would happen next. The mate then tossed a couple lengths of light line to Nugent's escorts. Each tied a line to Nugent's ankle nearest him and laid the loose end of the line out on the deck. Nugent removed his blouse and tossed it to Hugh Duncan. Then two others rolled the large barrel close up against Nugent's knees. Apparently knowing well what was happening, Nugent laid himself over the barrel and the ankle lines were tied fast to his wrists.

The two linemen then rolled the barrel a little forward until Nugent's feet left the deck. Tied thusly over the barrel, Nugent was helpless. The captain then said, "McAllister" and tossed down to him a peculiar leather crop with unraveled ends. Looking about at the crew, he bellowed, "If ye heed not yer captain, Mr. Nugent, perhaps ye'll be better schooled by the sting o' the cat ... ten lashes Mr. McAllister, if you please."

The captain then descended from the quarterdeck, turned about and retired down to his quarters. McAllister raised the whip high and struck Nugent full across the back. The ends of the whip left red welts on Nugent and by their fifth application, they tore Nugent's skin. At the first few stripes Lazarus felt vindicated and satisfied, but before the tenth fell he averted his eyes, repulsed by the bloodied back and the severity of shipboard discipline. At the end of the punishment, Hugh Duncan and Georgie Parker untied the bloodied man and helped him below.

Chapter 22. Initiation

Nugent did not appear on deck for four days. He returned to his station on the main deck on the first watch of the fifth day. Lazarus kept an eye on him from the fo'c'sle. Nugent moved deliberately and stiffly. He didn't speak, and his watch mates gave him some leeway. He did not seem to notice Lazarus or even look up on the fo'c'sle.

At the end of the watch Lazarus descended the ladder to the dark bowels of the ship and turned toward the forward crew bay and his bunk. A large hairy hand grabbed him by the front of his blouse and threw him against the bulkhead. An angry knee flew into Lazarus' groin, doubling him over. A hairy hand straightened him up and drew him upward. An angry dark face appeared in his and Percival Nugent whispered in a gruff voice. "You bes' keep yer eye peeled at all times Jew bastard. There be more than one way to ride the barrel an' ye'll find yer turn when least ye expect. This vow is mine own on my life." Then he dropped Lazarus back against the wall. Lazarus did not speak a word. He laid back against the bulkhead, breathing deeply as Nugent kicked at him and them turned and walked away.

Lazarus gathered himself, crept along toward his bunk and whispered to himself, "Mr. Clarkson insisted I work aboard a reputable ship because slavers are too dangerous. At least on such vessels cranky crewmen have other dogs to kick."

In the days that followed Lazarus suffered no further encounters with Nugent. The two men bunked in separate bays, Lazarus in the fore barrack with the younger seamen and Nugent in the aft with the sea veterans.

One day while in a forward storeroom, Lazarus jumped when a sudden noise sounded behind him. He whirled about and grabbed for the little cord knife he kept at his waist. He saw nothing at first, then from behind a crate he spotted the tail of the captain's tabby cat. "You gave me a start," he admitted to the cat as it scratched away at the bottom round of a basket. Likely a rat, Lazarus concluded.

The days were long and Lazarus could not sleep the three fours when he did not stand watch. Sometimes he took a book Mrs.

Symmons had given him in her father's grip pouch and read on deck. His gift, in addition to the leather case itself, was a biography of Dr. Samuel Johnson written by his young Scottish protégé James Boswell and just published in 1791, and a journal of blank pages to record his experiences and his thoughts. He could now smile when imagining how Mrs. Symmons might think of his celebration of Yom Kippur a week following his departure - when he had lain sick and smelly in quarantine.

* * * * * * *

The *Maidenstone* made her way on down to Cape Verde and through the archipelago passing several islands off starboard and one or two smaller ones off the larboard side. Rugged heights rose from the islands that looked to be dry and barren. Then the ship passed between two larger isles. Great plumes of smoke rose from the one to starboard. Flakes of gray soot fell like snow upon the ship and her crew from the sky. "Fogo boils over again," said Duncan, "as she did three years ago." Then he sang a ditty about fire in the sky. A few minutes later, Duncan gave Lazarus a shout and then sailed at him a soft hat with a brim all around it. "That, be me old bonnet lad. Keep it an' wear it in these latitudes or the sun 'ill burn yer brain wi' that li'l cap o'yourn."

The ship came around to the far, leeward side of the larboard island and up into a protected anchorage. The *Maidenstone* lay up there intending to stay four or five days before jumping off to catch the trades that would bear the ship southwest then due westerly to the New World.

Young crewmen including Lazarus, under guide of Second Mate Andrew Rowley, went over the side on lines and along the ship's water line in a boat. Rowley scratched at the sides of the *Maidenstone* with a poker and marked lines at her timber joints with chalk. Lazarus and his fellows then lined the marked joints with oakum, a black daub consisting of warmed tar, cut jute and chopped hemp fibers. With mallets and irons they stuffed the seams and then scraped smooth and covered over again with spirits-thinned tar. The job stained Lazarus' hands, arms, blouse and breeches. Some of it soaked through and stained the prayer tallis that he wore tucked away out of sight.

A party sent ashore reported back that the locals suffered from a severe drought and conditions were near famine. The ship carried mostly manufactured goods: cloth, kitchen pots, farming implements, fancy glassworks, iron barrel straps and rims, crated chandeliers and other decorative works for the houses of planters, gin in big 63 gallon hogsheads, and other goods from England. Supplies in its food lockers were barrels of fresh water and victuals for the officers and crew.

The captain now ordered the two small deck cannon cleaned and Mate McAllister drilled the crew in their use. These small bore guns, one mounted on either side of the foredeck where their height would improve their short range and permit them to be seen by those approaching, were mostly for show. These two were usually propped and lashed muzzle down, so rain could not enter. All vessels displayed guns to discourage pirates and privateers, Lazarus knew. He wondered whether this drill was also theater for the starving islanders within sight of the ship. While some drilled, others tidied and swabbed the decks with seawater. Since the island drought left no fresh water to haul and supplement his stores, the captain shortened the stay, lifting the anchor to catch the outgoing tide on the morning of the third day.

Clear of Cape Verde, the trades blew dry and fair and the *Maidenstone* rode at full sail. Ten days to the southwest she veered more westerly with the wind. No land came in sight. None was expected. Fair sailing put all at ease as well as could be for two dozen sailors and a few officers abroad the middle Atlantic weeks from the nearest dry land - which lay not ahead, but in their wake.

The captain now studied his sextant under clear starry skies at night to track his latitude. By day he checked his watch, set to Greenwich Time, under the noon sun to determine his longitude. He watched his compass more closely now and sometimes altered the *Maidenstone*'s heading.

Lazarus served his now routine watches. Not on watch, he slept below where it was always dark enough for the purpose. When he had slept enough he read.

The clouds covered the sun on the twentieth day from Cape Verde. Following his watch, Lazarus slept two hours, perhaps a little more. Then he took up on deck his prize possession, Francis Baring's satchel with the two looped handles. For a time, he stared at the mostly blank pages of the journal and admired their unspoiled whiteness. He had not written in it for many days. These days of alternating drudgery and boredom were not worthy to mar their purity. He deliberated on what future ventures across this dark sea would merit marks on his virgin pages.

His musings passed more time than he intended for he heard a bell ringing the end of the watch. He would shortly be expected on the fo'c'sle. He grabbed up the bag and started for the hatch ladder. At its top, he yielded to other first watch crewmen ascending. Climbers had priority over those descending. The four hands of the first watch main came up, one of which was Percy Nugent. His braid waggled about as he swung himself upright on deck. He faced Lazarus and glared at him from his dark sockets. Lazarus looked down at his bag and waited for the others to ascend. Once the four were up, Lazarus moved to take the ladder, but Nugent's big hairy hand stopped him.

"What 'ave ye there?" he demanded, looking down at the leather satchel. Lazarus did not speak but tried to turn and free his bag-bearing arm from Nugent's grasp. "No ye don't." Nugent said. "Lookie here lads," he said to the others, "this Jew dog keeps 'is treasure about 'im eben when 'e comes from below." Then to Lazarus he said, "We knows yer kind hoards the gold an' the silver, what truck have ye here?"

"It's mine!" Lazarus said as he again tried to pull away.

"Well mebbe 'tis an mebbe 'tis not," said Nugent as he grabbed the satchel and pushed Lazarus away in one motion. "Ye did not pull yer weight when the high wind spoilt the riggin', now ye must pay yer burden. Let's see what we 'ave 'ere," he said to his mates as he opened the bag, inverted it and shook its contents out on the deck. As the two bound volumes fell at Nugent's feet, he laughed. "Bloody books!" he said as if they were vermin. He dropped the satchel, reached down and hauled up one book, flipping through its blank pages. "Thar be no writin' in these 'ar books," he said, extending white pages toward his mates. Nugent and his mates laughed together. "What kind o' tomfool do ye be Jew boy?" he chortled. He threw the journal at Lazarus' feet, "Now we knows why this 'ar hook nose boy left 'is clan fer the sea - they casts out their lunatics." He turned laughing and strutted away. His chattering fellows followed.

Lazarus bent and retrieved his belongings. As he took them

below he thought, "That lout Nugent would not know treasure if it fell before him."

* * * * * * *

Lazarus tracked the days in his head and tried to be mindful of Shabbat, though he could not observe it on this vessel. He did think of Mordecai on those days and of the woven bread his father broke and shared.

Shabbat fell again on the twenty-third day from Cape Verde. When the bell rang the end of his midday watch, Lazarus went below to a storeroom that housed deck supplies. On his return down the narrow passageway, with a coil of cord over his left arm, he encountered a shadow that filled and further blackened the already dark passage. There was no way around and nothing to be accomplished by retreating, so he tried to act unconcerned as he approached the stationary hulk. He did not stop but merely turned his shoulders as if to pass to one side, said "by your leave" and proceeded.

Nugent turned sideways with his back to the bulkhead and waved his hand broadly, inviting Lazarus to pass. Lazarus took the invitation, but as he was just passed Nugent, the big man grabbed the coil of cord and pulled it back, turning Lazarus' face to the opposite bulkhead. Then Nugent pressed against his backside, pinning him against the slats. "My knife be sharp. If ye make noise, I'll slit yer throat Jew boy," he rumbled lowly in Lazarus' ear. He grabbed Lazarus right arm and bent it back. Then he wrapped the coiled cord around Lazarus' wrists and twisted it tightly. He turned and pushed Lazarus back down the passageway from where he had come. A left turn and then Nugent pushed Lazarus headlong down a step. Before Lazarus could right himself, Nugent was upon him again. He regained his hold, re-twisted the cord and turned Lazarus, pushing him forward. The two men stepped over a high threshold and into one bay of the upper hold.

Still pushing Lazarus before him, Nugent marched purposefully to a far, lightless corner of the bay. Holding the twisted wrists with one hand, Nugent tipped over a barrel with the other and forced the boy against it. Lazarus feared the beating he thought was to come. His breath was short but he drew it in and spoke. "I have no grudge with you, Mr. Nugent. Free me and I will not tell the captain."

"Tell anyone - and I'll - I'll kill you, you filthy Jew bastard," Nugent stammered as he tightened his grip on the boy's wrists. He leaned Lazarus forward and pushed him on the barrel as if to roll it, but it would not budge. "Arrgh, bloody damn," Nugent sputtered, then he grabbed and threw the boy up across the barrel. Lazarus struggled and tried to kick his feet but the heavy man pressed against him. Nugent grabbed Lazarus' blouse and pulled it from his breeches. Lazarus braced himself to feel the sting of a strap or a whip, but none came. Nugent seemed to be having difficulty positioning the boy as he wanted while holding his hands and pressing against his backside. He fussed and moved and grabbed and tussled. Lazarus thought that Nugent had loosed his wide leather belt and expected to feel it on his back at any second.

Then the big man grabbed at Lazarus' breeches and pulled them downward working them one side and then the other down below the boy's knees. Feeling Lazarus' prayer tallis underneath, the brute pulled it away as well. "What is this apron? Do ye wear your mummy's fringed apron Jew boy?" he demanded.

"What are you doing?" Lazarus asked with trembling voice as his entire body began to shake.

"I'll show you what happens to apron wearers," Nugent hissed. Then he placed one boot between Lazarus feet and kicked right and left, spreading the boy's legs and holding them apart with his knees. Lazarus thought he could feel Nugent's hairy legs against the back of his own now bare legs and buttocks. Then the man spat twice on the boy's ass, leaned in and rammed himself against and into the confused boy.

"What are you doing, stop ... please stop in G-d's name," Lazarus said, now crying.

The hairy man did not stop. Lazarus felt a painful burning in his ass and Nugent's thrusts. He began to feel sick. He struggled again to free himself or to reach Nugent's knife or his own small cord knife that was now on the floor with his breeches, but across the barrel with his hands behind, his legs spread and the heavy man on him, he could not move much.

"Keep it up you little bastard," Nugent angrily panted, "I likes it when ye squirm about."

At that Lazarus stopped his struggle and cried, "G-d, oh G-d, get off me you creature." He did not have to wait long for just at that moment Nugent thrust twice, even harder, and groaned and shook. Then once again he thrust deeply, cried "arrgghh" and laid his weight on Lazarus. After a moment of stillness except for heavy breathing and Lazarus' little sobs, Nugent pushed himself up, seemed to grab and pull at himself with one hand, fussed about for several moments more and stepped back off Lazarus. The boy just lay there on the barrel, sobbing, hurting, weak and shamed.

Nugent released Lazarus' hands but did not move him or face him. He cleared his throat gruffly, "Aboard a ship there be one lower 'an 'im what buggers," he said, drawing a breath. "The lowest and least is the weak lamb what's been buggered. If ye tell a bloody soul they'll all want some o' yer arse, Jew boy. They'll get it too, unless my knife finds yer throat first. Ye knows I keeps me promises now, don't ye?"

No answer came - only sobs. The boy did not stir.

"Don't cry mummy's boy, now yew has had yer 'nitiation, - without even gettin' yer locks wet." Then Nugent snickered lowly, turned and left.

Lazarus eventually gathered himself, slid off the barrel and sobbed on the floor. Later he rose slowly, fixed his clothes about himself and staggered to his bunk. The cord lay on the floor of the bay. The fat barrel remained on its side.

Lazarus missed the next watch and George Parker came below and looked in after him. He found Lazarus in his bunk, drawn up in a ball and unresponsive to his questions. He returned to the fo'c'sle and reported Lazarus ill of the stomach. "That lad be not made fer the sea," said Hugh Duncan. Below him, in his dark bunk, Lazarus shared the same thought.

Chapter 23. Shallow Water Man-Eaters

Lazarus had not thought of anything pleasant since his encounter with Nugent in the hold. He did think at times of Mordecai. He took relief that his father had not seen him splayed across the barrel like a starfish and would never know that he had been buggered by a Christian. Not a Christian really … he doubted Nugent knew any god at all.

He recalled that he had undertaken to keep a journal of his journey and his days abroad. The darkness of his berth and his illness early in the voyage had discouraged the practice. What would he write in it now? Would he omit the truth that he had been the prey of a sodomite? He could not write anything at all. If he were to write, his thoughts were simple: He had never had a woman, yet he had been taken by a man.

Nugent had not boasted of his conquest. Strangely, his threats that had followed the act gave Lazarus some assurance that Nugent, too, wanted the attack to be kept secret. But secrecy was not enough. Even if no one but the beast and his victim ever knew, Lazarus had been shattered on that barrel. He thought he would have preferred the whip Nugent had taken in sight of the crew on the main deck to the strokes he had taken below in the dark. Both men had been put over a barrel - a throne of justice in the case of Nugent, but an altar of secret disgrace in his own.

He felt despoiled and mightily wronged. Worse yet, he felt helpless to do anything about it. That brought him to think of the slaves who had made this same long crossing. Somehow, he believed he now had something in common with them. He, too, had been subjected to savagery at the hands of a white man.

Lazarus did not know what to do following the attack. He did nothing. He went about his duties and kept to himself. He did not speak to anyone.

He read the Boswell biography with an absent eye, - until he came upon a passage that jolted him alert. The writer claimed that Dr. Johnson had once observed:

> *No man will be a sailor*
> *who has contrivance enough*
> *to get himself into jail,*

for being in a ship is being in jail,
with the chance of being drowned.

In this instance, Dr. Johnson's famous humor did not amuse
Lazarus. Dr. Johnson had been more correct than possibly he knew.
As Lazarus went about his duties, his head and his spirits hung low,
and a darkness spread across his face. He pondered. He hated
Nugent, but he did not want to confront the large animal of a man.
Though the two men stood the same watch, Nugent was stationed
down on the main deck and the two never looked in the direction of
one another, - at least not at the same time. Lazarus wanted
vengeance, no - he wanted justice, but he did not want
embarrassment and shame.

He decided he would not report the beast to the captain. He
would not tell a soul, ever. He did not want anyone to know what
had happened, but he did want to find a way to punish Nugent and to
avoid another attack. That thought claimed much of his time, and he
knew that he felt somehow differently about himself than he always
had before Nugent's attack.

The good weather passed and a few storms rose up, but they
passed as well and none damaged the *Maidenstone*, though they did
slow her some. The captain had waited until middle September to
embark from London. His plans, with good fortune, would bear the
Maidenstone away from the north Atlantic winter yet send her into
the West Indies after the big tropical winds of late summer and early
autumn. Now he amended his plan with one addition. The breeze
must hold so she can make her way before fresh water runs low. He
explained this to his crew and imposed a new water ration. "It
should be sufficient," he told them.

Lazarus mused: We sail on a world of water, but sip half-cups.
Surrounded by the freshest fish, we choke down beans.

To the now bored crew, and especially to novice Lazarus
Perlman, the days seemed to follow without end. They passed the
time with sailors' tales, yarns of the tropics and confessions of past
misadventures, true or pretended. Lazarus listened in silence and
appeared to have little interest.

"The dark women o' the tropics are loud and limber," swaggered
young Georgie Parker with authority, though this was but his second
tour of the tropics. "In these latitudes, they sits astride a man and
rides him like a horse or they backs up against him and wriggles

about like a jellyfish. When they comes into their rapture, they whines and pants like big cats o' the wild. Along side them, the likely lasses o' Hampshire be stiff mouthed and thin lipped. Mostly they lies beneath like a split plank an' lets a lad do his best. Not so the dark ladies of Bridgetown. They be as hot as the tropic nights, and I be a lad what knows," Georgie proclaimed with a broad smile.

"When we return to England, you needs to cast about a bit Georgie," said Reggie Passingham of the fo'c'sle crew. "The ladies of London be lively enough you can be sure. I've fear you've missed the mark in your mother country."

"Aye," added Hugh Duncan, "No wonder that ye so ready leave the skirts of Portsmouth, Georgie." Then Duncan sang a ditty: *"The fiddle sings as the fiddler strokes and tickles the strings o' her narrow yoke."* Then he faced George Parker and said in mock earnestness, "Likely, my yeasty lad, ye be in need o' a more practiced style o' playin'."

The crew's laugh removed the grin from Georgie's face. Through it all, Lazarus remained expressionless. He knew himself to be as desirous as the next youth. Right now, all he really desired was to be delivered from this ship.

Lazarus lost track of the calendar. Was it Shabbat? Nugent had all but pounded the idea of G-d out of him. He no longer wore his tallis. It had not protected him. He felt ill though he had no identifiable ailment. On watch he went through the motions and daydreamed about exacting revenge on Able Seaman Percival Nugent. He thought, perhaps at the right moment, he could swing a boom and knock Nugent into the sea. Lazarus realized that he would likely be observed in such action, so he considered ways to accomplish his revenge without detection.

Lazarus laid out plans that were calculated to make his revenge look like an accident - but they were all too complicated and could easily go wrong.

Then it came to him. The light was poor below decks. He could come at Nugent as he slept and simply slit the man's throat.

No one knew of Nugent's attack upon him. If he were undetected, Lazarus reasoned, he would be no more suspected than any other man on board. Nugent had a number of enemies. All feared him - all save the captain and maybe Mr. McAllister. No one liked him or respected him one whit. His passing would not be mourned in earnest.

Lazarus would use the man's own knife and leave no trace of himself. He would remove his boots and move as silently as the Lord G-d of Israel when he killed the firstborn of the Egyptian slavers at midnight on the Passover. It was justice. Slavers deserve no mercy. Neither did Percival Nugent.

Lazarus watched Nugent to learn where he carried his knife. A few times he stayed awake during the second watch and looked in at the rear crew bay entrance to observe when those there began their sleep and where Nugent bunked. If he were detected during the act, he would claim he was seeking his friend, Hugh Duncan, who bunked near Nugent. He delayed action and became even more despondent. Then he finally decided he must proceed or count himself a coward.

On the selected night all went as planned. His nerve held, and his limbs remained steady. He crept into the aft crew bay undetected while Nugent and his berth mates slept. He approached Nugent still undetected. He readily obtained the man's knife. He bent over the man, grasped the knife firmly, raised it and readied to strike and slash at the snoring man's exposed throat. But something held his hand, something unseen. He could not do it! He began his lunge again. Again his strong hand, Nugent's knife well grasped, stopped in the air just above the man's jugular. Lazarus stopped and stood erect. Laying prone in his bunk Nugent appeared as if lying on an altar, awaiting his sacrifice to Lazarus' honor. Yet Lazarus' hand, like Abraham's over Isaac, was stayed.

Then he thought - Percival Nugent is no Isaac! Without planning, as if by instinct, he reached down and lifted the large braid of hair at the side of Nugent's head. He held it out away from the scalp as he brought the knife down forcefully in one quick swipe - and cut the braided hair cleanly from the man's head. Nugent stirred, turned away and continued sleeping. Lazarus returned the knife and left, braided hair in hand, as undetected as he had arrived.

At the next watch Nugent drew stares. Those who saw him immediately noticed that his braid was gone. He did not notice himself at first. Then he demanded the reason for the stares to which one near him on the main deck simply put his hand on the side of his own head and asked, "Did a pulley snatch ye?"

When Nugent felt his head he immediately flew into a tantrum, demanding to know what son of Lucifer dared to touch a single hair of his head. No one answered. The only one who could answer observed from up on the fo'c'sle, turned away and kept his silence.

On the third day after Nugent's rant, Lazarus noticed him step to the water barrel. Lazarus moved silently but quickly down the ladder from his post and stood behind as if to wait his turn for water. When Nugent turned about, wiping his wet mouth with his sleeve, Lazarus took Nugent's hand and in a single motion placed it in a fistful of braided hair. He looked right up in the man's face and said loud enough for just the two to hear, "You must sometime sleep, Mister Nugent. If you ever touch me again, I'll slit your throat as you snore, so help me G-d." Without more, Lazarus turned and returned to his post. Nugent stood and did not utter a sound.

* * * * * * *

Lazarus did not know if his ploy with Nugent would be successful. He remained watchful, in lowly spirit and tired beyond his youth. This crossing seemed interminable. He wondered if there really was a New World or if they would simply sail on until some new, unknown disaster struck and ended his boredom and his life. He feared it would all end with his drowning.

Then one morning, after the passage of an unknown number of days, someone cried out, "Look aloft, lads." There, above the waves off the larboard bow, a small white and gray bird with a split tail winged a little and then soared in the same direction as the *Maidenstone*. The bird moved faster than the ship and soon disappeared into the western horizon. Its sighting roused the crew. A day later more birds of the same species appeared. Their tails looked like scissors, cutting and shredding the sky.

As Lazarus watched the birds, Hugh Duncan's hand touched him on the shoulder. Lazarus jumped back as if jolted by a sudden blow.

"Ye be a skittish lad today," said Duncan. "What ails ye?"

"Nothing," he replied.

"Well, look there, fine a quarter," said Duncan, pointing back at the water near the rear of the ship.

Back toward the soft wake of the *Maidenstone* appeared five or six large dorsal fins circling about some and moving along behind the ship. Though not nearly as common as dolphins, sharks were not an unknown sight. Lazarus had never spotted more than one or two sharks at a time, though, and these fins were particularly large and dark colored. One of the fins came up along the starboard side and the fo'c'sle crew moved to the edge of the deck to get a better view. The creature didn't surface, but its wavy shadow of a form came near the side before it turned back toward the wake.

"Eleven feet, by my measure," said Georgie Parker to his mates.

"Near enough," said another.

"The monsters be lookin' fer their supper," Duncan announced to those on the fo'c'sle.

"Aye," said Georgie Parker, "but we've no dark meat aboard." Then the fo'c'sle crew laughed.

Lazarus didn't laugh. "What's your meaning?" he asked, speaking more than a single word for the first time in a week.

"They thinks we be a slaver," Duncan answered to Lazarus alone.

"A slaver?"

"Aye, we be approaching the straits o' the shark. The way be some narrow here as there be coral reefs below. When the slavers spot signs o' land and come upon these reefs, they inspects their cargoes and casts overboard such as ain't fit fer sale and ain't likely to mend. Slavers been feedin' the fishes here 'bouts so long that them bull sharks grow fat trailin' in their wakes. Bulls be shallow water man-eaters. They lives 'mongst the reefs. We be upon their feeding grounds, lad."

Dark in the water, the big sharks reminded Lazarus of the dark shadow of Seaman Nugent blocking the passageway below deck. Lazarus took a sudden shudder.

"Are ye ill, lad?" asked Duncan in a clear but lowered voice.

"I'm well enough," Lazarus replied. He did not know whether he lied. The thought of sickly black captives being thrown over to the sharks refocused Lazarus a little. Finally, he was entering the region where his work was to begin. He might be at the scene of some horrific crime this very moment. Nugent's attack had been terrible. Lazarus would never be able to forget it. Still, he breathed the sea air. Still, the *Maidenstone* made her way. Horrible as it was, there were worse fates. He looked again toward the sharks in the wake.

As he did, Duncan chanted with a lilt, *"Swallows in the sky an' bulls in the sea – my sweet Lord delivers me. Come now lads be o' good cheer, for land be near – dry land be near."*

The following day, the dark green sea began to lighten some and displayed shards and runs of light, bright water. Captain Graves doubled the water ration. Lazarus savored a full cup as the *Maidenstone* sailed past patches of sea plants. Colored coral walls could be seen at places where the sunlight penetrated the shallower waters. Lazarus now began to lift his chin and he spotted large sea birds sitting on the water, bobbing up and down with the waves. Some heavy gray birds with large beaks soared low over the waves, then one of them winged steeply higher and dived headlong into the water, emerging with a fish in its beak. For a time late that afternoon, the *Maidenstone* sailed into a patch of smooth waters where small fish, no more than three or four hands in length, occasionally jumped out of the water. It appeared that their fins held the shape of wings. This seems a strange latitude, thought Lazarus, birds dive below the water and fish fly from the sea; here the world seems upside down.

That night Lazarus again dreamed of drowning, but this time the teeth of large sharks tore at him as he was pulled to the depths. Sometime that night as well, the *Maidenstone* came within sighting distance of land. Before the morning sun could be seen over the eastern horizon behind the ship, the duty crew could see a dark, low bubble on the western horizon before it. As the sun rose, the bubble grew and lightened in color.

Lazarus rose to take his watch. As he climbed to the deck he heard a commotion. Most of the crew was already there, even some whose watch had ended. No one tried to hide his excitement at this sight, though the island remained too distant to tell exactly what land the *Maidenstone* had come upon. If she had sailed just a few degrees south from her intended course, it could be Grenada or Tobago before them. If her course had been too northerly, she could have missed Barbados and be bearing down upon Saint Lucia or even the French stronghold of Martinique. In the vast sea, the island in the distance seemed very small. If it were Barbados, Lazarus knew it would be shaped something like a squashed pear and measure perhaps 20 miles from northern tip to southern and about 15 miles across at its greatest breadth.

As the ship moved and the sun set, the island became a little larger and it began to look as if giant spiders crawled upon it. At this sight Hugh Duncan proclaimed to the fo'c'sle watch, "Dead reckoning, by God's grace, dead reckoning, she be Barbados fer certain. Captain Graves has done it again ... dead reckoning right on 'er just as 'e did last year." Lazarus did not understand how Duncan could be so sure, but no one challenged him.

As the *Maidenstone* drew about the southern end of the island the next morning, the spiders could be seen to be four arm windmills mounted on stone mill houses. They dotted the island's high ground and each faced the island's windward, southeastern shore from which the ship had approached.

The captain gave water and swung her wide as the ship began to round the island in a clockwise direction. He would not risk the *Maidenstone*'s belly to a reef or submerged outcropping. Off the starboard side the land jutted toward the sea and a stone wall rose from it. "Needham's Point and His Majesty's garrison," Hugh Duncan called out. "Carlyle Bay lies just beyond and Bridgetown across the bay. We be upon 'er now lads."

From a league distant this slavery island posed the picture of tranquility - peaceful, green and calm. Appearance could be deceiving, Lazarus knew. The most beautiful of seas encountered in their more than seventy days journey had been the coral straits approaching the south of the island - the home of the bull shark.

PART FOUR: The Caribbean Correspondent

Abroad – November, 1792–August, 1793

Chapter 24. Isle of Cane

Lazarus Perlman landed in Paradise.

He hadn't thought about a heaven, but here one was - or so it appeared. Once the *Maidenstone* tied up at the dock, McAllister assembled the crew. He assigned shipboard watch duties, warned against making trouble ashore and paid the crewmen their shore allowances, which was half their earned pay. Other than the unlucky two standing watch, the sailors of the *Maidenstone* then strode down the gangplank, making way for draymen from the docks to assess the cargo. On dry land, the sea weary mob broke into small groups and descended on the port of Bridgetown. Lazarus welcomed the shore more than he had at first welcomed the sea. He walked with Hugh Duncan and George Parker - east along the wharf skirting the gently rising town. They soon came to a stone bridge passing south over the mouth of a river. "I'm fer over the careenage and straight to the Bull 'n' Brew," sang out George Parker.

"Aye, that be the place fer ye, Georgie," said Hugh Duncan, "and fer me ownself jus' now." They crossed over and soon approached a two story building where a sign in the shape of a bull hung over the door and two dark women hung out from between second story shutters and beckoned with their hands. Their bosoms blossomed from their blouses as they did from their window perch.

Lazarus held back near the door with the excuse that he wanted to stretch his legs and look about. Duncan urged him to go inside. "Ye can get yerself stretched inside lad," he argued, "there be sights upstairs ye have not seen, I'll wager." Young Parker did not wait but marched boldly inside. Lazarus simply turned back toward the bridge. "Yer loss, lad," said Duncan. He shook his head and went inside.

Back on the bridge Lazarus faced an official looking building to the north and began to get his bearings. He breathed deeply, forcing himself to exhale all the stale, below decks air he could and take in the scent of Barbados. The place did not smell like London's suspended soot and open trench sewage. Its balmy air bore the odor of sea salt and molasses.

His feet on dry land, Lazarus grounded his mind as well. His crossing had been all consuming and at times frightful. But he remembered that he was not really Seaman Novice Perlman, not a cord boy required to climb and fetch, but actually an observer for the Abolition Society, Thomas Clarkson's eyes and ears in the Caribbean - a secret correspondent. Still raw from Percy Nugent's persecution, Lazarus recognized that all who looked on him saw first a Jew. If he took care, no one would suspect him to be an abolitionist. He would appear to be who he was – the son of a Jewish tailor. For perhaps the first time, he welcomed that role.

If he could only think how to convince the captain that he would not be returning to London on the *Maidenstone*, he could be about his mission. He had not dared to tell the captain when he had joined the crew. He had difficulty enough convincing the *Maidenstone*'s sailing master to take him on board at all. All the ship's hands were bound to complete the entire journey, not just the outbound leg. But Lazarus Perlman did not plan to return to London this year; and he certainly intended to avoid another ocean crossing in the company of Able Seaman Percival Nugent. No one on the *Maidenstone* knew his mind, but Hugh Duncan likely suspected.

When the swallows had appeared above the *Maidenstone*, Lazarus had taken Duncan aside and inquired of him concerning the protocols for a hand seeking to stay ashore. Duncan had provided little hope. Indeed, he alerted to difficulties Lazarus had not foreseen. "The capt'n can impress any male citizen o' seafarin' habits 'tween eighteen and forty-five years to 'is service. That be the law," Duncan had informed him. Lazarus had not been eighteen when he had joined the crew, and wasn't yet; neither had he been of seafaring habits – none of that mattered since he had volunteered. "Asides," Duncan had said, "ye would not want to risk being taken as a deserter."

"What?" Lazarus had gasped, "The *Maidenstone* is a merchant ship, not a naval vessel and we are not in His Majesty's service."

Duncan had looked at him with a smirk, "It do not matter one whit, Lad. Any crewman what quits a British trader wi' out leave o' her capt'n afore she returns to her home port may be called 'deserter' and hauled up on the charge." Duncan had said it as though it put an end to any notions the novice might have. To seal his point though, he had given a warning - Captain Graves had been known to retrieve crewmen from Bridgetown's public houses if so required. And the homebound voyage of those so retrieved had been unpleasant indeed.

Lazarus knew his position. He would require the captain's permission or would have to disappear until the *Maidenstone* left port - perhaps not so easy on this island. He worried some about it as he walked about and gawked at his new world.

Barbados was called "little England." As he strode about, Lazarus saw the reason. Bridgetown was something of a miniature London radiating from the mouth of a river just as London radiated from the Thames. The stone bridge was a diminutive London Bridge. As in London, the town spread from the north of the bridge and lesser structures lay across it to the south. Just as in London, small alleyways and narrow streets beckoned from the principal roadways. A few of the buildings here were of European design, but many others were a style to themselves with wide balconies and painted in pastel shades of pink, green and yellow. Some featured fine latticework and most had windows of louvered slats rather than of glass. The slats were in panels and tilted out away from their frames on hinges.

Lazarus walked up gently rising streets of cobbled ballast stone, crushed shell and sand. He watched people in the street, not minding his way. European looking people rode in carriages and walked among themselves. The more numerous Africans stayed apart, stood in shop doorways and swept walkways in front of the shops. But not all these Africans were really black, at least a goodly number of them were not. While the skin of some shined like polished ebony, some were a smoky ashen color, others a warm nutmeg, others still a soft dove-gray, and a few the color of cooked cream but with black hair and brows. More appeared to be of mixed blood than Lazarus had expected - and there were many women and some children among them.

Bridgetown was much smaller than London. Even though he walked slowly, looking this way and that, he soon stood at its northern edge. From here comparisons to England disappeared. A sweeping sea of tall sugar cane lapped the perimeter of Bridgetown not bordered by the bay.

On the wind, Lazarus heard some sound of a strange choir. A single voice struck a short lyric, then the group added a rejoinder. He could hear the cadence but not the words. Toward the east he could see black people clad in white on a terraced but still sloping cane field above him. In the distance they looked like a colony of ants. From the breadth of their hips, there appeared to be as many women as men. This island possessed a smell, a sound and a feeling all its own - nothing at all like England.

Of all the senses though, the greatest treats of Barbados were for one's sight. The bright pastels of the town, the deep greens of the cane fields rising from the red earth, the water of blues and green below, the striking shades of the people – this place spread a giant palette of vivid color. Lazarus could hardly blink.

Surveying the expanse of rising cane fields, Lazarus thought he could not have imagined a place so dedicated to a single endeavor. The east end London he knew, the only place he knew, was a virtual circus of commercial activity of every sort. Its clamorous streets drove inhabitants to their indoor sanctuaries. Barbados, though, seemed to move to a soothing outdoor rhythm.

Lazarus knew the reason for all this cane. To Britons the taking of tea was a dietary mainstay. British "tea" was more than that. It rose to the level of an addiction, a national epidemic - which no one sought to cure or even treat - except by ample gratification. Most thought of tea as a beverage from Asia and, indeed, most British tea came from India. Consumed in its most popular preparation, though, the beverage actually contained more sugar than tea when measured by weight.

Boiled molasses, dark muscovado, brown granular and refined white - sugar in its various forms - was also the largest single product imported to the British Isles by the nation's unmatched commercial fleet. Mostly it was shipped in hogsheads as dark muscovado and further refined in England. It had all started right here.

This island's dedication to the growth and processing of cane sugar came as no surprise to Lazarus. But at first look, its people did. He had expected to see Africans under whip, toiling in the hot sun. Yet these slaves worked paced not by whips but by their own melodic chants – or so it appeared from afar. Their movements and their sounds seemed almost tranquil and in harmony with the sweep of the wind across this isle of cane.

Lazarus headed back to the wharf by what he took to be a more direct route, but before he reached it he smelled fish and then he saw to his left a cluster of makeshift stalls and shelters where people milled about - a market. Lazarus strolled toward the market's center. There a big black woman sat on a tall stool hawking fruit and greeting those who walked near. A wrap around her head hid her hair. The yellowed smock wound about the rest of her looked as large as a top end sail canvass, yet both arms and one bare shoulder escaped it.

As Lazarus approached, the big woman smiled widely and spread her arms toward him. "Dis be me 'nanna 'nanna darlin'," she greeted him loudly as if she knew him. Then she swept one arm toward her colorful cart. "Come sah, come sah, try me ripe banana," she cooed as enticingly as if she were hanging out an upper floor window of the Bull 'n' Brew selling her favors.

He sampled her melon, examined what she called her "okras," her "pinas" and her "ackees." He tasted a delicious new fruit. The woman called it "mango." One taste was not enough, so Lazarus bought a large mango. He peeled and ate it standing in the shade of a very tall tree that stood nearby. The tree had pale bark and a trunk of great girth shaped as if several different pillars of odd sizes had been bound up in a single skin. Elongated pods and fibers from their centers were strewn upon the ground.

The big woman at the cart pointed Lazarus out to other 'nanna 'nanna darlin's as they approached. "See de mon 'neat de Kapok tree - dat be de hoppy, hoppy mon wit me sweet, sweet mango - come taste me sweet manga, manga, mango," she sang, "full an' firm, full an' firm, mangoes sweet an' full an' firm." As she sang her breasts heaved - full, not at all firm.

Lazarus spent a fitful night aboard ship. What if he asked the captain for permission to leave and the captain bound him onboard to prevent his departure? He knew that sailors not wishing to return to England usually disappeared and simply did not return to their ships. Lazarus could not bring himself to do that.

On rising in the morning, he felt melancholy. He thought to recite a prayer, but praying did not seem to fit the occasion. Then he bore himself up. The Atlantic may have wrung him out a bit, but he remained the same lad Mr. Clarkson trusted, the same Lazarus who, Mrs. Symmons said, had found his voice. He peeled off his old tar-stained togs that now looked much like sailor's slops. He shook out his duffel and retrieved from its bottom the fresh breeches, blouse and jacket he had stowed before he left London. He rolled the slops, gave a fold to Hugh Duncan's old bonnet and tucked them into the bottom and repacked the bag. As he did, he calculated: His courage may not have been tested by dunks in the sea, but he had passed his own ordeal – the attack of Percy Nugent. He had recovered to face the man down. He had left London just more than two months earlier. It seemed an age ago. As he had crossed the Atlantic, he had passed from boy to man. He felt it in his marrow. He could face the captain and he would – now, well in advance of the *Maidenstone*'s departure so that there would be time to sign a replacement. He wanted an honorable parting - one worthy of a man.

He hauled his duffel and grip and boldly took them on deck. For the first time ever, he stepped down and knocked at Captain Graves' cabin and answered strongly when he heard, "Who goes there?" He looked Captain Graves in the eye, thanked him for taking on an untested novice, announced his intention to leave the *Maidenstone* and respectfully asked permission to do so. Feeling his strength, he also requested to draw the balance of his pay.

The captain first sought to compel Lazarus to complete the voyage and return to London. He seemed surprised that the young hand sought to stay on this island and taken aback at the brashness of the boy. When Lazarus pressed his request, the captain stood with clenched fist and said, "I put a man o'er the barrel on your account." Then he softened. "Ye be a sickly lad and one given to troubles – gettin' yerself near keel hauled. I might press thee to service. But – but I allow, ye do not sit well with this crew. Perhaps, after all, ye be not yet ready fer the sea."

Lazarus and Captain Graves both heaved a sigh.

Then the captain cautioned, "Heed though, lad, the sea surrounds thee here."

"Aye sir," said Lazarus. "Perhaps I might ready myself for a return when the *Maidenstone* calls another year."

"Many vessels dock here lad," the captain said, his voice cooling. "I 'spect one 'aving crewed across can take 'is pick." Then the captain dismissed Lazarus without show of regret, but also without eighteen shillings - half Lazarus' pay earned for his two lunar months of service.

Freed, Lazarus made inquiry of a white man on the wharf and

walked about looking for the Spanish and Portuguese synagogue. From the directions provided, he found a large two storied building with a flat roof and rounded corners. Its four top floor windows rose to pointed arches. The sun had baked the building to a soft, bleached pastel pink.

As he approached, he detected a low walled cemetery to the building's rear. No monument bore the mark of a cross. This was the place. Inside, he introduced himself to a man who identified himself as Hazan Israel Abbady.

Lazarus told the hazan that he had come from London and had been trained by his father, a master tailor. He inquired as to the needs of the community for one with such skills. The hazan smiled politely as he told Lazarus in broken English that community Kahal Kadosh Nidhe Israel was comprised of exactly 147 members and their children, including an infant girl born to young Mrs. Mendes just last evening. The baby's grandfather, like the father of Lazarus, crafted clothing for his community and trained his son so that the community boasted two tailors. Lazarus, said the hazan, should have written before coming if he planned to make his way by sewing for the members of this synagogue. Seeing Lazarus' disappointment, the hazan did offer an evening meal and a sleeping room – just until Lazarus could find another.

Thinking to stay near the docks where he could watch the arrival of slave ships, Lazarus inquired for work along the waterfront. At the marine supply yard, the merchant grinned wryly and said he had work, but only "at a slave's wage." He nodded over his shoulder as he said it, where two Africans climbed on a scaffold. Lazarus fared no better elsewhere about the bay. Merchants offered no pay for labor. Slaves met their needs.

At the wharf Lazarus saw that some twenty-odd vessels were in the harbor or at the docks. The harbormaster - here he was called the harbor chief - claimed that only two vessels, anchored at some distance out, carried slaves. They stay well offshore, he said, to discourage any thought of escape by their captives. They had made few sales in Bridgetown and were bound for Jamaica. He said that the few plantation owners or others wishing to purchase slaves usually took boats out to inspect the cargo aboard the ship. "Seldom are more than a few at a time purchased at this port. It is not as it used to be," the harbor chief said. "Our island is small and now all but awash in slaves. They breed like rabbits."

This information took Lazarus by surprise. Mr. Clarkson's studies had shown that, in recent years, British ships hauled an average of 5,000 African's per month to the British West Indies, not including the slaves they transported to other places such as the former colonies in America. This one little slave island, the first of the British slave islands, had apparently just about reached its limit … finally. Lazarus could see that the Africans already on this island far outnumbered its Englishmen and other whites. The children about evidenced a source other than import for the island's workers. Judging by their skin, many of them were of mixed blood and likely born on the island – they were called creoles.

Advised by Hazan Abbady that some Jews had shops on Swan Street where their customers were mostly gentiles, Lazarus looked there for a tailor's shop. Seeing a busy street for trade, but with no tailor or haberdasher, he thought to open his own shop. He found no room on Swan, but then he located a narrow space on Tudor Street just a few doors south of Broad Street. It was a short walk from the wharf so that he could monitor the arrival of slave ships. The market, too, was nearby and along his path to the wharf. There was no flat above, but Lazarus thought he could establish a shop at the front and live at the rear. The shop had no table for cutting, but two cases where the prior tenant had displayed pottery lined one wall. Lazarus moved these to the center toward the front of the room and placed them back to back. Together their tops might serve as a cutting table, though care would be required where the two cases joined on the uneven floor. The case fronts could house his tools and supplies.

Satisfied, he took the place from the cobbler next door, who let it reasonably, Lazarus thought. He engaged a sign maker to craft a two-sided placard that would protrude from above his doorway and mark his shop. He commissioned for calling cards of the same design as his sign. From his duffel he removed the tools of the tailor's craft he had brought from Mordecai's shop. They were few but would suffice for the present. He cleaned the floors, obtained a rope, secured it wall to wall and draped a dark fabric from it to create his living quarters. Using more of his stipend from the Abolition Society, he obtained a cot, bedding, two wooden chairs, an oil lamp and a porcelain basin with pitcher.

He wrote Mr. Clarkson to confirm his safe arrival. He had arrived, but it had not been safe. Mr. Clarkson would never know that. He wrote that he had set up his shop and gave its location. He addressed the brief letter to Mrs. Symmons, asking that it be provided to "our mutual friend." He posted his letter at the British Packet Agency which he located near the official buildings just north of the careenage. "My first official correspondence," he mumbled to himself. Then he frowned and thought, "It contains nothing about slaves or slavers, but I will set about to gather evidence once I'm settled."

Outside his shop, Lazarus hung his simple rectangular wooden sign, "L. Perlman - Tailor" with a needle and a spool depicted beneath his name. Then he waited.

He waited still three days later when a man with stained brown hands finally called at his door. The man was not a customer, but rather a neighbor. He kept a leather and harness shop across the way at a diagonal. The man said his name was Piccard. He welcomed Lazarus and offered to advise the newcomer, as he had been born in Barbados.

Piccard's narrow face and his name made Lazarus think he was perhaps Portuguese and African. He spoke English well but with a pleasant accent different from the dialect Lazarus had detected among other creoles. Piccard hung on to his vowels and he emphasized the last syllable in a word, unless the word ended in a vowel, then he stressed the syllable before it.

"Is that your garden, in the alleyway?" Lazarus asked, with a thumb gesturing over the man's shoulder and directly across the street.

"Well," said the man, "I arranged it a bit, but the flowers grow without care."

"It's new to me," Lazarus said, "an alleyway that catches part sun at this time of year. I just came from London, no sun in such a byway there."

"Never been there," the man said, "but welcome to Tudor Street, if I can help you settle, well, just ask."

"Thank you, Mr. Piccard, since you kindly offered ..." Lazarus began and then set forth a barrage of questions to his new neighbor. Piccard answered them all straight away, until Lazarus inquired as to how to best obtain patrons. Piccard replied that he did not know since he had taken his shop from his father and had never lacked for business. He said, however, that many of the fine houses of Bridgetown kept a seamstress among their house slaves. He winked and said, "I had not thought it so, but perhaps some of them actually sew."

Lazarus called on his landlord, hoping for referrals. The cobbler seemed willing, but he had none to refer until he could inspect a bit of his tenant's work. "Reputations are hard earned," he said, "I'm sure you understand."

Of course Lazarus understood. Remembering old Rabbi Solomon's coat, he offered to make a piece if the cobbler would provide the cloth and stand for the measurement. The cobbler said he would think on it, but days later he had not shared his decision with Lazarus.

That night, Lazarus laid out his situation in his head. The number of new slaves arriving here had apparently dwindled and he had not found a way to earn his keep. He concentrated on how to best undertake the gathering of information that might assist Mr. Wilberforce before Parliament. Lazarus determined that he would focus on the island's numerous cane field workers and house slaves already present rather than upon new arrivals. He worried some, then he went to sleep.

In the morning he had found inspiration. He remembered the big woman in the market offering her fruit and flirting with passersby to make her sales. Lazarus remembered, too, that he had once encouraged Mordecai to take his work to the outdoor Sunday market on Middlesex Street near their home. Mordecai had declined to leave his shop.

Lazarus would not be so reluctant. Indeed, he would go one better. He would call about the island at the plantations like the country tinkers of England. He would take a few samples of his work and solicit orders from the gentlemen there. In this fashion he could move about freely and observe the treatment of the slaves on the plantations and at the same time supplement his stipend.

The island was much smaller than the English countryside Mr. Clarkson had repeatedly traversed. Lazarus would not even require a horse since he knew this island's windward eastern shore and central heights to be sparsely settled while its largest sugar plantations were located along its leeward plateau on the west. The majority of them were clustered in just a few of the island's eleven parishes lying from north to east and south east of Bridgetown. He could travel these on foot. He could use plantation tables for his cutting or return to his shop to fill his orders.

He would never be more than a few hours walking from Bridgetown. He could return frequently to fetch supplies and to post his correspondence. Perhaps he would call at the plantations with the most slaves. Their owners would be prosperous enough to afford new clothes. This plan might work very well. No one would have reason to suspect his true undertaking.

He took inventory of the tools and needles. He had most all he needed. He acquired a sharpening stone, a few more needles, large dark and small white buttons, and two bolts of weave. One was white and light, the other heavier and gray.

He recruited saddle maker Piccard as a model for sample pieces, but added an inch here and there to the measurements. Amiable Piccard made a fidgety mannequin, but Lazarus managed to avoid sticking him with a pin. From the light cloth he made a gentlemen's blouse with collar but without ruffles, and from the gray cloth he produced high-waist trousers. He thought he could also fashion doublets, cloaks, frocks and even cravats, but he did not know whether such were in much use in this tropical latitude. He believed he could reproduce most pieces using patron clothing as a pattern.

After some further preparations and further reduction of his stipend, he accorded himself as prepared as necessary - but for one thing. As most of the island's residents celebrated the eve of Christmas, Lazarus measured, cut and sewed a second blouse, to exact measure. Finished, he took it and crossed to Piccard's shop.

His new friend seemed please when Lazarus held the blouse up close for inspection, but not touching Piccard's stained leather apron. The blouse looked too prim for the harness maker with the stained hands, but Piccard said he would wear it at church that very night. Lazarus requested another favor of Piccard. He needed information on the island's largest plantations. Thinking that some of their owners might keep horses, he thought the man might know some of them.

Piccard looked back at his cluttered shop, then led Lazarus out to the alleyway at the south side of his shop, directly across from the tailor shop. He walked through a patch of fiery red and yellow flowers, "The pride of the island," he said, stepping around them. Then he led Lazarus through a wall of tall green bushes, pushing aside branches with big bright blossoms and calling them by name as he stepped, "hibiscus, azalea," he said.

Behind the alley of flowers and at the rear of Piccard's saddlery stood a portico with a latticed shade above, a table beneath and an earthen oven on a stone hearth in the far corner. Past the rear door to Piccard's shop, a cot with some sun-bleached cushions sat close against the back of the shop. Piccard stepped to a shelf near the oven and retrieved two flagons. He turned and offered one to Lazarus. "Sit," he said, motioning to a slice of giant tree trunk, "please share my Christmas punch." As Lazarus and his neighbor sat on sections of a giant tree, Piccard shared information as readily as he shared his punch. He easily named the largest few plantations in the surrounding parishes and their owners or overseers. He took a stick and drew lines in the dirt at his feet.

According to Piccard's dirt map, the island had a half-dozen public roads radiating in a half-circle from Bridgetown. Most of the large plantations could be found along roads one, two and three - headed north, north-east and east from Bridgetown - on the leeward side of Barbados in parishes named after St. Michael, St. George, St. James, St. Thomas and St. Peter. A few were to be found as far south as on road six toward Christ Church – the southern-most parish. Piccard twisted his stick in the ground, marking the locations of a few plantations, mostly the ones near Bridgetown where horses were kept. He also agreed to watch Lazarus' shop while the tailor called on customers and to take the name of any prospective client who cared to leave it. He would take no pay for it.

Lazarus wrote to Mr. Clarkson, addressed to Mrs. Symmons. He explained that most of the slave ships carried the bulk of their slaves on to Jamaica. His little island, the first British one in the West Indies to receive slaves, seemed well stocked with forced labor at present. No concern, he assured Mr. Clarkson, and he outlined his plan to direct his attention to cane field and house slaves. He outlined his clever guise of calling on plantation owners like a traveling tinker and his expectation that it would provide him a better vantage point as to the island's slavers.

Lazarus hoped he had not misled Mr. Clarkson this time.

Chapter 25.   The Red and Green Maharajai

With a sample case in hand that had been a sailor's grip sack and before that a book satchel, Lazarus boldly strode east from Bridgetown on Monday, December 27, 1792 and walked along road two toward the north-east. He soon came to a double-armed pole crossing the road at chest height like a frail gate. The poles protruded from a stanchion on the right side of the road, but had no gatehouse or gatekeeper. Lazarus tested the gate. It swayed but would not clear. He glanced about, saw no one, stooped and stepped under the gate. He walked on and stopped at the first sugar cane plantation he encountered. Piccard had said that the owner lived in London. In his absence, an overseer served as master.

Lazarus found the overseer before he reached the mansion house, but the man dismissed Lazarus in the middle of his speech. In truth, the speech was a poor one – too tedious. Lazarus revised and practiced it as he retook the road north-east. Satisfied with a shortened introduction, he determined to walk straight away to what Piccard had called, "the grandest plantation about – and with the best stable." Piccard had said its owner was in residence and was a leader among the sugar planters of the island. The man's name was Lord Harrington - Richard Malcolm Harrington.

For more than an hour Lazarus walked northeast, then he took a narrower road to the right through fields of tall cane to higher ground. Most of this land sloped gently back toward the sea, but bright flowers covered a steeper hillside off to Lazarus' left. The distant blossoms were of hues he had not before seen - not quite red, yet stronger than pink. He admired them as he walked and almost stumbled off the roadway. He turned his eyes back to his path and after several minutes stood within sight of the two-level mansion Piccard had described. The roadway divided into three like Poseidon's trident. The road left led to lower buildings around to the side of the main house. The roadway to the right sloped away a little, rounded to the south and descended from sight toward cane fields. The center roadway led right up to the wide porch of the broad, west-facing house. Lazarus followed it.

In a moment he stood before the impressive structure. On each side of its massive door, three tall windows rose from just above the porch to a height much taller than a man. Lazarus again practiced his speech. He took a deep breath and walked straight up as if he were expected at this place he had never been. Mounted on the front door was the brass head of a horse. A large ring ran like a bit through the horse's mouth and hung below against a metal plate mounted flush on the door. He drew back the heavy brass ring and let it fall against the strike plate.

No answer came. Lazarus looked back over his right shoulder at the roadway that led toward the cane field. Sugar cane, he thought, sugar is what brought the owner of this imposing mansion his riches ... sugar and the forced labor of African slaves. His life had been but preliminaries until this time, he thought. In the abolition crusade, he had served behind the lines. It was time for him to face the slavers and look them in the eye.

Lazarus turned again back to the large door and grabbed the ring bit in the horse's mouth. This time he confidently rapped, three solid strikes - three angry strikes on the knocker plate.

The large door slowly opened. In the doorway stood an ancient man dressed after the fashion of an English servant. He was thin with excess sagging skin. His gray hair and brows appeared greased into place. He looked neither African nor English and Lazarus judged him a mulatto. He stood erect as his years permitted, but they had left him with humped shoulders and a struggling neck that protruded forward from his oversized collar. Lazarus tried not to stare at the pale pinkish blotch of skin on the right side of his neck. His nose looked abbreviated, and he had little chin. His eyes appeared tired and low cast as if they had seen quite enough of life. His eyelids hung heavily over them. "May I help you, sah," the man said with better diction than Lazarus had expected.

"Why yes, thank you," Lazarus said. "I am a gentlemen's tailor, new this month from England. I am calling upon the gentlemen of this parish to introduce myself and display a sample of my work in hopes that I may be of service now or in the future as needs arise."

"You are not expected, then?" the old mulatto asked.

"Well, I suppose that I am not," Lazarus acknowledged. "I would take pleasure in speaking to the master of this house if I may - here is my calling card." He extended it to the ancient man.

Gnarled fingers of the man's slight hand, all curled in the same direction, slowly emerged from the cuff of his sleeve like a turtle from its shell. The turtle's mouth took the card. "Please follow me sah," the man said, stepping aside for Lazarus to enter and closing the door before leading the way. He walked just a few steps into a wide hallway, drew abreast of open double doors on either side and turned into the room on the right. Once inside he turned to Lazarus, and said, "Please wait here sah, and I shall inquire whether Lord Harrington will see you." With that he left at tortoise pace, closing the double doors behind him.

There were chairs and two richly covered divans in the room, but Lazarus kept his feet. He looked about but did not wander from his place near the doorway. Three tall windows ran to near the floor and lit the room from the front of the house. The windows were framed in maroon draperies, tied back at breast height with golden braided cords.

Large paintings hung on the wall opposite the windows. On the far wall, opposite the room's entrance, was a painting of a man on horseback. Lazarus could not see it very well. He stepped toward it, but just as he did, he heard the doors open so he turned to face the old tortoise.

"Lord Harrington cannot see you now," he said. "He asks if I may keep your card so that he may call on you at your shop should he choose to do so."

"Certainly you may," said Lazarus, "please thank him for me." Then Lazarus motioned to the painting on the far wall of the room, "Is that the master of this house?" he asked.

The old tortoise looked perturbed and drew in his head a bit toward his too large collar, "No sah," he tersely replied, "that is the first Lord Harrington." He emphasized the word "first."

Then the old man stood aside and Lazarus walked passed him, back out into the center hallway to leave. As he did, the glint of some bright object in the opposite room flashed in his eye. He peered across the hallway and into the room. He thought for just a moment that he saw a familiar sight. At a glance the room was shaped like the one he had just left, but a small table sat near its center window with a high-back chair at either side. On the table sat what he took at first glance to be chess pieces. He paused, rocked back a half step and looked from a slightly different angle.

It was not chess. The pieces displayed were shaped and colored different from chessmen. Those on the near side of the table were a light shade of red; those opposite were pale green. He could not determine their exact shape, but each looked to be an elaborately carved representation of some animal or fantasy. The ancient tortoise noticed Lazarus' pause and cleared his throat.

"Pardon me, but I thought for a moment that I knew that game," Lazarus explained, nodding his head in the direction of the table.

Now noticing that the table game had caught Lazarus' eye, the old man said, "That is Lord Harrington's prize."

"Prize?" Lazarus asked, "I do not know that game."

"It is called 'chess'," said the rich baritone voice of an Englishman, startling Lazarus.

Lazarus turned around and there, several paces down the hallway stood a tall, angular man. The hallway was not well lit, but Lazarus thought the man's clothes were all white linen. Lazarus recovered, "Oh, then it is chess, I do beg your pardon, sir."

"This is the tailor, Lord Harrington," said the tortoise, "I was just showing him the door."

The tall man ignored the servant and stepped toward Lazarus. "Do you know it, tailor?" he almost demanded.

"Pardon me?" Lazarus said.

"Chess, do you know chess, tailor?" the man impatiently asked.

"Why, a little, that is -" Lazarus started.

"Have you ever seen chessmen like those?" he asked, pointing in at the table.

"I cannot say that I have," said Lazarus, admiring their large size and their color, "though I have not seen many."

"Many or not," jumped in the tall man, "you never could have seen a set the duplicate of this one, I can assure you. There is no other like it! Come," the man said as he took Lazarus by the arm and marched him into the room and right over to the game table. The presumptuous touch of the man made Lazarus uneasy. As they approached, Lazarus could see that the squares on the table's top were also colored red and green. No two looked exactly alike. They appeared to be cut and polished stones, maybe gems laid into the table.

"The Governor of Bengal presented this set to me," boasted the tall man. "It came from the other side of the world."

"The other side," Lazarus repeated.

The man took it to be a question. "India, boy" he said, "India.

This set is a treasure carved by the hands of a great artisan of ancient India. It is called, *'The Maharajai of Bengal.'"*

This chess set has its own name, Lazarus mused.

"It was made for an Indian prince. Once it was complete, the prince had the right hand of the artisan cut off so there could never be another like it."

Lazarus stared at the man. He was perfectly serious. With his right hand, the man gently lifted a piece from the back row corner of the green side where the king's rook usually sits. He placed it upon his open left palm, raised it near Lazarus' eyes and turned it for display. The piece had the shape of an elephant. A rug sat across the elephant's back. From the center of the rug rose a squared box with its sides intricately cut into miniature pillars. It must be the representation of a castle, thought Lazarus, a castle on the back of an elephant. The elephant's feet were colored gold and small shiny stones were inlaid as its toes. Tiny stones also lined the trim of the rug on the elephant's back.

Lazarus remembered the charges that Parliament had leveled at Warren Hastings, the impeached magistrate of India. One of his lesser crimes was said to have been that he looted the treasures of India for his own coffer and those of his friends. Lazarus suspected that *"The Maharajai of Bengal"* was one of the stolen riches.

The man now held up the red king. He was not a king actually. Lazarus presumed him to be a Maharaja. He sat with his legs folded on a similar elephant. He wore a large turban pinned at the front by what might be a ruby. Jewels lined his robe. Lazarus looked down at the green Maharaja. His grand turban was pinned with a flawless stone that could be an emerald.

The tall man beamed and looked expectantly at Lazarus. As if commanded, Lazarus said, "Most uncommon, truly."

"Uncommon? Not just uncommon - one of a kind! Unique! Of inestimable value!" The man paused but to take a breath. "Do you play?"

"Sir?"

"Chess, boy, do you know the game?"

Though seventeen, Lazarus did not like being called "boy" in this tone. It had nothing to do with his age. What was it? Yes – it reminded him of Head Master Solomon from his early school days. He swallowed and said, "Yes sir, I have played, but never with pieces like these."

"I told you boy, there are no pieces like these," said the man. He reached and selected a piece from each side of the table, put both hands behind his back and presented them to Lazarus, palms down. "Choose," he ordered.

Lazarus pointed at a hand. The man inverted and opened his palm to reveal a green piece. Lazarus supposed it to be a pawn, but it held a sword diagonally across its body and wore a wrap on its head.

"Sit, lay your bag aside," the man instructed as he pulled the chair on the green side away from the table and firmly pushed down on Lazarus' shoulder.

"Well, sir, I suppose," Lazarus said timidly. The man took his seat at the red side, with his back to the door. As he did, Lazarus quickly studied the pieces. The kings or maharajai and the queens were particularly detailed. Lazarus did not know the title for an Indian queen and he did not inquire. The royalty had tiny demure faces rising from creased robes and each bore a large jeweled head wrap. The king was taller and the gleaming medallion at the front of his turban seemed to cast a hued glow across the board at the opposing pieces. Each sat upon the back of an elephant. Indeed, an elephant served as the base for each piece other than the pawns and the knights. The knights were horses in reared position. They were as large as the elephants and had golden hooves but no riders.

The man stared at Lazarus, who sat quietly and did not move. "The green plays as white," he said eagerly, "your open."

Lazarus did not play chess tentatively - until this moment. He was afraid to touch these pieces. He gently lifted his queen's knight pawn and moved it ahead one space. He would for now preserve his king's-side wall of pawns.

The man quickly advanced his king's pawn two spaces. "So you are a tailor," he said. It was not a question.

"Yes, I am," said Lazarus, and he moved his queen's bishop one diagonal space.

"And you play chess," said the man – also not a question. He ignored his pawn in jeopardy and slid his king's bishop across three spaces to queen's bishop four.

Lazarus thought to take the pawn, but curiosity stopped him. He moved queen's rook pawn ahead two spaces, biding his time, and replied, "I have played some, sir."

The man all but threw his queen diagonally out three spaces in the classic scholar's mate position. "Where were you trained?" This time it was a question.

Lazarus did not know if the man questioned his tailor's skills or his chess. He gave a single answer to both, "London." Lazarus had not fallen to a four-move checkmate since his first week at Mr. Symmon's chessboard. "This man is either a novice or he thinks I am," he said to himself. He lifted his king's knight and jumped it to face across at the man's queen, defeating the checkmate.

The man tried to hide his disappointment and looked unaware as if he had no intention of a four-move victory. "So you are a tailor trained in London and your name is Perlman." Perhaps this was a question.

"That is correct, sir," Lazarus replied.

"You are also a Jew, are you not?" the man said as if he had unearthed some concealed truth. Lazarus looked directly up at him. Either from concentration or to avoid Lazarus' gaze, the man's eyes remained on the chessboard.

"Yes," said Lazarus. "I am a Jew. My father is Mordecai Perlman, a tailor of Houndsditch Street near the Great Synagogue at Duke's Place."

"Very well," said the man. "My family is also of London. My wife and daughter live still at my house at The Adelphi. Jewish tailors and other Jews of skill have served my family for many generations."

There it was. The man's gambit for a quick checkmate had failed, so he now verbally placed Lazarus in check as a servant to his kind. He wanted it known that his London house sat near a bend in the Thames where fine homes of fine gentlemen stood. It was a short distance and a far cry from Houndsditch in the East End. Lazarus did not think the man's move particularly clever, and he thought to himself, "This man's manner is as crude as his chess." Clever or not, the match was joined. Lazarus, though, would play his out on the table between them.

Several moves later the man had left his queen exposed and on the same color as his king. Lazarus' knight stood but a jump from pinning the man in a royal split that would cost the man his queen. From there Lazarus estimated five moves to checkmate if the man were astute and three moves if he were not. He touched his knight.

Then, as if drawing inspiration from the chess piece, he decided that there was much more at stake here than chess. This man was the master of the largest plantation in Barbados. He could be the pathway to more "exact intelligence" on the treatment of slaves on the island than Lazarus might otherwise be able to gather. If Lazarus soundly defeated the man, this would likely be their final match. If Lazarus lost, the man might think him no challenge and lose interest. Lazarus could not bring himself to intentionally lose to this man who derisively called him "boy" and placed him as a servant anyway. He paused a moment then jumped his knight to a harmless position. At Lazarus' design, the match ended sometime later in a draw.

The man insisted they play again ... stalemate. Then a third time, but still no victor. The man now observed that there are great chess masters among the Jews. The man's tone indicated that he thought he had elevated himself by playing this Jew before him to a draw. Lazarus smiled inwardly. This man could never equal a chess master, Jew or gentile.

It had grown dark outside. Lazarus rose to go, but thanked the man for his hospitality and the chess. He openly admired the red and green chess set and said it must have brought him luck to be able to withstand the fine play of such a capable opponent. "Your servant has my card," Lazarus said. "Please call on me at any time if I may be of service."

"Jodhpurs," said the man.

"I beg your pardon?" Lazarus queried.

"Can you make me a new pair of jodhpurs? I have but one, given by the same man who gave me the 'Maharajai'. Since I ride daily, I am afraid they grow thin seated and I fear embarrassment - and blisters." The man enjoyed his jest.

Lazarus had never heard of jodhpurs. "May I see them?" he asked.

The man called for the old tortoise who eventually returned and handed some breeches to the man. The man stood and held them before him. "The nobles of India use these for riding costume," he said. "They allow comfort on horseback and control in the stirrups."

The breeches flared very wide at the hips, down to the knee, then suddenly narrowed and gathered at a strap well below the knee.

They had no buttons and closed by overlap and ties at the waist. One would be required to drop them to answer a call of nature. Lazarus had never seen anything like them, but he believed he could fashion near any garment if provided a pattern. "Sir, is this pair comfortable ... does it fit you well?"

"Yes, it is perfect - except just a little tight below the knee."

"The fabric is of a different weave, not like those of the Manchester mills available here. Is it to your liking?"

"Yes, I suppose so. It is soft, but not so sturdy. Something more durable than this Indian woven cotton might last, I think."

"That is fortunate, because I have not found any fabric quite like this one here in Barbados." Lazarus reached into his sample case and retrieved some of the heavy gray weave. He rubbed it between his fingers and extended it to the man to do the same.

"This might do," said the man.

Lazarus motioned to the worn pair, "If I may borrow these, I believe I can make a new pair for you," he said.

"When?" said the man, "as I told you, I ride daily."

Lazarus held them up and turned them about. He rolled the waistband and studied the inside. "Two, maybe three days," he said.

"Very well," said the man. "If you do well, I may like a second new pair."

"Thank you, sir - "

"You may call me Lord Harrington," said the man.

"Thank you Lord Harrington." Lazarus held up the jodhpurs with one hand, "I shall do my best," he said and took his leave. Indeed he would do his best, he thought, including his best to learn more of this man and what made him the Maharaja of the island's slavers.

Chapter 26. Bougainvillea Cascade

The morning after his chess match, Lazarus laid out Lord Harrington's worn jodhpurs for tracing. He chalked and cut leg panels. He could not lay the waistband fully out and save the worn garment, so he carefully measured, recorded the measure and pinned his marks, but measured once more before he cut. His constant checking slowed the process, but he chose to follow the habits he had learned from Mordecai.

By mid afternoon, the new jodhpurs began to take their shape. Lazarus held them up with both hands. They lacked but tie straps above the ankles. Then he remembered Lord Harrington's preference for light colored clothing and his comment about durability. He dropped his work and walked quickly to the waterfront. When he returned, he rolled out a few yards of sailcloth and started the process all over again.

Lazarus lit his oil lamp and worked into the night. The heavy sailcloth yielded to only his sturdiest needles and then required double stitching. Before Lazarus realized the time, the sun had risen and the sailcloth jodhpurs lay unfinished. He took some cold tea stirred in a cup and returned to his work. He required frequent pause now, but he labored on, throughout the day. Near evening, he proudly examined two pair of jodhpurs - one of heavy gray weave and one from lighter colored, but even sturdier sailcloth.

He could not wait to show Lord Harrington his work and probe his way into the man's confidence. Though it grew late, he reasoned that a brisk walk would bring him to Harrington Hall before dark. Lord Harrington would be surprised that Lazarus had completed two pair in just two days - well, two days and one night.

He began to tire as he neared Harrington Hall. Neither the urgency of his journey nor the hour prevented him from stopping on the roadway. For a few minutes he admired the sunset falling on the cascade of not quite red flowers which grew up over the steep rise at a little distance to the north of the road. He had noticed the blossoms before, but in the sunset they took his breath away. His nostrils flared as he inhaled deeply and continued on his way. The island that rose before him glowed in the setting sun. Such an irony, he thought, the slaves here have been imprisoned in a paradise.

He arrived at Harrington Hall at dusk. The old tortoise eventually answered his knock. Lazarus apologized for calling at a late hour, but explained that he wanted to deliver the riding breeches in time for Lord Harrington's morning ride. The servant showed him to the same room where he apparently deposited all callers. Once there, he said that Lord Harrington was absent. He did not know when the Lord would return, but he offered Lazarus tea and said that he could wait if he wished. Lazarus declined the tea, but said that he would wait.

After a time, the old tortoise returned. He had no news of Lord Harrington, though he seemed unconcerned. This time Lazarus accepted the offered tea.

Later still, the old tortoise returned again. He said that he did not know whether Lord Harrington would return that evening and, if so, at what hour. He spoke as if this uncertainty commonly occurred. "If you wish to stay the night, I shall prepare a room for you," he said.

The invitation surprised Lazarus and before thinking he declined. Instead, he opened his bag and handed over its contents. "Here are your master's riding breeches," he said. "And here are two new pair I have made for him. I know he commissioned but a single pair, but tell him the second is offered only on his approval." Then as Lazarus stepped down the front stairway and into what had become full on night, he turned back and said, "Oh, and please tell him that I will call back to assure his satisfaction."

The hour was very late, but half a moon and a thousand stars guided Lazarus' steps in the clear night. He had not walked far when he heard someone crying. He stopped. He turned to his right from where the sound had come. There it was again. Was someone in distress? Then he heard some strange noise - a high pitched, melodic chanting.

The noise beckoned him. He left the roadway and moved slowly through the edge of the thick cane field to his north. The sound stopped, so did Lazarus. It began again and Lazarus moved more quickly now, hoping to discover its source before it stopped once more. He could not be certain of his direction, but he hiked off to his right, up a rise and around the crest of a hill. He could not see far in any direction because the tall cane surrounded him. The sound that had grown louder with his progress now fell again silent.

He waited for several minutes. He heard nothing but the night. He decided to give up the search, but he realized that he was no longer entirely sure of his way back to the roadway.

Then he again caught sight of the moon and regained his bearings. Just as he turned and stepped off in the direction of the roadway, he heard shrieks. They sounded not too distant. He walked in the direction of the sound and then saw, just above the top of the sugar cane, the arms of a windmill jutting into the sky.

He had seen the big windmills of Barbados before. Dozens of them occupied the heights on the island where they caught the wind. From a distance they looked like giant spiders on the land. Their sails turned a shaft that protruded like a tail from the rear and drove the mills that crushed sugar cane. As Lazarus worked his way toward the windmill, he failed to mind his step and stumbled, but stood again and continued.

The chanting he had heard from the roadway returned, much closer now, and resonated eerily through the night, sad but pleasantly harmonic. He walked slowly toward the windmill, parting stalks of cane before him and turning his shoulders to move between them. As he came to the far, upper side of the cane field he stopped.

There in a clearing stood the broad stone base of a windmill. Many of the stones had fallen, and the sail arms, protruding from the far side of the base, stood bare. They were but frames of arms really, and did not turn. The mill looked dilapidated, perhaps abandoned. A glow and some shadows licked the tall wall of sugar cane that began again on the far side of the old windmill. The voices began again and sounded as if they were calling to him.

He moved clockwise around the old windmill, keeping his cover in the cane for he knew he had not been invited to this concert. Within a few steps, he began to see fire lighted black faces moving before the windmill in some sort of paced parade. As Lazarus continued his circle, he could see that a fire sat between the base of the old windmill and the dancers. Some hands now flew high in the air and swayed back and forth as the bodies beneath them danced. Wide black mouths made moaning sounds, occasionally punctuated with cries. The bodies all moved to the same rhythm, like stalks of sugar cane caught in a swirl wind. As they pranced, the bodies passed about an earthen jug. One by one each body danced with the jug a bit and then tipped its bottom skyward for a long moment before passing it to the next dancer.

Keeping his eyes on the spectacle before him, Lazarus continued moving to his left in a wide arc until he could see all of the fire. Then, behind the fire he caught sight of the corner of a pile of stones from the mill that appeared to have been stacked into a sort of a pier. Before the fire the dancers now quickened the pace of their chants and their movements. Suddenly they shook and gyrated about while standing almost in place. Their eyes looked big and all white as if their pupils were rolled back into their heads. Lazarus moved again to his left, where he could better see the dancers and the entire scene. Several dancers beat on their chests and slapped their thighs in unison.

Suddenly one then a second of the criers fell to the ground, rolled, wriggled and twitched about as if in seizure. None came to their aid but the dance continued. After a few minutes more, the two on the ground stopped moving. Then the others brought them to their feet. Where the aided fainters had been so supple before, their bodies now appeared stiff. All the dancers now faced the fire, but seemed to look beyond it.

With his eyes fixed on this fantastic sight, Lazarus slid his tired feet to the left to further improve his view. His left foot struck what he took to be cane stubble and he fell. He looked up from the ground toward the fire-lit Africans. One or two looked in his general direction, but soon turned away and resumed their celebration. Lazarus rose slowly, gripping his sample case, and moved still more to his left. Now he could see the full front side of the dilapidated stone mill house. There, directly below the terminus of the windmill arms sat a table like structure, breast high to a man. Its base was solid rather than legged and built of stones that looked to be borrowed from the mill house itself. A broad wood plank lay across the top of the stones, forming a mantle or perhaps an altar.

Atop the plank stood an array of figurines all facing the fire and the dancers. Some of the figures were as tall as a man's head. Others were only a few inches high. Each of the tall ones was a single color and shaped into a face with exaggerated features. No two faces were the same shape or color, but each had a long, rigid nose with large nostrils. The sides of their heads looked smooth, without ears. The smaller ones appeared similar, but with softer lines.

The dancers now closed upon the fire and almost stood in it. They all grew still and one raised his hands then moved to place them upon one of the stiff fainters. Lazarus moved still more left to better see this new part of the ceremony. Suddenly he tripped again and fell upon a row of cane that gave and waived under his weight. As Lazarus regained his feet, he saw that the dancer with raised hands shouted and pointed in his direction. Now two or three from the fire circle broke away and moved toward him. Instinctively, Lazarus turned his back and ran directly away from them. The cane impeded his flight, and he thought to run between rows back toward the roadway, but the field seemed like a single mass of thick cane stalks. He could hear his pursuers behind him.

He legs grew tired. He had worked through the night before and had eaten little. The cane field seemed much larger upon retreat than it had at advance. He became dizzy, tripped repeatedly, but continued his flight. Suddenly he ran out of the cane and into what appeared to be a thicket of what he thought in the night light to be the flowers he had admired during his walks to and from Harrington Hall.

He felt as if he were now running through an orchard of knives. He felt sharp points piercing his skin, grabbing at his clothing and scratching his neck. "Are they shooting darts at me?" he asked himself. Something grabbed his grip case and he pulled it sharply to his side. As he did so, he toppled to his left and headlong into more miniature knives. He tumbled and rolled and his body cascaded over a cliff obscured by the flowers. He did not know how far he fell, but where he landed the ground still gave way and he rolled through a thousand sharp points until he came to rest on his back where the land flattened out.

Lazarus tried to roll to one side to regain his feet, but he felt to be entangled and bound up by tendrils that gave a little but would not release. With each effort, the pain increased and he felt new punctures. His right ankle throbbed. He stopped struggling and just laid there panting, looking up through the vines into the night sky.

Soon he heard some talking and not long after some hacking, chopping and grunting. They sounded to be all about and growing closer. He tried again to free himself, but the pain and the plant wrapping prevented him. A moment later something struck through the vines nearby, then again. Then he saw the shadow of a man standing above him blocking the night sky. The man raised what appeared to be a short, broad sword and slashed. The blade just missed his left ear. The shadow raised the sword again and Lazarus called out a strained, "Please no!"

Then the shadow stopped, raised its head and yelled, "Here - here he be, dis way."

Other chopping sounds grew closer and Lazarus tried to roll to one side. He moaned and the shadow ordered, "Lie still, jes be still." Lazarus did as he was told. More voices spoke, ever nearer and soon he was surrounded by shadows, all breathing deeply and all bearing short, broad swords. Lazarus wondered for just a moment if he were to be hacked to death here or carried to the altar before the windmill to be sacrificed.

Then an older voice said, "Fetch de cane cart Andru whilse we lift him to de road." Then a figure at his side bent down toward him, placed a dark hand lightly on his chest and said, "Ya bees all right now, jes be still." Lazarus obeyed as if he had a choice. Several hands now moved about him. They cut and lifted vines away. Some sharp points tore more at him as they were pulled away. One of the bending shadows made a little cry and another said, "Eeccch - blasted."

In a few moments the older voice said, "We be goin to lif ya now. It will pains ya some, jes bite on dis bit o cane," and a hand fumbled for Lazarus' lips and stuck a soft stick in his mouth. He felt several hands grab and he rose. More hacking sounds came from above Lazarus' head, the older voice said, "Step careful now," and Lazarus was carried slowly headlong with hands upon him holding, slipping, gripping again and hurting with every move. He kept still. After what felt like miles, but Lazarus knew to be only tens of yards, he came to rest on what he took to be a roadway. He heard a light rumble drawing near. At command of the same older voice, hands took him again and laid him on some low planking with one high wheel at either side.

"Andru, draw him up 'round to Betts," said the older voice. A hand rested lightly again on his chest and the voice said in a lower tone to Lazarus, "Betts knows de way wit de bougain spines - she be fix ya up jes fine, no worries." The planks jerked forward and the voice cried, "Easy now - takes yer time Andru."

Andru rolled slowly, but it was not easy for Lazarus. The planks twisted a little as the big wheel at each side creaked and the planks ascended up a rising roadway. After a time Lazarus thought that the stinging had begun to dull some. The planks bounced and rocked a little now and with them Lazarus moaned some.

"Sorry, sorry, I is sorry," said a boy's voice from above his head, "it be jes a bit mo' now." Lazarus now paid no attention to the same half moon and star splashed sky that had guided his way an hour or two earlier. He could tell from the motion of the planks at his back that Andru drew the cart in a swooping circle off to his right.

"Starboard thirty," Lazarus whispered to himself for no reason other than his habit of trying to keep his bearings.

In a few moments more, the cart rolled to a gentle stop. "Betts … Betts," the boy's voice called out softly. Lazarus heard rustling sounds and steps on the ground. Now he saw a tall, thin figure of a boy at his feet.

"B-Bye de stars, what ya b-be doin' dis night Andru, is ya got no sense boy," stammered a woman's voice.

Andru did not answer but now grabbed up Lazarus' boots, one under each arm, and leaned back sliding Lazarus along the planks. Lazarus winced as a sharp pain struck his ankle. "Sorry, I be sorry," said the boy as he gently lowered one leg and then the other over the end of the low cart.

"B-Bye all de stars what be, what has ya breen me dis time," the woman mumbled in a feigned dismay. Then in real alarm and with a hushed tone she mumbled, "Andru, dis b-bees a white man. I gots 'nuf woes, why ya breens me dis buckra?"

"I know, I know," said Andru, "Singing Louis tole me draws him up to Betts. She know de bougain spines."

"B-Bye de stars - b-bougain spines?" asked the mumbling woman.

"He runned an dived down de bougain fall, dis one," Andru said with wide white eyes.

"De bougain fall. Bye de stars!" the woman exclaimed, "De bougain fall." Then she came around to stand by Andru, "Ya be one sticked man, bees ya black or buckra."

Lazarus did not know what to say. He simply acknowledged her with a low moan.

Andru and the woman helped him to stand and, as Lazarus

favored his right foot, walked him slowly into a small structure he could not see well in the night. They slowly removed his torn blouse and laid him out on a low, matted bed at one end of the building's single room. Andru departed and the woman came to the bedside with a candle that she sat nearby.

"Dey can snap in de skin," she said, "but most de bougain needles be cuttin', scratchin' and prickin'." Then she reached and rubbed her hand along Lazarus' side. She hit some sharp points and Lazarus jumped a little. "B-Bye de stars, yew did b-break some o de spines right off de bine." She stepped away and returned with a small cup from which protruded a thin stick and a sewing tweeze. She moved with the fingertips of both hands and pushed her tweeze down on a point. With a grunt she tightened and pulled.

"Aaeeech," Lazarus squealed.

"Dis gine to be a long night fo' ya," she said. "Mebbe, we kin help dat some." She stood and took her candle a few steps away to the center of the room. Lazarus' eyes followed her. She faced a dark shelf at the back of the room with her back to Lazarus. She busied herself with some spoon stirring around another handleless cup. In the flicker of the candle Lazarus could see up on the shelf a figurine like those he had seen on the alter behind the windmill fire. The woman turned back to Lazarus. She sat by his side, lifted his head slowly with one hand and offered the cup to his lips with the other, "Take dis," she said. Lazarus took a sip of the odorless liquid in the cup. "Take it all." Lazarus did.

Lazarus awoke with a jolt. He imagined he still ran from pursuers. He felt the sting of a hundred wasps over his body. His head spun and his legs, arms, neck and head throbbed in pain. His mind and his eyes blurred. As his eyes became accustomed to the light he looked up past a small beam and at the sloping underside of an uneven but steep roof.

He heard nothing. Then he moved a hand up to press his painful cheek and felt something layered against his skin. He pulled at it, and it came off his face. He held it away and saw what looked to be a piece of banana leaf. His thumb detected that one side of the bit of leaf was coated with a sticky smear, which he hoped was not puss from his own tender skin. He held his fingers away at eyes focus and rubbed the amber, translucent ointment between them. The salve had a pungent odor he could not identify. He felt at a pull on his neck and found more bit of leaf held in place by sticky salve. As he peeled this bit of leaf away from his throat, he jumped as a woman said, "Ya b-best leave dat poultice if ya 'spects to heal."

Lazarus sat up and threw his feet over the left side of the low bed and faced a small black woman. He moaned as his right foot struck the floor. He looked up at the woman. "Who are you?" he demanded.

"Never ya mind who I be," said the woman, "I knows who yew be. Yew is da b-boy tailor what plays de elephant game wit de masta."

Lazarus began to stand but his right ankle gave way. As he caught himself, he discovered that he was naked beneath a thin bed sheet that covered him. Looking at his arms and chest he saw a few more bits of banana leaf adhering to his skin with the aid of the same amber balm. He felt more below and held the sheet away to examine himself while keeping it between his body and the woman. Still more banana leaf stuck to his side and legs. He felt funny at his core and saw then felt that his penis was entirely wrapped in a length of leaf with amber oozing from its edges. "My Lord," he said out loud, "have they butchered me?" He felt with his hands and found, beneath the wrapped banana leaf poultice, he remained intact. In the effort the cover dropped down to his knees, and he looked up to see the woman staring at him as he grasped his groin with both hands.

He felt a blush and pulled the cover back up to his waist. The woman remained somber and said, "De b-bougainvillea did not do dat cuttin I 'spects. How did ya lose dat skin? Do it be hurtin' too?"

He looked at the earnest puzzlement on her face. He did not understand what she asked - but then he realized that she had probably never before seen a circumcised man. He could not explain. He looked at her bare feet and said, "It is an old cut from when I was very small. It does not hurt."

He now looked at the woman more carefully, from her feet upward. She was with child. Her belly was not big, not close to her time, but its round firmness stood out from the rest of her thin frame. When his eyes finally left her belly and climbed to her eyes, he cleared his throat and in the calmest voice manageable asked, "Where am I? How did I get here?" Then he remembered and held up one hand, palm toward her as if signaling a halt. "Wait, I remember … I think I know," he said. "You are Betts, are you not?"

"Bye de stars, yes, I be Betts."

Lazarus examined her face. She looked young but for two exceptions. One of her eyes drooped, her left, and about her mouth her skin drew inward and folded together with little sign of any lip. When she spoke, her lips emerged from their fold and pursed out from her mouth. She worked her words out past her pucker with effort and no sign of a tooth. The room around her was very simple - a single door at one side, a single window opening at each end, all brought together by frame and slat. The windows had no glass, but horizontal jalousies hinged on angle to admit some light and air while rejecting rain.

"Thank you Betts for your aide to me," Lazarus said.

"I best go tells de house yew is here so de masta do not miss ya," Betts said.

"The master? What master?"

"Masta Load Harrington. Dis be he's plantashun, dis be he's slabe b-billage and dis," she waved her hand around the room, "bye de stars, dis be he's chattlo house."

"And you, Betts, you are his as well?" Lazarus asked.

The woman laughed a small, nervous laugh. She smiled enough that Lazarus could see she had no teeth, at least none he could detect. "Bye de stars, I be de masta's too, all me days."

Then they both laughed a little laugh. The poultice must be magical, thought Lazarus. Hours before he had never known such pain. Now he was sore, but without the sharp stinging pain - and able to laugh.

"By the stars," said Lazarus.

Chapter 27. Home Bred Slaves

Lazarus limped from the chattel house, squinted in the bright day and looked about. Betts' house stood at the end of a row of near identical houses. A few hundred yards away, on higher ground, a bit of red tile roof that looked to be a rear corner of Harrington Hall was just visible.

Lazarus took a few steps and looked about the village. It appeared that several rows of the same style little house were lined behind Betts' row. Each of the tiny houses sat a few hands width off the ground on beams or blocks. The beams had been rounded on the ends as if they had been slid into place. Several Africans and a few more he judged to be of mixed race stood, sat or walked about the place. Some were gathered at what looked to be an outdoor kitchen across and two houses up the slightly inclined wagon way that passed in front of Betts' house. Nearly all eyes were on him, though a few pretended to pay him no mind.

A small mulatto girl with one shock of hair bound up at the top of her head skipped right past him and into Betts' house. Not wanting to be a spectacle, Lazarus followed her back into the house. The little girl was up in Betts' arms. She stared at Lazarus then turned and whispered in Betts' ear.

"No b-baby, dis man do not be takin' our house," Betts said. The child again whispered in Betts' ear. "Bye de stars chile, 'course yew can eat." Betts turned about, took down a saucer from the end of the long shelf at the back of the room and placed it and the child at a small table at the left of the room, beneath the side window. She stood again and turned to Lazarus. "Can yew eat?" she said.

"Yes, please," said Lazarus. He could not remember when he had last eaten. Obeying her motion, he sat at the table opposite the child. Betts took down again from the shelf and sat at the end of the table, facing the window with the child on her right and Lazarus on her left. They ate cold yam fritters, short bananas and tea - cool tea, tasty fritters. The little girl acted coy and giggled but did not speak except to whisper to Betts. Lazarus was unsure how to talk to her.

"Her name be Shayala," said Betts, proudly. "Load Harrington calls de womans he takes by de names o' de fine English ladies. But I names dis chile o' mine. No English name fo' her."

Now someone outside was singing. The singer approached the front of the house and walked right inside. The singing ended, but a still tuneful voice said, "Eliz'beth, how bees de buckra boy ta ..." The man stopped. Then he spoke to Lazarus, "Oh, ya be up, an lookin' jes fine." It was the older voice from the night before. The face belonged to a sturdy black man with a ready smile. He looked mature but not as old as his voice.

"B-bye de stars," Betts said, "does ya got no work Louis?"

"Don't hags me dearheart," Louis grinned at Betts. Then he put Lazarus' grip sack on the table. "Dis belong to da buckra boy?" he hummed.

"Why, yes," Lazarus said, "where did you -"

"Andru fetched it from the bougain fall," Louis said. Then he playfully swooped up the child, causing her to giggle. He swung her around and swung himself into the child's place with her on his lap. He bounced the child on his knees and sang,

> *Gootie, Gootie hop up girl,*
> *Gootie, Gootie got no curl.*
> *Gootie come and Gootie go,*
> *Gootie need a big red bow.*

The girl giggled again and Betts lectured with a half smile, "Man b-be comin' 'round here in de light o de day, havin' no mind fo' he's work."

In a lower tone Louis said, "Betts me dearheart, ya know de cutting be startin' soon. Deese be 'bout de only peace'ble days fo' dis ol' boy, don't ya know. Asides, me gots to see me li'l Gootie girl," and as he said it his first finger tickled the child under her arm. Then Louis sang, *"Is dem fritters dat I sees - fetch some fo' me purdy please."* Then he moved one hand to his little Gootie's stomach and said, "Les see, puts dem fritters right 'bout - here." His hand pounced into a full five-finger tickle and the little one squealed and squirmed. Betts retrieved two golden fritters and leaned on Louis' shoulder as she placed them before him. He took two big bites, then he stopped. He fed the next bite to the girl on his lap.

"How many o' de points did he snap?" Louis said to Betts while looking straight at Lazarus and still chewing.

"I'll show ya," Betts said. Lazarus wanted to thank Louis, but he could hardly get a word. "Dey be nice 'uns too," Betts said as she returned from the shelf and placed another cup without handle in front of Louis.

Louis took another bite. Then he quickly inverted the cup on the table between him and Lazarus and held it there as if to avoid spillage. He suddenly lifted the cup high as if unveiling a surprise and sang, *"Well lookie here an lookie be."* There on the table laid half a handful of sharply pointed needle shaped tines. Most were green, a few had some brown and some had traces of blood on them. Each was at least half an inch in length, a few were nearly two inches. Lazarus hurt all over again looking at them.

"I b-believes I got 'em all," said Betts.

"Did ya feel every bit o' dis boy searchin' fer 'em?" Louis asked. Then he broke into a wide smile and dodged Betts' hand thrown halfheartedly at the back of his head.

Louis fingered the tines. He whistled a prolonged two toned note, "ssreeiit-rrooo" and looked at Lazarus. He shook his head slowly and proclaimed, "Dat be de most points I seed in jes one man." Then he smiled a little at Lazarus. "Ya be a fortuned boy," he said, "ya be fevered and mi-i-i-ty sick widout dis angel." He nodded toward Betts with his wide grin. "Some, dey fevered up an' joins de ole ligaroo if de tines stays in."

"Ligaroo?" Lazarus questioned.

"Um, de ghost o de dead – " Louis began.

"B-Bye de stars, Louis, stop it now!" Betts said, mocking anger and retaking her seat at the table.

Gootie now reached for the tines and Louis backed away from the table so her little arms could not reach. "Dose tines do not be fo' me Gootie girl," he said. "Ya knows, me girl, we don't play 'mongst de pretty bougans wit' de nasty tines."

Lazarus spoke now, earnestly thanking Betts for her nursing and Louis for his rescue. "Please thank the others from last night," he said to Louis.

Louis suddenly frowned and set Gootie down to the floor on her feet. "What others?" he asked.

"Why, the dancers and the boy who brought me here. It was dark, I would not know them now, so if you . . . ."

"Dat be jes as good," said Louis. He sounded anxious now. "Sah - please sah," he plead, "Jes forget what ya seed las' night and forget where ya seed it. Please sah."

Lazarus understood. He had seen more than he should have. He reached out a hand and touched Louis at his forearm. "My name is Lazarus Perlman. I came recently from England and never saw bougainvillea before I got here. I would still be wound up in it but for you. I am in your debt." He looked at Betts and back at Louis. "I will do as you ask. I saw no fire, no dancing, no altar last night. I shall never tell. You can trust me."

"Tank ya Mista Laza," Louis said. Lazarus doubted he had convinced the man as apprehension remained in his eyes. He decided to lighten the moment.

"This is a beautiful child," he said motioning to the now perfectly behaved girl clinging to Louis' leg. "I thought her name was Shayala, but you call her 'Gootie,' is that how she is called?"

"Oh, hay-he-he," Louis laughed, "no sah, I jes calls her after de li'l furred Agouti hare what lives in de cane field. Like de English calls um, de li'l ... um ..." Louis smiled and placed his two fists together, but with the first two fingers of each sticking in the air at a curve. He jumped his fists together across the table toward Lazarus, a few inches per jump.

"Rabbit?" asked Lazarus.

"De baby rabbit, all wit de fur, de ... a ... li'l ..."

"Bunny rabbit?" Lazarus guessed.

"Jes so - de bunny rabbit! Gootie bees de li'l bunny."

"She is a beautiful child," Lazarus repeated.

"Dat she bees," said Louis. He took her by the waist and sat her again on his knees. She smiled back at him and he rocked his knees under the child, "Dat she sholly bees."

Gootie girl was mulatto, but Betts and Louis looked African. Lazarus decided to probe without seeming to do so. "You must be proud to be the father of a fine child like this one," he said, patting Gootie once on the head.

Louis looked at Betts. She looked at him and then softly at the child on Louis' knees. "Tank ya Mista Laza," she said, "b-but she be de masta's chile - "

"Betts!" Louis said.

"B-Bye de stars, Louis," Betts shot back. "Mista Laza be de only one in dis billage what do not know - half de chiles on dis plantashun be made by de masta." Then she leaned back in her chair and its legs screeched a little sliding away from the table. She placed both hands spread wide on her round belly and said, "Dis be his work, too ... bye de stars."

Lazarus did not know what to say. He told them that he was merely a tailor to Lord Harrington and not his confidant. He said he was not expected at the manor house but had left some of his work there for Lord Harrington and was returning to Bridgetown when he fell at the bougainvillea cliff. "I must have mistakenly thought I had found a short cut," he said, practicing his story.

Louis nodded approval.

What Lazarus had witnessed, he would keep to himself. He swore it again. "There is no need for anyone to tell Lord Harrington I was in this house, or have ever been here," he assured them. He thanked them both and said he thought he now felt well enough to walk to Bridgetown. He rose to do so and knew that he was wrong. He felt dizzy, his right ankle hurt him and he sat back down.

Lazarus stayed with Betts and Gootie another day, sleeping in their mat bed as they slept on the floor. He did not like the arrangement, but Betts would not, b-bye the stars, have it otherwise. She also gave him a cup of her poultice in case he burned or itched while she slept. He used a little of it on his right leg sometime in the night.

Lazarus awoke before Betts and Gootie. He stood slowly, stretched from side to side and looked about the room. He limped over to the back of the room and faced Betts' long narrow shelf. Now he could better see the figurine that had earlier caught his eye. He saw that there was not one figurine but one large one, about two hands width tall, and several smaller ones less than half as tall. Each appeared to be the bust or head of a stern looking African. Each had closed eyes in the shape of upended eggs - or perhaps spaces where eyes should have been. The tall white one appeared to have been carved by a skilled craftsman. It had a strong rigid nose with flared nostrils and thick lips that protruded some from its face.

Lazarus looked back over his right shoulder at Betts sleeping on the floor next to her child. These were Betts' pursed lips on this white figurine. The smaller figurines looked smoother with somewhat softer features and were of various colors. He touched a small blue one with his left hand. It felt cool and appeared to be made of clay or of stone. He moved his hand to a few of the others, in turn touching a green one and then one the color of shallow seas in bright sun. He started to touch a reddish one but stopped as it reminded him of bougainvillea blossoms.

"Dose b-be de Obeah Gods," a voice behind Lazarus startled him, and he knocked the big white figurine off the shelf. He caught it before it struck the floor. He stood slowly, clutching it with both hands and looked over the top of it to see Betts still on the floor but propped up on one elbow and looking over her still sleeping daughter at him.

"I am sorry, I just - I did not mean to - "

"Dat one bees Obatala, de God o de Gods," Betts said as Lazarus carefully replaced it to its position on the shelf. "Obatala made man, woman an he made all de Gods . . . de God o war, de God o de sea, de God o de b-blowin' wind an such."

Without showing any concern for Lazarus' near accident with Obatala, Betts rose and gathered some things from her shelf. She walked out the door. Lazarus stood just inside the doorway and peered out after her. She walked diagonally across the wagon way and stopped at the outdoor kitchen where a few others were gathered. Then she appeared to go about making some preparations for a morning meal while talking with the others.

Lazarus was startled again by a light brush stroke against the back of his hand and a sudden pressure at his leg. He jumped a little and looked down to see a shock of Gootie hair pointed up at him and the arms of its owner now wrapped around his thigh. He smiled down at the little one who looked out across the way at her mother.

Chapter 28. Eyes On the Ground

Hobbled and swollen, Lazarus stayed a few more days with Betts. He ate fritters and sat Gootie girl on his good leg. Louis called every day at dusk. Some village slaves milled about in the alleyway near Betts' home each evening – perhaps Lazarus had become a curiosity or maybe they just liked Louis' singing. He sang songs, teased Betts and cuddled her daughter. He talked graciously with Lazarus. Betts fussed about, spoiling them both. Each night and morning she unwrapped and inspected Lazarus' ankle and his healing, now very itchy skin. She dabbed more amber poultice. Her light touch on the sores sent tingles along Lazarus' limbs.

Louis brought him a bent pole with a top cross-piece, wrapped in rags – a crude but sturdy crutch. "Yew ain't de firs 'round here to need dis prop," he said. Then he tucked it under his own arm in demonstration. Within a moment he began to sway, dance and hop around Betts' little house with the crutch, producing giggles – first from Gootie girl and then from her mother - and finally, a hearty laugh from Lazarus.

"Chew de cane and wuking up, wuki, wuki wuking up," Louis sang, twisting about and alternating a mock pout with a huge grin.

"Stop dat pompasettin," Betts scolded, with a little smile.

Standing on one foot, Louis handed the crutch to Lazarus. It was awkward at first, but he got the feel. He did not try to dance.

"Yew bees da strangest buckra eber I sees," Louis told him. "Colored all hoppy in de chattlo hut."

On a sunny morning, nearly a week after his fall, Lazarus dressed in his newly washed and dry clothes, hugged Gootie girl, and took her mother's arm with a fond press. His throat tightened as he took his leave, grabbed his grip sack and began his walk home. He looked back before he lost sight of Betts' house and lifted his crutch toward two women - one round bellied and the other very small, watching him and waiving as he left. He avoided Harrington Hall and found his way to the main road to Bridgetown. His armpit soon ached and his grip sack slipped. He tucked the leather grip up under his arm and over the crutch some. He moved slowly, but he managed to make his way.

He had gone but a little way when Singing Louis and a trim,

handsome African lad came up behind him in a low, narrow two-wheeled cart drawn by a single sway-backed brown horse. The young African appeared to be almost Lazarus' age. His features were uncommonly fine and his shoulders well muscled.

"We got errands in Bridgetown," Louis said. "Sit yersef in de back, Andru," he nodded to the boy. Andru climbed in the back and sat with palms flat on the planks. Lazarus handed up his crutch and gingerly took his place next to Louis on a narrow board that was more railing than seat; and the old horse started slowly down the red dirt roadway. The cart's two big wheels creaked as they slowly turned. Bridgetown was not far, maybe five miles, but Lazarus was still weak from his bougainvillea "shortcut."

"Tell me about Lord Harrington," Lazarus asked Louis. Louis had been free-spoken before, but now he just shook his head and said, "He be de masta, dats 'bout it."

Lazarus did not press. He told Louis something of himself: that he liked books; that he had crossed the ocean as a deck hand; that he had eaten sugar all his life, but never seen sugar cane until he arrived on this island. He was tempted to confide in Louis and disclose that he came to spy on slave holders. Confidences beget confidence, he thought - but he barred the thought - bad idea.

Louis willingly talked about sugar cane. The planting and ratooning season, he told Lazarus, runs from August to October. Ratoons, he said, are cane roots that grow without replanting, but require cultivation. The cane is "holed" in rectangular plots and planted over a period of months so that it can be harvested, not all at one time, but some nine to twenty months later, depending on rainfall and wind damage. Like planting, the harvesting revolves from field to field and generally takes place between January and June though, Louis said, sometimes it can be completed by May if the mills do not break down or run too far behind the cutters. The island is never completely bare of cane as, even after the harvest season, some slower growing stands remain to be cut early in the next cycle.

"Louis, you explain the sugar cane business better than any white man I have asked about it," Lazarus said.

"De buckra don't be in de field an don't cut de cane," Louis said. "De buckra don't be boilin' in de suga' house."

"Buckra?" Lazarus asked, though he thought he knew what it

meant.

"Yew be not long on dis island. De slabes calls de whites de 'buckra,'" Louis said, then he continued unprompted. As the cart passed among fields where slaves worked, Louis nodded at them and explained: The field slaves work in three gangs. The first gang is the largest and consists of the strongest workers, like Andru, though nearly as many women as men. They do the heaviest work, the hoeing, tilling, holing of squared plots for planting, planting, chopping out encroaching underbrush and the ratooning. The first gang does all the cutting of the cane.

The first gang also suffers the most injuries, as Louis told it. Field workers fall from axes, from harvesting blades Louis called "choppa," from snakes, from overseer cruelty and mostly, just from spending daylight to dark for months every year bending over. "Dis ol' boy gots some de cane back he self, so I gits me to da boilin' house."

"Cain back?" Lazarus muttered.

Louis didn't hear him. Looking back over his shoulder a little, Louis winked at Lazarus and spoke a little louder, "Andru here gine keep he's straight back. No mo' cane row fo' dat boy."

"Snakes?" asked Lazarus.

"No, snakes ain't ya trouble at all - is dey Andru? Not 'less ya calls de masta de ol' serpent."

Lazarus looked back at Andru. The boy tapped at his temple with the forefinger of one hand and pointed the other one up at Louis as he shook his head, "Not dis again, Louis," he said.

Louis grinned, he nodded back over his shoulder and said, "Now dis one growed, he be pretty-pretty, de front house boy - ain't dat so, Andru?"

Now Andru shot back, "Dat be fuh-lie, Louis - nobody be fetchin' yew from de boilin' house to serve de suppa in de big house, not wit dat bougeley ol' face."

Louis' old face grinned all the more.

"He serves in the house?" Lazarus asked.

"Not yet he don't but," Louis began to hum, "de masta say he gwine get he's try."

"Do not fling dat chune Louis!" Andru growled.

Louis glanced back at Andru and then back at the horse. "Ya be tru Andru, I bang de teet too much," he said and then he quieted.

After a few moments of no sound but the horse and squeaking cart, Lazarus asked, "What about the second cane field gang?"

Louis breathed as if relieved and continued. "Dat gang," he said, "be ol' ones, women with small ones or 'specting da chile and big chil'rens. Dey does de soft work - haulin' and spreadin' manure, firin' de underbrush an' cane stubble, stackin' de dry stalks, tendin' de fire, fetchin' de tools.

Louis described the third gang as those too feeble to do much but carry a little water from carts to thirsty workers. Many of them have crooked backs and cannot straighten – cane back. They tend oxen that pull the heavy cane carts, and they clean up chaff from mill floors.

Odd, thought Lazarus, the words "cane back" imply comfort to me, but mean something much different to Louis.

"And Betts, does she work in the field?" Lazarus asked.

"Betts done all afore," Louis said. "When she gits de chile, she leave de cane. Dat one, she gots de obeah charm - " Louis stopped. "Um ... most she nints up de sick an' de injure - when da masta leave her be."

According to Louis, one task or another kept the slaves busy in the fields except for two weeks or so about year's end and another break when a celebration is held throughout the island at cane season's end. Louis' voice peaked and his eyes sparkled when he spoke of the harvest festival. He said it most often occurred in late June or in July. "De masta calls it de 'crop-ober,' but I calls it de 'ka-doo' ... 'cause dis ol boy be showin' he ka-doo de cane one mo' time." Louis half sang the ka-doo part.

If the field work were not enough, sugar slaves also labored at heavy tasks in the mills and boiling houses. Louis said he was a "boiler" and that afforded him some privileges denied to others. It was skilled work, but if he made a mistake and cooked the juice from the squeezed cane too long, too hot or too little, it could be costly and he would be punished severely.

Harrington Plantation is one of the island's largest, with nearly a thousand acres, Louis said proudly. Six hundred acres are planted with cane, but some land is devoted to Lord Harrington's stables and horse pastures, to other livestock, to Harrington Hall and its out buildings and to gardens. The slave village, including a small vegetable garden for each chattel house and outdoor kitchens all occupy some of the plantation, Louis said. A few acres are just not usable, he explained, "Ya seed some dem lands by de light o' de moon."

Louis estimated that Lord Harrington held more than 300 slaves, field slaves, mill slaves and boiling house slaves. "One field han' fo' two acres o' cane," said Louis. Lazarus shook his head. Slave ships count slaves per ton capacity of the vessel, he thought; here, sugar cane slavers count them by the acre.

But there were still more slaves to be counted. Lord Harrington had a number, maybe 30, Louis said, that were "house slabes." Not all of those work in the house, though a number do. "Some," said Louis, "helps da Masta entertain he's guests." Then he quickly added that several cleaned and constantly polished Harrington Hall and its contents, others worked in the stables, keeping the grounds, in the kitchen and in Lord Harrington's own gardens.

Louis talked freely now, so Lazarus risked asking more about his master. "How does he treat his slaves?"

Louis changed his demeanor immediately. He stared at Lazarus as if to charge that he already had his answer. "I mean, he takes the women, but what of the field gangs?" Lazarus asked.

"He be sharp if dey be stiff er talks back. He's boss mens, too. Keep de mout shut, dat be de way to keeps de whip off de back o' dis ol boy," Louis said. "De women he takes as it please him, field slabe or house slabe. De ones he fancy most he put in de house. Betts be in de house 'til Gootie chile, but de masta fetched her up to de house some mo' 'til dis new chile be comin'."

"What happened to her teeth?" Lazarus said, assuming that chewing too much sugar cane could not account for missing every tooth.

"Dis be jes fo' ya ear and not fo' ya mout, Mr. Laza," Louis was somber now. Lazarus understood, he promised not to repeat what Louis was about to tell him. "Betts, she bite de masta's man dickey when he be foopin' she mout," Louis said. "De masta got some dem teets an she eye too wit he's temper," Louis said, then he lowered his voice and turned toward Lazarus, "den he taked de rest o' she teets fo' he's pleasure. Den de masta say to Betts, 'See if dose teets bites me now.'"

Louis could not mean what Lazarus thought he had heard, but the slave's voice and his eyes told Lazarus he had heard correctly.

"Have you ever thought of running away?" Lazarus asked.

Louis shook his head. "Runnin', dat jes' breen de woe." He moved his hand out in a sweeping motion. "Dey ain't no place to run on dis island – aside, cane bees all dis ole boy do," he said. "I seed de slabes run afo' - dey gits catched. When dey catches me, only bad tings gwine ta happen."

"What would happen?"

"Den - den de masta beat me good or else he sell me to de bad masta."

"The bad master? There are masters worse than Lord Harrington?" Lazarus asked.

Louis looked at him, then back at the road, "Load Harrington ain't de worse masta dey is if ya bees a cane boy - an stays out he's house, an dats de troot." Louis took a deep sigh, then spoke lowly, "He be beatin some an kilt some what despecs him, but he leave dem be what keeps dey eyes on de ground."

As if to qualify his opinion, Louis said, "Mebbe some dem town boys gots it easy, but not de suga boys. Been tole de gangs wit de oberseers be like libin' wit de debil when dey mastas be gone." Louis leaned in and Lazarus felt an elbow at his ribs and a whisper on his ear, "Some de boss mans drinks de rums."

Lazarus smiled, the old horse walked as slow as a man in his rum. He was glad of it. This singing man beside him had not only rescued him from the bougainvillea, in just an hour he had schooled Lazarus in the life of sugar slaves. Lazarus placed a hand lightly on Louis' back. "Thank you again for aiding me – and for your trust," he said. "I think you are a stronger man than I … I could not work the cane fields or the boiling house."

Louis looked at him for a moment, then he turned back to the road and with the hint of a smile he said, "Mista Laza, ya could so. Dey is tricks to it."

"Tricks?" said Lazarus. "What tricks?"

"When de boss man speak, keeps de eyes low an de mout shut. Move when he say, but hold yo pace. Sings de songs ebery day an dance 'neat de moon fo' Ob'tala and de gods. Dat be de way fo de cane boy," Louis said with confidence. Then he turned toward the back of the cart, "Eyes on de ground, Andru. Do not forget boy, eyes on de ground."

Louis drew back - suddenly quiet now and stomped his foot

where it rested. "Blasted - I be lickin' dis mout no end. If I gits trouble, dat fa' like dis ol' mout." He took a finger and thumb, and pinched his lips together.

"I think I understand – you are worried you have told me too much," Lazarus said calmly.

Louis nodded and looked sideways at him.

Lazarus touched Louis' arm, looking directly at him. "Have no fear, Louis, have no fear." He then lifted his hand and put a raised first finger on his own lips with a pronounced "ssshhhh" and a nod.

Louis smiled his big smile again.

The cart arrived near the edge of Bridgetown, and Louis pulled up the horse. He looked Lazarus in the eye as if he were not used to meeting the eyes of white men, but wanted Lazarus to seal the secrets the two men shared. Lazarus returned the stare and again nodded a knowing acceptance. Then Lazarus climbed down from the cart, favoring an ankle.

Louis handed down the crutch and grip sack. "Ya be needin' dis fo' awhile," he said. Handsome Andru hopped up to Lazarus' cart seat and the two men turned about and headed back up the same roadway, apparently forgetting their errands.

Chapter 29. Jodhpurs

His fall over the bougainvillea covered cliff did not leave any serious injury, but for a few days more Lazarus ached and his body still seemed weary from the shock of so many little lacerations. He tended to himself with honey, cold tea stirred in his cup, bed rest and a pungent amber colored salve which he dabbed on with his finger tips from a cup with no handle Betts had sneaked into his grip sack. As the swelling in his ankle receded, he began to take slow, short walks around Bridgetown. For the moment, he had enjoyed quite enough of the cane field countryside.

Lazarus measured his exertion. He did manage a letter to Mr. Clarkson, addressed as always to Mrs. Symmons. This time it took the form of an affidavit. As he finished it, he knew that he had lied to Betts and to Louis. He would tell someone of his adventure and particularly of the village of slaves - where a British Lord sired many of the children, and even removed teeth for his pleasure. That someone, though, would be 4,000 miles across an ocean and would use the information in opposing the slave trade. Lazarus did not count it a betrayal. The clerk at the Packet Agency readily witnessed Lazarus' signature, and that he had sworn to the veracity of the affidavit. He melted a rust colored wax and embossed his seal, all without requiring disclosure of the document's contents.

Mr. Clarkson, Lazarus knew, tried to cull the best quality evidence of the cruelest acts and most onerous practices of the slavers for presentation by Mr. Wilberforce to the House of Commons. Mr. Wilberforce preferred live witnesses when he could get them. He also favored evidence that the slave trade damaged not only the slaves, but those engaged in it and the British nation as a whole. In their attempt to inundate law makers and British society with proof of slavery's abomination, the abolitionists used a broad array of evidence in ongoing dialogue with members of Parliament and opinion leaders. This could often be done without disclosing the identity of the informant. To indicate the accuracy of the report, Mr. Clarkson liked to say that he had it "on sworn affidavit." An affidavit meant that the informant subjected himself to a charge of perjury if the information proved false. The slave lobby could not dismiss it as rumor. Lazarus' affidavit did not provide a first-hand account, but it was recent and came from Barbados which had not supplied much evidence. It is good evidence, Lazarus thought, even if not "exact."

Lazarus checked at the waterfront for slave ships. One had just departed for the leeward islands, reported the harbor chief, after selling only a small number of its Africans at Bridgetown. No others were at port. He cut out some breeches for himself to replace the ones torn in his fall. He saved the heavy gray weave for the patrons he hoped to have and used the sailcloth left from Lord Harrington's jodhpurs.

On the fifth day back in Bridgetown, as he shopped for a teakettle along Roebuck Street, Lazarus noticed Lord Harrington approaching him on horseback. He made a smart horseman with new gray jodhpurs that looked to Lazarus out of place in the town. Lord Harrington spotted Lazarus and pulled up but did not dismount. He inquired as to the location of Lazarus' shop and arranged to call there later that morning.

Lazarus hurried back to his shop without the teakettle. He tidied the place and tried to make it look as prosperous as possible. When Lord Harrington did call, Lazarus pretended he had been in the process of pinning a vest.

"Thank you for timely delivery of my jodhpurs," Lord Harrington said, "but you failed to submit your bill of account. I cannot bear indebtedness to any man, we must settle."

"I beg your pardon," Lazarus said. He did not know what fee to charge. He knew Mordecai's charges, but this was not London and he was not a master tailor. He quickly calculated the cost of the fabric and his supplies. He considered Mordecai's usual charge for breeches. "The jodhpurs are four shillings, six if they will suffice."

"Suffice?" said Lord Harrington, "they are just as I hoped. The heavier light colored pair even better. They are most sturdy and will suit well save perhaps in the heat of August."

"You did not order but the one pair," said Lazarus, "the second pair was a trial, please accept them with my compliments."

"Nonsense," said Lord Harington, "I shall pay twice your price; let me see, four shillings and six pence doubled comes to nine shillings. Let us make it ten shillings, fully half a pound, and at that I am sure I have the better of the bargain."

"Thank you Lord Harrington, but that is not necessary," Lazarus said. "If you wish to reward me for the second pair, may I have your reference rather than your coin?"

"Pardon me," Lord Harrington said, "but you are a peculiar lad for a Jew. I am afraid I do not understand you."

Lazarus ignored the implied slander and explained, "I know you to be a gentleman of considerable importance in Bridgetown and among the parishes. I am new here and young. It would be of benefit to me to advise those I seek as patrons that I have sewn for you and that you were pleased ... well at least satisfied, with my efforts."

Lord Harrington smiled broadly. "Why, yes, you may certainly have my reference to that purpose. Perhaps you are shrewd after all." Then he stopped and looked about the shop. "You could use a boost no doubt. I have an idea - a proposition for you." Lazarus looked expectantly at him and he continued, "Each January, just before the cane harvest begins, I entertain the gentlemen of the turf association at Harrington Hall. It is a grand dinner. I am told it compares to the finest of feasts served anywhere. Several horsemen of Saint Michael Parish attend. They also come from Christ Church on the south and a number from the north leeward parishes, as far as St. Peter. They are select friends of the oldest and most prosperous planter families. They stay on for two or, if they like, three days as my guests. We talk of horses, plantation affairs, and our petitions to mother England. In the mornings we ride."

The more Lord Harrington talked the more excited he became. "In the evenings we entertain ourselves. We play at darts, draughts, backgammon, cards or chess. I confess that there is gambling, good spirits and companionship." Lord Harrington placed emphasis on the word "companionship."

Lord Harrington paused, he had gotten carried away and he could see Lazarus' head was swimming trying to imagine it all. He lowered his voice. "Each year I also present a person skilled in matters of interest to horsemen. Our skilled guest provides instruction or services. This year we were to have the company of retired Major Francis Gildart. Major Gildart served in His Majesty's Light Dragoons." Lord Harrington rolled his eyes a little and said, "Unfortunately, the Major, God rest his soul, had the bad manners to break his neck in a fall while riding near Mount Misery three weeks past ... loss of a beautiful stallion as well, I am afraid. The man survived a career of armed campaigns and then died while out exercising his mount on a peaceful Sunday morning. I thought it too late to obtain a replacement, but you - you might do ... and gain a patron or two if you would care to attend my guests."

Lazarus had never sat upon a horse. "But I do not ride," he admitted.

"Aahhh, yes, but you do sew," Lord Harrington replied as he pulled at one leg of his jodhpurs. "Bring your tape - you may obtain some orders."

Lazarus could not believe his ears. What good fortune, he thought. Then he remembered the bougainvillea and decided his fortune was in balance.

He readily accepted the invitation and noted the date. He thanked Lord Harrington and both excited men forgot the payment for the jodhpurs. Whether four shillings six or half a pound, it remained in Lord Harrington's purse.

Chapter 30.   Pandy

Lord Harrington did not exaggerate. Lazarus had never seen a feast like the one spread before him in the room with the painting of the first Lord Harrington. A long linen-covered table now spanned the room from side to side. He knew none of the guests present. He did not even recognize several of the preparations on the table. No matter - Lord Harrington, in his manner, stood at the far end of the table, facing Lazarus, and introduced the guests. By their familiars with one another though, Lazarus could tell that he was the only stranger in the room.

"We are pleased to call Mr. Leland Mayford our neighbor," Lord Harrington said, extending an open hand to the first gentlemen on his right. "It is our pleasure to have ridden this morning with Sir Ian Adamson, a fine horseman and our friend." The words "we" and "our" utilized by Lord Harrington this evening seemed as much the regal as the plural.

He tapped his glass with a spoon and waited until he had full attention. He moved his upturned hand toward the next gentleman without actually pointing at him. "None of us would share the good fortune we have known these years without the able efforts of Lord Wallace Pennington who has managed our petitions to Parliament and made passage to his London home each year to assist the West Indies lobby in their efforts on our behalf. Thank you dear Lord Pennington for joining us this evening." Polite applause had followed each introduction, but hearty clapping and cheers welcomed Lord Pennington. He tipped his head to acknowledge the appreciation.

Perhaps it was fortunate, Lazarus told himself, that Mr. Clarkson kept me toiling away at 18 Old Jewry Street and did not often let me go to Westminster during the parliamentary sessions. Had I frequented Westminster, my face might have become familiar to Lord Pennington, Barbados' own member of the slave lobby.

Lazarus looked along the table. There were six men on each side with himself and Lord Harrington at the ends. Mr. Denis Lyman, Lord Ernest Gilbert and Lord Rodney Swain completed one side of the table. After the first six were introduced, Lord Harrington omitted Lazarus and next introduced Mr. Abner Doland, seated to Lazarus' right.

Lazarus became anxious and wondered why Lord Harrington had skipped over him. He thought he had been invited. Indeed, the old tortoise had taken his cloak and sample case upon his arrival and said they would be placed in the corner room, third on the right from the top of the stairs - Lazarus could retire there when he grew ready. As he had slowly seated Lazarus at this place nearest the room's entry, the old servant had even indicated that Lord Harrington had designated this particular seat at the table for Lazarus. Yes, Lazarus was certain he was invited.

As the heated food cooled, Lord Harrington completed his introductions working his way back toward himself. "Our gathering would be incomplete without the presence of Mr. Allen Hindsall. Mr. Hindsall has favored us again this year with two kegs of fine rum from his Christ Church distillery." This drew renewed applause. "If you should fall ill next year or your dear wife keeps you at home, please advise us Mr. Hindsall for we should miss you indeed," said Lord Harrington. "We shall also forthwith send down to fetch up your rum, but we shall miss you." Lazarus would have laughed with the others were he not thinking on why he had been overlooked.

"Mr. Chester Phipps also bestows on us the pleasure of his company this evening," Lord Harrington continued. "I see we also have the pleasure of his spoon already in the carrot pudding - please be patient a little longer Chester, if you can." Phipps was a round faced old man with a flat, upturned nose that exposed his large nostrils. He snorted and his chins vibrated as the others laughed lightly. George Creighton, "Baron of North Saint Michael" sat next in order, followed by Mr. Norman Hindergast and, finally, Lord Arthur Cockrell.

What a gathering, Lazarus thought. He knew that in the prior century, nearly twenty early English planters on Barbados had been knighted by the crown. A half dozen more were recognized with baronies. While Barons ranked the lowest among the English peerage, Lazarus knew they were British nobles nonetheless. He had read that the descendants of most of the island's nobility had since relocated back to England, leaving their plantation estates in the care of trustees and overseers. Of the noble families remaining on the island, Lazarus believed that most of them were represented at this table. Here among them sat a common English boy and a Jew at that.

The room buzzed with light conversation. Then Lord Harrington, still standing, extended his left hand at one side of the table faire and called out to be heard over all, "Now to our feast." Then in rapid succession he called out, "Here we have sweet potato soup, roast lamb, fried flying fish, carrot pudding, island citrus, kidney beans with onions, stewed fish from St. Lucy, asparagus, Bajan black cake, boiled leek and apple chutney." Then he extended his right hand toward the opposite side and said, "This is kidney pie, roast fowl - but not as foul as Baron Creighton's flatulent gray gelding - giblet gravy, cous cous, radishes, rice and peas, real English cheddar, and near the young man at the far end, roast pork, steamed mussels and crabs."

As if waiting for the moment, four servants entered the room from behind Lazarus and two marched along either side of the table behind the seated guests. Each young man was costumed much like the old tortoise. Two carried glass carafes with flared lips in each hand. The other two carried a large pitcher resting on the palm of one hand while the other hand clutched its neck. "These attendants" said Lord Harrington, "will pour for you Hindsall House Rum, ale, Madeira wine, juniper gin, punch or good old Bajan swank."

Lazarus looked up at the attendants. Three were young creoles. The fourth, an African, was Andru. Andru stood stiffly and his face showed discomfort. He was obviously new to this duty. Lazarus nodded almost imperceptibly to Andru. If he noticed the gesture, Andru did not acknowledge it.

Lord Harrington took a deep breath now and launched in again. "Now gentlemen, it has been my pleasure at each of our annual fore-harvest gatherings to bring to Harrington Hall a guest expert in horsemanship or horse keeping." Lazarus now felt all eyes fixed on him. "Last year a Spanish riding instructor spent two days with us." Lazarus feared what Lord Harrington might say next.

"Despite his instruction," Lord Harrington said, "our ride this morning confirmed that several of us still encounter difficulty finding our 'seat.' Am I correct, Chester?" The men laughed loudly now.

"You may have noticed that a young man has joined us here at the table. May I present Mr. Perlman, a craftsman, new from

London. Many of you admired my breeches from India during our ride this morning," Lord Harrington proclaimed. "Actually, the originals given to me by the Governor of Bengal are worn through. This young man made the ones I wore today. He is prepared to serve you and will be roomed here in Harrington Hall these few days. If any of you wish to seek his assistance as to your riding attire, please do so at your leisure. I do believe this tailor may help any one find his 'seat.'" Now grunts and feigned coughs proved the guests understood the pun. "I warn you, though," said Lord Harrington, "be cautious if you discuss your wardrobe with him over a chessboard."

His preliminaries complete, Lord Harrington spread his arms "Gentlemen," he said, "to your plates." As he sat to dine, he fixed his gaze on Lazarus, "Mr. Perlman, from what I have seen of the 'seats' of these fellows, you may be kept busy for some time. I suggest you take sustenance while you are able. Will someone please offer our tailor some of the pork and shell fish on the table there near him?"

Lord Harrington laughed a little at his own joke. Most of the guests joined him, perhaps out of courtesy, because Lazarus sensed that few of them understood Jewish dietary restrictions. Mr. Phipps defended his riding and his breeches. Then he slopped gobs of food onto his plate, stirred it all together and devoured it in large gulps.

Lazarus could not fathom Lord Harrington. His humor was harmless if unamusing and his speech was perfect. These men likely would not dine with a Jew as equal, but as their servant none seemed to object. Lord Harrington was almost charming. Lazarus knew him to exploit slaves and abuse women. How could he be the same witty man entertaining this evening?

Lazarus ate only vegetables. He did try the Madeira since he recalled that Captain Graves had treasured it. He did not know whether it was good or bad, but it made him lightheaded.

After dinner, led by its host, the group retired across the hallway into the equally large room with the red and green maharajai. Now there were more chairs and more games. Lazarus doubted he was welcomed to join the play. He stood quietly by himself near the doorway, but to one side so as not to interfere with the busy wine attendants. Andru stationed himself two or three steps to Lazarus' left. Maybe he did recognize Lazarus. From his station, Andru kept his eyes low, but just so he could see a guest signaling for more of his rum punch.

By twos and fours games commenced. Baron Creighton approached Lazarus briefly and arranged to be measured for a pair of jodhpurs the following afternoon. Corpulent old Mr. Phipps stepped up, purposely raised his double chin and walked away to signal his disregard. Lord Cockrell approached Lazarus and inquired about the latest fashions for London gentlemen. Lazarus knew little but answered from his memory of the clothing worn by Mr. Sharp and the other members of the Abolition Society who were neither Quaker nor clergy. He quickly turned the conversation to admiration of Lord Cockrell's attire. Cockrell's frilly blouse shined like silk and his breeches fit tightly. The man clearly took pains with his appearance. Sometime later, Mr. Doland said he would like to discuss Indian riding breeches after the group ride the following morning.

As the attendants poured, the men grew louder and soon wagers floated about the room. The wealth of these slave holders, if measured by their friendly bets, staggered Lazarus. One lost the spring foal of his prize mare at cards. Mr. Phipps seemed to offer the grandest wagers to his most inebriated comrades.

There arose a clamor at the far end of the room as Lord Swain lost his creole blacksmith to Mr. Phipps on a roll of dice. Lazarus thought that the wagers were becoming excessive. Lord Harrington may have thought the same, Lazarus decided, for he interrupted the games and reviewed accommodations for the night. Lazarus and five more were to stay in the mansion house. The others were to sleep in guest cottages around to the north side of the house. Then the host instructed that glasses be refilled and offered a toast, "God save George the Third, by the grace of God, King of Great Britain and Ireland and of this British soil of Barbados, the first of his royal colonies in the West Indies."

"God save King George," the guests chanted in unison.

"God save his Queen, Charlotte-Sophia of Mecklinburg-Strelitz," proffered Lord Harrington.

"God save Queen Charlotte" all concurred.

"Raise your glasses to the noble horsemen of Barbados," neighbor Mayford proposed, "may they long ride this island turf."

"Hear, hear, to be sure," several guests rejoined.

Mr. Hindsall stepped forward, "Drink now to rum and to sweet muscavado sugar," he said, "may our barrels flow abroad as smoothly as our island rum meets the palate."

"May it always be so," spoke Lord Pennington. He offered forth his glass and added, "and may Mr. William Wilberforce, sitting on his high horse in the House of Commons, be blessed with boils on his arse."

Lazarus had feigned a sip at each toast. Now, as the sniggers erupted, he merely moved his glass a bit without really raising it past his chin.

"Yes indeed," said Lord Harrington, "and may we enjoy a fruitful harvest of the cane this year of our Lord 1793!" All joined in, including Lazarus. Lord Harrington, though, was not finished. "We may all be too engaged to enjoy our island's bounty within a few days. Perhaps this evening's pleasures will ease the days to come."

At this he drew congratulations, thanks and praise. "Since, you have managed to tolerate the evening so far, may I trust you will enjoy one final treat." Lord Harrington smiled broadly as he said it. He raised his glass still once more and motioned to the doorway with his free hand, "To the dark ladies of Barbados, may they comfort your loneliness and keep you company in your good health." As he then drank, a parade of slave women walked in line to the center of the room. Each was attired in the modest dress of an English woman. A pannier overskirt, each of the same design, scalloped and open at the front, had been tied around the waist of each woman to make her simple dress look more like a fuller, layered gown. The women were mostly very young. As they entered, two especially young ones tried to hang back, but were pulled along by their sisters.

Lord Harrington only thought his toast to be the final one. "To the ladies of Harrington Plantation," said Lord Cockrell, sounding quite proper.

" … and to full lips and ready hips," added old Chester Phipps as his belly and his chins all shook together in a nasty laugh and the others either laughed a little or rolled their eyes at him a bit.

Lord Harrington again took the floor. In line he introduced "Vivian, Clarice and Margaret." Next he held an open palm out toward Rebecca, Charlotte, Abigail and Penelope. Most of the women dipped a slight courtesy as they heard their names called. A few stood with blank stares. "This new young lady is Emily," Lord Harrington said as he stepped a little down the line, "and this one is Sarah. Here we have Marion and beside her, Miss Priscilla." Priscilla was a slight and especially dark girl. Her white eyes shone and her lips were pursed.

Andru stood to the left of Lazarus with his eyes cast heavily on the floor. As he heard the name "Priscilla" he looked up immediately and choked. He covered the choke with a light cough so that none but Lazarus took notice.

Lord Harrington completed his stroll down the line of girls pointing in turn to Caroline, Pandora, Victoria, Emma and Anne. As he did, Lazarus saw that Priscilla caught sight of Andru. Her eyes looked pleadingly at him and he looked back, but finally hunched his shoulders slowly and then looked back at the floor. It looked to Lazarus that both had water in their eyes.

"Where is Elizabeth?" old Chester drunkenly blurted.

"Elizabeth expects a child," said Lord Harrington. Then with feigned austerity he said, "You have not been coming 'round my south camp this year, have you Chester?"

"No," Phipps spewed, "but if you wish to es - extend an in - inbitation I shall be happy to oblige you. Remember dear Harrington, ev - every slave bred is one less to be bought and pa - paid for."

Lord Harrington cleared his throat and changed the subject - well at least the tone. "This year we shall select in order of property from north to south. Dear Mr. Hindsall, enjoy your rum. As you chose first last year, this time we shall require your patience. I believe you and your St. Peter's fellow there have the honor," he said, nodding toward Mr. Lyman.

Two men stepped forward, each to a lady in line and offered her his arm. Then the two couples strolled slowly back toward the perimeter of the room as each man began some low conversation with his companion. Lazarus took a quick count. Excluding the attendants, there were two more girls in the room than men, three more without himself.

Chester Phipps cried out, "I be next then." He staggered forward and grabbed Priscilla by the arm and jerked her toward the doors. She turned her head as she passed by Andru with pleading eyes.

She spoke one weak word, "Andru."

Andru was wide-eyed now and could not seem to help but cry out "Prissy," as he dropped his pitcher, splashing all about with his punch. He jumped forward, grabbed Priscilla's arm with one muscled hand and tore old Chester's hand away with the other. Chester moved to stop him as did Lord Harrington who shouted Andru's name. Andru paused for only a second. He looked straight in the eyes of Chester and Lord Harrington then down at Priscilla. The two men stepped to front him, and he swung one big arm knocking old Chester flat out on his back and rolling along the floor.

Lord Harrington sternly called "Andru" at him again and grabbed at his arm. This time, without hesitation, Andru threw his master aside with the sweep of an arm. Lord Harrington fell against two guests who managed to catch him just enough to break his fall as he reached the floor at their feet.

As Andru and Priscilla ran from the room, Lord Harrington was uprighted, and he walked rapidly out after them. Shouted words could be heard in the hallway and a heavy door slammed and shook the manor house.

All were suddenly silent in the game room. The slave girls dressed as English ladies stood with open mouths. Within a few moments, Lord Harrington slowly reentered the room. He was disheveled, red faced and he apologized to his guests.

"That boy needs a lesson," Lord Swain offered.

"I demand he be pun - punished," drunken Chester Phipps shouted, still struggling to his feet.

"I assure you that he will not go unpunished," Lord Harrington declared. Then he straightened himself a bit, caught his breath and said, "Please gentlemen, you have all seen rebellious slaves before tonight. No doubt you have owned one or two yourselves."

Guests grunted their agreement.

"Please do not let my discourteous attendant ruin your evening," Lord Harrington said, signaling the remaining three attendants to refill glasses. "Now, where were we?"

The next while seemed most awkward to Lazarus as, now a little more reluctantly, guests paired themselves with slave girls. Chester Phipps found himself another, older girl. Two couples left the room with the male partner politely asking that they be excused, apparently to retire for the evening. At the end, Rebecca stood by

Lord Harrington and three women remained in the center of the room. All were paired except Lord Cockrell. He gave a little bow and took the arms of two of the women, one with each hand. Lord Harrington, now seemingly recovered from his earlier humiliation, hunched a shoulder and nodded his approval. That left one conspicuous, skinny girl standing alone. Lord Harrington looked about and his eye caught Lazarus still at the edge of the room. "Please, be my guest," Lord Harrington said to Lazarus and he motioned Lazarus toward the skinny girl with a nod of his head.

Lazarus had neither expected nor desired this. After a brief silence he said, "You are most thoughtful, but I think I should decline ... thank you."

"Come now," said Lord Cockrell, "be a sport young man."

Lazarus looked at the girl. Her unruly hair rebelled against the coif imposed on it. Her thin body and face were unremarkable except that her lips were either thin or pressed together tightly and her eyelids did not fully open over her large oval eyes. This gave her the appearance of being sleepy though awake. She stood rigidly, with arms straight at her side. She had narrow hips and appeared to have the thighs of a boy. Her form provided little to indicate she was a woman except small conical breasts that pushed against the too tight bodice of her gown. She looked to Lazarus to be as embarrassed as he was, but he could not tell if she were relieved to go unmatched or forlorn to go unclaimed.

Lord Cockrell momentarily released the two arms he held and walked over to Lazarus. With rum heavy on his breath he stood too close and whispered, "She is the last of the litter tailor, but do not despair. Lord Harrington trains them to please. This one may be boney, but I know women and let me tell you, they all look the same in the dark." Lazarus did not reply and Lord Cockrell unsteadily backed away, reclaimed the two arms and began to move them toward the door.

Lord Harrington now looked the impatient host. He seemed desirous of retiring himself if he could just get his guests to do so. He walked about the room with Rebecca in tow, reminding his guests that the morning ride would commence an hour after sunrise. "Tomorrow we climb to the highlands and Mount Misery. Rest well and ready yourselves horsemen, the long eastern trail requires strength."

When he came to Lazarus, he paused just long enough to throw his eyes toward the lone girl still motionless at the room's center and say, "I regret she is not to your liking, Mr. Perlman, would you have preferred a boy?"

This took Lazarus off guard. "No," he said, "it is just that I, well - well, perhaps just some conversation and punch." Then he hesitantly stepped toward the girl and she readily took his arm. Lazarus and the thin girl stepped slowly to a far corner of the room without speaking. He removed her hand from his sleeve and obtained a glass of punch for her. He apologized for not recalling her name.

"I be Pandora," she said, "but most dey calls me Pandy. I know who yew be - Mista Laza."

"Yes, indeed" said Lazarus, astonished that she knew him. "But how do you - "

"I seed ya at Betts' house. Most de billage know who yew be … Louis, he sing yo song all de day."

"My song?" Lazarus' jaw dropped.

"Yes, ya know –" then she turned her back to the room and hummed slowly a little under her breath …

> *"Mista Laza los' he's way*
> *Into de bougain he do stray*
> *He tumble and he snap de tine,*
> *He roll all up into de bine.*
> *Betts she wrap him up so fine*
> *Out o' he skin she pull de spine*
> *Mista Laza los' he's way*
> *May-bee he come back some day."*

Pandy's voice was soft but not weak. Lazarus did not know how to react. He could not help but smile, and they laughed a little quietly together. When Pandy smiled, her eyelids rose a little more; and her lips seem to fill and turn up at the corners, showing straight white teeth. Her smile also immediately produced a most endearing feature not at all noticeable until then - her cheeks sank into deep dimples that transformed her face from plain to quite pretty.

Pandy said that she knew Lazarus to be a tailor. She seemed to admire him for that fact and said she could sew some herself when she could obtain the thread. Unexpectedly, Lazarus enjoyed her simple conversation and within a short time he felt more at ease with her than in speaking with any of the men in the room.

As the room slowly began to clear, Lazarus determined that he should not keep Lord Harrington waiting. He took Pandora's thin hand, looked at her slender fingers and then awkwardly shook it in a gentleman's clasp. He told her that he found her delightful and enjoyed speaking with her. "Thank you, too, for singing Louis' song for me."

Then he wished her good evening and turned to go. As he neared the door, he noticed that she followed right behind him. He turned and said, "I suppose you are free to retire Miss Pandora. Perhaps we shall meet again some time."

She frowned at him and crooked her head a bit. "Ya does not want me in yo bed?"

Her directness paralyzed Lazarus for an instant. His throat felt tight and he took a slow deep breath. "It is not that you, um ... what I mean to say is that you ... I mean - it is not required." Now when he turned to leave, he made certain that she stayed behind. He walked up the stairs to his guest room. He did not sleep for some time, but when he did, he did not dream of drowning.

After he had slept a while, he stirred and thought there was someone in the room with him. Before he could sit up, he felt someone sit lightly on the edge of the bed. He blinked his eyes and squinted. Given to vivid dreams, he did not know if he saw a shadow or an illusion. He cleared his throat and started to speak. "What are you - " Fingers pressed against his lips and stopped him. He saw beyond them in the dark to the outline of a face - it was Pandy.

"De Masta say 'it is require,'" she whispered. As Lazarus lay on his back, she leaned down and kissed him softly on his neck, sending a tingle throughout him. She moved her hands down his chest and rubbed his sides through his nightshirt, pulling down his bed cover as she went.

He could not do this. She was a slave directed by her master to please him. That is not how it should be, not how he had envisioned it. He was here to benefit slaves, not to take advantage.

Pandy reached the hem of his nightshirt and now moved her hands against the bare skin of his thighs. He almost jumped, and she rubbed harder as if to calm him. Then she slid her hands up his body. He closed his eyes and tried to think on how to end this. He would do so … in just a few moments more.

He breathed deeply. She released him and stood over him. In a smooth almost single motion she lifted her gown up over her head and threw it aside. Lazarus could see the protruding nipples of her sharp little breasts, and he sighed involuntarily. She bent down a little, took both his wrists and placed his hands on her warm, soft cones. He squeezed a little and felt himself stiffen.

Now she knelt on the bed and threw one leg over him. She lay full on him, squirmed a little, and moved his nightshirt up under his chin and quickly over his head. He could now feel her skin on the length of his body. It transcended any dream he had ever had. Both Pandy and Lazarus breathed very deeply, but neither spoke. She kissed his ear with her open mouth, then she pushed herself up and sat straddling him. She reached down, held and rubbed him up and down against herself. Pandy then took a deep sigh; she rose up a little and held him with one hand and herself with the other as she slid down upon him. Lazarus told himself that he must not … he would not … he could not … he could not stop.

Pandy rocked just a little up and down on him, very slowly at first and then with a little more movement. Lazarus just lay there, tight as a violin string, and took her movements. He shuddered and gave up any thought of telling her to stop.

A few minutes later, without thinking about it or intending to do so, he found himself arching his back and thrusting his hips skyward each time Pandy lowered herself on him. He knew he was now completely beyond restraint and he did not care. At that moment he was gladly her slave and she his master. In just a few thrusts more he made a little "aaahhh" cry aloud and positioned himself with arched back for several seconds jerking in seizure. Pandy now moved wildly on him and rocked forward throwing herself upon his chest. She straightened her legs, slid downward and almost ground herself into him and panted "iieee, oooh, oooh, ohwaaa." Lazarus could feel his heart beating inside her and hers throbbing around him. He lunged up several more times and then collapsed with her breasts nipple to nipple upon him and her open mouth wet and panting against his neck.

Neither of them moved for several minutes. Then Pandy gently lifted her hips as he fell from her. She slid just a little to one side, still touching him from her cheek to her toes. They matched breaths in a slow recovery, and without a word both fell asleep.

Chapter 31. The Fish-Boning Knife

Lazarus woke to a ruckus in the distance outside the window. He felt then looked for Pandy, but she was not there. He had slept well and long. He again heard men talking in strained voices. He rolled to his right, sat upright on the edge of the bed and breathed in the musky fragrance of his night with Pandy. He rubbed his eyes and stretched as he stepped to the rear window and parted the drapery.

He squinted against the low, early sun coming directly in from the east. He looked away from the light and could see a part of the slave village off to his right. Off to his left and well to the rear of the manor house sat some short buildings and to their right a railed paddock. Several horses stood about the paddock, bridled, saddled and tied to the railing by their reins. Two black men stood back by the horses, as if awaiting instruction. His eyes began to adjust to the bright light and he shaded them with a hand. To the right of the paddock and just left of the rising sun stood the tallest kapok tree he had ever seen. It had few leaves and those were high up and gathered in clusters near the ends of branches. Its pale gray buttressed trunk grabbed the ground like a giant fist.

A black man was thrust up with his back against the largest knuckle of the fist and his arms outstretched as if bound to the trunk behind him. The man faced in Lazarus' direction as did two burly men, one at either side of him. A group of a dozen or so men half encircled the tree facing the trunk and the black man against it. Two or three at the center of the group moved about and raised hands in the air. Even at this distance, Lazarus could see that the men were dressed in riding costumes and that the tall man at the center of the group wore flare-legged jodhpurs.

Lazarus threw on his clothes, ran fingers through his hair and surged out into the hall and against the stair rail. He loped down the broad stairway and straight out the front door of Harrington Hall. He ran at a canter to his left around the house. Coming around the rear corner of the big house he again caught site of the scene under the kapok tree. Out of the corner of his left eye he saw steps from the rear of the house telling him that he had not taken the shortest route. The ancient mulatto, in his usual costume, stood on the rear steps craning his neck to see the gathering back beneath the kapok tree. Lazarus slowed to a hurried walk but came up behind the men at the tree within a minute.

He had not been invited to this gathering, so he stayed back but moved off to the right so he could see the base of the giant tree and the men there. The black man on the tree trunk was young Andru. In his attentions toward Pandy the night before, Lazarus had all but forgotten about handsome Andru. He looked wild-eyed and angered now as he struggled against the lines that wrapped and leaned him back against the giant trunk. He gritted his teeth, and his nostrils flared. He panted as if he had been running, and his skin shined. Lazarus had never seen the two burly men, one white, one mulatto, who seemed to stand guard at either side as if to assure that Andru did not break free and attack the dozen men who faced him.

Those men, the noble horsemen of Barbados, did not seem to notice Lazarus but were either fixated on Andru or engaged in debate about what action to take. Lord Harrington spoke above them, addressing Andru. "Where is Priscilla?" he demanded. No answer came from Andru. "Speak up boy or you will regret it," Lord Harrington said.

"Flog him," said Mr. Adamson, as he whip-snapped a horse rag in his hand.

Andru snorted like a stallion and mucus trailed from his nose.

"You will tell me or pay your price," Lord Harrington said. Andru stopped his struggle and stared defiantly at Lord Harrington.

"This is a fine tree for a hanging," said Mr. Lyman.

"He thinks he is a ladies man," grunted fat Chester Phipps. From a safe distance, he shook a black riding crop toward Andru and shouted, "I say we castrate him."

Lord Harrington looked askance at his guests and shook his head. "This one may not make a house boy, but he has become one of my best cane cutters," he said. "If I can break him, he will sire some fine additions for my cutting gang."

"A fair point," said Lord Pennington, "cutters born to it fare better than new blood from Africa. They have no memory of running free or of capture."

Lord Harrington seemed to deliberate while the horsemen argued Lord Pennington's point. Lord Harrington turned back to his right, glanced at Lazarus as he turned, then yelled back toward the house, "Fetch my fish boning knife."

The old tortoise disappeared into the house. While he waited, Lord Harrington turned to Lazarus and said, "Good morning tailor. You are just in time to see how we must maintain order on a sugar cane plantation."

Lazarus stepped slowly to the right of the circle of men. He raced his mind to find a way to deter Lord Harrington from whatever punishment he planned for Andru. "Your plantation looks already well ordered to me," he said.

Andru apparently recognized Lazarus' voice and shook his head at Lazarus, signaling him to not intervene. This black boy is not only beautiful, he is brave as well, thought Lazarus.

"You saw this slave assault my guest last evening, Mr. Perlman," said Lord Harrington. "Such action cannot be overlooked."

"Well yes," Lazarus said, "but I also saw that he thought he was aiding a lady. While he was foolish, we have all acted the fool where ladies are concerned, have we not?"

Lord Harrington's eyes flashed now at Lazarus, telling him to mind his tongue.

"Harrington, I will flog him if you like – until he tells you anything he knows and begs like a dog," offered Chester Phipps. He raised his nose in a long snort, stepped toward Andru and spat a ball of phlegm into the air. The ugly mucus fell short, but Andru snarled and jerked toward Phipps – which made Phipps jump back faster than Lazarus thought the fat man could move.

The two burly men tugged at the ropes about Andru, pulling him up tighter.

Harrington ignored Phipps except to shake his head. After a few moments more, Lord Harrington grew impatient of waiting on the ancient tortoise. "Henry, fetch the knife," he said. This command sent the mulatto at Andru's right running toward the rear of the house. As he reached it, the old tortoise reappeared at the back entrance and handed him something. The man turned, ran back to Lord Harrington and made the transfer.

Lord Harrington spun back around to face Andru, stepped closer to him and said something in a low, threatening tone that Lazarus could not hear. Andru did not speak but stared into Lord Harrington's eyes. Lord Harrington held before him a leather scabbard in his left hand and drew from it a knife with his right. It was a thin knife with a narrow blade a bit longer than the length of Lord Harrington's hand. He held up the knife, displaying it, as if acting out a familiar scene to which he was happy to have witnesses. He signaled the two burly men toward him and spoke to them beneath Lazarus' hearing. Then the three men descended upon Andru. The burly ones held his head tight from either side as Lord Harrington moved the knife back and forth before Andru's eyes, motioning as if he were about to cut Andru's throat.

"Will you speak now?" he shouted, and he glanced back at the noble horsemen. Andru remained silent but his eyes flashed back hatred.

The circled horsemen quieted but nodded approval. Lazarus wanted to speak, to cry "stop this," but he did not.

"You think you can defy me? You think you can attack my guests?" Lord Harrington screamed at Andru, pumping himself into a frenzy. "You think your pretty face will save you?" he threatened, twirling his knife about under Andru's nose. Still Andru made no sound.

"Surely a generous man as you can manage some other way ..." Lazarus heard his own voice, but it was too late. As he said it, Lord Harrington grabbed Andru's hair with his left hand and then slipped the tip of the thin knife blade into Andru's left nostril and pulled it quickly upward splitting Andru's nostril to the bridge from the inside out. Blood squirted out onto Lord Harrington's hand and his collar. Andru now cried out, "aaahhh," but stopped himself and slumped back against the tree.

Lazarus grabbed his own nose and gasped.

"We shall see how the women like you now," Lord Harrington yelled at Andru. Then he turned away and faced the gathered horsemen, proudly displaying the bloody fish knife.

Andru then muttered something that sounded to Lazarus like, "Dey likes me still better'n you."

This froze Lord Harrington for a moment. Then he turned back toward Andru in a rage and pointed his knife, motioning with its blade and a nod of his head for the two brutes to again hold Andru. As Lord Harrington's thin knife cut into Andru's right nostril, the boy reared back to avoid the blade. Lord Harrington yelled, "hold him now," and the two brutes at either side regripped Andru's head, jerking it forward. As they did, Lord Harrington's blade slipped up through the boy's nostril and in a quick single motion, plunged into the socket of Andru's right eye, adjacent to the bridge of his nose.

Andru reared back again, crying but another brief "aaahhh" and the knife handle slipped from Lord Harrington's grasp as Andru whipped his head wildly from side to side as if trying to throw off the protruding knife lodged deeply in his eye. This gruesome sight shocked even some of the noble horsemen of Barbados, and a few turned away. Fat Chester Phipps leaned closer for a better view.

Lord Harrington cursed "Bloody Goddam, Henry," grabbed at the knife handle and ripped it roughly from Andru's head. As the knife came away, Andru's bloody eyeball came partly from its socket and Lord Harrington dropped his knife and pushed the eye back in with the fingertips of both hands. "Gimme a kerchief," he hollered and Mr. Adamson stepped forward and held out his filthy horse rag. Lord Harrington grabbed the rag, bunched it in one hand and pushed it against Andru's face - a face that was now just forehead and blood.

"Take this Henry," he said and handed the slave and the rag off to the burly mulatto. Then he turned, bent down and retrieved his knife. He took a kerchief now offered from Chester Phipps and began to wipe his own chin, hands and his fish boning knife. "Bloody, stupid slaves," he said to no one in particular as he wiped. As he and his guests strode away toward the paddock and their morning ride, he turned back and shouted to the burly men, "See to him … better take him 'round to 'Lizbeth."

Some of the guests could be heard to congratulate Lord Harrington. "Least the boy's still got 'is balls," said Chester Phipps. Lazarus wanted to rush to Andru's aid, but instead found himself turning away, bending at the waist and spreading his feet to avoid his own vomit.

Within a few minutes, Lazarus managed to straighten and turn back toward Andru. He was no longer at the tree, but with hands to his face and a burly man at each arm was walking him down to the right, toward the slave village.

Lazarus stood alone at the scene. Not knowing what else to do, he walked toward the slave village, following Andru and his handlers at a little distance. The two brutes walked Andru along the first wagon way, past the outdoor kitchen and straight to the end chattel house. Betts met them at her door way and ushered them inside. Lazarus held back near the kitchen, but when the burly men soon departed, he quickly walked to Betts' door and stepped inside. Betts sat on the edge of her bed, tending to Andru stretched across it at a diagonal. She glanced up at Lazarus, then fussed over Andru, inspecting his damaged face through his fingers. Then she turned back to Lazarus with a puzzled look and said, "De 'nana leafs do not heal dis boy."

"I'll be back soon," Lazarus said, and he bolted from the door and ran. He reached Harrington Hall, went in at the rear entrance, flew around the banister and up to his room taking two stairs per stride. He grabbed his grippe and retraced his path back to Betts' door. He came in panting and straining in the low light. Singing Louis stood silently over Betts, still perched on the edge of her bed. With her left hand she pressed what appeared to be a ball of kapok fibers at Andru's right eye. With her right, she dabbed at his nose. Andru moaned a little and pressed his hands at either side of his head, covering his ears.

"Feed him some mo'," Betts said.

Louis lifted a handle less cup and poured from a red earthen jug Lazarus recognized. He bent to the front of Betts and tipped it at Andru's lips.

"How is his eye?" Lazarus asked.

"I pushed it in," Betts said, "I does not know."

"… and his nose?

"Poorly, it do not stay," Betts answered, glancing up at him.

"Let me see," Lazarus pled, "Louis, please open the shutters."

Louis floored his jug and cup, stepped around and let in more light.

Lazarus slowly peeled back Betts' fingers. Andru's nose lay on his face like a gutted fish ready for the pan. Blood filled his eye socket and he would not let Lazarus touch it. Lazarus nodded Betts back to tending the eye. "I cannot help the eye," he said, "but I can try to stitch the nose. Daub it with your brew, Louis."

Louis did so. Andru started a scream but stopped himself.

Lazarus slid his grip sack with a foot and reached inside. He took a needle last used on jodhpurs. With trembling hands he poked at its eye with light thread, kept Betts at Andru's eye and placed Louis to hold Andru's head. With his left hand he pinched Andru's nose and with his strong right he applied a cross stitch last used to baste a cuff … then a second one on Andru's left nostril and a single one on his right. Andru's nose was more difficult than sail cloth. Lazarus had never sewn a man before, not counting his own fingers. When he finished, he cleaned away some blood. Then he rose, lifted Louis' jug to his lips and gulped. He lowered the jug and took up his grippe. Without another word, he left out the door, leaving Betts at the eye, Louis wiping the head and Andru moaning lowly on the bed.

Lazarus hauled himself back into the manor house and up to his room where he curled up in a ball on the bed and sobbed. He all but forgot what had happened in that bed during the night. He dearly hoped Andru would survive, but he had lost so much blood and the knife to his eye socket had surely pierced his brain. Lazarus had done nothing to prevent the mutilation. His few stitches would not heal a brain or make more blood. It was a crude patch, nothing more. If the boy lived, he thought, it would not be due to any assistance from Lazarus Perlman, the abolitionist, the champion of slaves … the coward. This was not the first time he wished he had never left London. He told himself he was a failure. Then he thought of poor Andru, lying in the slave village suppressing screams of pain from a bleeding brain and a torn, swollen face. Now he felt guilty for his self-pity and he started to recompose himself.

He did not know if Lord Harrington had heard him cry out as he had maimed Andru. Lazarus felt guilty and ashamed. He told himself that he should have done something more, anything more to stop the attack. Then, after a while, he told himself that he served a larger cause, one that could prevent other Africans from suffering Andru's fate, but that did not help the feeling in his gut one bit. Neither had it helped Andru.

This same Andru had found Lazarus at the foot of the bougainvillea cascade, cut him free and carried him to nurse Betts who healed him and prevented the infection that could have brought a deadly fever. He might be lying at the foot of that cliff still were it not for this slave. Andru had even gone back into the treacherous bougainvillea to retrieve Lazarus' sample bag. Andru had likely saved Lazarus' life and more. Lazarus had not returned the favor. Surely Andru would die of fish-boning knife to the brain.

Later in the day, when the noble horsemen of Barbados had returned from their ride, Lazarus stood groomed and ready in the game room where they gathered for refreshment, entertainment and to be measured by a young Jewish tailor.

Apparently few of them had paid attention to Lazarus' weak attempts to intervene in the morning's mayhem. Only Lord Harrington and Chester Phipps made comment, but both attributed Lazarus' behavior to a weak constitution. After all, he was but a Jew and could not be expected to possess the strength of these nobles.

Lazarus feigned a little timidity and minded his business. He seethed, though, as he measured four fat asses for jodhpurs and one pompous Lord for a waistcoat. If Lazarus hated slavers before, he now loathed these monsters.

Here Lazarus found himself, though, bending to serve these creatures. As he did so, Lord Harrington instigated a chess tournament across the room. "He seeks to recapture some of his dignity lost last evening," Lazarus told himself.

One after another the boastful host readily disposed of three challengers. Then he caught fat Chester Phipps in the four-move scholar's mate. After his embarrassment on the floor of the prior evening, Lord Harrington was quickly recovering his prestige among these men. "Is there no one among you as can match me?" he openly dared. There were no takers. Lazarus concluded his measurement of Mr. Doland, stepped forward a little and with all the propriety he could muster said in a deferential but determined tone, "If there are no others, I should not want your Lordship to want for a game."

Lord Harrington paused, looked about the room where all eyes starred at him. "By all means, it is a match," he said. "Come be seated Mr. Perlman." Though he had achieved only stalemates against Lazarus before, Lord Harrington looked unconcerned. "I warn you that I am in fine form today," he told Lazarus, "and not the tired man you faced when last you sat at this table."

As Lazarus took his seat behind the red elephants, he wished a wager turned on this match. He knew Lord Harrington's game. For Lazarus, opposing him was no gamble, but it was too late to play against Andru's punishment.

At first Lazarus thought to feed Lord Harrington his own

medicine by trapping him in a Queen-Bishop mate like the one stupid Chester Phipps had not detected. Lazarus would decoy his attack, however, so that Lord Harrington would not see it coming until he was already finished. Then Lazarus decided that would be too easy and lack satisfaction. He therefore set about to utterly demolish the green elephants in a lopsided war of attrition. Given the difference in their skills, Lazarus' war was more an exercise in annihilation. Twenty minutes later there had been very little loss of the red, but the green stood mostly on the table at the side of the board. Lazarus did not stop until he had taken every single green piece. Once he lifted the last green pawn, he effectuated checkmate of the fleeing green king in a single move.

Lord Harrington sat red faced, but quickly fell upon his wit and strained humor to right himself. "I suppose the long ride may have proved more tiring than I thought," he said, "especially as I was required to attend to some man's business before it commenced."

How callused, Lazarus thought. This "noble" now boasts of cutting Andru as if the young African had not been bound beyond movement and outnumbered thirteen to one, no fifteen to one, adding the burly men. Had Andru been loosed, Lazarus thought, he may have taken all fifteen.

Lord Harrington was not finished. "I suppose," he said, "that even a Jew should have some little talent beyond that of a seamstress." There was strained laughter. "Let us drink," Lord Harrington called out, "bring on the rum."

Lazarus was not satisfied by the game. Now though, he smiled at last too, but he laughed at the man, not with him. "A nobler man than you lies with his face in pieces," Lazarus thought, "and a better man than me."

Chapter 32. Meddling

In the weeks that followed Andru's punishment, Lazarus grew despondent. He regretted his failure to prevent Lord Harrington's attack as much as his inability to stop the assault he had suffered at the hands of Percy Nugent aboard the *Maidenstone*. No one looking at Lazarus could detect his injury. Andru's could never be hidden - if he lived.

Lazarus also told himself that he regretted his night of pleasure with Pandy the slave girl. "How could I?"

He wrote to Mr. Clarkson of the cruelty and abuse he had witnessed. He identified Lord Harrington and he named each and every one of the accomplices - the "noble horsemen of Barbados" – among the largest slave owners on the island. He included a separate note to the letter's addressee, Mrs. Symmons, urging her to read his affidavit before delivering it and to share it with the King Solomon Club, especially with the two boys who had questioned Mr. Clarkson about "savages."

The crimes against Andru – and even those against the "hostesses" all "trained" by their master to service his guests - would be powerful evidence before the Parliament. No one could charge that this evidence was stale or that these slavers were reformed. His affidavit provided first hand "exact intelligence," of outrageous brutality. Lazarus had hoped to make precisely this kind of valuable contribution to the abolition crusade when he had undertaken this expedition – his mission, his mitzvah. Now it seemed much too costly. Mr. Clarkson would likely congratulate him, but that would not soothe his nauseous stomach. Politics, he had learned, was a messy business. Espionage, he thought, can be worse. Even this wonderful exact intelligence didn't seem as valuable as one solitary slave boy – or even as his nose.

Lazarus felt he must know whether Andru had survived. He must speak to him. He also longed to see Pandy - to apologize for – for his … abuse.

He walked near Harrington Plantation on his way to deliver completed garments to Lord Cockrell and another horseman who had placed an order with him the day of the disfigurement. He could not bring himself to enter Lord Harrington's domain either coming or going. He felt ashamed to face the slaves. He had stood by during the attack on Andru and they might view him as complicit. Finally, one afternoon headed south back to Bridgetown from St. James, he took the road from the north turnpike to the left and climbed the gentle rise up to Harrington Hall. His pretext for the call would be to confirm with Lord Harrington that his services to the master and his guests in January had been satisfactory, and to see if his seams in the sail cloth jodhpurs actually held up to rigorous horse riding. He hoped to see Pandy and, as he left, to perhaps creep around to the slave village to inquire about Andru.

As Lazarus mounted the step to the veranda of the house and reached for the knocker in the mouth of the brass horse, Lord Harrington, in the company of two other horsemen, came round from his left and startled him. All three riders were finely attired, not in riding costume.

"I beg your pardon, Lord Harrington," he managed to sputter. "As I was nearby, I took the liberty to – "

"You are a bold one," interrupted Lord Harrington. He turned his horse about but did not dismount. Then he bellowed, "If I had wanted my field hand mended, I would have called my own surgeon."

"Yes," Lazarus said, "but I was just – "

"Take heed tailor Perlman," Lord Harrington sternly cautioned, "One should not meddle in the discipline of another's workers. Stay away from my slaves!"

Without more, he reined his horse back to the west and trotted away with his company after him.

Lazarus did not know what to do. He took a moment. Then he rapped at the door. The old tortoise answered promptly, apparently having been called forward due to the commotion at the front of the house.

"Miss Pandora," Lazarus inquired of him, "may I see her?"

"I am afraid I do not know who you mean, sah," the tortoise readily replied.

"You know, the young lady who entertained me at the gathering of the horsemen, Pandora, she called herself Pandy."

"Sah, I am instructed to tell you, there is no such person at this house," the old man said. He started to close the door, but reopened it a bit and said, "I should not make any inquiries here sah. If such a lady were here, Lord Harrington would not take kindly to your notice." Then the door closed.

The words confused Lazarus a little, but he understood their gist. The old man had followed his orders, while at the same time letting Lazarus know he had been told to lie. He thought to walk around to the slave village, but having just been warned by Lord Harrington, he hesitated. Perhaps another day, he reasoned and he retreated and left as he had come, without seeing Pandy, Betts, Gootie, Singing Louis or Andru – if Andru was alive to be seen.

He walked toward Bridgetown with slumped shoulders. As he neared his shop, he suddenly straightened as he recalled that Lord Harrington had accused him not only of meddling, but of mending. If Andru had mended, that likely meant he had lived. Lazarus took heart.

In the following days, Lazarus called at the manor houses of his other customers, biding his time. At the residences of other planters, he found circumstances much like those at Harrington Hall, if not quite so opulent. They were all large, well appointed homes of two levels staffed with Africans or creoles. Each sat among broad fields of sugar cane. Each plantation had its village of slaves in small movable houses, or just as often in mere tiny huts.

His work for the slave owners soon produced other customers among their households and a few beyond. Lazarus tried to keep his mouth closed and his ears alert as he smoothed the wrinkled shoulders and tugged at the snug waistlines of slavers. He kneeled at their heels to measure for trouser length, as if he were supplicating himself to their power. He had no difficulty prostrating himself to these slavers. He learned much in doing so. Besides, he had violated a slave girl himself.

Still, these inseams were the most uncomfortable measure. He would hand one end of his measure tape to his subject and instruct him to press it tight into a leg crevice while Lazarus knelt to check the reading. It is astonishing, he thought, what a slave master will talk about while pinching the top end of a string against his privates.

Lazarus learned of more abuse and even saw a few easily avoidable cruelties himself. He compiled them into a couple of affidavits, with the names of the offenders, and sent them to Mr. Clarkson. Some involved greater numbers of slaves, but none were more ruthless than carving up the face of handsome Andru. Lazarus did not travel far from Bridgetown. He avoided walking as far north as the plantation of Chester Phipps. He would not sew for that animal even if it meant failing to obtain evidence against him.

Though mid-winter, Lazarus took no coat as he called upon his clientele. Winter or not, the cane fields did not whistle so much in the wind as they had weeks earlier. Near and far on this isle of cane, gangs of slaves dressed mostly in white descended upon the cane stands. They chopped at the sturdy stalks and gathered their cuttings into tall stacks. Hulking, lighter colored men stood near most crews and barked their orders. The slaves worked dawn until dark but never in silence. As they worked, they sang and chanted music of their own composition. Even in his downcast mood, Lazarus could not help but be buoyed a little by their songs.

Curiously, Lazarus thought, the plantation owners themselves seldom tended their own expansive and valuable cane fields. He saw only two or three in the fields, and these had been on horseback and paying more attention to their steeds than their slaves or sugar crops. Overseers attended each gang of workers, either closely barking at them or idling nearby as if daydreaming. He casually inquired about their supervision on occasion while fitting a newly completed item on its wearer. The slave owners preferred to talk of weightier matters. At least, they deemed them of greater interest.

Tuning his ear to what at first seemed simple-minded prattle of Lord Cockrell, Lazarus gained insight to the society and governance of Barbados. Cockrell's plantation was situated in lower St. Thomas Parish and straddled its border with St. James. His holdings, while not adjacent, were situated a little to the north-west and not far at all from those of Lord Harrington. Lord Cockrell fancied himself a dandy. He lavished all the trappings of his station upon himself - especially new clothes. Despite any discouragement he may have heard from his neighbor, he often received Lazarus and spent many hours in front of three full-length mirrors in his own salon at the corner of his manor house with the Jewish tailor fussing about him. He liked attention, found the tailor's exacting habits in his favor and Lazarus played to his vanity.

Lazarus knew that the daily affairs of Barbados were conducted by a governor, appointed by the crown, and a two-chamber legislature loosely modeled on the British Parliament, but he had thought the latter to be mostly ceremonial. Lord Cockrell's conversations revealed that, in addition to their annual January equine gathering, the noble horsemen of Barbados, with a cadre of their friends, also dominated the legislature.

He claimed that the legislature, together with the island's trade council also controlled by the noble horsemen, had successfully procured the recall of the island's governor, a fellow named Cunninghame, in the recent past. That governor had galled the leeward plantation owners by imposing fees which required their assistance in repairing the often storm damaged roadway from Bridgetown to St. Phillips Church near the southeastern, windward point of the island. Then he had cut the planter's access to gunpowder by allocating it to wasteful official use like conducting cannonade salutes to ships rounding the far northern tip of the island at St. Lucy. Thus the richer parishes were assessed to the benefit of the most remote and least populous portions of the colony.

Fortunately, Lord Cockrell confided, the leadership of Lord Harrington had procured this new Governor Parry, a fellow of milder and more pliable constitution. The islands major thoroughfares had become "turnpikes" like those in parts of England where travelers using the road dropped a coin to engage the pin that allowed them to rotate or lift a crossbar. Those using the road should pay for its maintenance, Lord Cockrell insisted. As Lazarus well knew, one without carriage or mount could simply duck under the bars.

Like Lord Cockrell, the slave owners not raining cruelty on their slaves merely neglected them and the neglect was not benign, for then they were left to the whims of the overseers whose treatment ranged from indifferent to savage. Well, Lord Cockrell did relate the concern of the noble horsemen with one fellow he called "the arrogant Joshua Steele." Mr. Steele apparently owned three odd-parcels which, taken together, amounted to a sizable plantation. To manage his spread holdings he had denied his overseers the discretion to punish slaves. Instead, he had created an informal court among the slaves themselves, with their elders acting as judges and imposing discipline for most charged offenses. For this, the noble horsemen judged Mr. Steele naïve. "His foolishness does not end there," Lord Cockrell scoffed, "He has taken to paying his workers according to their completion of tasks and awarding premiums to his best workers." For this, the noble horsemen verbally charged him with sedition. They found Mr. Steele's alliances with unnamed but powerful friends in London most inconvenient.

"Mr. Steele thinks he is immune," Lord Cockrell said, "but he meddles with the wrong mob."

Lazarus stifled a chuckle. Another meddler, he thought, I am in good company. Then he remembered Mr. Clarkson's disclosure that he had occasional correspondence from Barbados, including from one most unlikely sympathizer. Lazarus thought perhaps he had uncovered a clue to that mystery. He sought out the manor house of Mr. Steele and discovered he actually lived in Bridgetown. The house man said that his master had "removed himself for a time to England" but would return in the autumn.

Lazarus located and looked about Mr. Steele's three cane fields. "Odd-lot" or not, they were substantial. In the man's absence, his fields looked at least as well kept and more tidy than any Lazarus had seen. Though cane field roads were often deeply rutted, Mr. Steele's were smooth. He came upon two crews harvesting Mr. Steele's cane and stood observing them for a time. Both seemed industrious and content. Their pace felt a little livelier than others he had seen at the task. One gang had no detectable overseer at all. That's what comes of such "naïveté" and "sedition," he thought.

Having seen much in a short span of time, Lazarus determined that one of the greatest cruelties of all was completely overlooked by the neglectful slavers, and not imposed by knife, whip or hot iron of their overseers. It was the disfigurement of large numbers of slaves by years - decades of bending their backs in long days of heavy toil for thousands of hours every year. He had seen scores of bent slaves who could not straighten and hundreds permanently hunched over more than Mordecai at his sewing table. The term "cane back" had identified Lazarus' comfortable chair at 18 Old Jewry Street. On this isle of swaying sugar plants, cane back was a widely shared disfigurement causing unceasing, sometimes excruciating pain. No wonder the slaves tried trances and appealed to Obatala and the stone gods. Singing Louis had identified this scourge for him many weeks earlier, he realized, but he had not suspected the condition was nearly as pervasive or painful as he had found it to be.

Lazarus drafted an affidavit about cane back. He crumpled it and wrote another. It still failed to convey what he had seen. Cane back was a torture. He called it that in his third attempt, but remained dissatisfied. He had it attested and sent it to Mr. Clarkson anyway. He included a letter about the "enlightened" Mr. Joshua Steele and his unusual and successful approach to the maintenance of slaves. He conceded, the slave lobby had been right about "reforms" in at least one instance. But Steele remained an exception, a notorious one who dared to vary from the ways of the Barbados slave masters - a meddler.

Chapter 33. Droopy Eyes

When March came Lazarus found that his business prospered, but his spirit still suffered. On visiting the harbor one morning to inquire of slave ships, he encountered a line of sailors just coming ashore. He overheard their chatter. Their ship, the speedy 18-gun sloop *Trusty* of His Majesty's fleet, had arrived from mother England in the early dawn. As it had departed, the sailors had heard the report – the French peasants who had stood for a republic had beheaded their king. Lazarus grabbed his neck and shook his head. Somehow Louis XVI's loss of his head made the burdens on Lazarus' shoulders less weighty.

That very afternoon, he finally found the fortitude to set off for the Harrington slave village. Lord Harrington's demand to stay away from the slaves still sounded in his ears. That didn't alter his determination. He admitted to himself that he was more desperate than courageous. He carried his sample case for cover and took precaution not to be seen from Harrington Hall. He took the crutch that had stood some weeks in the corner of his shop. When he arrived at Betts' house, the village looked the same except there were no people about the wagon way and only one enormous old woman at the outdoor kitchen. Also, the nearby cane fields had been cut back away from the village. He remembered that nearly all of the slaves would be in the fields, so he sat near the old woman and watched her chop and add vegetables to a big boiling pot suspended from a tripod above a fire on the ground. She dipped and offered him a cup of her stew. The vegetables were still firm in the spicy brown broth.

It is a peculiar land that grows vegetables in the winter, he thought, though it did not feel like he had passed a winter on this island. It had remained as warm here in January as a London June. He sat back, rested his head on his leather case and dozed.

He awoke to an indigo sky straight above as night approached. His mouth was agape and dry. He closed it and saw Louis standing over him. "Mista Laza, ya looks like a jumbie … do ya wants some o' dis peppa pot?" Louis said, extending a crude bowl toward him with both hands. Lazarus did not know what Louis meant by "jumbie." He extended the crutch to Louis, but all he could manage to say was, "Andru?"

"Follow me," Louis said. He took the crutch, turned and walked across the way and without slowing right into Betts' house. Lazarus followed him several paces back. Inside the house all was as Lazarus remembered, Betts and Gootie eating from bowls at the table and the stone gods on the back shelf. Gootie girl bounded from her chair and wrapped up Lazarus' right leg as if he had been gone but an hour and had left her fonder of him than he recalled.

Lazarus pulled from his sample case a length of red ribbon he had obtained in Bridgetown for this purpose. He showed it to Gootie. Then he pulled it through her grasping fingers, carefully wrapped it twice around her shock of hair and fashioned it into a two knot, four loop bow. *"Gootie come and Gootie go, Gootie got a big red bow,"* Lazarus sang off key. Gootie again hugged his leg.

"B-Bye de stars, dat Singin' Louis always breen me de strays," said Betts, not moving from her place. "Sit Mista Laza, eat, bye de stars, eat," she almost begged.

"No thank you Betts, it is good to see you, by the stars it is," Lazarus said.

Betts beamed her pursed-lipped smile up at him.

He did not know quite how or what to say so he merely started, "I must know about Andru ... did he, I mean do you know if he -"

"Bye de stars," Betts interrupted, she stood and picked up Gootie with her as she did. She did it with difficulty. Betts was large and near her time now. Gootie straddled Betts above her belly, one child atop the one about to come. Betts waddled a few steps passing Lazarus on his right, then turned sideways, as if to clear the view and nodded her head toward the far side of the room. Past them, across the little house, in the low light of the night, on Betts' low mat bed, lay Andru. He sat up slowly toward Lazarus but with his head bent low.

Lazarus turned fully and took a step toward the bed, but he stopped as Andru spread both hands over his face. Before he did, Lazarus could see for a moment. It looked raw, as though scabs had just come off the nose and been replaced by a thin smear of Betts' poultice. Andru peered through his split fingers. His right eye was in its socket, but it was just a rolled-back white ball, ribboned with red veins. His lid fell partly over it, matching Betts' droopy eye. Lazarus put his own hands to his face, aping Andru, and then he said

"Andru" and slowly removed his hands. Andru then mimicked Lazarus, lowering his hands. Andru did not turn away as Lazarus feared he might. He did not want to see Andru's back to him. He would rather confront his scarred face. It was that, broadly scarred – longer on his left than right. The knife had slipped, sparing half the right nostril when it had plunged into Andru's eye. His nose tilted a little to the left, as if pulled too tight there. The stitches had held, Andru was healing and the nose remained a single piece. It really wasn't Andru's nose now, but it was still a nose.

"I am happy to see you alive," Lazarus said. He had never really spoken directly to Andru. He had difficulty doing so now. "I am so sorry, I tried, I mean I should have tried … that is, I know that I failed you after you … after you …" he turned back and looked at Louis, "after both of you …" he glanced at Betts, " … after all of you helped me. I – I have no excuse … I mean," he could not go on.

Betts stepped to him, thrust out Gootie against his chest with both hands, and said, "Bye de stars, hold dis chile whilse I'll gits up yo dinna."

Lazarus now embraced Gootie even more fondly than she had hugged him. He had never heard better words than Betts' "bye de stars" and to make things better still, he now felt Louis' open hand resting on his back and moving up to his shoulder in a light squeeze.

"Andru had hisself a hard time dese many days," Louis said. "He's blood would not stop. At first, we feared we would lose him to de ol' ligaroo."

Lazarus remembered the ligaroo.

"But Betts, she wrap he's head wit de 'nana tree," Louis said, "and Andru, he rob dat ol' ligaroo ghos' like de fingasmit thief."

"But he cannot see." Lazarus said. "His right eye, he cannot see."

"No, not out he's cut eye and he gots de great pains in he's head, but maybe he gits some betta … maybe no."

Betts brought food, but Lazarus could not eat. He sat, keeping Gootie on his lap as he tried again to tell Betts and Louis that he had witnessed the attack on Andru. He said he had made a feeble attempt to intervene, but had not really lifted a hand. He confessed his shame, his regret and his anger. He could not tell them that he had tried to soothe himself by destroying Lord Harrington at chess – it was a mere game. It was ludicrous. He could not even tell them of his work with Mr. Clarkson or his true purpose in coming to Barbados. That, too, was far too little and seemed no justification at all for his failure.

Betts and Louis consoled him. Louis told Lazarus that every slave comes to know the terror of standing by helplessly while another, sometimes his own brother or his father, is attacked and damaged for life or even killed by "de Buckra." Andru rose from the mat bed and joined them at the table after placing a cloth wrap around the middle of his face. Betts told Lazarus that he could have done nothing to help Andru. Louis told him that the master is not to be crossed and that Andru was young and had forgotten that. Andru, Louis thought, would be back cutting cane before this harvest was over. Andru said nothing, but he did not turn his back to Lazarus. Later, Lazarus thought he could hear Andru hum along as Louis sang ...

Andru cut de cane all up
   And pour de rum in Masta cup
He knock de Masta on de flo'
   He run wit Prissy tru de doa'
De Masta cut he wit de knife,
   An' Andru hang on fo' he life
Mista Laza sew de nose, an'
   Jes' like cane de t'ing regrows
Now Andru cut de cane all up
   He pour de rum in Louis cup.

Louis sang more verses, all identical except for the last line. His song filled "Miss Betts cup," "Gootie cup," and "Mista Laza cup." Andru hummed to each and Lazarus rocked Gootie girl and her red bow on his knees.

Then Lazarus gathered himself a bit and asked, "Miss Pandora, um, I met a girl in the master's house that night, she called herself Pandy. Do you know her."

Louis smiled.

"Knows her, I looks afta her all her days," said Betts. "Partic'lar now."

"Has she been ill, did the master punish her?" Lazarus asked anxiously.

"Yea, in a manner – she b-bees wit' a chile now."

Lazarus paled and looked at the floor. He stirred his foot about, then looked up at Louis and Betts. "It is my child," he said, "I am responsible."

Louis cleared his throat with a "hummpf."

"Pos'ble, if you says so," Betts replied, without emotion. "But mos' likely it be de masta's, she tell me. He been afta' her afore yew and much since."

Lazarus knew that information should not have taken him back, but it did. His fantasies shattered, right there in front of witnesses. Anyone could surely see it in his eyes. He knew he could not have Pandy any more than he could have had Mrs. Symmons. She belonged to Lord Harrington – in the real sense of ownership. Wrong as it was, it was true. If meddling with slave discipline angered Lord Harrington, stealing away with Pandy would likely cause Lazarus to be prosecuted as a criminal or worse and he knew it. It stung and Betts' amber plaster would not soothe it. He calmed himself by communing with these people who faced deprivation from the moment of their birth.

Lazarus talked with Louis for hours. He had missed the slave with the melodic mouth and a trove of information in his head. Lazarus asked Louis about the bad masters he had once mentioned. Louis did not leave Harrington plantation often, but he did sometimes drive a cart loaded with boiled sugar to the wharf at Bridgetown. He said that the slitting of nostrils occurred on nearly every plantation. The masters humiliated their rebellious slaves that way, without the cost of replacing them. Splayed noses, though a badge of subjugation, didn't hamper hands, feet or backs needed to plant and harvest sugar cane. He had "heared on de wind" though, that the temperament of some masters hurt their pocket books. One fat one who rode each year with Lord Harrington was particularly feared. He had crippled a few slaves. He also "fooped" slave girls before their child years and "likes to rubbatail on he's boys," Louis said.

Another buggering white man, Lazarus thought.

This master's plantation was north, in St. James Parish, east of Holetown. Lazarus had not walked that far north. Louis said the slaves secretly derided the cruel St. James master with slurs. "Any hole will do fo' de Holetown hog" they said of him. Louis had no song for him. "Dis ol' boy chants fo' happy," he said.

As Lazaus walked home in the night, he thought more of Pandy. She had not replaced his boyhood fantasies of auburn hair, but Lazarus knew she would always be with him, in a place of her own, in his best of memories. Walking in the moonlight, Lazarus could still hear the echoed chants of the slaves in the cane fields earlier that day. He could still hear Louis' voice pouring rum. As if a slave in song, he talked aloud to himself as he walked along. "What an irrepressible, spirited, resilient people these Africans are," he said to the night. "They 'chant for happy' in the face of unspeakable horror ... hardly an inferior race." Then he thought of the noble horsemen of the island and mused, "... more likely superior."

Chapter 34. De High Monkey

The days now passed better for Lazarus. He kept up his sewing. He fashioned a carefully drawn affidavit about the Holetown slave master. It wouldn't be much help, cast in the third party and omitting the name of the monster. He suspected Chester Phipps, but couldn't be sure, so he avoided defamation. Lazarus began to call at Betts' house each week. She and Gootie girl lifted him as did Singing Louis. Louis, too, proved a bounty of information. Lazarus learned that Priscilla had been found and returned to service in the Harrington manor house where Pandy also remained.

Lazarus tried his Hebrew best to feel remorse for his brief liaison with Pandy. She might, at this moment, carry his child. Reason and his sense of justice commanded him to regret his culpability. He simply could not bring himself to it. A fearsome master may have ordered her to the third guestroom at the top of the stairs, but Lazarus himself had not forced her, not even a bit. He had not even invited her. He had declined suggestions that he do so and refused her offer – at least initially. Still, Pandy may have feared a report to Lord Harrington if she had failed to please his guest. Lazarus told himself it was not true. Even if she remained in "service" in Harrington Hall the rest of her days, Lazarus could not deny his feelings - and his belief that the skinny slave girl with the seductive eyes had shared them, however briefly.

Keeping up his work, both apparent and clandestine, helped him think of other things. Still, sometimes – often - he closed his eyes in bed and felt Pandy, every bit of her, lying on top of him. In his dreams she remained thin and seemed innocent. Even his imagined reenactments brought no guilt. Rather, they produced gushing juices and a longing for dimples.

In late March, Louis reported that Andru had regained his strength and returned to work in the cane fields. Andru had gone right back to the first gang. He would not hear of less, though he still suffered headaches and retained vision in but one eye. Lazarus still felt guilt for standing by during Andru's ordeal, but he had learned from Louis, Betts and Andru himself to live with it. These people and others in the slave villages had endured even worse, Lazarus knew, and had done so on this very island for well over a century, nearer two.

Louis also boasted that the slaves of Harrington plantation were signing a new chant – the story of Andru's attack and of the nose sewn by the master's tailor – the song Louis had composed. The entire village focused on Andru's face and the saving of his nose. They chanted it while at their work and within hearing of the field bosses. Lazarus smiled to hear this news, but then grew concerned. Surely Lord Harrington did not know the song?! Perhaps that adds to the man's anger, Lazarus thought, and perhaps an apology - even if insincere – can calm him.

Lazarus practiced a carefully worded appeasement and called at the Harrington manor house, but Lord Harrington would not receive him. "Mr. Perlman," said the old tortoise, "Lord Harrington says you are no longer welcome here."

Lazarus did not know what "here" meant. Did Lord Harrington mean at Harrington Hall, the entire plantation or maybe even the entire island? He would have to be on guard. He told Betts' and Louis that his visits at the slave village might have to be curtailed. Betts fretted. Louis acted as though it were inevitable.

"Ya can not hide what yew is," he said, "jes' like de high monkey."

"The high monkey?" asked Lazarus.

"As dey says, de monkey he mus' climb, but de higha de monkey climb, de mo' dey sees he's tail."

Louis didn't really know what Lazarus was, not all of it. No one on this island knew. Lazarus had taken care to disguise himself from detection as an abolitionist – and an informant. Surely no one suspected. But his one act of compassion to a brutalized slave had revealed him as sympathetic to slaves and willing to interfere in their discipline. Suddenly, his work became more difficult. Fewer planters ordered clothes and, even when they did, they seemed to speak guardedly in his presence. Louis is right, Lazarus later thought. He felt a bit like a monkey that had exposed its tail.

Lazarus stayed more in his shop. He did call on a few in Bridgetown who had left their names with Piccard. And he worried.

He had little time to fret. Early April brought rumors then confirmation in the *Barbados Mercury and Bridgetown Gazette* that France had, on the first day of February, formally declared war on Britain. The new French Republic had lost no time seeking retribution on those who had supported their tyrannical monarchy, whether among their own countrymen or foreign powers. However strategically inadvisable, they took on several nations at once. First they engaged Austria, but before many weeks they added Britain to their list of declared enemies.

Lazarus knew that war between Britain and France was hardly new. After a protracted conflict, they had signed a treaty less than decade earlier. Indeed, the two powers had been at war, declared or otherwise, as often as not for many decades. Bridgetown residents murmured, "What would war mean for the West Indies?" Lazarus knew the pattern, for a century and more, whenever war broke out in Europe, the participants would export their dispute to their colonies and, in particular, would use the occasion to attempt expansion of their holdings in the crop-rich West Indies. Most of the islands of the region had flown more than one flag; some of them had flown several. Portugal, Spain, France, England, the Dutch and even Sweden and Denmark had held island colonies in the West Indies. Spanish and French interests had contested dominance of Saint Dominique almost constantly and had each taken to occupation of the big island – the French at its west end and the Spanish at its east. Surely someplace in the West Indies this new war would put island occupants in the shadow of a foreign power's cannons.

Traffic to the garrison near Bridgetown increased and many more of His Majesty's war ships began to appear in Carlyle Bay. The military, in lesser strength, stood vigilant also to the north at Speightstown, or "Little Bristol" as some called it, and at Holetown on the island's leeward coast. The island's planters talked of a militia to repel invaders, but the proposed recruits were still cutting cane.

May brought news of naval skirmishes in the lesser leeward islands to the northwest of Barbados. Concern spread and a few slavers drilled their slaves as the harvest wound down. Two plantation owners ordered grand military officer styled uniforms with epaulets, high collars and brass buttons. They ordered no clothing for their subordinates. Merchants in Bridgetown made good trades as some panicked slavers bought up and hoarded supplies.

Barbados remained the gateway to British presence in the West Indies. It was strategically located since ships from England, cut short of it, would be compelled to remain on the high seas – low on rations, fresh water and supplies at the end of the long Atlantic crossing. It made sense - the planters knew their little island would be at the center of the battle for the West Indies.

A sharp debate quickly arose. One planter at southern Christ Church Parish was said to have sought to procure arms and, using just a few old Brown Bess muskets as samples, trained his slaves in their use. Most of the plantation owners strongly objected. Perhaps they knew, as did Lazarus, that the slaves were as likely to turn weapons on their masters as on people they did not know. The argument grew heated but a general agreement was reached – slaves had their cane choppa knives, they would serve well. French military muskets, made in France's Charleville arsenal, were inferior to better crafted British designs, the planters had been informed. While the longest range of the French muskets was 200 yards or so, they were known to be accurate for only a quarter of that distance, and young slaves were fleet footed and dodgy targets. They would do well against the French. The military confiscated nearly all the black powder not already in their stores anyway.

The planters of various parishes now competed for priority from the military, each arguing that their location would be the first attacked. As the plantation owners bickered and quarreled, the British commanders scoffed at them. The ports, especially Bridgetown, they advised, would become the targets if the French were not cut-off out at sea.

Apparently the French did not share the views of either the planters or the British commanders. French warships never showed anywhere near Barbados - not a single one. After some days, fevers cooled on Barbados. A new opinion grew that the French would not dare to strike Barbados. Though commercially long out-produced by Jamaica, this first British outpost remained a military stronghold. Strategic as it was, if the French attacked it, they would face grave risk of a sound and early defeat. They were more likely to attack softer spots, not this fortified and courageous citadel.

All this amused Lazarus. These suddenly bold slavers turned so easily upon one another and from fear to vanity. What would they do if French warships appeared? What if the French invaded the island? What would they do then? They were foolish and very openly so. Like the high monkey, their tails were showing. And as these monkeys scrambled, they pulled each other down by the tail.

Lazarus thought next of the slaves. What would they do if Barbados came under attack? Would the slaves take the occasion to rise up for themselves?

Then Lazarus turned to himself. Just what would he do? Would he run to Harrington plantation and take Pandy under his wing? He imagined himself doing just that. He spent early war-time nights safely in such dreams.

Chapter 35. Crash and Ka Doo

Lazarus' Barbados life, real and imagined, came to a disorienting crash one beautiful June morning when he received a parcel from London. He opened it to find a number of tailor's tools … all well used, all familiar, all Mordecai's. He fumbled through the parcel pawing Mordecai's scissors, two awls, a measure tape, some button blanks, a worn brass thimble and a leather palm pad into which were anchored several needles of various tensile and length.

Beneath the tools lay two envelopes. One was in the handwriting of Mrs. Symmons. He opened it and verified … his father was dead. The death of a man in his sixties was hardly unusual, but Mordecai had not been ill. He had been found in his bed with his hands neatly clasped at his chest. He was cold when discovered.

He had been buried the next day in the Jewish Cemetery at Alderney Road where his Leah had rested for nearly eighteen years. The community of his friends and devoted patrons at Duke's Place had properly mourned Mordecai. Mrs. Symmons said she knew Lazarus would be saddened but she reminded him that the extended period for a son to mourn his father continued. She provided Mordecai's date of death as the sixth of April.

Mr. Symmons had added a post script providing his own condolence and advising that several bolts of cloth, some furnishings in the shop and the rooms above and some "fixtures" had been sold to pay the expenses of care for the body, funeral service and burial. Lazarus wondered if Mordecai's headless mannequin was among the "fixtures." Mr. Symmons wrote that Lazarus might be able to keep many of Mordecai's customers if he returned to London without delay.

The young tailor who sewed clothes, suddenly tore at his. His chest felt ripped like his blouse. He looked for a mirror to cover or break, but his shop did not have one. A fine tailor, he thought, with no mirror. He dropped the letter to the floor, then he threw the package down as well, bouncing Mordecai's tools off the floor. Then he sat down among them. He wrapped himself in his own arms and rocked in place, crying and moaning until he drooled. He lost the time and sat there all day. At dark, as if the axis of his world had shifted, he tipped over but remained on the floor, a pile of sudden sorrow, until the morning.

When he awoke, Lazarus rolled on his back and looked at the ceiling. He thought and felt so many things at one time. One given to sense and order, he could not begin to catalogue all he felt. Had he abandoned his father and hastened his death? Would Mordecai still live if his son had not sailed an ocean, not taken up the cause of abolition, never have met Thomas Clarkson? Lazarus meant what he had told his father as they had parted – he fully expected to find the man still at his work when Lazarus returned. Mordecai had always been there, in his shop, plying his skill as long as Lazarus could remember. That was the order of things - constant like the sea and the sun, but he was no more – not in his shop, not in the synagogue, not on this earth at all. Now, Lazarus knew, he lies cold and buried in it.

Lazarus had felt deprived of a mother. He examined himself – had he failed to value his father, who had been there for him every day? Remorse catches the guilty, he thought. Those at the synagogue would already have lamented Mordecai – the poor tailor with the ungrateful son who had left him alone in his old age –and they would be right.

He rose, gathered the tools and papers on the floor and placed them on his cutting table. There, atop the pile he saw another letter. Then he recalled, there had been a second one. What could it offer him? – nothing, he was sure. Resigned, he opened it. It came from Mr. Clarkson. It was dated "2 April 1793" and had been routed through Mrs. Symmons as planned. In the letter, Mr. Clarkson thanked Lazarus for his correspondence. Finally! Until now, he did not know if Mr. Clarkson had even received his correspondence.

The letter made no mention at all of Mordecai. Mr. Clarkson was all business, as always. He said he had provided all of the evidence Lazarus had sent to Mr. Wilberforce. He also informed that the Parliament would not likely be willing to consider a move to halt the slave trade in its upcoming session. Many members had responded to the Abolition Society that the matter had not achieved passage after several attempts in the prior two years, and there was now this war with the French occupying so much attention. The Abolition Society would feel its way and try again as the opportunity presented in the parliamentary session of 1794 or perhaps 1795.

Mr. Clarkson also wrote that he had expended his health and most of his fortune in the campaign. He regretted that the society could send no further stipend. He well understood, he said, if Lazarus determined to return to England. Mr. Clarkson did not say so, but Lazarus could tell that the great man had at last become disheartened.

Incidentally, Mr. Clarkson wrote, Mr. Wilberforce had a message for Lazarus. He implored that if Lazarus did stay in the islands, he should try to direct his efforts to the treatment of slaves newly arrived from Africa rather than those long in the islands or born to slaves after their arrival. Cane back, deplorable as it may be, is too subtle a torture to sway members of Parliament. Mistreatment of slaves and creoles long in service is really a different issue from the importation of new captives. It is the latter matter that must be the focus in ending the traffic, Mr. Wilberforce advised.

Given Mr. Wilberforce's advice, Lazarus realized, all his efforts had been futile. The attack on Andru apparently served as little testament for ending the slave trade. No member of Parliament would be moved by Betts' absent teeth. The House of Lords would not take notice of the slave-keeping nobles of Barbados who populated their plantations by sleeping with dozens of their own slaves. If they did look at the evidence, they would not much care. The noble horsemen of Barbados could commit mayhem and butchery to their heart's content - it would not count in the struggle against slavery. It would not be "exact intelligence" against the slave trade in the debate before the House of Commons, because there would be no debate – not this year, and perhaps not the next. All of the affidavits – none would be of use this year at all.

Oh wait, this letter too held a postscript. Mr. Clarkson congratulated Lazarus on the most potent affidavit – the one about the plantation owning English lord who put out the eye of his slave. Mr. Clarkson had found it quite compelling. Even though no formal debate would be held, he had tried to keep up some pressure and had used the incident described by Lazarus in the effort. One or two of the Lords had pressed for the name of the offender and, as Lazarus had provided it, Mr. Clarkson had disclosed Lord Harrington's name, though not the identity of the informant. Mr. Clarkson had assured the Lords, however, that he had the information "on sworn affidavit."

Lazarus was stunned. Yesterday's letter had gutted him, and now this one had taken out his legs. He did not know what to think or where to turn. As both letters mentioned, he could return to London. There, though, he would be just the son of a deceased tailor. Here, his efforts had not produced any help to the abolitionists.

Such injustice! Lazarus had felt such purpose two days before, but he now felt useless. He had not intended to denigrate his father's ways. He had hoped to fulfill their larger promise. His father had not understood and, now, he never would.

Now, Lazarus realized that his father and his own identity as a Jew had always provided the foundation on which Lazarus Perlman stood. Perhaps he had taken this foundation for granted, even resented its limitations at times, but he had never rejected it in his heart. He was confused. Had he abandoned his father? Would Mordecai be breathing still if his son had not left him? Was his entire expedition to this time meaningless? Was this obeying a mitzvah or a calling at all - or just vanity?

All this was too terrible and too real. He had not eaten and he tired. He lay on his bed and escaped to fantasy. He tried to envision himself stealing Pandy away, but how and away to where? Louis was right – one could not run far or hide well on this island. Harrington plantation sits within a dozen miles or so of its most remote tip. Then what of her child? Pandy would need Betts' help and he couldn't steal Betts as well. His mind swam in a confounding stew. His head pounded. His stomach burned.

Lazarus did what he always did when seeking clarity. He stirred his muddled mind and he went to sleep. This time, though, he did not arise in the morning with even the beginnings of a solution. He did not arise at all. He stayed in his bed for most of three days - grieving, disheartened, depressed - sick.

On the third day he arose in the late afternoon and faced reality. He had to go to the market or starve. He prepared to meet the world as sparingly as he could and descended on the streets of Bridgetown. He had barely done so when he noticed he had awakened to a wholly different world. The entire place had thrown out the old order and replaced it with a gigantic celebration.

Slaves, free blacks and creoles of all shades danced in the street to drums he thought to have been outlawed. Cane cutting rags had been exchanged for brightly colored and daring costumes. Painted faces laughed. Men walked on stilts and he spotted one dressed up in leaves being chased down the street by others. Servants and masters stood in the streets, both openly drinking spirits in sight of the other and singing. At the market the higglers and hawkers gave away slices of melon and embraced customers. Lazarus thought he still might be sleeping, but he knew what he saw and heard – and he tasted the melon. Lazarus wandered about gawking at the celebrants.

Men down near the water stood over piles of fish and raced one another to see which man could bone his fish first. He caught sight of a boning knife and it brought him a little to his senses. He walked back to the market. From a vendor's cart, he picked up one of his favorites, a mango, and asked the woman, "What is this, is the war over?"

"Wat war darlin?" she said. "Dis be de crop ober kadoo don't ya kno ... and it don't be done fo' days." Now Lazarus knew he had not gone insane. Louis had told him about this festival, but not prepared him for this. Lazarus walked home and took greater care in grooming himself. As he did, he caught sight of the parcel and the two letters open and lying on the cutting table. He tore his mind away from them and went back out in the street.

A few minutes more and Lazarus lifted a glass of rum punch with three complete strangers who did not know if he were Jew or gentile, resident or visitor, sailor or tailor - or abolitionist - or spy. He stumbled home by torchlight held aloft in the hands of revelers and plopped in his bed. He slept late, into the afternoon, then went back out for rum, revelry and the companionship of strangers. He repeated the day for two more. He did not know himself, but this new Lazarus had few worries and laughed easily. He thought, no one would know me now – not Mordecai, not Mrs. Symmons, not Mr. Clarkson, not even Betts or Singing Louis. With the help of the entire island, Lazarus was throwing himself a grand kadoo.

Finally, one evening, a grand procession moved through the streets - the real kadoo. Paraders wore painted masks or painted faces. Stilt walkers in costume led the way. Animals pulled small colorful carts. Flowers were cast before a "king and queen" of cane cutters as they passed by in island royal garb and crowns of blossoms. A scarecrow called "Mr. Hard Times" was burned up on a bonfire. Lazarus thought he saw Louis in the crowd, but he could not locate him again or be certain that the yellow and red painted face really belonged to his friend. No face appeared unhappy. No man was the slave of another. It was a fine fantasy - a world void of intolerance, a bizarre but happy place. He drank and paraded himself until he could no more. Then he just made it to his little shop home and collapsed.

Lazarus awoke late in the day with a throbbing head. He could not remember feeling so poorly since the bougainvillea, but he knew what he would do. Rather, he knew what he would not do. He would not let Mordecai's death deter what he had undertaken during his father's life. He would not let Parliament's delay defeat his purpose. He would not abandon the Gooties and Andrus of the future now unsuspectingly living in Africa – or in the belly of slave girls like Pandy. He would not let the slavers of the world have their way – not without a fight from Lazarus Perlman. He knew no better way to honor his father – a descendant of slaves. He would have to formulate a plan. He didn't know how he would resist or how to prevail – only that he would not cease the struggle.

Chapter 36. Hiding

He got up some food and took it to his cutting table. He paced, chewing and pausing at his table to sip tea. Then he heard the shop's door open over his shoulder and turned about to see Andru, his face still streaked with kadoo colors, panting in the open doorway. Before he could extend a welcome, Andru breathlessly blurted out, "Ya mus' hide Mista Laza, ya must flee. Louis say de Masta hunt ya, ya mus' go – de Masta an' he's bulls bees on dey way."

"Andru?" Lazarus said. "What is this about?"

"Mista Laza, I runned in de field, I pass dey horses, dey is close. Ya mus' go – no time!" Andru panted.

Lazarus thought a moment, but Andru tugged at his sleeve. "Hmm ... this way," Lazarus said, and he ran across the street and pushed aside giant flowers, to the rear of Piccard's saddlery and out of sight of his shop, with Andru on his heels. Behind Piccard's shop, he turned to Andru and said, "Now catch your breath and calm down some, then tell me what this is about."

Andru didn't wait, but said, "Louis tole me, 'run yo' bes' Andru, warn Mista Laza, de Masta he read de letta' and he be in a rage. He say he gwine kilt dat boy what sew."

"But why, Andru, did he say why?" Lazarus pled. Before Andru could say a word, Lazarus heard a stir in the street and peered back through the alleyway hibiscus to see Lord Harrington and two familiar bulky men in the street, sitting on their horses facing his shop. The horses and their riders moved about restlessly, casting tall shadows against the front of the building before them.

"Tailor," yelled Lord Harrington. "Come out – now. I know it was you – you were the only one there who it could have been. Come out Jew boy, show yourself." Without waiting longer, Lord Harrington barked, "Henry, haul him out here, time for him to visit our kapok tree again."

His big mulatto overseer swung off his horse and threw open the door to Lazarus' shop. He bolted in but emerged a minute later. "He's not here," he reported, "but his tea is still warm."

Lord Harrington roughly jerked his horse about and Lazarus slunk down to stay out of sight. Lazarus heard the irate slave master bellow, "Perlman, I know you can hear me. You are a criminal, giving false witness that I mistreat my slaves. I know it was you who snitched to London – I'll have your skin you bloody Judas." He slid off his horse and sent his bosses scurrying along the street. Then Lazarus saw the back of Piccard, stepping toward Lord Harrington. The two men spoke and Piccard motioned toward the north. Lord Harrington remounted and called his men. Then he spurred his horse which reared a little and the three men bolted off together.

Lazarus shook his head at Andru and took a deep breath. He waited, listening, then he gasped again as Piccard suddenly emerged from the back of his saddlery. "You won't be safe here. Better find a place. Not sure where that could be."

"Where has he gone?" Lazarus asked.

Piccard propped one foot up on a stump, scratched his head and said, "Somehow he got the notion that you may have gone to the market. It should take them a while to sort through that evening crowd."

"Thanks for not giving me away. This is Andru," Lazarus nodded to the man at his side.

"Andru," repeated Piccard with a nod of his own. "Harrington is a good customer," Piccard said, "but he is no friend. I do not like the man. But I don't know how you can escape him."

"Come wit me," Andru said, again tugging at Lazarus' sleeve.

"Again, thanks Piccard," Lazarus said, and he returned to his shop with Andru at his elbow and shut the open door behind them. "Let me gather some things," Lazarus said, taking up his grip sack, "Where should I go, is there a cave on Mount Misery or a hidden glen on the windward coast?"

"I knows betta," said Andru. "Load Harrington don't looks dere."

Within a few minutes Lazarus found himself out into the street and following Andru through alleyways and toward cane fields. They walked for a time and Lazarus asked where they were bound.

All Andru would say is "follow me" and he kept walking as the sun set. Twice, when Lazarus heard noise on the road, Andru headed into a nearby cane field, motioned Lazarus to the ground among the stubble and waited until travelers passed. Andru's stride was long and he grabbed away the grip sack so Lazarus could stay with him. After a while, he veered off away from the road to the right, across a rising field that would have been much slower going before the harvest. Despite their new route, Lazarus knew the direction. Andru seemed to be headed to Harrington Plantation.

Lazarus stopped. "Wait, are you taking me home?" he asked.

"Follow me, dis be de short way," Andru said and resumed his march.

Lazarus asked himself why he followed, but he did. At dark, they arrived in the cane field to the south of the slave village, the side away from Harrington Hall. Andru walked to the left, at the edge of the village. Lazarus had only visited its first row of chattel houses; he didn't realize the size of the village. Andru passed several rows of houses and came to that first row and up to the rear corner of Betts house. He tapped on the west-end shutter and then lifted it up. He threw up a leg and crawled in through the window. His big arm reappeared and his hand beckoned Lazarus near. Then it reached around under Lazarus' arms and hoisted the winded tailor right in after it. Inside, Lazarus landed on the bed. He rolled off it and rose to his feet.

Betts and Singing Louis stood inside. Gootie girl sat at the table. A small package cried from the foot of Betts' mat bed. Where Lazarus and Andru had been healed now lay a new baby.

"My goodness," Lazarus said. "It's so small. I'm glad the baby was at the foot or we would have smashed it coming in the window. What is its name?"

"My sista, my sista," Gootie clapped as she spoke.

Louis, Betts and Andru didn't reply but talked together in a circle. Unlike their custom, they spoke lowly. Lazarus didn't hear what they said. He straightened his skewed clothing and dusted himself. Then he stepped closer to hear the conference.

"Yes, yew be right Andru, dat will do fo' now," said Louis.

"How did you know to warn me?" Lazarus asked Louis. "And why did Andru bring me here?"

Louis had always been polite, even deferential to Lazarus, but now he sounded urgent. "Not jes' now," he said. "Firs' we gits you tucked away." Louis then told Andru to go out, look about and whistle twice if the way was clear. "No winda' fo' dis ol boy," he said.

Andru left, but before Lazarus could say anything to Louis, a *"schreeet – schreeet"* sounded and Louis said. "Follow me, Mista Laza an' pull yo' colla' up 'round yo' buckra neck."

Outside, Lazarus followed Louis. He turned right around the corner of Betts' house and made his way into the heart of the slave village. Even at this late hour, a few slaves in doorways and wagon ways looked at them with wide eyes as they passed. Several rows in, Louis stopped, turned left and stepped just inside a hut with only a suspended cloth in the doorway. Then he emerged and pulled Lazarus in by his sleeve. Lazarus couldn't see much. A tall stack of large cotton or jute sacks stood at one end of the hut. Louis dragged two from the top and slid them to Lazarus' feet. Then he looked at them, stepped around and hauled down two more which he laid next to the first two. "Sleep easy here," Louis said. "I sees ya wit' de sun," then he left.

Lazarus fretted some, more than a dozen people had seen him in the village, they knew where he slept. Lord Harrington owned them all. He didn't know what else to do and he ached from Andru's strenuous pace through the cane fields. So he slept.

In the early light, the curtain door flew aside, and someone came inside the hut. "B-bye de stars," she said, "I brung yo' breakfas'."

Lazarus sat up and smiled. He rose and surprised Betts' with a hug. "Where is your baby?" he asked.

"Careful, o' yew eats from de flo'," she said with a no-tooth smile he could still see. "De baby be wit' Shayala," she said. Lazarus liked the soft way Betts pronounced "ba - by" as if were two words; and he had nearly forgotten that Gootie's name was really Shayala.

Halfway into the dried fish and the yam fritters, the head of Singing Louis, quiet as Lazarus had ever heard it, poked around the curtain. He entered as Betts left. He re-stacked a few sacks of grain from the end pile, sat on them and took up a lengthy conference with Lazarus.

Louis had learned from Master Harrington's house man, the old tortoise, that Lord Harrington had received a letter in the post from England. He had read it, cast it on the floor and gone immediately mad. He raged at everyone about and swore he would kill that tailor – the Jew boy. After he had stormed off, the old tortoise, who Louis said could read, picked up the letter and looked at it. The writer was Lord Pennington. Lazarus knew that Pennington traveled frequently to London and was the liaison of the island's planters with the slave lobby. The letter, the old tortoise had told Louis, said that some lords in London had approached its writer at the office of the West Indies lobby and inquired concerning Lord Harrington and his mistreatment of his slaves. They knew of a report that he had bound one slave against a tree, slit both his nostrils and put out an eye. It was a new offense they said, not a stale one, occurring in January of the present year. They said the report was from a credible source. Lord Pennington had tried to rebuff the lords, his letter said, but he cautioned Lord Harrington that word of such matters made his efforts much more difficult.

Hypocrite, thought Lazarus, Lord Pennington had witnessed the event of which he complained, but like Lazarus, had not stopped it. Pennington had not even tried. Apparently, though, it was not the event itself but rather the report of it reaching London that disturbed Lord Pennington. The letter concluded that he could think of only one witness to the event who could have produced the report.

"How do you know this," Lazarus asked?

Louis had been hurried the night before, but now he patiently explained. When Lord Harrington had stormed from the house to call to his stable boys, his house man had read the letter, gone to the second level of Harrington Hall and waived his kerchief outside the window of a corner room. The signal had been used before and meant that he had urgent information for the slave village. A runner had fetched Louis who met the old tortoise at the rear steps. His message had been brief, but it had allowed Louis to send Andru with the warning as Lord Harrington had called in his brutes, waited for three horses to be bridled and saddled and trotted off for Bridgetown. Louis had met the ancient house man again this morning and learned the details of the letter.

Hearing all this, Lazarus sat silently - astonished. These slaves had saved him before. This time even the old tortoise had come to his rescue. Warning signals he had never imagined, likely from the window of a room where he had once slept, and a one-eyed slave boy who out-paced trotting horses – these slaves had conducted a whirlpool of intrigue, and all for his benefit. Lazarus was not the only spy on this plantation.

Louis brought him back with the name of Lord Harrington - he and his bosses had rode out early this morning in the direction of the heavy country to the north-east, where slaves had sometimes tried to hide, in search of Lazarus. Lord Harrington, Louis said, had repeatedly sworn to take his revenge on Lazarus.

"What can I do," he asked Louis.

"Stay right here fo' awhile," said Louis. "De masta and he's bosses don't come in dis slave town. Dey neva' fines ya here."

"But the slaves, they know I am here," Lazarus protested.

"Yes, dey do. But Mista Laza, dey kno' ya sewed Andru's nose. Dey will not give ya up." Louis smiled confidently and whispered, "De boss mens don't be cummin' in 'mongst all dis many slabes at one time."

Lazarus talked to Louis about sending a message to Pandy by way of the ancient tortoise. He had run of Lord Harrington's house. He had sounded the alarm and told Louis all about Lord Pennington's letter. Lazarus had noticed that the old man moved reluctantly to Lord Harrington's orders, and that he usually called the slaver "Lord Harrington," but seldom "master." Apparently the old tortoise could be trusted.

Louis said that the ancient one saw himself above the slaves, but he secretly hated Lord Harrington. He was, Louis said, the bastard offspring of the third Lord Harrington, born to a house slave, not accepted by his father but manumitted, freed by will, when his father had died. He had been freed, but not provided for in any way. The old tortoise was Lord Harrington's grand uncle. Harrington let him stay on to serve so that he could thereby provide for himself, but to Harrington he remained no more than a slave, manumitted or not.

Lazarus could not help but be amused. In this manner Richard Malcolm Harrington, the fifth Lord Harrington and the leader of the island's plantation slavers, honored his own uncle. He clearly had more regard for his chess pieces. The old uncle had confided in Louis, but then, everyone shared their secrets with Louis. It would not be necessary to trust the old man with a message to Pandy, Louis said, as Betts looked in on her every few days.

Again, Betts' brought food and water and emptied an earthen necessary pot she also supplied. She seldom stayed but a moment, but she did answer Lazarus when he asked her, "How is Pandy, is she safe - and her baby, how ... um –"

"Pandy bees jes fine. No worry," Betts said. "Dat chile, he bees half de ways to he's birth. B-big chile, whoeber's he be."

"Tell me about Pandy," he asked, "what will become of her?"

Betts pursed and skewed her lips and wrinkled her brow, "What will become of her?" she parroted, but she didn't understand his question.

"Will she be punished? Will she go in the field? – and when her baby comes, what will happen with the baby?"

"Mista Laza," said Betts. "Pandy don't be de only slabe to birth a chile 'round here. And dat babe, it don't be da first one I bringed out its momma's b-belly. Dey do as we all does on dis suga' lan' – what de masta says - an' we gits by. De masta mebbe keeps Pandy in de house o' she go to her brudda - she gits by. Yew seed ya ownse'f - we all gits by."

"Her brother?" Lazarus said to himself. He never thought of Pandy as having a family. Of course she has a family. All these slaves have family - likely right in this village. How stupid I am, Lazarus thought.

"Betts, will you tell her ... tell her ..." Lazarus was not sure what to tell her.

Betts helped, "Mista Laza, please take care what ya says to dat one. She bees a babe herse'f. Ya don't wants to git in 'til ya knows yer way out."

Lazarus realized that Betts was right. But perhaps he had already gotten himself "in" without any clue of an "out" for himself – or for Pandy. He didn't even know how he would get himself out of this hut and out of danger from Lord Harrington.

Cooped up in a small hut all day with a vexed mind tired Lazarus more than work. Although it had become too warm of late, he had enjoyed Barbados where scented tropical breezes lulled him in slumber. On this island he seldom dreamed of drowning – if he dreamed at all. After a few nights on grain sacks, though, he knew he couldn't stay in his hut much longer and he needed a plan. One had begun to take shape when Andru had run to warn him and hauled him from his shop. He remembered – he had resolved that he would carry on in his mission. That hardly seemed possible now. Lord Harrington had found him out and his alarm would have, by now, alerted most of the noble horsemen and their allies. There would be no place for an abolition informant on this island.

Lazarus knew he had somehow been the architect of his own predicament. He should have told Mr. Clarkson that he was the only non-complicit witness, but what good would information about the attack on Andru have been if it could not be shared? He had been so excited about providing a bit of exact intelligence that he hadn't even considered a way to avoid detection. He lectured himself - "Brilliant!"

Another night passed. Again he slept little. He calculated: The crop-over kadoo was over. Lord Harrington looked to kill him. He couldn't stay in the hut forever, but no other place on Barbados would be safe for long. He could move constantly about, but his usefulness here had ended even if he avoided capture. He had no choice. Lazarus' stay on this island of homegrown slaves was also over. He had to leave – but to where and how?

Mr. Wilberforce wanted evidence of "new arrivals," but perhaps the man of Parliament did not realize that this small island had started receiving new arrivals more than 150 years earlier. Now, plantation owners and their slaves bred their own new generation of slaves and relied on raw captives for less than 10 percent of their needs. This island had long been saturated with slaves. The slave ships stopping in Bridgetown sold but a very few of their cargo. They stopped mostly for water and respite from the long sea crossing. They carried the bulk of their slaves to a much bigger island with an interior yet to be tamed. Where the new slaves were bound, Lazarus would also go - to Jamaica.

He must find a way and think more carefully. He thought for days.

Each day, Louis came morning and night.

Each day, Betts brought food and water.

Each day, Lord Harrington continued his search.

Each night, Lazarus slept in a small hut with a curtain door within a quarter mile of Lord Harrington's own bedroom – in the middle of 300 slaves - the safest hiding place on the entire island of Barbados.

PART FIVE: Jamaica Bound

August–September, 1793

Chapter 37. Disguise

Lazarus Perlman had to flee for his life.

After a week that passed like a month hiding under Lord Harrington's nose, Louis brought some relief. Lord Harrington had tired of riding out every morning hunting Lazarus. Even so, all was not well, as he had put his fellow noble horsemen and some other allies on alert for Lazarus in at least six parishes. Unless Lazarus wanted to exile himself to the windward side of the island, he could not show himself. Even that exile could likely only delay his capture.

Lazarus knew his plan or most of it. He said quick farewells to Betts, Louis and Andru – less painful for all he thought – and asked them to convey his love to Pandy and Gootie girl. He lit out for Bridgetown in the middle of the night, thinking to use Andru's route and his method of hiding whenever he heard a noise on the road. He didn't encounter a soul. He hurriedly slid into his shop and changed from his tailor's clothes he had carried from London and back into his smelly sailor's garb from his passage on the *Maidenstone*. He packed his few belongings by shielded candlelight. He left rent money on his cutting table with a note to his landlord that he relinquished his lease.

Lazarus wrote a hasty letter to be shared by the Symmons and Mr. Clarkson. He thanked the Symmons for their service regarding Mordecai. He advised that they could dispose of property remaining in the shop and flat above and retain the proceeds for the Jews' Free School. He asked though that the Symmons keep for him three items: Mordecai's old seven-candle menorah, a silver goblet they would find near it and Mordecai's Torah. Mordecai's shop could be turned back to its owner.

Lazarus told his friend Mr. Clarkson to take heart from the society of others he had so often lifted up himself. He advised of his decision to go to Jamaica and the reasons for it - citing the advice of Mr. Wilberforce. He said he had been found out and could not wait the three or four months required for a reply, but planned to be in Kingston, Jamaica as Mr. Clarkson read his letter. His work was not complete. He had come most of the way already. He had survived and grown these last ten months and was better prepared than the

Lazarus Perlman they knew to face the prospect of danger in Jamaica. At the end, he gave them each his fondest wishes and asked Mr. Clarkson to guard his health. He slipped the letter into his grip sack.

Lazarus checked the sky and thought he had another hour or two until dawn. He looked about his shop and tested himself on whether he had done all he had intended. For all his rest in the slave village, he tired and needed sleep – but not here. He tugged Duncan's bonnet well down on his head, lifted his duffel and grip sack and stole back out the door, across Tudor Street, through the alley and onto Piccard's portico. He dropped his load, threw his bonnet on it and fell onto Piccard's cot and into a sleep.

The sun rose high before he stirred in the morning. "I worked quietly and let you sleep," said Piccard, standing at the foot of the cot and sipping from his cup.

"Oh, Piccard. Thank you," Lazarus said as he sat up. "I apologize, I didn't want to endanger you, but I feared sleeping in my bed."

"Yes, Harrington's man has 'dropped in' a few times. Where have you been? You look like you've had a time," Piccard said, nodding at Lazarus' stained garb.

"Andru, the boy you saw – he hid me, but I couldn't stay there. If they had found me here, you may have had trouble, I'm sorry – "

"Ah, take no mind," said Piccard. "You can stay out here as you like, and sleep," Piccard said, nodding to the cot. "If Harrington finds you, well, then I hadn't seen you here - you are a trespasser-sorry."

"More than sufficient, what a friend you are Piccard," Lazarus said. "But I can't stay here – or anywhere on Barbados, I've got to sign on or stow away. Not quite sure how, but that's the only way."

"You are right," Piccard agreed, "nobody can be Harrington's rabbit for long without ending up in his stew pot."

"Yes, well, I expect to look about the wharf at dusk this evening and make inquiries."

"Let's get some food in you," Piccard said. Then he turned to his corner oven and shortly provided a plate of corn meal cou cou, a spicy sausage he called "chorico" and a small ball of bread flavored with marjoram.

Piccard spent most of the day on his portico with Lazarus, going into his shop only when he thought he heard someone enter at the front. As the sun sank, and he understood Lazarus' plan, he offered advice on how he thought one might flee undetected. "Take that for what it is," he said, "I've never been off this island. But whatever you do, you'll require more disguise than that stained costume." He went into his shop and returned with a stone dish and a pestle. He sat it on his now cool oven and reached inside, scratching off some black ash. He ground that to his already brown dish, then dipped his already stained fingers and smeared Lazarus' cheek. "Hmm, perfect," he said.

"What is it?" Lazarus asked.

"Diluted brown leather dye and wood ash," said Piccard. The ash blackens it and will shorten its effect. Don't worry," he laughed, "on live skin it may last a fortnight - more if you don't bathe." He continued the application with a smirk on his face. As he finished with face and neck, he handed the stone dish to Lazarus. "Best coat your hands and ankles and re-touch that left ear." He held his own wrist up next to Lazarus' face and proclaimed, "Welcome to the family, Senor Alvares. From your skin, I would say your mother was African and your father from Lisbon. Yes, Miguel Alvares – I like the name. No one on the docks should take you as a tailor from London if your tongue doesn't betray you.

Then he faced Lazarus and said, "We'll need to give you a few phrases to go with your complexion. Can you say: "Voce pode usar uma mao deck, capitao?"

"Vo-kay pod oosar … I don't think so," said Lazarus.

"Well, try this: Estou com fome. Mostre-me para a galera," Piccard enunciated with a grin.

"Yestoo cum fo, fo - what?" Lazarus shook his head.

"Well," said Piccard. "Just try to speak English like I do. That might do."

I think I can do that a little," said Lazarus. "Par-done may, Cap-i-tan, have you need of crew,?" he said.

"Humm," said Piccard. "Work at it – and say as little as possible."

The sun set just as Lazarus left Piccard, but not before he pulled the envelope from his grip. He entrusted it to Piccard who had never posted a letter. The man could be trusted, Lazarus knew. That is a comforting thing to know about a man, he thought. Then he caught himself. Lord Harrington could be trusted too – trusted to find Lazarus if he could and trusted to kill him if he did.

Chapter 38. The *Benevolent*

As Lazarus approached the darkened wharf, he couldn't see well, but naked masts piercing the sky told him that thirteen sea vessels sat dockside or at anchor in Carlyle Bay. This was many fewer than normal, as he knew that some forty or fifty cross-Atlantic craft reached Barbados each month. The masted craft bobbed easily in place while one small boat scurried about and a launch moved out toward a ship at anchor.

He recounted masts. Then he noticed that north and beyond the usual anchorage sat a frigate and beyond her a tidy line of other naval vessels. He could not make out their number. From this distance he could see the frigate's black cannon lined through square holes along her sides. He tried to count her guns, she carried at least thirty and they were not the small show cannon like those of the *Maidenstone*.

Since he had waited for the cover of night, Lazarus now realized he had arrived after the work day and he could detect no promising activity along the wharf. All quiet, he thought, and then he remembered - he knew someplace that would not be quiet at this hour.

Lazarus turned about and walked toward the bridge over the careenage, toward the Bull 'n' Brew. Perhaps he could learn more of the vessels at port from drinking crewmen than from the harbor chief. Either source might tell him where a craft was bound and her cargo, but crewmen could also advise on the skill of the sailing masters, the vessel's seaworthiness and her victuals. Lazarus knew what he had wanted when he sailed again: a competent ship's captain, an agreeable crew, a sober cook and a dry bunk in a tight ship. Of course, he had made that list when thinking of his eventual return to London. He couldn't be particular now – he was not returning with his mission complete. He was escaping - a fugitive from Lord Harrington and the leading planters on the island.

A few sailors had already found their way to the public house. They sat in a few clusters, talking among themselves. Lazarus looked about, seeking one who might be loose lipped, but perhaps the hour was too early for much inebriation. Well, there were two who may have spent the whole day in their cups, but they were beyond comprehension. At home among sailors and confident in Piccard's leather and ash skin stain, he bought a cup of swank for each of three already with drink at a square table and sat himself without drink at the fourth side. Lime water, sugar, perhaps lemon and possibly rum flavored the local drink. This time "double the rum" Lazarus whispered to the barman. After downing his swank, the youngest of the three said they were off a ship tied at the north dock. She had delivered her load and waited for a below-the-waterline repair to set before taking on the mountain of sugar barrels that sat near her on the wharf. The sailors had "been about the place some" or at least they had heard others talking over their cups. They did not know of any vessel bound for Jamaica, but they knew the destinations of only a few.

Throughout the evening more customers arrived and Lazarus questioned his way around the room. Lazarus tried to bury his London accent and picture himself as Piccard. He knew he didn't do it well, but nobody here raised an eyebrow at language when the speaker bought rum. As he did, his purse grew lighter but he learned nothing that would help him make his way to Jamaica. There were too many now and the place became loud.

Just as he thought to return to Piccard's portico for the night and stepped outside the door, five or six smelly men went in through it. They had been drinking up the road, he thought, because they appeared already drunk. As he stepped aside he heard a thick tongue spit out an epithet and a slurred mention of Spanish Town. He stepped back inside, toward the sound but heard no more. He approached the smelly group, gathered near the end of the bar. They stood grumbling with their heads down. Lazarus stood by and waited for an opening. When it came he leaned in and said, "Pardon … pardon, but did you say you were in Spanish Town?"

"Ne . .ver be … never been there," said the same voice from among the bowed heads.

"Who wants to know?" demanded a more sober and older one. This one raised its head showing the weathered face of a white bearded older man. "What do you care?" he as much stated as questioned.

"Well, take no offense, mate, I am, um - I'm looking to sign on for Jamaica," Lazarus said.

"Blood - bloody fool," said the thick tongue and its owner tried to signal the bar maid.

"Don't need any swabs," said White Beard, "and I ain't yer mate."

"May I offer you drink?" Lazarus said, "a round for the lot?"

"Humpf," said White Beard.

"Bloody hell yes," blurted Thick Tongue, "I'm yer bloody mate."

Lazarus raised his hand high until the barmaid took notice and circled his hand about to signify a round of drinks. When they came, they included one for him. He sipped at it as the smelly men gulped at theirs. He did not speak, but listened and followed as White Beard led the group to a table at the far side of the room. There, Lazarus sat with them, though not invited, and listened more.

Thick Tongue finished his rum before the others and held his cup aloft as if it would be refilled from heaven. Then he slammed it angrily to the table and said, "He lost near half them black devils, and he'll like kill us all afore we see England again." Then he hiccupped, only once, but so loudly that he brought stares from neighboring tables. His fellows ignored him.

"The *Benevolent*, haw! More likely the Curse," Thick Tongue declared. No one responded. "We ... we, hell, we should - "

"Mind yer tongue, Geoffrey," White Beard instructed. Two of the others grunted.

So it continued for two more rounds which the smelly men paid for themselves. Lazarus continued to nurse on his first. When the group was ready for still more, Lazarus again raised his hand in the air.

"Ye do not want any of this," said White Beard.

"How's that?" Lazarus asked.

White Beard looked at him, shook his head, then motioned him nearer. "We be off the old ketch *Benevolent*, scourge that she be."

Lazarus did not know the vessel, and merely raised his eyebrows.

Then White Beard leaned toward Lazarus and said lowly, not wanting to be overheard, "She be a guinea ship, lad."

"A guinea ship?"

White Beard shook his big head, "aye, lad," he almost whispered, " ... a slaver."

Lazarus tried to look disinterested, "Where is she bound?"

"To Kingston, Jamaica," said White Beard, "with a consignment of Africans for the plantations near about Spanish Town ... well, but half a load just now. If ye be a mate, drink with me to drown my misery," he said.

Lazarus didn't like the word "drown" but he lifted his cup against it. "Aye, I be against such miseries," Lazarus said, and he drank again.

Lazarus awoke still in his chair, but with his arms and head upon the table and a bell in his ears. Only two others remained in the room and light came from the windows. He sat upright, gathered himself and stepped out into a bright morning. Lazarus walked straight to the wharf and located the *Benevolent*. Being a slaver, it anchored several hundred yards off shore. He hired a boatman to row him. Another boat with its boatman already stood bobbing along her starboard side.

The *Benevolent* looked a curious old craft, perhaps half the draft of the *Maidenstone* and missing a foremast. On her low foredeck this morning gathered a row of Africans and a few crew. After a curious delay, Lazarus got permission to come aboard. He climbed up amidships and turned about to face a hollow cheeked old salt with skin drawn up from the sun. Lazarus asked to speak to the captain. "He be engaged," said the sailor and he nodded over his left shoulder up toward the foredeck. "I be 'is mate, what be yer business here?"

"I would sign for Jamaica," said Lazarus, and looked toward the group on the foredeck. He could not tell with his glance what transpired there.

"So ye be a slave seaman, then?" said the mate, looking mildly skeptical.

"Aye, I be a seaman sir," Lazarus said, "I crossed on the ship *Maidenstone* of London last year, seaman novice on the fo'c'sle and cordboy."

"Well, we seek no crew here," said the mate.

As the mate ushered him back toward the boat, Lazarus thought quickly and said, "I can pay - I'll pay for my passage."

"This is not yer way, lad," said the mate, and he reached for Lazarus' arm and escorted him back to the rail gate.

"But no others here are Jamaica bound," Lazarus protested.

"Hold on there," said a quivering voice. They turned about to face a pot-bellied man who stood several paces behind them. He looked strangely pale for a seaman, except for his red nose.

"I was just showin' this lad ashore, captain," the mate said.

"What be yer business, here?" the captain demanded.

"I would sign on for Jamaica," Lazarus said.

"No need," the captain said flatly.

"I can pay," said Lazarus. "I must go to Jamaica."

"Well ... stand by whilst I finish here," he said, nodding over his left shoulder, "and we shall see." Then he turned and walked back to his business on the foredeck. The mate shook his head and departed aft without another word.

Lazarus followed the captain a few paces so as to watch him at his task and held up. There on the foredeck with his back to the starboard rail stood old Chester Phipps in tall black boots with a riding crop in his hand. He faced a row of eight or nine Africans, half small-breasted women, half boys, naked but for their ankle shackles laced together, one chain for each gender. Their hands also appeared bound behind. A crewman stood at each end of the line and one to the rear.

"These be but all? There be no more?" said Phipps, his fat chins shaking.

"Aye, there be near eighty more, but ye asked fer the best girls an' the boys. Fer yer cane, we carry a grand lot, why, a big 'un below be as powerful as yer ox team. He could cut ye a swath, er I'll be - "

"No, no, no, I need house boys and a girl to train as seamstress," Phipps exclaimed. "I told you, I have my own for the sugar gangs."

"These be good 'uns," said the captain. Then he grabbed the boy on the end by the neck and drew him forward and turned him about. The ankle chain drew and the next boy in line slipped and fell. The Captain kicked the fallen boy and cursed, forgetting himself, then regained his composure and turned again to Phipps. "Look here," he said, then he bent the first boy over. "Grab yer ankles," he shouted as if expecting to be understood. He nodded to the seaman at the rear who stepped forward and held the boy bent over. The captain roughly spread the boy's cheeks and probed at his ass with both thumbs, "See fer yerself, no sores, no blood, stick yer crop here if ye have a mind, no bloody flux with any of 'em. Never had any on my ship."

"Very well, very well," said Phipps.

Then the captain straightened the boy, abruptly turned him about to face Phipps and jerked him forward by one arm. The next boy fell again and the captain started to kick him, but stopped himself, glancing back at Phipps. As the fallen boy stood on his own, the captain turned back to his inspection of the end boy. Having thumbed the boy's ass, now he pried the boy's mouth open with his thumbs. "Look here, all 'is teeth, not one knocked out ... if you bite, I'll ..." he said, then holding the boy's jaw open with one hand, he reached and grabbed Phipps riding crop from him with the other.

He jammed a finger and the end of the crop in the boy's mouth. "See fer yerself," he said. As Phipps stepped up, the boy bit down some, trying to swallow. The captain yelled, "bloody goddamn," and he again gripped the boys jaw, jerked it down and rammed the crop to the back of the boy's throat. The boy tried to suck air, and then he gagged. He suddenly wrenched forward and threw his head to one side, dislodging the crop and the captain's hand. He reared up, made a gurgling sound, gagged again and spewed vomit straight out at Phipps and the captain. As the captain raised a hand to strike, the boy spewed again and the captain dropped his hand to wipe his cheek.

The crewmen now descended on the boy as the captain and Phipps turned away and walked toward the rail. As Phipps turned, he spotted Lazarus watching him. Lazarus lowered his gaze under the brim of his bonnet. Phipps paid him no mind. He raised up his snout, turned toward the railing and brushed vomit from his vest. The captain bellowed for water, and a seaman brought a pail. The captain and Phipps argued as they washed in the pail held by the seaman. Then Phipps turned away, walked to face Lazarus, again raised his nose and walked past to the rail gate and with difficulty climbed down to his boat.

"Ha!" Lazarus told himself, "He didn't recognize me at all."

The captain hollered, "take 'em below." Then he stopped, pointed back at the sick boy and hollered, "give 'im his due - then double it." The crewmen roughly followed their orders, beating the sick boy while moving the lines toward the hatch. The captain continued cleaning himself. Then he turned and stepped toward Lazarus, whom he seemed to have forgotten. "You still wants to pay yer passage on a slaver, lad?"

Lazarus was certain. Mr. Wilberforce wanted evidence on mistreatment of new arrivals, he told himself. This mean, potbellied little captain already had begun to accommodate. "Aye, captain," Lazarus said, "I'm for Jamaica if you will."

"Haul up your duffel, and then come to my cabin to settle," said the captain. With that Lazarus became a passenger on the *Benevolent*. She was, he learned from White Beard, an old navy ketch, decommissioned to a seagoing fishing boat then refitted to carry Africans. With no foremast, her low foredeck had been suited for cannon load, mackerel and now slaves. Lazarus was not her only passenger. The captain also accepted payment to take on an old Bajan woman in a dull white wrap. Her master had died in Barbados and bequeathed her to his brother in Jamaica.

Chapter 39. Bucklehead

The *Benevolent* struck out for Jamaica under power of her two masts. Her cargo included eighty-odd African men, women and children, but no old people among them. He looked back at Barbados as the *Benevolent* got underway. He saw it differently now than he had only months earlier. Its green and yellow, swaying beauty against the blue sea remained, but now he saw it as the home of Betts the healer, of ribbon-haired Gootie girl and her cooing infant sister. This place, too, was home to handsome but now disfigured Andru and Singing Louis.

Lazarus breathed deeply and consciously instructed himself to soak up all that was good about the island. He closed his eyes and thought of dimpled Pandy. She was the vision of Barbados he wanted to take with him … not the image of Lord Richard Malcolm Harrington and his deceitful grimace. Just the thought of Harrington shattered his daydream and inverted his grin.

* * * * * * *

Below decks, the old ketch was configured like nothing Lazarus had imagined. She had been partitioned with the slaves fore and the crew aft. All below shared a common deck ladder, save the vessel's two officers in their separate rearward cabins. Two rows of iron bars divided the slave bay into two chambers and provided a narrow passageway between them. Men and older boys were kept in the starboard chamber, the women and children in the larboard. Despite their separation from the men, a few of the women were round with child.

Lazarus bunked with the crew. The old Bajan woman slept on bundles thrown about a rearward storeroom.

The smelly lot from the Bull 'n' Brew comprised near half the crew. These were barefoot sailors. They lacked the discipline Captain Graves had required aboard the *Maidenstone*. The thick tongue, which Lazarus learned belonged to Seaman Geoffrey Neeland, confided that nearly half the slaves and two crewmen had been lost enroute from Africa, mostly to the bloody flux. The captain had lied to Chester Phipps. "The cap'n made us pack their arses with oakum tar, like they was a leaky ship," admitted Neeland.

The cure had failed. When a slave girl had grown too weak to stand, the captain had her thrown overboard. This practice had continued until those stricken had all been disposed of into the sea at his orders. The cargo had been so depleted that there was no need to replace the lost crewmen.

"Blood and runny shite soaked the deck and puddled below" during the middle part of the crossing, according to Seaman Neeland. The *Benevolent* still smelled of death and of its past decades as a fishing vessel. During the passage, the captain had kept apart from the others. Even when on deck, the captain had required his crew to stand four paces off so that he would not breathe in what he called "the airs of pestilence."

"He keeps close to his woman, though," said Neeland. "He has her brought to his cabin every few days. Same woman every time, and by his order, none but him touches her. Baffles me what she does that the others will not," Neeland winked. "I'll show ye the cap'n's woman so ye don't take her when yer blood is up."

"No need to that cause," Lazarus replied. "I do not expect to take any as are aboard." He did want to see the captain's woman, but he did not want Neeland to think he would take a woman, any woman, against her will. Pandy, he told himself, had been willing.

Neeland looked at him with raised eyebrows. "The dark ones not to yer likin' then? I expect ye would turn to it all right, if ye had but one."

Lazarus could only shake a bowed head, like he had so often seen Mr. Clarkson do. Then he brought Neeland back to recounting the vessel's Atlantic crossing.

Even before the bloody flux had set in, the captain had ordered two of the male slaves thrown over the side after a short but violent revolt that had killed a crewman. "A third was to join them," Neeland said, "him what done the killin', but the captain's woman wailed and pleaded for him so the cap'n had him bound up special."

From Neeland's account, Lazarus soon discovered what he supposed had caused the rebellion. The captain allowed the crew to lie with the slave women that would have them. This was common practice in the slave trade, Lazarus had heard, but this poorly supervised crew withheld food from the women and the children on board in order to procure consent. Lazarus now supposed that trick was not uncommon either. While the crewmen usually took their women to their own bay or into a storeroom before returning them to confinement, Neeland boasted that a few of them took the women right before the eyes of the bound men.

The slaves were fed twice a day. They ate mostly beans boiled with a small bit of salted beef and rice. They were brought on deck in small groups for exercise on alternate days. Occasionally, the crew "bathed" them by pouring over a pail or two of sea water. The slaves brought up and emptied their own waste buckets. Out of port, the women came on deck with no chains through their leg shackles, but the men came bound two together. Many were entirely naked, though some had wraps about their hips.

The captain seldom came on deck. Nobody seemed to check the heading or set the course, but as the *Benevolent* sailed northwestward, it often came upon the next island in the string of the Antilles. The frequent sight of land assured Lazarus. At least this part was better than the long, landless crossing from Cape Verde to Barbados.

On the third day the slaves brought on deck included a tall man with a head as big as Lazarus'. He was not coupled with another, but his hands were bound behind him. He had shackles at both ankles and the short chain between them clanked on the deck. He wore a muzzle – an oval metal plate perforated with tiny round holes and, at its edges, small slots with three leather straps, each buckled behind his head or neck. The contraption obstructed some of his face, but his eyes looked big and wild. Lazarus had not noticed him below. As the man stretched and rose to full height, Lazarus caught his breath. He stood a head taller than any man about him. Shinning in the sun, he looked too perfect, like a polished ebony statue. His name must be Goliath, Lazarus thought, and he sought out Seaman Neeland to satisfy his curiosity.

"He's a mad one," said Neeland. "We calls him 'Bucklehead.' The captain would have fed him to the fishes were he not of such value ... and because of the woman." Lazarus had waited for years to see this, the bound noble savage enroute to his unworthy master. He could not resist being drawn to the man. He walked around the muzzled African inspecting him with care. Then he walked around again. The man was a young specimen with broad shoulders, a rippled stomach and large hands and feet. Lazarus came back around to face the man, looking up as the man stood fully a head above him. Lazarus studied his muzzle, his face and his piercing eyes. The man's entranced clear eyes stared back. From beneath his muzzle he said in a low tone, "Mo nlo iku." It sounded like gibberish.

"Why the muzzle?" Lazarus asked.

"Stay clear if you know what's good fer you," said White Beard, from near the larboard railing. "This one will eat you for his dinner. He bit clean through the jugular of a seaman bigger 'n you."

Lazarus backed away, paused, stared and then approached again, fascinated with the shiny big man. As he did, the big man said, "Mo nlo iku." Lazarus again leaned forward to better hear him. Suddenly the big African snarled like an animal and pounced in Lazarus' direction. Lazarus jumped back, startled. Then he saw that the man had merely feigned an attack. Lazarus would swear that the big man smiled behind his muzzle. Then the man laughed two, three deep fierce sounding chorts.

White Beard laughed. Neeland guffawed. Lazarus blushed and imperceptibly trembled. "Throw some water on 'im and take him back down," White Beard told the younger Neeland.

Lazarus watched as Neeland and another complied. Then he stepped to the rail near White Beard and looked west, shading his eyes from the afternoon sun. "Do not let him fool you," White Beard said. "He be bound up well now, but even hobbled that devil could snuff yer life in an instant if he threw his fit. Bound as you see him, he bolted when we came within sight of Barbados and it took six to hold him."

"Thank you," Lazarus said. "I shall hereafter keep my distance." Then he walked across the deck to the opposite rail and looked out at the sea.

The old Bajan woman soon approached him. He had spoken to her before, but she had not replied. In fact, he had never heard her speak that he could remember. Now she looked up and caught his eye. "He be de Aremo," she whispered.

"What?" Lazarus said.

She turned her head to each side, satisfying herself that no one stood near them. "He be de chosen one, but now he be taken. De zoms got he spirit."

"Wha, What do you mean?" Lazarus asked.

"He be de son o' de Yorubaland king, - de firs' born. Dey taked he in de raid from de slabe fort. Dey keeped he tied down in de sun an de bloods run out he eye. Den he taked de oat' to de chief God, Obatala. He say he kills all de Buckra what be lookin' in he eye."

"How do you know?" Lazarus asked.

"He muddah, be below," she said. "She be called 'Yobanna' … she who plead wit de Gods. She be lie wit de cap'm to keep he alive." Lazarus looked intently at her now with more questions in his eyes. "Me own muddah be from the land o' de Yoruba. Me talks a bit o' de tongue."

"Which is the mother?" he asked. He did not recall seeing a woman who looked old enough to be the mother of this big man, young though he was.

"She be de one wit de hair. De cap'm, he leebes her grow." Lazarus did not know what she meant. Unnatural though, Lazarus thought, that this big beautiful prince of Africa would be a captive of the pale man with the pot belly and red nose. Still, Bucklehead was the most fearsome man Lazarus had ever seen. Lazarus' purpose was to free Africans from their chains. Somehow, though, he was content that this one man was well bound up in his.

The next day some women were brought up to get their air and stretch. They mulled about the foredeck under the eye of two crewmen. Now, in the light, Lazarus noticed that one of them did have hair. All of the women in this group were close shorn except one. She had a waist wrap, big eyes, a comely figure and she had hair. It curled and twisted making her head look enlarged. As Lazarus stared, the Bajan woman approached him. "She be de one," the old woman said.

"She is the mother of the big man?" Lazarus asked. She did not look like a girl as did some others, but neither did she look like a matron.

"She be Yobanna - de muddah," the old Bajan said, "an she be de woman o' de cap'm."

Lazarus and the old woman just stood and watched. Soon Yobanna went to the starboard rail near the bow and turned away from the sea. She crouched down on her haunches and leaned back against the bulkhead. Her hands fumbled and separated from her waist a thin leather strap. She pulled at the strap with both hands, rotating it around her until her hands came upon a small pouch of the same leather bound up by the strap. Lazarus had not noticed either the strap or the pouch.

Still squatting against the bulkhead, Yobanna widely parted her knees, sliding her wrap up her legs and exposing her inner thighs. Her fingers spread open the pouch and she inverted it, spilling several shiny stones onto her spread lap. Though Lazarus had seen that several of the women aboard were naked, Yobanna's posture looked disturbingly immodest from the angle of this distance. He stepped closer to see her lap and the shiny stones now nestled there rather than the terminus of her thighs. The old Bajan stayed by his side.

Each of the lap stones looked oddly the shape of Lazarus' thumb, but a little larger, more the size of the pawns on Master Symmons' chessboard. Each stone appeared to be carved into some figure, not intricate, but with a face of some sort. The features were rounded and smooth and each a little different from the next, except that each one had a distinctively rigid nose like Lazarus' own.

Yobanna fingered each stone. Then she returned a blue one to the pouch, followed by a speckled gray one and one the yellow green color of the Barbados cane fields. She held up the two stones left in her lap, a white stone and one that looked reddish streaked with jagged shards of white, the shape of lightning in the sky. She said something to herself or to the stones, and then held them aloft, one in each hand. She returned them to her lap, raised the white one to her lips, whispered to it and then returned it to the pouch.

Lazarus had seen such stones before, or ones much like them, on the big altar behind the old broken windmill just before his fall in the bougainvillea and again on Betts' shelf. Some of those had oval eyes and some closed eyelids and thick, wide lips. Some smiled. Some frowned. These little stones were the Gods of Africa, or at least of these Africans.

The stones seemed to resemble people. In fact, he thought, they look something like human features he had seen on this very vessel. Then some words jumped into his head. "So men created God in their own image, in the image of man created they him." He thought it was something he had learned from the first chapter of the first book of the Torah, but he knew the words that now came to him reversed the meaning he had earlier learned. "Stone obeah gods – made by the hands of a man," he said aloud but under his breath.

The Bajan woman heard him. "Ya kno de Gods o' Obatala?"

she asked, surprised.

"No, I cannot say that I do," Lazarus said, now speaking to her while still looking down at Yobanna. "But I have seen them before - in Barbados. Those gods will provide her no help, but I suppose they are as good as any." Then a question struck Lazarus – were all gods creations of men like these stone ones and the ones on Betts' shelf? He knew the thought had occurred before, but until now he had pushed it aside.

Yobanna now held the little red streaked with white god in one cupped hand and stroked it with the other much, as he imagined, she might stroke the captain in his cabin. He tried to put that unwelcome image out of his mind. Then with both hands she held the little streaked stone god against the tip of her left breast and moved it in three slow little circles while it touched her nakedness. She repeated the motion with her right breast and then she rubbed it up and down between the two. Then she brought the little god to her thick lips. All the while she whispered to the stone god in the soft tones of a lover.

Yobanna now held the stone god before her eyes and seemed to caress its eyes with her thumbs. She spoke more loudly at it now, as if pleading with a child to obey. "What is she doing, do you suppose?" Lazarus said to the old Bajan.

"She pray to de god," the old one said, as if it were quite obvious. "Come, let we ask for what she pray." With that, the old woman walked right up to Yobanna. Lazarus followed slowly and stayed a step behind the old Bajan.

Seeing the old woman's feet, Yobanna looked up, but she did not stand. "Mojuba," said the old woman. Lazarus knew this to be a greeting.

"Mojuba lya," Yobanna replied.

Then the old woman said something that Lazarus did not understand, and Yobanna replied in a soft, but also strange tongue. Lazarus listened to the two women talking, not quite sure where one word left off and the next began. He thought he heard a few words that he had learned on Barbados. "Busi tie lle," the old one said. "Bless your house," Lazarus guessed to himself.

Yobanna scowled, then talked rapidly, but Lazarus thought he heard "okun" – sea, "arun" – sickness, and "mi omo" – my child.

The old Bajan spoke now in an almost reverent tone.

Yobanna spoke in a plaintiff one. From Yobanna's lips Lazarus thought he could pick out the words, "shango, dide, abebe, afefe," and "ara."

Lazarus could not remember these words, and he gave up on them and watched Yobanna's angry face as the two women talked. Within a few moments more the old woman said, "Moducue" – ah, Lazarus understood this word – "thank you." Then the old woman turned to Lazarus.

"She say de men o' dis boat kill she girl chile an many o' she people and thro' dem into de sea when dey gits sick. She say she pray to Shango, de god o' de tunder an lightnin', fo' to bring de big wind an kill de men o' dis boat. She say she give she self to Shango an she rub he's eyes and she sing fo' him and pray fo' he fabor."

"She offered to give herself to Shango?" Lazarus was not sure that he had really heard that.

The old woman looked into his eyes. "So she say."

Lazarus said nothing for a long minute. He did not know what to say. Some of the slaves on board were completely naked. None had more than a bit of a cloth wrap. How had Yobanna managed to possess such a treasure as her pouch and stones? He looked at her again. Then he told himself, "Likely the same way she keeps her hair."

Lazarus looked up at the old Bajan, "Thank you," he said. Then he looked back down at Yobanna. All the while she had stroked the stone god, Shango, the god of thunder and lightning, as she had talked to the old woman. She continued to do so now. "Mojuba" – I salute you, he said.

Yobanna now looked up at him, surprised, he thought. Then he said, "Moducue."

Chapter 40. Blockade

The *Benevolent* provided none of the amenities Lazarus had sought for his passage to Jamaica, not even a dry bunk. No one tended to her hull and she seeped and creaked. The almost absent sail master shared the same title as the master of the *Maidenstone*, but he did not compare with Captain Rodney Graves. The crewmen were a lowly sort, and the cook was miserable, if sober. Lazarus could hardly wait to reach Jamaica and be rid of them all. This sorry boat must not be a good measure of anything, even of slave vessels, he speculated.

The *Benevolent* wended her way up the chain of the Antilles until she came upon Nevis, a smaller of the British controlled isles in the West Indies. Then she turned to near due west, intending to pass to the south of the greater islands of Puerto Rico and Saint Dominique and on to Jamaica. She had been so directed for two days when she came upon three of His Majesty's war ships. A heavily gunned brigantine hailed her down and sent a boat along side. The captain greeted the brigantine's boat party on deck, and spoke to them from several paces apart as was his custom. From this distance the men spoke loudly enough that many on deck could hear.

"Where be ye bound?" a junior officer of the brigantine asked the captain.

"Jamaica, Kingston harbor," the captain replied.

The officer inquired whether the captain had encountered any French war ships and what he had observed as the *Benevolent* had passed by Bay Fort de France at Martinique. The captain had no intelligence at all.

Not so for the officer. He told the captain that French warships had appeared off the southwestern peninsula of Saint Dominique. "It looks to be a make-shift squadron," he said, "mostly privateers but a few of their line." The French, he said, had sunk a British naval ship and taken several trade vessels bound for Jamaica into their custody. "You lie now just south of Danish Saint Croix," the officer said, "and the French squadron awaits you but three days sail to your west. They have been losing the war and I think we have them bottled up in the Mediterranean. In their desperation, they are borrowing our tactics and blockading well outside Kingston harbor to intercept vessels headed for Jamaica." The French war maneuver made sense to Lazarus. Jamaica was clearly both the most valuable and the most remote of the British held islands in the entire West Indies.

"My captain says you should turn back," the young officer explained.

"How can I do that?" said the captain. "My cargo is consigned to Jamaica."

"Even so," said the officer, "you are advised to reverse or alter your course. When you come upon the privateers, they won't just turn you back. If you remain afloat, they'll claim this vessel and its cargo as bounty even if they have to slit your throat to do it. We will not order you about, but we cannot run afore you as we are bound to Saint Christopher on orders." Without more, the young officer returned to his boat and his brigantine. Within the hour the three warships were behind the *Benevolent* and shrinking out of sight.

For once, the captain stayed on deck. He paced back and forth. He lifted his hat to scratch his bald head. He paced some more, then retired to his cabin. As soon as he did, the crew began to buzz. They debated as if they had any say in their fate. Most wanted to turn back, but a few said they could not draw their pay if they did not deliver the Africans to the Jamaican planters. All the while, the *Benevolent* sat dead in the water. Lazarus had little doubt the captain would retreat to Saint Christopher.

"There be others hereabouts as will buy the blacks," said White Beard.

Just as he did, the captain came back in view and stood above on the quarterdeck. He stepped forward and bellowed, "Ye all know our trouble." Then as if he had heard White Beard, but without acknowledging him, he announced, "There be others, not on Jamaica, as might value this cargo. Some in the small islands might afford a few, but we have eighty-seven. Yet, there be no need to turn back and prolong our voyage."

He did not say more. The crew looked up at him with puzzlement. Then the mate, also standing above asked, "Captain, what heading, sir?"

"Head 'er north by west, Mr. Stiles," he said, "and set 'er sails for Carolina." Then he walked back and again disappeared.

The crew buzzed about and then set about redirecting course at the mate's orders. A few seemed troubled and grumbled, but White Beard spoke up again and quieted them. "There be a rich slave market, Carolina," he said. "She may be a wee bit farther than Jamaica, but Carolina lies right on our course home to England. We'll be home a fortnight sooner, God willing."

The crew seemed content and, Lazarus thought, even a little surprised that their red-nosed captain had a likely solution. To Lazarus' mind it was a terrible idea. He followed the captain to his cabin and knocked. The captain came to the door, but did not admit him.

While standing in the doorway, Lazarus caught a glimpse of Yobanna, standing naked in the cabin, but with her back to the door. Lazarus redirected his eyes, asked the captain's pardon and questioned whether it might do to follow the warships back to Saint Christopher. It lied just northwest of Nevis and, even tacking against the fair winds, not more than two or three days behind. "The British likely gather a fleet there and lay plans to attack the French squadron," Lazarus said. The captain said nothing and so Lazarus continued, "Once His Majesty's fleet counter attacks, our way to Jamaica will be clear."

The captain looked perturbed. "God knows when that might be. I will not go back. No, I think not." He began to close his cabin door.

Lazarus held his hand out to keep the door open, "But captain, you agreed to take me to Jamaica, I have paid you already." As she heard Lazarus becoming more assertive, Yobanna turned to face him, unashamedly exposing herself.

Lazarus' insistence only angered the captain. "It cannot be helped," he barked, looking at Lazarus' hand against his door. Lazarus managed to move his fingers just before the door banged closed.

As he climbed back on deck, he wished he had asked to be taken on board the brigantine. The navy may not have allowed him, but had he known this captain would fail to turn back, he would have tried. Then the thought came to him that the *Benevolent* would likely encounter another friendly vessel in these waters. Perhaps one headed to a British port from which he might still make his way to Jamaica. If so, he could hope to make his transfer then.

As the *Benevolent* proceeded, Lazarus kept a lookout for passing ships. He thought he may have seen one in the distance, but too far away to tell for certain. Jamaica was only days to the west, but as the *Benevolent* moved north it was becoming more distant.

The old Bajan woman noticed his watch, and he enlisted her in his vigil. She apparently thought her plight better in the hands of her deceased master's brother in Jamaica than likely resold in a Carolina slave market.

As Lazarus' searched the horizon, he saw some islands to the east he thought to be the Virgin group and the *Benevolent* passed a large one far off its larboard side. This, he thought, must be Puerto Rico. Two days later he finally saw a ship far off the starboard bow. Despite Lazarus' request, the mate held the helm and would steer no closer.

Lazarus rushed excitedly to the captain's cabin. The captain refused to come to his door, but bellowed from within, "Go away! Don't trouble me again unless you seek a bunk with the slaves."

There seemed no way Lazarus would now find his way to Jamaica … unless it came by way of Carolina. Now he hated the captain and felt the need to rub his own little stone god, or perhaps, the need for the G-d of Moses about whom he had not recently thought. "Where are the plagues upon this little pot-bellied Pharaoh?" he asked himself.

Chapter 41. Shango's Rage

The captain's mate kept Bucklehead, the muzzled African, below when the *Benevolent* sailed within site of land. He feared that the big African might bolt at the sight. Shackled, hobbled and bound as he was, he still seemed capable of making good an escape if he put himself to it. Moving through the Antilles, the big man had not been brought on deck as often as the other slaves.

Lazarus understood the fear. Mr. Clarkson had convinced him that slavers produced savagery in their captives, but Lazarus had quickly judged Bucklehead a monster of no man's making. Such extreme ferocity did not seem merely the product of chains and whips. It must be innate. He imagined Yobanna invoking African war gods during Bucklehead's conception and screaming in agony at his birth. Lazarus, the abolitionist, thought Bucklehead to be one African he would exempt from freedom, at least until standing at a safe distance, and that to be measured in nautical miles.

Sailing within sight of land had always comforted Lazarus. His recurrent fear was of drowning. It was irrational, he knew, but his worst nightmares were drowning dreams, usually the same one repeated. Even though he could not swim the length of a mast's shadow, he somehow felt better with land in sight. With Bucklehead below, he favored it for another reason. Land sightings had been frequent on this voyage. Sometimes another island had appeared before the *Benevolent* while one could yet be seen in her wake. With Puerto Rico behind, there was suddenly too little land to be seen.

On the morning of the second day past Puerto Rico, Seaman Neeland and two others brought up the big African and left him on deck for some time after they threw some pails of sea water onto him. Whenever he appeared, two of the small crew stayed not too distant.

Chains hobbled the African at his ankles; other chains bound his hands behind him. Leather straps with three metal buckles secured the muzzle that obscured the man's face. He could hardly have been more restrained and yet be free standing. The man could not even eat except when the muzzle was briefly loosened for that purpose.

Still, Lazarus did not argue at the treatment. Just now, he had no objection to it. He kept his distance, but he could not help but stare at the man. Following his first encounter with the big captive, Lazarus had thought to avert his eyes from the man's view, but he found Bucklehead a fearsome fascination. The big African seemed to understand his impact upon Lazarus and took pleasure in staring savagely at him, or so Lazarus believed. Before the crewmen took Bucklehead below, he stood near the hatch, looked at Lazarus and the old Bajan woman leaning against the railing and said, "Mo nlo iku." Then he raised his head to the sky, stretched his neck and bayed like a wild dog through his muzzle, "Ashe Obatala, mo nlo iku." His cry seemed to echo back from the empty sea like a war chant. Then he was gone below.

Lazarus turned back toward the sea. As he did he caught a glimpse of the old Bajan watching him. She looked unsteady and she nervously dropped her eyes to the deck. "What is it?" he asked her.

"De mad Prince," she said, "he talk de debil."

"Well, what … what did he say, exactly," Lazarus looked sternly at her now.

She looked back up at him. "He say he kills ya. He say, 'by de powers o' de chief god,' he kills ya."

"Nonsense," said Lazarus. "He does not know me. I have done him no harm."

"Yea, dat be so," said the old Bajan, "but ya be de buckra what always look in he's eye."

Lazarus looked at his forearms and the back of his hands. In the hot, humid days Piccard's stain had mostly faded from his skin. Apparently each day he had become more a white man – a buckra. The crew had not commented or cared. Only this Bajan woman and the fierce African below took notice. His disguise revealed, he went below and changed from his sailor's slops to the attire of a passenger.

The following morning Lazarus noticed large sand bars and a few dotted islands off the larboard side. During the next two days the vessel passed an assortment of low and mostly barren tiny islands. Lazarus calculated that some of them must shrink to half their size or disappear altogether in a storm swell or even the highest tides. Still, these were land enough to keep the big, frightening African locked behind bars below.

When Lazarus came up on deck one morning after a fitful sleep, he noticed that the *Benevolent* followed a heading that seemed a little too north in relation to the sun. He inquired of Geoffrey Neeland about the course, but the young seaman paid little heed to navigation. White Beard overheard. He told Lazarus that on a return trip from Jamaica to England, the captain had once been set upon by Spanish privateers off Eleuthera. Since that time he had avoided the Bahamian Archipelago altogether when weather permitted. The captain, said White Beard, preferred to sail past the Bahamas to the east and to come upon the land at a line somewhat north of Spanish Saint Augustine and south of the Oglethorpe settlement at the mouth of the Savannah River.

Lazarus realized that he did not know White Beard's name. The man spoke to other crewmen and they spoke to him, but no one called him by name.

Lazarus decided that avoiding the Bahamas and Saint Augustine might be prudent indeed. With England and France now occupied at war with one another, who could tell what adventures the Spanish in the area might undertake. Perhaps the captain, holed up in his quarters, was not a complete fool.

Yet sailing out of sight of land meant that Bucklehead would be brought on deck more frequently. The creature had, for reasons Lazarus did not understand, vowed to kill him.

For a week past Puerto Rico the journey remained uneventful. Uneventful on a sea voyage is a good thing, Lazarus' experience told him. The days were hot and the nights stayed warm. Thunder and some rain came up in the afternoons with some regularity. But for that, the sailing itself remained steady and unremarkable. With every hour, though, Lazarus knew he was passing farther from his real destination and his purpose. It was maddening.

For Lazarus, the boredom gave way to apprehension for two hours or more on the days Bucklehead came up with his deck escorts. The escorts gave Lazarus little comfort. Lazarus doubted they could deter the gigantic slave if he determined to attack.

"Land, ho!" The call came one morning as Lazarus climbed the deck ladder up to daylight. He walked to the larboard rail and looked for himself. A low, dark green wide expanse of land spread from off the larboard bow to the quarter deck.

"She be land for certain and she be no island," said White Beard.

Within, Lazarus conducted a private celebration.

The *Benevolent* now followed the coastline north with land in sight by light of the sun and glow of the moon. With land off the larboard side, at least the brute Bucklehead remained below. Lazarus' spirit lifted a little. Jamaica lay far behind, but so did Lord Harrington. Here at least was dry land.

Unlike Neeland, White Beard did give attention to navigation. He estimated that the vessel might now be within two or three days sail of the river harbor at what he called "Carolina's Charles Towne." Lazarus knew of the place. Charleston was the principal southern port of the American Atlantic coast. It was also the nation's slave capital. To its port came more Africans bound for American slavers than to any other place. Perhaps from this slave port Lazarus might make his return to Jamaica. "My return … my return to Jamaica," he whispered to himself. He could not help but both smile and frown at once, "I have never been there."

That night the clouds covered the mood and stars in a dark gray blanket. The land could not now be seen in the darkness. The wind, which had aided almost constantly since Bridgetown, now blew from the east. The *Benevolent* tacked a little to starboard, quartering the wind, to avoid being driven too near the land in the darkness. This slowed her progress. Such seems my fortune, Lazarus thought, as soon as relief appears, some new opposition arrives. The new destination laid quite close now and land was near, seen or not. He retired to his damp little berth content that the captain's mate, always it seemed on watch, would bring him safely toward Charleston and its river harbor.

Lazarus awoke in the night to the groaning and creaking of the vessel. The *Benevolent* swayed and rocked from side to side. Lazarus' stomach told him that she also rose and fell on sea swells of some height. The lamp in the crew's bay, hung from a head timber, swayed widely back, forth and in a circle. The motion, though, had not awakened him. It was the sound of the timbers and, perhaps the cries of a few of the African women, forward in their barred slave bay.

He rose and went to the passageway from the crew's bay and lunged forward, staggering against the roll of the ship. Beneath the hatch, he hung on the rungs of the deck ladder. Rainwater from above fell on his head. He wiped his eyes and looked between the rungs, forward into the slave bays. With just the reflected light from the crew's cabin, he squinted to see. To the right, the white eyes of the black men stared at him. He thought he felt the eyes of Bucklehead peering intently. He looked away. To the left, some of the women and girls cried. The children clung to the women. In a near corner, he could see Yobanna with the hairless head of a girl in her lap. She patted the girl with one hand and held the leather pouch about her waist with the other. Lazarus climbed the ladder.

On deck, the crew had its hands full. The wind now bore down, still from the east and blew the rain at angles before it. The mate, though, continued to try to tack into it and to make headway in the storm. Lazarus spotted Geoffrey Neeland standing hard by the main, checking her shroud and rat lines. A few paces away, White Beard tugged on the backstays. Lazarus approached White Beard. "How does she hold?" he asked.

"She fares well enough," White Beard said. Then he added, "Nice little blow." The aged man could hear him in the wind. He had likely stood in a hundred such winds in his days.

The night began to give way, and in the light Lazarus could see that the clouds had thickened. The wind kept steady from the east, the sea swelled the height of a man, a big man the size of Bucklehead, but the mate managed to make a little headway as he busied the crew with his tacking.

As the day passed the storm did not. It grew steadily. Lazarus stayed on the deck and assisted the crew. Near the end of the day, some became sick from the pitching and falling. Lazarus saw lightning off the starboard side and he spotted a peculiar sight in that same direction. In the distance a part of the sea rose up to a point to meet the clouds that seemed to reach down to grab it. "Look," he cried at White Beard in the wind, "the cloud pulls up the sea."

"God a' mighty," White Beard said, looking for the first time just a little alarmed. "That be a water spout, and a grand one, too." One or two others saw the water spout, then it descended back into the sea.

"What does it mean?" Lazarus asked.

"It means that this be no small storm as shall soon pass by. It means we best find our port soon, 'er we may get caught up in the 'cane."

"Caught up in the 'cane," Lazarus wondered? For a moment he

envisioned a blowing sugar crop, then the growing storm blew him back a step and he hollered in the wind toward White Beard, "Oh, you mean a hurricane?"

"I mean we be on the edge of her, and we best run light and away afore she draws us to her eye." Lazarus had not sailed the tropics in September and though he had survived Atlantic gales, he had never been at sea in a hurricane. His face told the old man as much. "Lad," said the old man with a strong voice, "mebbe this li'l blow of ours ain't so little at all." Then as if called up to his purpose, lightning flashed then flashed again to the east and in its light another water spout appeared. Thunder clapped and waves slapped against the *Benevolent*.

When the sky briefly paused, Lazarus turned and faced White Beard. "Should we not bring her straight into the wind, strike sails, anchor down, batten her up and hold fast to ride her out?" It was the way to ride out a storm he had learned aboard the *Maidenstone*. He knew it to be right.

"We best find the shelter of a port if we can make 'er," White Beard said insistently.

"But should we not bring her into the wind?" Lazarus said, pointing eastward with one hand and hanging on a line with the other.

"That be the way in thunderstorms, in short lived squalls and even in gales," White Beard explained. "God help us if this storm catches this old ketch in open water, she could break us if she be a 'cane … and," he said pointing to the east where the lightning had revealed the water spouts, "them be the signs."

"The signs of what?" Lazarus couldn't hear well and he shouted now.

"Of a hurricane, yes lad, a hurricane … a blow and a commotion of the devil himself, as calls many to the depths for good. If we try to face this devil and ride her back, we may survive, and we may not. A 'cane don't blow through and be done, she can last fer days and roll this sea to turn its downside up. Like as not, a real 'cane'll throw the sea atop us and break this old boat. Even at harbor she may be dashed or grounded, but we as rides 'er would find ourselves a better chance."

Lazarus looked at him, apparently in disbelief, for then, for the first time, the old man met him eye to eye. "Believe me boy, I knows, I knows!"

Lazarus did believe him. Throughout the night he did all he could to assist the crew. The first storm he had encountered at sea had made him violently ill. He had since learned to ride with the movement of the ship in heavy weather. This storm though, grew and grew and, aboard this unworthy vessel, made him fear for his life.

Before day came again, the winds began to scream and the rain to fall sideways in buckets. The sea tossed with surges that rolled and washed up on the deck. The mate did not strike sails. There was nothing but shreds to strike. He screamed to the crew to drop the anchor, but it gave no help and one man followed it into the sea. The mate then bellowed an order that could not be heard, but was passed from man to man. "Go below er else tie yerself down."

The mate began to lash himself to the helm. White Beard posted himself at the foot of the main mast and circled himself to it. Lazarus started to help him with his knots. "See to yer ownself," White Beard shouted. He obeyed the old man, struggled to the hatch and climbed below. At the bottom of the deck ladder he stepped off into water near deep as his knee. Now he could hear the slaves wail, joining the screaming storm. They were now all standing. The women gathered at the door to their cell, extending their hands, pleading. The men hollered some, but stood on line in their chains. Some crewmen stayed below, but most who descended climbed back to the deck when they found water in their bay. They all showed terror in their eyes, but none of them took any note at all of the slaves.

Lazarus looked about, peered back into the crew's bay and saw three sailors on upper bunks. Geoffrey Neeland was there. He stepped toward Neeland and yelled, "You are a slave keeper, where are the keys to the cells and the chain locks?"

"Right O!" Neeland hollered, "If we be doomed, might as well have our way one last time ... I'm yer mate."

"No, no," Lazarus could not abide this fool, "we must free them or they will have no chance at all." Just then the whole ship seemed to shudder and a long, low cracking sound could be felt as well as heard. Then another shudder and snap sounded, louder than the first. A scarph has separated, he thought, the futtocks are free. The very ribs of the old vessel were cracking and coming apart. "Where are the keys?" Lazarus demanded of Neeland.

"Only the captain has keys - and his mate," Neeland said. "He provides 'em with his orders."

The ship now rolled to the larboard a measure and did not rock back. The water covered Lazarus' knees. Lazarus had not seen the captain in days. His cabin laid all the way aft, over the transom. The mate was lashed at the helm above. Both were distant. The mate was closer.

Lazarus hesitated. He remembered he had hesitated before and had failed Andru at the giant kapok tree. He would not fail Yobanna and these slaves. At least he would try his best.

Lazarus turned and waded his way to the deck ladder. He pushed aside a sailor milling about in the water in a daze, doing nothing. As he climbed above he could see that the roll of the ship left the African women and children in water above the waist of the tallest and near the head of the shortest. Children clung to women and women clung to bars of iron and reached through in his direction, grasping handsful of water and air. He did not stop to comfort or gesture to them.

He climbed the ladder. He could see White Beard lashed to the main mast, holding up an arm against the torrent. Lazarus worked his way toward the quarterdeck stairway and pulled himself up the ladder. Against the wind and the wave tops, he dashed from one handhold to the next until he could see - nothing. The mate was not there. Lazarus quickly concluded that the sea had taken him.

Without pause he headed toward the captain's cabin. He lunged rearward, caught the aft railing and pulled himself along it until he reached the raised coaming that protected the captain's entry from the wind and the water. In this storm, the coaming was useless. He dropped down the few steps of the entryway and found the captain's door closed. Water stood against it. He rapped hard and could hardly hear his knock himself. He tugged at the latch, but the door seemed swollen against its jam. Lazarus turned his back to the door and propped his feet against a stair riser. He leaned against the door, reached back over his shoulder and struck the latch as he straightened and struggled wedging himself between door and stair. Nothing happened. He hit it again, uncoiling his body with greater force. This time the latch sprung, the door swung free and Lazarus slid into the cabin on his backside.

He jumped up and looked about for the captain. The potbellied man sat calmly at his writing desk at the far side of the cabin. He looked as comfortable and unconcerned as if he were lounging on the veranda of a Barbados manor house. He did not even seem to take much note of Lazarus. Lazarus walked right up to his desk. As he did, he saw a keg on the floor next to the captain's chair and a deep mug in the captain's right hand. The man's red eyes and red nose, and now the odor of strong drink told Lazarus why the captain kept to his cabin - and why he did not help his crew in this storm.

"Where are the keys to the slave bays," Lazarus demanded. "The water rises and they will drown if they are not freed."

This focused the captain a little. "They will drown ... they will drown anyway," he stammered, "as will we all."

"Perhaps they will," shouted Lazarus, "but then they will drown free ... or at least without their chains. Now, where are the keys you sorry slaving bastard?"

The captain just sat, glassy-eyed and silent.

Lazarus hurried around the desk and opened its drawers ... no keys. He went to the captain's chest near his berth. It too was locked. A tall, narrow armoire fixed to the cabin's planks stood against the bulkhead opposite the bunk. It yielded nothing. Then he saw the rear of the door he had forced open. A large ring hung from a steep peg at its inward side. From the ring hung a few iron skeletons, large and small. He grabbed the ring, untied the line about the waist of his sailcloth breeches, put one end of his waist cord through the ring and then retied the line. Then he took a deep breath and bolted from the cabin and back up the short stairway.

At the top the storm had worsened. Lazarus had not thought that possible, but now he could not stand at all against the wind. He grabbed the aft railing. Hand over hand, he moved across the rearward rail. Suddenly, a length of the rail gave way and sent him skidding on his belly until he caught a spar bale and uprighted himself. He worked toward the hatch amidships and grabbed anything fixed in making his way, walking first and then crawling. He clutched a deadeye, the edge of a deck plate, a pulley block, a tie chock. He grabbed, yank tested and pulled along a line whipping loose at his end but still held fast at some forward end he could not see.

Finally, he came on his belly to the hatch and slid like a snake

over its raised edge and fell headfirst down the rail ladder and into
the water below. He reversed ends and stood in the water, which
now nearly reached his armpits. The only light now came from the
hatch and the storm sat dark and low upon the *Benevolent* and upon
the sea. He fumbled in the water for the ring at his middle and lost
one end of his waist cord in retrieving it. His breeches drooped and
twisted in the water. He forgot about his breeches and pulled
himself around to the door to the women's bay. He jammed in the
first skeleton key in the lock as small black hands reached past the
flat bars and tore at him. It opened the door, and the black hands
pushed it and him away. The women and the children held on to the
outside of the bars now, moved toward the deck ladder and pulled
themselves up its rungs and out the hatch. Lazarus helped the last
few as the water rose still. He feared that the winds grabbed them
up as they emerged on top.

One woman stayed below. She grabbed at Lazarus and clung to
his neck. Her wet hair brushed his face. Now he knew her, even in
the dark. She cried in his ear, "Moducue, moducue," as she
embraced him. Then she pulled him toward the backside of the
ladder and the slave bays, toward the men's bay. "Mi omo, mi
omo," she cried as she clung with one arm and pointed to the far end
of the bay with her free hand. Lazarus could not see much, but he
knew Bucklehead was chained, hand and foot, to the bars at the far
end of the men's cell. The other men lined along the bars before
him in two rows, each secured with a single chain through a shackle
clamped to each man's ankle. He could free the men by removing
the lines of chain and do so without freeing Bucklehead.

He tried to quiet the woman as he moved to the men's door. He
tugged at his sagging breeches and almost jumped along, half
bobbing in the water. The men's cell door unlocked with the same
key as fit the women's door. He entered the bay with Yobanna still
about his neck. Once inside she released him and moved toward the
back. Lazarus squatted in the water and felt about for the chain line.
The men all shouted and moved about making his task more
difficult. He grabbed the leg of the first man in one line and worked
his hands down the man's leg to his ankle. There was no shackle, it
was his free leg. He switched legs and found the shackle and the
chain.

Now he had to hold his breath and drop below the water to

follow the chain. He readily found the chain end and the clasp lock that held it around a bar. The clasp was too small for the door key. He bobbed up, took a few deep breaths while he felt for a smaller key. Finding one, he gasped air and submerged again. It was the wrong key. He resurfaced, tried to pull up his sagging breeches, found another key and dived again. The clasp opened and the first man had pulled the chain through his shackle by the time Lazarus stood. Then all the lined men held by that chain lunged forward and fell upon one another and upon Lazarus. As they stood together, Lazarus yelled over the storm as if speaking to Englishmen, "In order, one at a time or we will all drown." From somewhere in the dark, the woman was yelling too.

The men acted as if they understood him and in order reached down and pulled the chain through their ankle shackles. As each man came free he moved as quickly out the door, around and up the deck ladder as the high water allowed him. Lazarus then moved to the second line and, with the correct key, unlocked the chain on his first dive. The men of that line then pulled the chain through their shackles and moved in order as they had seen those of the first line do. Lazarus stood by the door and felt each go by him and watch the escape of each up the ladder further darken the little light from the hatch. When the last in line had departed he started to move to the ladder himself. He almost tripped over his breeches, which now clung to his legs below the waterline.

Then he heard the woman pleading at him from the end of the chamber. "Wa, wa, wa," she called, then "sofun, sofun, wa wa." He did not know the words. He knew for certain what she wanted. He took a strong chill and shivered in the water. He could not bring himself to free Bucklehead. Lazarus knew the big man despised all buckra and, for some reason, especially him. Bucklehead destroyed all whites he could reach with a free hand. He had vowed to kill Lazarus. He could not know that Lazarus was not a slaver. It probably would not matter to him.

Lazarus stood on the ladder and began to pull himself up. As he did, a bright light flashed and a simultaneous thunderous boom sounded. For a minute he thought he was blinded and deafened - but he could still hear the cries of the woman. Now she cried, "Shango … Shango … Marerefun Shango."

He dropped back down, still with the key ring in his hand and his sturdy sailcloth breeches about his ankles. He fingered the ring and hobbled back into the slave bay and back where he could not see at all. If Bucklehead attacked him, he would never see it coming. He felt his way and grabbed a metal buckle. He felt another - the back of the big slave's head. The woman's hands pried his away and began to unbuckle the straps of the muzzle. In a moment, Lazarus thought, she had it off. Lazarus half expected to feel Bucklehead's teeth ripping into his neck. Bucklehead did not even speak.

The ship creaked and screamed, and it seemed her aft dropped into the sea. The woman was pleading with him. Lazarus moved quickly now and selected one key, then another. He dropped into the water at the big slave's feet and pulled at the shackle pins. He could not find a piece to fit them. He rose, gasped for breath and again submerged. This time he freed the chain from about Bucklehead's ankles. Lazarus stood. He found that the water had brought back some of his sight for he could detect some light. He had left the bound hands of the big slave until last, but he did not now hesitate. The key turned, the lock slid and giant hands came free.

Lazarus held his breath. He felt the big man stand erect in the water and move to the door. With the woman before him, he soon darkened the hatch and was gone.

Lazarus waited a moment, relieved, then he began to follow them. As he stepped toward the door, or tried to step, he found himself caught up at the ankles by the legs of his breeches. He kicked to free himself, but could not move much in the rising water. Something besides the water and his bunched wet breeches restricted his kicks. He took a breath, bent down and felt for his ankles in the water. He could feel a part of a chain between his legs. He pulled toward one end, it gave a bit but would not pull free. He rose up, took air and squatted back into the water. He grabbed the chain, pulled at the other end and felt it tighten around his left ankle. Somehow he had gotten caught up in it.

He thought quickly now and tried to calm himself. He must have stepped in a loop of the chain, but how had it come to lie across and through his breeches? He would simply loosen it and slip away. He submerged and tried to loosen the chain. It would not budge more than a link. He stood, now leaning his back against the iron bars. His head seemed to spin, and the *Benevolent* tilted more bow high. He thought he could feel it slipping deeper, aft end first. The water rushed to his shoulders now and there was no more light from the hatch. Then came a jolt and the squeals of twisting wood as the vessel struck the bottom or perhaps fell upon a shoal.

Lazarus dove again and pulled down at the left leg of his breeches. They were twisted about, caught up in the chain and he could not free his foot. He felt about for his knife but knew it was gone with his waist cord. He pulled at his breeches. They were of his own making. He had cut them from sailcloth and double stitched them. They were much too sturdy to yield. He stood to breathe, but his head stayed in the water. He reached about and grabbed an iron bar, but could not pull himself up enough to find air.

He thought he felt something push at his head, then pull at his hair. He reached to grab it but felt nothing but water and iron. He thrashed about but could not kick free. He held his breath as long as he could. He remembered the slaves of the *Zong* pulled into the sea by their ankles. He thought he saw a soft light and the vision of a clear face surrounded by soft auburn hair billowing around it in the water. Then he felt something pulling him down by his ankle. "Here is my drowning," he thought, and he opened his mouth to breathe in the sea.

Chapter 42. Salvage

Lazarus felt something move against his cheek and his lip. He thought he could feel. A little light, too, appeared to come in at the right edge of his vision. He stirred. Something pinched his upper lip. He rolled a little from his stomach to his left side and grabbed at his face with his right hand. He felt the offender and knocked it away. Sitting up and shading his eyes, he squinted as a many legged shell creature nearly the size of his hand scampered awkwardly away on the sand.

He spit sand from his mouth and brushed it from his face as he looked at the stretch of sand that ran to the horizon. He rose to his knees and then unsteadily to his feet to get a better look. The wind blew steadily and the sky remained low and gray, but no rain fell. He brushed at the sand coating his front side and found that he stood naked below his blouse. Wind caught and filled the blouse which blossomed away from his skin. His breeches lay in two, each half wrapped around an ankle and covering a foot planted in the wet sand. To his right, large choppy waves rolled up on the land but spent themselves just as they reached him.

He turned left and scanned the view landward. Beyond the sand, clumps of low dull green trees and ground growth whipped in the wind. Then, continuing counter clockwise, he completed his turn and caught his breath. Just a few feet away on the sand to his sunward side lay a completely naked large black man, also belly down in the sand. From his size alone, Lazarus knew him.

Beyond him some distance were a few scattered timbers, some upon the sand and some rising and falling with the oncoming waves. Further away and out in the water stood a large piling of jumbled wood. Just seaward from the piling, the forward ribs of the ship rose stiffly out of the water at an angle, laced together by remaining planks near the bow and some along the hull. The waves moved flotsam up and down among the skeletal remains of the vessel. Other timbers, planks and debris spread, scattered still farther down the beach.

Lazarus dropped his eyes and studied the big man. He did not stir, but his sides filled and fell some. He looked dead except that he breathed shallowly. Lazarus decided to leave him be. He walked widely around the big man and on down the beach to see if there were any others. His halved breeches dragged in the sand. He stopped, sat on the sand and pulled at them. They would not pull away. He worked and twisted them, one then the other. Finally and with great effort he managed to disentangle each piece and pull his foot free of it.

Then he stood. Other than the black pillar of a man lying prostrate on the sand, he could not see another soul, yet he felt exposed. He pulled his arms from his blouse and worked it down until its neck opening encircled his waist. He lifted the empty sleeves and tied them before him converting his blouse to a covering for his lower nakedness.

Then he continued down the beach. He found a few barrels, most of them smashed, but one intact. He thought it contained drinking water, but he could not tap it. A few scraps of sail canvass were strewn about, and he spotted one wet blanket, mostly buried in the sand. He picked up a piece of the sailcloth. He looked about for other survivors. He was not sure whether he hoped to find the old Bajan woman, Yobanna and White Beard or rather hoped to confirm that the captain had perished. He found no survivors and not even a floating body.

Then he recalled that he had not seen any of the crew for some time before he opened the slave bays where he had drowned - or thought he had. He had managed to loose the slaves some time before he felt the *Benevolent* strike the shoal - or this land. Had he unchained them too early? Would they have survived if he had left them locked in their bays until the storm had beached the ship? He could not know, but as he walked about the debris on the beach and looked out at that wreckage standing in the water, he could not detect a living thing. Then he wondered how he had come to be on the sand rather than in the sea with the others. He shook his head and walked back toward Bucklehead.

He stopped short when he came back to his breeches. He stooped and retrieved one piece and looked at it. Then he dropped it and examined the other. The breeches looked as if they had been ripped apart. It would have taken a force that may have broken his legs to pull these sturdy breeches apart beneath the water. Or - he looked over the top of the piece he was inspecting and caught sight of the black man - or an inhumanly strong creature.

He dropped the torn garment, still clutching the piece of wet sailcloth and walked straight away to the body on the beach. He bent over the man. He laid the sailcloth over the big man's middle, covering his buttocks. He reached and touched, then pushed a little at him, but the man did not stir. He did breathe, though, but in a labored manner. Lazarus set his bare foot lightly on the man's back and pressed down a little ... nothing. He crouched and slapped the man between his shoulder blades ... no response. He slapped again, harder and then twice more. The man coughed and sputtered some and rolled a bit and back in place. Lazarus could tell that the mighty man was damaged, but he could not see the injury.

Lazarus kneeled next to the man and slid his hands under the man's middle. With great effort he lifted, pushed and rolled the man to one side to tuck the sailcloth about him. Then he closed his fist and struck the middle of the man's back three times as if he were angrily pounding at the strike plate of Lord Harrington's door. The man wrenched and spewed water from his nose and mouth. He convulsed and coughed out still more. Then his eyes twitched and he rolled over just a bit more. As he did so, Lazarus saw a narrow strip of leather across his chest and running up around his neck. Lazarus grabbed at the leather line and dug a little in the sand near its terminus. Something came loose, and he pulled it up from the sand and away from the wide black chest. Lazarus recognized it immediately and wiped sand away from Yobanna's leather pouch.

He felt the pouch and knew it contained the small gods of stone, one of them white - Obatala, and one a red stone streaked with jagged shards of white - Shango. He did not know what god, if any, had a hand in his rescue. Perhaps the Lord G-d of Abraham, Isaac and Jacob had helped him as he had Moses at the Red Sea. He lifted the pouch slowly, moving it away from the sandy black chest and began to work it and its lanyard up past the man's face and over his head. A huge black hand suddenly grabbed his wrist and wrapped around it just as his own hand clutched the pouch. Lazarus started but could not pull away. He looked up into the face of the man he knew to be his rescuer.

The man's eyes were open and he stared right at Lazarus. For a moment neither man moved. Then Lazarus looked down toward the pouch and back into the face as the man began to crush Lazarus' wrist. He dropped the pouch. The man sputtered, coughed and released Lazarus. The two men just stared blankly at one another. After an interval and with some difficulty, the man propped himself up on his right arm, slowly lifted his left arm and held up Yobanna's pouch in his open palm as if making an offering. His eyes rolled, his whole body trembled as though taken with delirium, and then he sprayed out a garbled cry which sounded like: "Memaa Iya ... Yobanna lo okun ... Yobanna lo a Shango." Then he shook his head, poked a finger in his ear and twisted it around.

Lazarus knew only three of the man's words, but he understood. The man had not managed to save his own mother. The Thunder God Shango had finally heard her prayer and accepted her sacrifice. The man could not save his mother, but someone had saved Lazarus, for here he knelt on the sand before this black god of a man.

For hours the two men sat in the sand looking out at the water, then at one another and then back at the sea. They did not speak again. Bucklehead wheezed, choked and spit water. He took air in large gasps. He tipped his head and slapped at its upper side. It seemed all he could do just to breathe. A little later the sun dropped below the row of trees behind them. Later still, they settled back down on the sand within reach of one another and fell asleep.

Lazarus woke to the sound of men shouting in the distance. He sat up. The sun rose high behind the clouds. The wind blew much lighter and now from a direction opposite of the storm that had broken and grounded the *Benevolent*. The sea swelled with lower waves. He heard voices again and saw a launch with two pointed ends, pulled up near the sand down by the beached wreckage. Several men milled about and shouted to one another - white men. The big man near him rolled, coughed and also sat up. Lazarus stood and motioned with both of his palms downward for the big man to stay put. He stepped a few paces down the beach, turned and motioned again. The big man seemed to understand or to be too weak to stand.

Lazarus then walked slowly toward the men and shouted out, "Ho, ho, here I be." They spotted him and a few ran to meet him. They drew up a few paces away.

Before Lazarus could speak, their questions flew. "Are you from the ship?" Where is the captain?" "Are you alone?"

"I am from the vessel, I was a passenger. I am not alone, but there be only one other that I have found." Lazarus motioned back along the beach with one hand.

The men looked up the beach at the big black man. "Where was she bound? What was her cargo?" one man asked.

"We claims her salvage!" said another.

"She was the ketch *Benevolent* of Bristol. I came aboard at Barbados where she stopped, bound for Jamaica," Lazarus said.

"Jamaica?" a few said at once. Then one with raised brow added, "That was a big blow, but you say she was bound for Jamaica?"

"The French blockaded Jamaica, she diverted," Lazarus explained. "Do you have any water or perhaps some bread?"

A thin man turned to another, "Fetch water," he said and one departed toward the launch. Then the thin man turned and added, "biscuit as well." Facing Lazarus again he asked, "Diverted? Diverted where?"

"To Carolina," Lazarus said, "Charleston."

At this the men laughed.

"There be few stores hereabout," another man said. "What was her cargo?"

Then again one said, "We lay claim on right of salvage. We be first at the wreck."

Lazarus lost patience, now he asked the questions. "What is this place?"

"This be Folly Island," said the thin man. Lazarus looked puzzled. He had never heard of Folly Island. "Southerly Carolina," the man said. "You stand but two leagues from the mouth."

"The mouth of what?" Lazarus was insistent.

"Why, the mouth of the Cooper and the Ashley rivers ... the entrance to Charleston harbor," the man said.

A stout, shorter man stepped around the thin one and stood right up to face Lazarus. "The cargo boy, the cargo - what was her cargo?"

Lazarus leaned back from him a little. He looked back up the beach at the giant, still incapacitated man, propped up on an elbow. He turned back to the stout man and said, lowly, "Slaves, her cargo was African slaves."

"That be a fine cargo," said the stout man, "but where are they?"

Lazarus swallowed hard. "I do not know. I expect they lie with her crew." He pointed out to the sea.

The men milled about the washed up wreckage for an hour or so.

Lazarus took the water flask and a biscuit back up the beach and handed them to the big black man. After a while, three men followed him. As they approached, the big man stirred and sat up. He managed to stand stooped over, looking fatigued; he panted and his lungs whistled some. Lazarus again motioned to him with both palms turned downward and pushing toward the sand. The big man sat back down upon his haunches.

The approaching stout man looked at the big black and said, "Will you look at this one? He will fetch a price. We claims this slave by right of salvage."

Lazarus stood immediately between the stout man and the weakened big one. He drew a deep breath. Without thinking he heard himself say, "This man is not cargo. He is my servant. He belongs to me." His voice stayed strong, he sounded convincing he thought.

"Is that so?" said the stout man.

"Yes it is so." Lazarus firmly replied.

The stout man looked past Lazarus at the big man, "Is that so, boy?" he loudly asked the African. "Does you belong to this lad?"

The big man remained still.

"If'n he be your servant why don't he talk?" the man demanded. Again to the big man he yelled, "What be your name, boy? How does they call you? Is this your master?" He pointed at Lazarus.

The big man stirred but made no sound. Lazarus calmed him with a slight movement of his hand.

"He do not answer," said the stout man to the two others with him. "If this one be his master, he could talk at him. I says he be new from Africa and slave cargo."

"You are right that he is not long from Africa," Lazarus said. "He does not yet speak our tongue. I bought him off a ship in Barbados just last month. I intended to take him with me to Jamaica. I have a bill of sale, that is - it went down with all else I own." He motioned toward the wreckage in the foamy surf.

"Yeah, that be likely, a lad like you," the stout man mocked. He started to step around Lazarus and push him aside with one hand. Lazarus resisted and they struggled a bit. As they did, the big black man slowly came to his feet. The stout man needed no help from his two mates. He got the better of Lazarus and grabbed him by the throat.

Just then his eyes got big as he saw the black man at his full height. A big black hand flew to the throat of the stout man. The two mates started in, but Lazarus shouted, "Stop, stop." The big black hand lifted the stout man to his toes and he released Lazarus. The big man then allowed Lazarus to pry his hand away from the man's throat finger by finger. The stout man's two mates stood still. The other men of the launch party had now come up the beach at the sight of the struggle. They stood off a bit as it concluded.

The thin man said, "Back away Michael." The stout man looked again at the big black, and stepped back several steps without a word. His two mates retreated as well.

The thin man approached the little gathering, "What is your name, lad?" he asked.

"Perlman sir," came the reply, "Lazarus Perlman."

"And what do you call your slave?"

Your slave thought Lazarus. He did not like the sound. "My slave?" he said aloud, then he corrected, "um … this man, my servant, is called Buckleheaa … that is," he cleared his throat, extended a hand toward the black man and said, "his name is Buck."

"Lads," said the thin man to the assemblage, "there be not much for us here but some timbers and a bit of railing. We shall return with a barge." Then to Lazarus he said, "Well then, Master Perlman, let's to the boat and we shall haul you and your 'servant' up to Charleston bay."

"Thank you sir," Lazarus said. He stepped to the big man, stood at his side and lifted a heavy black arm that he rested around his shoulder. With Lazarus and an ailing Buck setting the pace, the troupe made its way slowly down the beach, into the surf and aboard the launch. Lazarus and Buck sat back a larboard near the thin man who took the rudder as the others strained at the oars.

For an hour or perhaps more they passed by the land to their west. They moved past a rock tower as tall as a big ship's main mast and bore a little left. They now rounded past a little rocky shoal and the thin man at the rudder steered still more to the larboard side. Across from them now, in the distance, was another stretch of sand upon which sat some sort of low-lying fortification.

The thin man saw Lazarus staring at it. "Fort Moultrie," he said.

In just a little time more they were in a harbor with many more ships at anchor than Lazarus had ever seen in Barbados. Signs of the hurricane lay all about and some vessels lay close upon others. Buck gazed about as if in a world he had not imagined. He looked at Lazarus and, taking his lead, remained calm.

Ahead and a little to his left, Lazarus could see the buildings, waterfront and wharves of a city sticking outward into the harbor toward them. At its point was what looked to be a low, uneven white wall or field of some sort. The wharf laid to the right of the white wall. There Lazarus counted a long row of docks. Masts rose next to many, but some of the masts were at angles as if the wind and water had pushed their vessels up against the land. Beyond a little and near the middle of the city he could see the tall white steeple of a church.

Lazarus watched wide-eyed Buck. He clutched Yobanna's leather pouch in his big hand as if it were his salvation. Near drowned and laboring for air, he still seemed the better of any man in this boat, but hardly the same fierce African prince. He now looked bewildered, confused. Lazarus felt disoriented himself. A wartime blockade and a hurricane – events he couldn't control or even foresee had changed everything. If his life were a chess game, G-d or providence had scrambled the pieces.

Still, when one nearly dies of drowning, one suddenly sees patterns through the details of daily life. Now he reflected: Whether God created man or man created God, Lazarus could not say - but the creator of this black man sitting next to him was an artist. Lazarus had found a bit of that same artist in selfless Mr. Clarkson, dedicated Mr. Symmons, generous Piccard, singing Louis and once-handsome Andru. He remembered angelic Mrs. Symmons, nurse Betts, little Gootie girl and precious Pandy. He thought of his mother, the dainty songbird he never knew. Certainly such women were the artist's masterpieces.

It was September - a year since he had left London aboard the *Maidenstone*. It seemed much longer. Though he had never worked as hard, he had accomplished nothing in that year. Could today be Rosh Hashanah, the New Year – the time to start anew? He dwelled a moment more on the past, recalling places left behind – the synagogue at Dukes Place, The Jews' Free School, Guildhall Library, The Abolition Society at 18 Old Jewry Street - and the shop of Mordecai, the father he would never again see. He had sailed to Barbados in an effort to help slaves, but he had failed – and the slaves had saved him – from his fall down a treacherous cliff covered with lacerating spines and again from the wrath of a vengeful slaver, Lord Harrington. Lazarus had left Barbados, too, disguised, fleeing for his life. IIe had left those places to begin this expedition, this mission, this life - and to continue with it. He had at last freed slaves, dozens of them from a terrible slave ship, but only to send them to drown in the raging sea. Now he was entering the Carolina slave capital - someplace he never meant to be. Now he claimed to be a slave owner himself - something he never meant to become.

He told himself it was pretend. He had lied to protect this slave. He was devoted to saving slaves. Yet for all the help from all the people, for all his efforts in all the places, this weakened big man here beside him was the only African he had managed to save … and, Lazarus knew … the slave had actually saved him.

The End

Historical Afterword:

The British Parliament finally outlawed the slave trade, but not slavery itself, in 1807.   The role of the Society for Effecting Abolition of the Slave Trade, its decades-long campaign, the Parliamentary leadership of William Wilberforce and the efforts of Thomas Clarkson in amassing evidence against the slave trade are matters of record.

Though fictionalized here, the Jews' Free School is now known as JFS and is coeducational. At this writing it continues to educate students and to promote tolerance.

African slaves first came to Barbados in 1627.   The British Parliament passed the Slavery Abolition Act for the United Kingdom and most of its colonies in 1833 – three decades before Abraham Lincoln issued an executive order known as the Emancipation Proclamation. - BLW

About the Author

Byron Lee Wade is an American nomad, having lived in the Rockies, on the west coast, and the east coast.

He now resides near the Texas gulf coast. He has never learned to sail.

Readers may contact Byron via email at byronleev@gmail.com or visit his web presence: www.tolerancetriumphs.com.

www.ingramcontent.com/pod-product-compliance
Lightning Source LLC
Chambersburg PA
CBHW031249170626
46807CB00001B/57